STRAY CATS

GEOFFREY MEHL

For Judy

This is a work of fiction. Names, characters, places and incidents are products of the author's imagination or are used fictitiously and are not to be construed as real. Any resemblance to actual events, locales, organizations, or persons, living or dead, is entirely coincidental.

STRAY CATS

There's a great deal more money to be had."

Tommy shook his head. "Carter, I've taken everything you are and everything you ever were. You're just a gelding now. Guys, this is – "

Yenchenko growled. "Josef Rabemann. This wolf has become too old. I fail to recognize old man in photo. But I know this voice from many year ago. He is Josef Rabemann. He is Blackbird." Yenchenko glared at Blackmann. "You cause death of many good soldier, many innocent person." He stepped forward to complete a ring surrounding Blackmann and asked, "Who is woman?"

The anger welled up again in Tommy's throat. "Myra Fielding. For a long time, I believed she was on Blackmann's side. But she was a mole, helping Campos. Maybe others."

Ian sighed and in a sad voice mumbled, "What these bastards call 'collateral damage.'"

Blackmann seemed to sense the gravity of his situation and promised his captors "Anything, anything you want. I'm still very – "

"Extraneous," Tommy injected while he released the clip from the Glock. As he walked toward the farmhouse, he tossed the weapon into shrubbery. A few steps further. Behind, two gunshots. No need to look. He grunted and climbed the porch steps.

CHAPTER FORTY THREE

Narrow, open wooden stairs creaked during Tommy's descent into a ordinary cellar. Cool, faintly musty, but tidy. A swept floor, no cobwebs, ground zero for utilities. Heat. Air. Electric. Washer, dryer, utility sink. The space ringed with shelves. Opened and new paint cans, cleaning supplies, small tools and equipment. As expected. *Richtige ordnung*, everything correct.

And a portal to a small space that would have been directly beneath a sitting room. More cans of paint on shelves about chest high. A table, chair and a full-sized Draper & Sutton safe door.

The kind used for bank branches. Old fashioned, five tumbler. Tough to pain to crack. At least it's better than the new electronic styles. Here comes Sergei and Ian. I'm not going to ask.

Yenchenko said. "So. Is this prize? Or trap?"

"There will be a walk-in vault on the other side. Has to be the prize. The door's real enough, and it's going to take some effort to open."

"Perhaps there is bomb on other side? Remember, Koshka, your careless moment in California. Also Dieter."

Tommy squatted to spin the dial. "Hard to believe Blackmann would risk a booby trap in his most critical stash."

"Be most careful, Koshka. This is poor place to die."

Tommy sighed and worked the lock. It took nearly five minutes, but when the last tumbler clicked into place, he reached for the handle to open the font of secrets.

"*Nyet! Ne dvigat'sia!*"

Do not move!

Tommy's hand froze and he very slowly turned his head toward Yenchenko.

Sergei stepped past, toward the shelf of paint cans. He worked with great care and a soft touch to moved several aside. A shiny, new, unopened can. No label. Then another. And then several more.

Yenchenko wiggled his fingers to fill them with dexterity. He reached out and lifted a nearly invisible brown wire and used the tip of his finger to follow it from one can to the next. "*Da, da*. Too many can of paint. This is old, most clever KGB trick. How you say, *lovushka?*"

Trap. Booby trap.

Tommy's hand remained safe door handle.

Ian stepped forward. "I suggest you hold that hand quite still, Thomas. Even pressure, no movement." He pointed to a second thin lead crossing the portal and disappearing into the paint shelf of the outer room.

They removed two more used paint cans.

Ian said, "Black box, about ten centimeters square, plastic, three leads, opposite directions."

"There is red light, which make slow blink. There. And once again."

"Right. Two second intervals. A five says it's the trigger, Thomas."

Knees tightening from squatting too long. Shoulder stiffening. "There's got to be a key or switch or something."

Sergei stood very tall and peered into the line of cans connected by the wire. "I see nothing."

The casino. Lester Finn had pulled a tiny little black box with a hinged lid. He had flipped it open and there was a button. When he pressed the button, the guy at the end of the aisle won a jackpot. "Ian, see if you can get back around me without bumping me. Take a look in Blackmann's pockets for

some sort of a remote control."

"Right. But if perchance I squeeze it the wrong way?"

"You can have our shares. But not the Gulfstream."

Sergei nodded. "*Da, da,* Koshka. Most reasonable. There is enough explosive here to blow entire house into small pieces."

For three minutes, Yenchenko and Tommy struggled to ease tension with light banter about good vodka, bad women and fun times. Ian's footsteps on the stairs.

"Got the damn thing, Thomas." He unfurled his fingers to reveal a rectangular object on the palm of his hand. "I suspect the hinge is on the left side."

"Open it."

"You're quite certain?"

"My fingers are killing me on the handle. Open the damn thing."

Ian scowled. "Bloody hell. You're getting on, Thomas. No stamina at all."

Yenchenko leaned in to observe. Wells used his thumb to tug at the right edge of the object, and with a gentle snap it came open. Everyone exhaled.

"Two buttons, mate. Left and right. No labels."

One to turn off the booby trap, one to set off the whole thing. The wall safe in Rashid's bedroom: a gray block of Semtex, a whole mess of wire, thin wire, brown wire. A trigger next to the card that said "Goodbye, Mr. Kane." A blinking light. It was Ian who told him to ignore what everyone sees and look past, into the shadow. The trigger in the safe. Two buttons. One pushed in, one still out.

"Try the one on the right."

"Odds are only fifty-fifty, Thomas."

Sergei concluded a moment of silence. "Koshka is always man of good fortune. I make trust with my comrade."

Wells nodded, took a deep breath, and his finger pressed the right button.

Yenchenko winced. "Light become green, no blink."

They all exhaled a sigh of relief.

Tommy stood, flexed his fingers and twisted the handle. The heavy steel door swung open. The vault room.

Wells offered the trigger. "You keep the filthy thing. It'd be my misfortune to squeeze it improperly and blow us all to bits."

Tommy's hand worked across the wall and settled on a light switch to expose everything. Two rows of file cabinets. A document shredder. On a table in the center of the room, a computer with a collection of storage devices. A stack of manila envelopes, maybe a dozen. As they crept into Blackmann's collection of files, Yenchenko, then Wells, pointed to another line of canisters that ringed the walls about six feet off the floor.

Ian murmured, "Oh, my word – "

"*Da*. We are inside very large bomb."

Tommy sifted through the sealed envelopes, which varied in thickness and names neatly lettered in the upper right hand corner. On each one was a handwritten note: "Terminate." Several he could not recognize. But the last three: *Sterling, Warren. Campos, Walter. Tommy, Thomas.*

His eyes scanned the file cabinets. "I don't even want to think about what might be inside."

Yenchenko picked up a flash stick from the table, studied it for a moment and dropped it back on the table as if it were the carcass of a locust.

Ian sounded reverential. "The mother lode. Blackmann likely used all of this to extort, to blackmail, to... I can't even begin to imagine the value of this material."

Tommy grunted and studied the envelope with his name printed in the upper right hand corner. He tapped the edge against the fingers of his left hand and turned it over several times. Then he sighed and put it with the others. "I can. It could cost us our lives."

Yenchenko said, "What is plan?"

Tommy tapped his fingertips on his face. "Round up the bodies. Bring them into the house. I've got a lot shredding to do."

Ninety minutes later, they walked away from the farmhouse, down the bridle path, past the horses placidly grazing in the meadow. Dandy, still wearing the saddle, had joined them.

As soldiers do after the battle, they slowly found the banter of comrades. Who made the better shot. Who saved who from certain death. Who was careless, who was lucky. But after a couple of hundred yards, they fell silent and Tommy displayed the detonator in his hand.

"What the hell." He pressed the button.

A moment later, the earth shuddered. An enormous ball of fire rolled up into the sky. Concussion pushed them forward. A second blast followed. The helicopter was gone, too.

None of them looked.

They simply walked away, toward tomorrow.

CHAPTER FORTY FOUR

Somewhere in Pennsylvania

Wood plank floors creaked under foot. The man named Charlie guided the tour of a log cabin, high on a bluff that overlooked a gray lake. The snug house had two small bedrooms, a rustic but adequate kitchen and an expansive, airy den with a fieldstone fireplace and a modest stable of liquors. Dark leather, polished brass, a small library of used books and woods of different colors and hues defined warm, worn, comfortable, masculine.

Charlie was shorter than Tommy and barrel-chested. A thin strip of light gray hair circled his nearly bald head, and under his rimless glasses he sported a very thick brush mustache. "You got electric, and a well, o'course, but no phone and no god damn TV."

"Fine by me."

"Just telling you, because I don't want no whinin' later. You're too far out in the woods for them services. Goddamn electric was hard enough when we set this safe house up." He scanned the room. "Lotta books anyhow. Maybe you can do some reading."

'Maybe." Not only was there no television or phone, but no stereo, computer or appliances of any kind. *Paradise and prison, at the same time. The thick file from Lucy in the rucksack will keep me busy for a long time.*

Charlie's tone softened "Anyways, it's the best I got on

short notice. You know anything about witness protection?"

"People in trouble disappear, get a new identity."

"Yeah, well, I ain't really in the business no more. I only brought you in because Moses Clay's an old friend. I don't expect your kind knows much about loyalty. People who give up their partners don't have much."

"And what kind do you think I am?"

Charlie shrugged. "Some kinda criminal on the run. White collar maybe. Probably got a contract on your head or something."

"No. It's not that way at all."

Charlie shook his head and waved Tommy off. "Don't make no difference to me, bub. Round these parts, people are judged by what they do, not where they come from. Don't gimme no shit now: you got anybody looking for you?"

"No."

Because when Lucy got through the back door at Gulf Chemical and Gas, she got through the security walls of the Central Intelligence Agency. Because after a long, long day of interviews and notes, she erased every record of Thomas Kane. Because he wanted to keep his name, she fashioned a whole new identity. Because Blackbird's lapse cost him, Lucy went deep on technology. And details counted. *Damn, she was thorough.*

"They give up, did they?"

"No. They're all dead."

Charlie stared at Tommy. "They ain't never all dead."

Heat in his ears. Restraint in his attitude. "This'll be fine. I'm grateful for your help."

"Yeah, well, we'll see come spring. You're up in the woods of northern Pennsylvania, sonny. You're in the dead center of a fifteen hundred acre tract. Town is fifteen miles down a two lane with nothing between here'n there. Not too bad now, but before long, you get a lot of god damn snow. Comes off the Great Lakes. The last guy, the one with all them books, well,

he kinda went nuts and decided to take himself a short walk on a long day. We found him froze when the snow melted at the end of April. 'Course, he was a city fella, probably couldn't live without that god damn TV."

"I'll be fine."

Charlie led Tommy back into the kitchen. "There's some grub in the pantry, just the basics. I'll bring up some supplies tomorrow. You gonna be needing some kind of truck or something?"

"Eventually, sure. I can pay."

Charlie shrugged. "Okay by me. Just don't go gettin' nothin' too fancy. You're supposed to blend in. This ain't New York City, Mister, uh, Kane."

No, I don't think I'm hurting for money. Lucy's still got some loose ends to tie up, but Gulf Chem is sold and gone and Lucy's made a whole new company to go with that identity. Two hundred and forty three million dollars worth of new identity. Babu said, "what is money but paper and metal?"

"Tommy. Friends call me Tommy." *But Babu also said something good can come of it. Like, maybe redemption.* "Or whatever works."

Charlie countered with a long look of appraisal and tugged the collar of his canvas field jacket up around his thick neck. "Yeah, well, we'll get to names if you keep your nose clean and make it through the winter."

Charlie sounded like the sort of man who'd spent a career solving the problems of people on a path to immunity from prosecution because they pointed the finger at bigger fish. He couldn't begin to expect Tommy to be an exception. *And maybe I'm not. Time to hold your tongue, pal.* So he silently followed Charlie through the creaking door onto the broad porch.

"Once the ice gets thick enough on the lake, you can cut yourself a hole and maybe do a little fishin'. You do any fishin', son?"

Tommy softly smiled and heard Paw-paw's voice. *"If you*

ain't fishin', you ain't doin' nothin' worthwhile." It had been many years since dropping a lure into the still backwaters of the bayou in quest of thick catfish to make a hearty platter of real food.

"Yeah, well," Charlie finally said to silence from Tommy, "nobody's perfect. I'll come by tomorrow with supplies, make sure you ain't dead yet."

Tommy watched the retired deputy marshal hobble with a slight limp to his truck and drive off into the dense forest that surrounded the tiny clearing. The woods were bluish-gray in the weak light of late afternoon, and a raw breeze floated across the lake and up the hill.

Sergei Yenchenko and Ian Wells were long gone by now, on their own paths again, following their own instincts and dreams. They had parted with a brief handshake and a long, shared look of trust, and when he was alone Tommy recalled the phone number given to him by Moses Clay in Las Vegas, the number to call when he wanted an absolute out. Charlie's number.

Now there was the taste of chilly air, the quiet of complete isolation and the memory of his grandfather's funeral. Old cronies spun hilarious tales of fondness and the tears came from laughter, not sadness. Paw-paw's last words to him whispered on the wind: *When you do good things on purpose, better things start happening by themselves.*

Tommy turned to the shelter of the cabin. *Not exactly an Alden,* he sighed. *But it'll do.*

Epilogue

Doc bought a small ranch near Santa Ana, Mexico, where he and Miguel rescue and shelter wild mustang horses. Miguel's son plans to become a large-animal veterinarian.

Moses Clay won the Mega Millions lottery, closed his bail-bonds business and retired to renovate a plantation near Baton Rouge, Louisiana. He married Adrienne Tillman and they are foster parents of five children.

Duffy O'Neal went bankrupt in San Pedro and returned to Ireland, where he tends bar at a pub in Barefield, County Clare.

Lester Finn was briefly detained by police in Monte Carlo, but managed to escape. His whereabouts are unknown.

Margaret still maintains a stand in the open-air market on Tortola, and Percy and Old Stanley continue to hustle tourists at dominoes.

Sammy bought a new van and still operates a taxicab business in Nassau.

Nassau Dave sold his adventures business and relocated to Australia with an American divorcee. He owns a hardware store in Sydney.

Daniel Akintunde reconciled with his father and moved to Cat Island. They bought a rum shop in Arthur's Town and launched a thriving Internet business specializing in West African artifacts.

Sandy embarked on a solo circumnavigation of the globe aboard *Freckles II* and was last seen off the west coast of

Panama.

Walter Campos bought to an estate near Palm Springs, California, and became a philanthropist who supports human rights initiatives in third world countries.

Mandy Owens returned to New York. Her notes and materials were impounded by the Department of Justice on national security grounds. She works as a freelance writer, and Tommy Kane thinks of her often.

Cesar Hernandez manages a corporate charter jet service based in Allentown, Pennsylvania.

Lucy Tramanian reconciled with her father. After an extended vacation, she formed TKA Associates, a private investment and equity firm headquartered near Wall Street in New York City.

Ian Wells and his niece purchased a chateau and vineyard in southern France. She operates an art gallery and he paints impressionist landscapes.

Sergei Yenchenko bought a cattle ranch in Uruguay and promised everyone he will not start any more wars.

Tommy Kane became a close friend of Charlie and settled into a quiet, unobtrusive lifestyle in rural Pennsylvania. Some of the time, anyway.

The remains of bodies found at the Carter Blackmann farm were interred at undisclosed locations near Washington, D.C. Their identities are classified, the documents stored there could not be recovered, and Blackmann's nationality remains a mystery.

CHAPTER ONE

Beverly Hills, California

A ticking bomb. The last thing a burglar expects. But there it was, right in front of Tommy's nose when he opened the wall safe. A gray block of Semtex, nestled in a thicket of wires with a motion trigger. Off-the-shelf SD-24, popular as a trigger device. A green diode winked hello.

A thin card, scribbled words, said "Goodbye, Mr. Kane."

His heart missed a beat. Like a speedy spider, a tingle scampered up the back of his neck and into his hair. Just a couple of seconds left to live, and three things were true:

I've been black flagged.

There's a second bomb in the room.

It's time to go.

The green light winked again. *I might be middle aged. Over the hill. A relic. A pain in the neck. But I'm also a hard kill. And I'm going to prove it to Mather.*

The little green light winked for the last time. Window. Roll. Down, away. Duck head. Form a ball. As the device exploded, his body punctured the glass and the white flash of the second bomb splattered his shadow onto the trees. A low rumble billowed into a roar, screamed past. Concussion hammered his back and pushed him further into the night. The light withered from white to yellow and sparks flew in all directions.

A thousand eager fingers of shrubbery reached up and then collapsed under his weight after a long drop from the second floor. The first debris rained down and Tommy went into a roll. Air exploded from his lungs. His legs fought a snare of branches. He shoved out a hand and yelped when a broken twig pierced his flesh. Just as the entire wall of the stucco mansion crumbled onto the shrubs, Tommy tumbled onto the grass.

The fireball billowed upward and heat swept the lawn. Smoke and dust settled into surreal fog over a landscape littered with concrete and stucco. *Shards of glass. Splinters of furniture. Chunks of a corpse. The guy in the bedroom who didn't make it.*

Tommy crouched to find a point of balance. Pain from a dozen wounds stomped across his back and tore down his left leg. He gulped for oxygen but gagged on dust. Bloody clothes clung to his skin like paste. He exhaled a hoarse whistle and blinked his eyes to dismiss tears of agony. Chagrin floated in to whisper admonition: a black bag job so easy it could have been a training mission for a rookie, the lowest of all the lousy assignments of the past year, the expendability signal that his career had ebbed. Hints he should have heeded, but with denial ignored.

And so he was surrounded by bomb debris and embarrassment and his eyelids felt heavy as the soft lawn seduced him with a promise of comfort and rest and dreams. But from far away and long ago came the wisdom of his grandfather: *"If I die, I forgive you. If I live, we'll see about that."* He shook his head to banish throbs of pain, set his jaw and grasped for annoyance, then resolve. He opened his eyes.

A shadow moved. Then another.

Wet team. Tommy muttered a curse and hobbled to a large nearby tree and peeked to scan the perimeter. Shadow number two settled behind a shrub in a pool of orange street light.

Think. Four contacts at the Hollywood Park racetrack parking lot the night before, a straightforward mission. Break into Rashid al-Hassan's house, plant their compact disk and leave. Now they were out there. Now he was the target.

Tommy patted a pocket, felt the phony evidence destined for the safe, and flung it toward the debris.

At the meeting, Mather was the principal agent and said little. A guy named Trotter issued detailed instructions. Trotter was tall, thin; the third man was stocky, pugnacious; and the fourth was average height, blond crew cut and looked like he worked out a lot. He decided first shadow was the third guy and Number Two must be Trotter. He wondered about Mather and the fourth man. Trotter said Rashid was dirty and the FBI needed a little help to move their case along. Tommy wondered just how true that was, but Trotter said it was need to know and classified.

A quick burst from automatic rifles tested the air. *Colt Commandos. Weapon of choice for younger guys on wet teams.* Tommy's tree took several hits and chips whizzed past his head. *They were supposed to take charge of the mess. Now they've got to deal with me.* More slugs punched impact craters into the soft earth near his feet.

Again, Tommy set his jaw. *Ignore the pain. Focus, focus.* A familiar nine-millimeter Beretta found its way into his right hand, but his fingers were unable to close tightly around the pistol. Frustration gnawed on his spirit as he realized adrenaline had tamped down the severity of wounds on his right shoulder. He shifted the weapon to his left hand, unfamiliar with the grip. His body flattened to the ground, slithered slightly right and put a lot of faith into the shadow of the tree.

Easy, easy. Slow, steady breath. Relax. Wait.

A tentative burst of fire through a large bush near the street revealed the first shooter. Just as neighborhood windows came to life, Tommy took careful aim. When faces appeared in the windows, the first man too eagerly pulled the trigger. Three rounds went high. Tommy locked his arm, held his breath, and felt the punch of the grip. The recoil shot into his shoulders and spread out across the frayed nerves of his back.

He winced while his target gurgled a cry and collapsed.

Tommy remained still. Distant, plaintive cries of sirens drifted across the battle zone. *Wait.* People began to step from their houses, transfixed by the mess. *Wait.* Sirens wailed louder now and the second man panicked into a scamper across open ground.

Foolish mistake.

Tommy picked up a lead with the barrel of the Beretta, pulled the trigger and watched the body drop. It shuddered for a moment and then went still.

Flashes of blue and red ricocheted off houses half a block distant.

Another moving shadow. Let it go. Time to leave. Stand. Move. Get to the car. So far away.

Witnesses found courage. One man began to yell while Tommy lunged toward escape.

Don't look. Don't give them a face to remember. Get to the car.

The car rocked back and forth like a boat in choppy water, in and out of focus. When his hand found it, he paused to steady himself against dizziness. He fumbled with the door and suppressed a groan as he stuck his right leg in and his body collapsed behind it. The first police cars burst into the scene. He found the ignition and brought the car to life.

Tommy pressed the accelerator and evaporated into a shadow.

CHAPTER TWO

Near Ventana, Arizona

The fifty-foot racing yawl first surged into Tommy's mind at Doc's weathered shack, twelve miles from town and just this side of hell. The gentle pop when the mainsail filled with air, a smooth tack. Hull speed on a close reach. Everything blue, bright.

Alternatives were good. If he was dead, he was in that place in eternity where the sun was always warm and the salt air sweet. But if it was only a dream, then he was still alive. And if he was still alive, he could snuggle down with the dream in the whispered light of daybreak, a lazy Sunday morning, before coffee. And linger with a dream.

But if he was dead, there was no hurry to go anywhere. Except to follow a course, savor the tranquility....

Tommy's right shoulder screamed. The dream popped like a child's balloon. His eyes snapped open, terrorized and confused.

"Goddammit, Tommy, wake up!"

A bony hand reached out to jostle him a second time. Tommy's left arm blocked the attack and he raised a finger in warning. His voice lowered to a growl. "Don't. Do that again and you'll die."

Doc retreated to an expression of smug satisfaction. "Nap time's over, boy. We got company."

Tommy blinked to beckon consciousness. Behind the

grotesque face of Doc, pale curtains danced in the desert wind
and everything on the other side of the frame was yellow or
reddish brown or gray. Inside, dry heat pounced on every pore
to chill him to the bone.

Doc asked, "You want coffee? I got coffee. Six, maybe sev-
en hours old. But it's coffee."

Tommy tested the dryness of his mouth and nodded. He
began to drift back into the shelter of closed eyes, where a
murky fog offered sanctuary. Doc's long finger slithered toward a shoulder thick with bandages. Tommy saw it coming
and pulled away with a sigh. "Yeah, yeah, I'm up."

Doc's bloodhound eyes were filled with a blend of compassion and anxiety. At the bottom of his long face, a thin
smile formed on a heavy jaw under a bulbous nose. Doc stood
six-four but probably weighed not more than a hundred and
fifty pounds and every joint in his body stood out like sandstone hills eroded by wind and heat. His hairline had crept
high onto a knobby skull and he looked odd without his usual
wide-brimmed hat. But he had coffee and news of a visitor.

Doc said, "Just figured you'd want to know. I'd get my
thirty-thirty, 'ceptin' it's a woman comin' and it don't hardly
seem right to shoot a woman."

The coffee was very old and very strong, barely warm and
intensely bitter. "You don't know some of the women I've
known. What's she look like?"

Doc scampered to the window to double check. "Not too
tall, city clothes, black hair. Set of hips that look like she'd be a
whole lot of fun in the sack, but she walks kind of tight-assed."

Tommy sighed. "Myra Fielding."

"You know her? I mean, damn, Tommy, that's fine – "

"She is – was – my case officer. My boss. She alone?"

Doc turned to answer. "Yep. Jeez, Tommy, how come you
always get these women? Only one who ever come on to me is
ol' Minnie Tohono, who's a damned ugly ol' whore down at
Covered Wells, in the Papago. She charges ten bucks and all

you get is the clap."

"Myra's just my boss." He was safe for the moment,. When Myra wanted someone killed, she sent a team of five or six. Today, she was alone.

Doc abandoned his post at the window. "Too bad. I can still shoot her if you want. Only got seven rounds left in the shack for the Winchester, but I got me an old Colt 44-40. Could plug her at the front door."

Tommy rolled his eyes. "Poor idea. You'd better let her in and I'll try to ignore my shoulder."

Doc grunted. "Three hundred eighty stitches, Tommy. Gotta be some kind of record. Wasn't enough blood left in you to transfuse a god damn squirrel. Had to make a run to Tucson to fetch a bunch of units from a feller I know. I figure if the injuries don't put you down, the blood's probably loaded with HIV or Hep-C."

"Thanks. I *really* needed to know that. Get the door."

Doc chuckled through a half wave, half salute. "Yup."

It would be good to stand, with maybe a bit of indifference, to prove he really was all right even after riding a bomb blast through a second-story window. It would be good to grin past the pull of stitches in his shoulder and leg, just a routine day on the job. Instead he'd have to slump against a pillow that felt like it was stuffed with coarse gravel, weak, pathetic.

Myra marched into the room, each step planted with the assurance of young command. She wore a conservative tailored suit that accentuated assets and minimized liabilities. Her black hair tumbled through a thousand waves and curls to her shoulders and the contrast gave her pale blue eyes an icy warning that kept lesser men at bay.

He spoke in a tone reserved for the prettiest girl in the bayou. "Hello, Myra." Optimism without certainty, hopefulness without anxiety. The smug heat of his words and the twinkle in his eyes intended to annoy her. As always, she rose to the bait.

Myra pursed her lips and spat admonition. "Save the southern charm. I don't need the aggravation. And don't even think about that pouty look. It may work on farm girls, but not me."

A nice try for not trying. "Nice to see you again, too."

Myra crossed her arms and glared as if about to order him to write a good behavior pledge on the blackboard a hundred times. "You want to tell me what the hell happened in L.A.?"

He chose a quiet, calm voice and studied her eyes for betrayal while he spoke. "I was set up. An SD-24, to trigger a larger device. A guy named Mather was the primary."

She nodded. "Barry Mather. He's in the two-thirteen group. Damn. You've pissed off the wrong people." She nodded toward the door. "Who's the goofy guy eavesdropping just outside?"

"Doc? A good friend. I work with him sometimes. Helps to have someone you can trust."

Myra shook her head in slow disappointment. "That's one of your problems. You freelance too much work outside the firm. You ought to know that it annoys the people at the top."

Tommy chuckled. "Like now? What was I supposed to do? Stroll in and file a field report and complain that Mather's people missed?" *Take a chance.* "Besides, who'd I send it to in two-thirteen?"

She rocked her foot on the heel of her right shoe, the way she always did when she struggled to contain frustration. "What did you expect? Have you ever read your personnel file?" She looked up and read the first comments from an imaginary projection on the ceiling, then returned her gaze toward him. "Let's see. Insubordinate. Reckless. Irresponsible. Failure to follow protocols. Ignores regulations. Many reports incomplete. Loose cannon. Violates policies. On and on."

He winced. "Ugly rumors. Some misunderstandings. An occasional distortion." *Press again.* "I can't imagine why it would bother the two-thirteen group."

She studied the floor. "Think about it. Times have changed, but you haven't. The Company is no longer a bunch of cowboys running around shooting Indians. You're a dinosaur. A relic. You've been bounced from one unit to another because you just can't adapt."

She's right. But I've got no use for those smug little computer wizards and their exotic toys. The endless planning meetings. The touchie-feelie debriefings. The stacks of field reports. I'm a field man, plain and simple. Could care less about crap like policies. Rules. The law. No need for those dismissive bureaucrats who can't cope with an empty file folder.

The price, understandable. Bottoming out. Assigned to a rent-a-goon squad, where new control officers like Myra Fielding had their first experiences with command. *Myra, on the way up, mostly because she still hasn't risen to the bait.* He lifted his eyebrows and forced a smile. "So you've come to give me an evaluation and pep talk? Is that what two-thirteen wants?"

Myra looked at him directly and spoke with deliberation. "No, I didn't. Not this time. I stopped by to tell you to run like hell. Disappear. 'Black flag' is an understatement." Her voice softened. "I owe you that much. You're a pain in the ass, but you're loyal."

"Okay, then, I quit. Go back to Washington and tell the two-thirteen group I got the message and cheerfully retired."

She had begun to pace back and forth but abruptly turned her path into a tight circle and when she stopped, her hands were on her hips. "It's not that simple. You're a loose end."

He lowered his voice. "You should know that if they come for me, it's going to get ugly. I won't just fold."

Myra glared. "I wouldn't do that if I were you. You can't take on an entire ops division of the CIA. They'll squash you like a bug."

Tommy shrugged. "So what did Rashid al-Hassan do to the two-thirteen group to deserve being diced up into shark chum?" Time for a direct challenge. "So who's pulling the strings in two-thirteen?"

Myra looked away. "Sorry, that's need to know. And you don't."

"It's against the law for the CIA to operate inside the United States. I could hold a press conference, maybe write a book, one of those tell-all things that shakes up the establishment."

Myra laughed. "Okay, just think about that for a second. You and your associate Rashid al-Hassan made all the papers. Federal officers were killed trying to apprehend you. That CD you were carrying? It's been found at the scene. The FBI and ATF forensic people have already pegged you as an assassin, a double working for al-Qaeda. You're a wanted man, wanted in a post-nine-eleven world where everyone's scared, everyone wants vengeance, nobody trusts anyone and no one gives a crap about one faceless little asset-turned-liability."

"And Rashid?"

She shrugged. "Collateral damage, I suppose."

Tommy flexed the fingers of his right hand to test the level of resulting pain in his shoulder. "You set this up?"

"No."

"You're sure about that?"

Myra looked offended. "Yes. I am. I had no idea assassination was part of the plan. Mather's team requested support and specifically asked for you. I should have guessed it was a wet job. But I swear I didn't know the details." She glanced out the window and sighed. "No. Don't get righteous. Your character is short on morality and devoid of ethics. You wouldn't last twenty seconds under media scrutiny. Trust me on that." Her eyes returned to study his placid face. "Your kind belongs in the shadows. If I were you, that's where I'd go."

She was probably right. Not many would care if he quit, ran, hid. *Hell, nobody would care.*

She dug into her bag and drew a wad of currency. After a quick count, she looked at him and said, "Have you got money? Probably not. Look, two hundred and forty dollars is all I have."

"Keep it." Another mention of two-thirteen would be a wasted effort.

"Take the two-forty. You're off the reservation and on your own." She stepped forward to press it into his hand. "Buy a funny tee-shirt or hat or something." Her fingers lingered on his hand and they shared their most intimate moment. After a few seconds, she pulled away and Tommy tucked the cash into his pocket. "Look, I can't stay. I'm not even supposed to be here. I should go. You should, too. How soon do you think you can travel?"

There it is. Tommy suppressed a smile. It couldn't possibly be this easy to guess the Company's next move. He forced a thoughtful expression. "Maybe tomorrow."

She nodded. "You take care. Heal up, then find someplace to hide. But remember you can't contact me again, okay?" She bit her lower lip while she marched to the door with the same measured step she used when she arrived.

Doc shuffled back into the bedroom. "Damn. I ain't never known a woman who smelled like raspberries before. You think she's got money? I mean, that blood cost me a couple of hundred and I can't exactly send a bill to your company insurance, now can I?"

Tommy pulled the wad from his shirt pocket and offered it to Doc the eavesdropper, who beamed and said, "Say, you up for some *caldillo* with extra chilies? I got a pot going, and we'll get drunk on Tecate beer after. I probably should've invited Miss Stick-Up-Her-Ass, but it's a man's meal." He studied the window for a moment. "Probably melt them plastic tits, anyways."

Tommy's eyelids drooped. The image of the yawl began to form on the wall opposite. *An old yawl. Made of wood. A racing yawl.* It sliced through bright blue water on a smart heel, pushed by a fresh breeze of sweet spring air. It vanished when he jerked himself awake and agreed to Doc's legendary *caldillo* and the Tecate.

Crap. The car.

Tommy winced and asked Doc about it.

"That fancy sports thing you come in? It's in one of them rental places where folks store stuff. Town about forty miles northeast. I couldn't drive the damn thing, so I got a neighbor to help. He's handy with cars."

Damn. The Beretta was in the glove box, and there's probably enough blood on the seat to provide a million DNA samples.

"Don't worry none," Doc assured him. "Ain't nobody gonna find it. I got the bag you was carryin', but that's about it."

No value to arguing the point. But Myra probably tracked the car, which was how she knew where to look. Tommy asked about the Beretta.

"Sorry."

Tommy grunted forgiveness. "It's all right. You didn't look in the rucksack?"

Doc seemed annoyed. "'Course not, Tommy. A fella don't go messin' with another fella's gear."

"You'd have found money for the blood."

"Mebbe so. Just didn't seem right, though." He studied the cash from Myra. "This is fair enough, I reckon."

Tommy began to drift again.

Doc said, "Supper's at six. I'll wake you. Easier next time."

The simplicity of Doc. Accept people as they were, respect a man's privacy and space. He'd found some sort of monastic peace in the desert. As his head turned, the yawl surged past, its starboard gunwale just barely above water. The main and mizzen masts soared into the rich blue sky. At last he saw the stern and the name he'd give her when he took the helm.

CHAPTER THREE

They took their *caldillo* and beer on a thin and weathered porch where Doc kept a tiny table and two chairs, one for himself and one for visitors who were as rare as rain and just as welcomed. A raggedy outpost in a wild and dangerous place, a sanctuary as fleeting as tracks in the sand. The temperature tumbled as purple shadows slithered across the valley, and the oozing chill took the edge off the sting of injury. Out in the shadows, scorpions stirred and rattlesnakes tested the air. For their prey, the time of terror began anew and only the wily, the cautious, would see the sun again. Tommy, the hunter, now the prey, waited his turn. He bit hard into a potent chile and tingling crept across his jaw an into his ears, an act of defiance in the face of a force not yet on the horizon.

"Kinda bites back, don't it, Tommy?"

"Oh, yeah. For true."

"Tomatoes seem a bit nasty. Got 'em off a truck that come by recent. And the taters, they seem a bit weathered."

"Rabbit's good, though."

Doc chuckled. "Bagged that bunny yesterday. Beats hell outa reptiles. Never was much good at skinning lizards."

Tommy filled conversational pauses by organizing a workable plan, one that now saw the Caribbean as a destination because that seemed the best place to find an Alden yawl. It certainly would not be the desert, which might be fine for Doc.

When plates were empty and bellies full, Doc rolled a ci-

garette and relished every breath of it without apology. "It's
my only vice, Tommy. Well, 'cept for the occasional whore,
but I figure that's more out of a sense of relief, like when a
man's gotta take a leak so bad, any spot'll do."

"Like Minnie Tohono?"

"Minnie's stubby and round like a cactus, with a personal-
ity about as prickly. Her house is maybe three quarters of a
mile outside of town." He sucked fire from the cigarette into
his throat. "Sometimes there's a truck parked in front, so I set
and wait for the fella to finish and he'll kinda creep back and
vanish in a cloud o'dusty shame. Pretty much like me, I guess."

Tommy shrugged but said nothing.

Doc stared into the purple shadows. "So the way it works
is I leave ten dollars on the table by the door and, you know,
tell her what I'm needin' and she hitches up her skirt and,
well, I take care of business."

Doc's voice wandered into a quiet melancholy. "Yeah, like
Minnie Tohono. She was the property of a Mexican named
Jorge, y'know."

"I didn't."

"Yessir. He won her in a poker game, and pimped her from
a truck on both sides of the border. One day Minnie got tired
of the beatings. Cut ol' Jorge with a ten-inch skinning knife,
left him to die real slow in the desert. I hear the buzzards
started chewin' on him as soon as he couldn't move no more,
but before he was dead. They go for the eyes first, you know."

He flicked the corpse of the cigarette into the fine sandstone gravel and the tale hung in the cool air for a few
seconds. "When do you think they'll come for you?"

Mather. Until the briefing, he'd never met Mather, yet the
face then, as now, seemed vaguely familiar. Mather spoke
carefully, in well-groomed English, the kind that came from a
sophisticated background, maybe somewhere in the Mid-At-
lantic states. Pressed for details, Mather didn't wish to share
and his voice became more agitated. It was then that he sensed

a faint accent, maybe German, neither distinctly northern or southern, and stuffed with arrogance.

"Are you from the valley of the clueless?"

A strange turn of phrase then, and still odd in recall on the porch at Doc's. The words were clipped and over-enunciated and the word "valley" became "falley." But as much as he nursed the reminiscence, he could not place Mather's face and, after much too long a pause with Doc, said, "Tomorrow. If Myra knows I'm here, so does half the CIA."

"Reckon you're probably right. Too damn tricky to come killin' at night around these parts. You got a plan?"

"No." Seven rounds in an old Winchester meant planning on the fly, a style that would appall Myra Fielding.

"They pretty good?"

"Very good. You'll want to take off early to visit Minnie Tohono."

Doc leaned into a post and looked into the fading light. "Nah. I oughta help out. I owe you, Tommy. Big time."

"There's no markers between us, Doc. It's not your fight. I'll be okay."

Doc scowled and changed the subject. "You hurtin' any? Been a while since I done any doctoring."

Doctoring. A big-timer in large animal veterinary practice, proud and elegant and respected, trusted to care for multi-million-dollar thoroughbred horses. And then came the day when media people swarmed like summer mosquitoes around a tall and confused man trapped in a scandal, played out on an imaginary screen once again in the darkness beyond Doc's shack. A dozen race horses dead and dying behind Doc that awful day, and dirty owners pointed fingers at a vet who'd played ball and now had a career stomped into the dust at Arlington Park. The reporters pressed in, tight, to jab with microphones and camera flashes, demand confession, shred Doc's dignity to nakedness. Tommy shouldered in to push them away from his friend. But for the first time he saw Doc bend his torso into a droop of misery and shame, and for long time after, Doc said that was the day he died. He fled punishment and notoriety, but admitted that anguish was rekindled with every morning when the sun erupted from a rumpled sandstone horizon to stab and torment anything alive. For a dozen hours, the devil's own breath raked the thirsty desert and roasted Doc's three-room, half-wood, half-adobe shack.

For Doc, the shack served as neither retreat nor sanctuary, but rather punishment for sins past and penance for transgressions imagined, a sentence he accepted without complaint and where nature keeps death close, maybe just half a step away.

You hurtin' any? "Some," Tommy lied. It hurt a lot; not more than he could bear, but bad enough that sleep in the cool of the night appealed to him, if only to recharge strength as much as possible before the showdown he believed was surely under discussion at a large table somewhere in the CIA complex. If Myra was truthful in her slip about a special ops unit called two-thirteen, they'd run at least a dozen scenarios to decide the best way to exterminate Tommy, who had the good fortune to be in the center of a broad, desert valley that all but snuffed the element of surprise. So although the repaired wounds yelped with each flex of torn muscle as distant shadows grew, Tommy was tough enough to say only, "Some. But not too bad."

Doc said, "I used to have some ol' Apache Magic,. "They'd mix it with *pulque* and feel no pain for two, three days. 'Course, they'd see a lot of them spirits, some good, some bad, some goddamn nasty. I figured you'd want to keep your mind clear."

Tommy poured the last of the beer into his throat. "Sure hasn't been too clear lately. Probably misplayed this hand, big time."

Doc grunted and shook his head in sympathy. "How you gonna know when your boss is gonna screw you over? Them

Washington-types is all farts and lies, anyway. What's black flag mean?"

"Expendable. To be killed." The pain in his shoulder had consolidated into a throbbing ache and he'd have to get back to bed soon.

Doc seemed to absorb the explanation in a methodical way. "Sorta like getting fired, eh?"

"Yes, sorta."

"'Ceptin' without the usual gooey recommendation and two week's walkin' money?"

Tommy laughed. "Not even unemployment compensation."

Doc lifted his hat and scratched a spot behind his ear. "Damn. That's a bit rough, Tommy. But I guess if you're dead, it's hard to collect anyways."

A rattlesnake, a four-footer en route to supper, crossed the road in the shadow of a power pole. Tommy dusted away a pair of flies while Doc rolled another cigarette and spoke. "'Course, that Myra woman could freeze sand on a day like this." He plucked a shred of tobacco from his tongue, then spat to clean out what remained. "I swear she was so rigid she must have had a long rod shoved up her ass. Anyways, I wouldn't of let her shoot you or nothing. I can handle that old Colt pretty decent."

"It's not your fight, Doc."

Doc's slight scowl betrayed him. "There's gonna come a time when just sayin' fuck'em ain't enough. One of them times when a fella gets just tired enough to not give a shit." He grunted, and put a sly grin on his jaw. "Besides, I don't reckon you're gonna be worth spit with a bum shoulder and a lever-action Winchester and just seven cartridges. You want another beer?"

Chapter Four

Tommy stirred just before sunrise and tested stiffness in his shoulder. It would have been good if some sort of foul-up would delay the CIA team, or if Myra was smarter and more honest than he thought, or that he hadn't done any one of a thousand things that brought him to this moment in time.

But it was not going to be a good day.

He had ladled up a platter of self-pity when he heard his grandfather, from long ago and far away, snort an epithet. "Don't show up to my party," Paw-paw asserted with his nose high and chin thrust forward, "less'n you plannin' to dance."

A faint thutter fouled the warm memory. The distant sound of air disturbed, the methodical rhythm of the main rotor of a helicopter, a chopper that followed the line of the ridge and descended into the wide, flat valley.

Yeah. Oh, yeah. Time to dance. Tommy rolled off the bed to gather Doc's Winchester.

From the front of the shack, Doc called out, his words laced with excitement. "Just like you said, Tommy! They're comin' out of the east with the sun behind!"

The aircraft flew a hundred feet off the ground, unhurried, straight toward the shack.

"Doc, get to the truck! Get out of here, and don't argue."

Doc nodded and scampered from the shack toward an ancient red pickup truck fifty feet distant. The old Colt revolver holster flopped up and down from his right hip while the chopper banked left into a slow turn.

The aircraft door opened. A man who in a baseball cap, bill backwards under thick earphones, lifted his weapon.

A tech nine. Mather.

The full auto burst of fire cratered sand near Doc's feet. Tommy stepped from the shade, fired once out of annoyance and anxiety and then a second time to distract the gunner in the chopper. He lunged for the cover of the shack. *Five rounds left.*

The chopper banked again and retreated to a few hundred yards east. Dust raced in mad circles below it, and the scream of the jet engine roared across parched earth. Mather and the pilot probably paused to organize a plan. Time to think. The shack as a target might not stand up well to a tech nine, but would distract them from Doc, so he dragged his wounded leg across the plank floor, into the back room and bit his lower lip when his eyes measured the little window.

Outside, the chopper began to move.

Tommy took a deep breath and put his mind somewhere else to discard anticipated agony. He dove through the opening and tumbled out into the rocky sand. Misery raked his entire body and for a couple of seconds he felt so dizzy that he thought he might faint. He pushed himself with harsh orders: *Get to your feet. You're not going to die today. Steady. Focus.*

At last he stood and pressed his back to the wall. A long breath of air tumbled from his chest. Adrenaline poured into his veins. His jaw slackened and his eyes and hands relaxed. In an instant he found himself fifty yards from the shack, near an outcrop of sandstone rock, and a cactus guarded his left. He growled when he chambered a round. "C'mon, Mather. Time to dance!"

The chopper rose just above the roofline of the shack and hovered like an excited dragonfly.

Oh, crap. Mather had discarded the machine gun and began to pull a long, olive drab tube to his shoulder. *Anti-armor. AT4. Eighty-four millimeter warhead.* Serious damage was headed his way. Tommy pulled the trigger and the recoil slammed into his wounded shoulder. His third shot was way low. *Four rounds left.*

Now it was Mather's turn.

Tommy struggled to chamber another cartridge while the chubby AT4 shell floated down toward Doc's house. *Here it comes.* He curled into a fetal position and pulled his arms over his head. And he hoped Doc did, too.

Doc's shack blew apart, ripped in all directions.

Tommy peeked through his fingers. A shower of building pieces floating, floating, falling mostly over his own position. Scraps of lumber, metal and furnishings tumbled toward earth and then the fireball pushed them away. He yelped when a chunk of a door dropped on his leg. But not a moment to complain.

An AT4 is a one-shot weapon. My turn.

He popped up from his position. The back wall of the building wobbled but still stood. Mather had discarded the empty fiberglass tube and reached for another AT4. Struggling with aim, he pulled the trigger for the fourth time. He hit the fuselage, a wasted and ineffective shot. His target looked up. Tommy gritted his teeth, ejected the spent shell and tried again. The shot was too high and again he winced while he chambered a new round. *Two rounds left.*

The sixth bullet just missed, but this time Mather must have felt it fly past. Mather's expression remained firm and focused and this time he began to take very careful aim on Tommy's position.

One round left.

Next to the cactus, beads of sweat rolled across Tommy's forehead. Out of time. His right hand thrust the lever to chamber the last round. A searing shockwave tore through his right side. The chopper pilot bobbled momentarily in a gust of hot air, then lifted the craft slightly to give his gunner a better angle.

A hundred yards distant, Tommy gave himself a pep talk and chose a boulder as a tripod for the rifle. Then Doc marched toward the aircraft, hovering just thirty feet above the ground. He gripped the revolver tight in his right hand, squared his shoulders and stood very tall.

"No! No!" Tommy cried into the noise.

Doc snarled words lost in the scream of the jet engine. He lifted the Colt to a point of aim and began to pull the trigger. Again Doc said something. Two more rounds went off.

Mather turned his attention to Doc.

Tommy's eyes widened again and his jaw dropped. *Mather's made a terrible mistake. He should have stayed on me, not the old man with a handgun.*

He lifted the rifle just as Doc fired again. The Winchester recoiled. His last bullet caught Mather's left shoulder. When Mather spun away, his right hand tensed and the AT4 went off. A split second later, the aircraft's tail blew away and the entire front end vanished in a fireball that sank to the ground.

Tommy hugged the earth as debris whizzed past again. The roar of fire dissipated into a crackle, a sizzle and then eerie silence. Doc was much closer to the blast and he heard his own voice murmur, "Dammit, Doc, why didn't you stay put?"

Ribbons of pure black smoke swirled in the air and the acrid scent of burned metal and jet fuel seared his nostrils. He fought for air and he knew that when the adrenaline evaporated he would face an even worse ordeal with wounds torn raw. Within the aircraft wreckage, the blackened remains of two men were held in nearly seated positions by their flight harnesses. Mather had evaporated.

Tommy set his jaw and got to his feet. A few feet away, his rucksack lay in the dust, otherwise undamaged. He tucked the rifle under his left arm and picked up the bag with his right hand. Before him wreckage smoldered, but through the smoke he saw the bed of the truck. Tommy staggered across the burned ground toward the charred pickup. "Doc!" he cried out. "You okay? Doc?"

Tommy paused. The only sound was the devil's breath whistle through the carnage. His shoulders slumped and he called out again in a voice that begged more than demanded.

Then, from behind a mound of rubble, came the sound of adobe being shoved away and a soft voice. "Yeah, yeah. I'm okay."

Doc took his time, but stood, holstered the revolver and dusted himself off. "Shit, that was some goddamn explosion, weren't it?"

Tommy exhaled relief. "Yeah, Doc, it was."

"Bastards wrecked my house."

Tommy surveyed the rubble. "They did."

Doc stepped through debris. "Yeah, but we showed them sons of bitches, didn't we?"

"We did. We surely did."

Doc picked up his revolver and thrust it into his holster. "Damn. I reckon one of their aircraft is missing."

Tommy mustered a grin and laid the gun barrel on his left shoulder while Doc examined the remains of the helicopter. "I think your shot was the one."

"You think?"

"I do, Doc. I really do."

Doc cracked a smile of satisfaction. "Man's gotta defend his house." Then he shrugged. "I reckon we're up to our ass in trouble now, aren't we?" He found one of the porch chairs and stood it up on its legs, dusted off the sandy earth, then settled into it.

Tommy's eyes roamed the mess and he spotted the still functional second chair. He parked it next to Doc's, leaned the rifle against Doc's leg, dropped the rucksack to the ground and joined him. "Yeah, we're in real trouble. You got somewhere to go?"

Doc glanced at the remains of the truck. "Hard to say.

Don't believe my truck's goin' nowheres."

They winced as the wind swirled and blew the stench of the burned helicopter into their faces. But mostly they remained quiet and motionless to let adrenaline settle and get past what had just happened. A surreal silence swept across the scene. Tommy took shallow breaths and closed his eyes to rest.

The sound of a truck revived him. It crawled in low gear to make its own path through the desert. Trailing wind caused a cloud of dust to billow slightly to the front. A large stake body, it paused two hundred yards from the wreckage, then crept forward.

Tommy reached for the rifle.

The truck stopped at about twenty yards. A short and stocky man in white peasant clothing got out and left a boy in the truck.

Tommy instinctively lifted the empty Winchester to a loose aim.

The stranger lifted his hands to surrender. "Please, *señor*, I do not wish to die. Especially in front of my son. I have no weapon."

Doc reached out and pushed the barrel down with his hand. "It's okay, Tommy. This here's my neighbor. Howdy, Miguel."

Miguel's eyes surveyed the scene, and his words were timid. "What has happened here?"

A calm pride filled Doc's voice. "Couple of government people shot up my house, so me'n Tommy dusted 'em. Blew them bastards right out of the sky."

Miguel's eyes showed shock and awe.

Doc asked, "Maybe you can give a couple of old farts a lift?"

"*Si, si*, of course. To town?"

Doc and Tommy turned to study each other's eyes. Tommy remained silent, so Doc turned to Miguel and replied, "No. To Mexico. You know the way?"

Miguel rubbed his chin and then reached to scratch the back of his neck. "*Si, amigo*. I know all the back roads across the border. But I do not wish to bring my son. He is legal. And we will need some supplies."

Tommy hoisted the rucksack.

Doc watched and asked, "You been luggin' that thing around during our little gunfight?"

Tommy said, "When they blew up the house, it came flying out and dropped within reach. There's enough in here to replace your truck, and also to make it worth your while to do me a favor: destroy the car and everything in it. Then you go to Mexico. I've got some business in Vegas."

Doc discarded curiosity, nodded and turned his attention to the rucksack. "Damn. You know something? You're the luckiest sonofabitch I've ever known. One of these days, boy, you're gonna use up the last of them nine lives."

Miguel cocked an eyebrow. "You are *El Gato*, the cat," he declared. "Doc has spoken of you many times. Mostly when he is very drunk on pulque or when he takes the mescaline."

Tommy chuckled. "Apache Magic, eh?"

Doc scowled to mask embarrassment. "Yeah, he's The Cat all right. But he's sure's hell a stray cat now."

CHAPTER FIVE

Las Vegas, Nevada

Fluorescent light oozed from doors and windows of a three-store strip mall halfway between the strip and I-95. It slithered through a thicket of parking lot weeds and expired just a few feet ahead, under a burned-out street lamp.

In the store on the left, a lone patron thumbed through a rack of second-hand compact disks. The cashier tried to look indifferent while he browsed a newspaper, but peeked at the customer. Tommy had a better angle and watched the customer slip at least three disks under his shirt.

On the right, a coin-operated laundromat named Qwick Wash appeared to be vacant until a man, probably the manager, entered from a restroom door in the back and zipped his pants as he went. Tommy was about to return to his sweep of the three stores when a woman came through the same door and tugged a tight, short black skirt down around her thighs. *The Qwick Wash guy did better than the CD guy.*

Sandwiched between the CD store and the Quick Wash, an unevenly lit sign above an unadorned storefront said, "Moses Clay, Bail Bonds, 24 Hr. Service."

The bus ride was long, and the hike from the terminal even longer. Weary, maybe. Vulnerable, certainly. Caution, definitely. That's what shadows are for, but, sooner or later impatience overwhelms prudence. His eyes scanned the perimeter one last time. The person in Clay's office was not on a search team. She was alone and nobody was stationed outside.

Tommy went straight to the door and slipped in to a large open area in which a handful of blue plastic chairs on bent-tube legs scattered like strangers in a field of beige tile. At the far end, perhaps fifteen feet from a partition punctuated with a door labeled "Office" stood a high counter skirted in paneling and crowned with a pale green laminate countertop, just below chest-height for Moses Clay but elbow high for most visitors.

Moses leaned into the counter and cradled his jaw and cheek in his left hand. His right hand clutched several sheets of paper and before him stood a young woman whose attire advertised sexual favors, discounted to street prices.

Moses glanced up. Tommy signaled he could wait. The woman turned and sneered, the way they do when they see a guy that looked like he'd already been rolled. Just visual garbage.

Moses Clay lifted an index finger to gesture he'd only be a minute.

Tommy settled into a molded plastic chair and winced when the exhausted leg and the stitches in his shoulder objected.

"Bobbi Jo, it doesn't matter," Moses continued in a quiet and measured tone. He looked over the top of eyeglasses in gentle patience.

She protested. "It should. It's Larson with an 'e' and not an 'o' so these papers are on a different man and I should get my money back."

"I know. The court clerk is a stupid person." He stood erect but allowed his shoulders to slump. "But the court clerk and the judge and you and I know that the bail on Freddie Larsen – with an 'e' – is seventy-five thousand. Ten of that is yours, but the rest is mine, Bobbi Jo. Any idea where he went?"

She shrugged and looked around as if to appeal to invisible supporters for a plausible lie. When her eyes paused on

Tommy, he shrugged to suggest he, too, was ignorant of Freddie's whereabouts. She wore the pout of spoiled rural belles destined to become Miss Something-or-Other. The look may have been successful with boyfriends clumsy with panty elastic or lecherous contest judges who craved the opportunity to press a palm against a firm breast, but it was probably not going to work with Moses Clay.

Moses softened his voice. "How many times have I posted bail for you?"

"Once in a while. Maybe six. Or ten. Or so." She stood a bit straighter and tugged her shoulders back a bit. "I didn't know I was going to have to add them up." She pulled her shoulders back even further, turned slightly and dropped her chin.

Tommy was amused, but Moses ignored her chest and rolled his eyes instead. "And I've always been straight with you, haven't I?"

"Well, sure, o'course. But that don't mean – "

Moses sighed. "It means that if I tell you Freddie Larsen skipped, the judge keeps your ten thousand and my sixty-five."

Her fingertips found a strand of hair just in front of her right ear and she began to roll it through her fingers. She lowered her voice and chin, but raised her eyes in an exploratory way. "O'course, if you found your way clear to sort of give me ten thousand, then only one of us would be out any money at all and you could draw the blinds and have a really, really good time."

Moses grunted and shook his head. "Dryden tells us that it's better to shun the bait than struggle in the snare. And you're still on the very wrong side of twenty-one."

Bobbi Jo chewed gum with ferocity and loud smacks while Moses explained that the only way she'd get her ten thousand back is if she persuaded Freddie to turn himself in and take the fall.

Bobbi's shoulders relaxed. "You and all your fancy sayings.

They don't mean shit, do they?"

The voice of Moses Clay remained gentle but insistent. "Tell Freddie to turn himself in."

The tableau remained frozen for a long moment before Bobbi Jo heaved an enormous sigh, designed to demonstrate she was not only well endowed but unfettered by a bra as well. She turned and stalked toward the door and brushed Tommy when she passed, her air haughty and her self-esteem artificially inflated.

Under the fluorescent light, the features of Moses Clay were chiseled into a coarse sculpture. His wiry hair had tinges of gray now, and the beard was not so neatly trimmed. His shoulders sank, and his hands lay limp on the counter. And his dark eyes were astonished and mournful as he studied Tommy. "You look like hell," he said at last.

"Been there. Don't recommend it."

Moses Clay nodded, the way he always did when trying to figure out something polite to say or exercise restraint. He grunted and cocked an eyebrow above the whisper of a smile. "Milton reminds us, 'Long is the way, and hard, that out of hell leads up to the light.' The last time I saw you looking so awful was that night at The Chimes you bet you could drink a whole bottle of Southern Comfort." He extended his right arm to beckon Tommy to come forward, take a seat.

Tommy complied. "Yeah, and I would have beat that boy if the bartender hadn't stopped serving us. I believe he was a Tackett, one of those Ole Miss boys."

Moses studied the ceiling to prompt recall. "I believe so. Harlan Tackett, I think his name was. It took him two days to recover in the hospital. And all you did was puke all over me."

"It was a matter of honor." It was the best bar within a hundred miles of Baton Rouge, cozy in its dark wood décor, expansive in its beer menu and exceptional in the quality of po-boys.

"It was stupid. Everyone still believes that you'd have

drunk yourself to death to win twenty dollars. I certainly do. All I remember was all those oysters heaving out of your face and all over my favorite silk shirt. I haven't been able to even look at an oyster since."

Tommy shrugged off shame. "Ah, well, you know how it is. Live fast, eat well. You look good Mo. The years have been kind."

Moses rolled his eyes to feign modesty.

"You still got great hands? We could get a football, toss it around, pass some good time. I always said you had the best hands in the Southeastern Conference."

Moses used a thin smile to hide embarrassment. "And the worst knees. Nobody in the NFL would even look at me. So my criminology degree got me a job with the DEA. I went back to school on the side, got a master's in literature. I thought about teaching for a time, but nothing turned up." He looked around the room. "It's not much, but it's my business. I get by. Remember Freddie Larsen?"

"Can't say that I – "

"Freddie was once a decent middle linebacker for the Crimson Tide. And that made him useful to Bobbi Jo, you know, to keep the hitters and cutters away. His enchantment with sports betting began in college and because everyone except the NCAA knew he was addicted to point spreads, he was ignored in the NFL draft."

A hazy memory came into focus. "Oh, yeah, the – "

"Yeah, he was the one. Now he's killed a bookie in a casino parking lot. Tourism boosters wanted to make an example, so instead of manslaughter, it's a murder two arrest to prove the city's still safe for the weak and the wicked."

Freddie. A jerk that could have had it all, but blew it. *Like me.*

Moses Clay changed course. "No matter. Can I buy you a drink?" He rummaged through a file cabinet and came up with a fifth of Macallan, only partly gone. "It was you who got me to appreciate the good stuff. After all those years of share-cropping and all those years of locker rooms and tape and an-esthetics, I wanted to feel, well, cultured, civilized. You were a good model, Tommy. In some respects, anyway." He passed the bottle.

The silky taste of twenty-five-year-old single malt coated Tommy's mouth and tongue and caressed his throat. *Oh, yeah, I earned that one.*

Clay's eyes were filled with disappointment. In his hands, two chubby glasses with weighted bottoms.

Tommy looked down at a pair of dusty shoes, a good thing to study in the depth of shame and embarrassment. Especially when Moses used long seconds of silence to grind it in a little.

At last, Moses gently hung compassion on every syllable. "It's that bad, is it?"

"Sorry. I didn't mean – "

"Yes you did." He accepted the bottle from Tommy and rationed a small amount in each glass. When he finished, he returned the cork stopper to the bottle and set it aside, picked one glass and gestured toward the other. He swirled the scotch in his glass to allow the rich scent to fill his nose, and sipped. "They put this up while we were still putting down Dixie and Turbo Dog by the pitcher at The Chimes."

Tommy gathered up his glass and hoisted it. "Here's to old friendships." Moses Clay was hopefully still a tolerant man and wouldn't be angry for very long.

"Just as long as it doesn't include oysters. Damn, Tommy. That was something."

"Yeah. It was."

"So. After all these years, Tommy Kane shows up, looking like he's been in a knife fight in some honky-tonk parking lot. I don't believe you're here for the scotch."

"No. And it wasn't a knife fight. It was a bomb. Then a bunch of guys who tried to shoot me."

"How'd they make out?"

Tommy took a very soft sip of the sort of whisky that could make a man feel human. "They're all dead."

"So you called in the cavalry?"

Tommy eased the empty glass onto the counter. "They *were* the cavalry."

Moses Clay shook his head. "Okay. You've finally touched bottom. Your own people want you dead. I'm actually surprised that you lasted this long."

A flash of anger. Defensive. Emotions on autopilot. Acceptance. "Yeah, you're right. Finally found the bottom the manure heap."

"You know, back in Baton Rouge, everyone thought you were just a wild and crazy guy, party animal, the fellow who knew more angles than you ever could find on all the pool tables at Click's put together. A lot of us envied you. You come from tall cotton, man. Good family. Good money, the cultured kind. Had the smarts and the looks, too." Moses paused to fondled and admire his scotch. "But now I'm not so sure. In retrospect, I'd say you were, well, self-destructive."

I didn't come here for a –

The door to the office swung open. Moses muttered an epithet. He gestured for Tommy to remain seated and hidden from view behind the counter. While Moses stood, Tommy scanned the surroundings for an escape route. Maybe Moses or the woman tipped the feds. *Just too damn paranoid.*

"Evening, Jerry," Moses said. "How's the CD shop today?"

"Yo, Mo," a voice called. "Didja see the news, man?"

"No."

Jerry's tone was overloaded with excitement. "Yeah, well, they killed Freddie Larsen. It's on the fucking TV, man! Coupla blocks from here. Musta just happen'd. When they said the guy was out on bail, I figure, maybe he's one of yours 'cause of the hooker he ran with."

Moses spoke in a soft and patience voice. "*Who* killed Freddie?"

"I dunno," Jerry replied. "Some fuckers got him. Maybe the cops, maybe the mob, who gives a shit? All I know's that he's on the fucking slab, man." Jerry's voice brightened. "Hey, you got anything with his autograph on it? We could maybe make a couple of bucks, you know, on one of those Internet auction things."

"No, Jerry," Moses answered. "I don't have his signature."

A pause suggested Jerry was pacing in circles, hunting ideas, but ultimately came up empty handed. He wondered aloud if Bobbi Jo was around, and then decided it didn't matter. "Yeah, well, it was on the news, Mo." Jerry voice faded to dejection. "Look, I gotta get back to my place. Don't want to get ripped off by nobody."

"Have a good evening, Jerry," Moses said and returned his attention to Tommy.

"You know, I've been wanting to say just that to you for a long time, that I really do think you're self-destructive. I'm your friend – at least I still hope I am – and I think I have the right, the duty, to be honest with you."

Tommy sighed. "Okay. Make your point."

Moses began to speak, but fell silent to rephrase. "Maybe not. You wouldn't get it. I'm still holding a stuff for you." He unlocked a file cabinet drawer pulled out a small canvas bag. "I'm guessing there's a lot of cash in there. Nope, I never looked. It comes with a suggestion. Why don't you remake yourself, do some good for a change? What are you trying to prove, and to whom?"

"I need a gun."

"No, Tommy. You need redemption. Pope tells us – "

"Right now, I just need a gun. I'll pencil in time for redemption next week."

Moses pursed his lips and sighed, his eyes mournful again. He reached into a drawer and returned with a nine-millimeter Browning. "It's the best I have to offer, Tommy. I only keep the damn thing because of the cash. It's never been fired."

Tommy released the clip to check the load, then reassembled the parts and chambered a round.

Moses Clay finished his scotch. "They close? I'd rather not have a problem."

"No, there'll be no trouble here. I'm off the reservation." He stood and tossed the remaining Macallan down his throat, licked his lips and savored a moment of luxury. "Retired. Quit. Done with it. And no, I don't come from tall cotton. My daddy was just a coonass, too poor to paint and too proud to whitewash."

Moses cocked an eyebrow.

"For true, Moses. For true. And for what it's worth, I'm pretty good at my job. Old school, maybe, but that's where you find the loyal people. These days? Just names and numbers, like some kind of video game." He grunted. "Even the guys who flagged me are just some number, two thirteen."

Moses Clay leaned back and wore the expression of a man sifting scraps of memory.

Maybe he's heard it before. "Ring a bell?"

"We were doing some field intel once," Moses answered. "Can't remember the exact particulars, but there was some chatter about a group called 'C Two Thirteen.' An up-and coming cartel in the coke trade. Thought it might have been one of those crazy revolutionary groups down in some banana republic, but not much came of it."

"How come?"

"We got called off by Washington. The reason I quit was every time we'd make some progress, some honcho in Justice would move us to something else. We spent forever pushing paper, accounting stuff mostly. You know I couldn't stand that kind of stuff, so I packed it up after I got my master's and moved on."

Tommy waved off a refill. There was a lot more to the story, but it was a story Moses would have to tell.

"Narcotics people are nasty, Tommy, worse than you know.

No scruples at all, no loyalty, no mercy. If you've somehow gotten wired into that..." His voice trailed off. He drew pen and a small slip of paper toward him to neatly print ten digits, which he then handed to Tommy.

"What's this?"

"It's an absolute out. If you ever want to really slip away, to vanish, drop out of sight, you call this number from any phone, anywhere, any time, and ask for Charlie. You must ask for him by name and tell him who gave you this number. He'll take care of the rest."

Tommy studied the paper. "Do you mean, like right now?"

Moses sighed. "No. When you're done with what you have to do."

Their eyes met and they exchanged a deep understanding for a long moment.

"We're even, Tommy. Don't come back. And no, don't tell me where you're going. I don't want to know."

Tommy nodded. Numb. Understanding. Acceptance. But...

Moses sighed and said. "I don't know. I guess because I'm a crazy old son of a bitch. Now, get the hell out of here. I've got to deal with that damned Freddie Larsen business."

Tommy shook the hand of his oldest living friend and was halfway to the door when Moses called out, "Life can be like the lottery, Tommy. I buy a ticket every week and every week dream about what I'll do with all that money. I never win. But I'll still buy a ticket next week."

Tommy had paused to listen, studied his shoes and then offered a faint smile and nod. "Maybe you'll get lucky, Moses."

"You, too. You take care, out there in the dark, hear?"

CHAPTER SIX

San Pedro, Belize - Six years later

A ten-knot breeze dusted off dive shops, little hotels and souvenir huts, flowed along the white clapboard buildings of Pelican Street, and carried the voices of Flora and Antonio to Tommy's ears.

"*Señor* Tommy, wake up!" Flora called to a shapeless form inside a makeshift hammock. Created from a worn-out cast net Tommy had bought from a desperate fisherman for nearly the price of a new one, it was a perfect haven for a nap. Everyone in the bar thought Tommy daft at the time, but the fisherman was back at sea with a replacement and Tommy enjoyed a daily siesta behind the pub.

And so when the children arrived, Tommy pretended to sleep.

"*Señor* Tommy!" Antonio cried. "*Señor* Duffy needs you right away!"

Eight or ten feet away, the children whispered, debating how to safely arouse Tommy. An enormous gray tomcat named Nudger, known to be hostile to the very young, snoozed on Tommy's chest.

Flora was creeping closer to plead in Spanish. "Please, *Señor* Tommy. He has offered us money, but will not pay if you do not come."

Nudger opened his yellow eyes to glare at the children.

Flora circled to the top of the hammock and crept close.

Her voice fell to a whisper. "*¿Por favor?*"

The tip of Nudger's tail twitched.

Tommy suddenly opened his right eye and the two children jumped. Flora laughed and showered him with a bright and innocent smile, echoed by her younger brother. "*Señor* Duffy says you must come right away. It is *muy importante.*"

Tommy yawned and spoke in Spanish. "How much will he pay you?"

She stuffed her words with pride. "A dollar for me and fifty cents for Antonio."

The amount suggested the mission was terribly important and therefore given only to the most reliable of the children available for an errand in the sandy streets of San Pedro. "Only fifty cents for Antonio?"

The little boy looked down in shame.

Flora shrugged and tossed her hands out in a gesture of ignorance to any other possibility than that which she was about to concoct herself. "He is younger than me, *Señor* Tommy, and I am smarter."

Nudger hopped off Tommy's chest and parked a dozen feet away to tidy his fur. Antonio and Flora lunged forward to grab Tommy's left arm and urged him to stand and follow.

"How did you find me?" he wondered in mock complaint.

Flora masked her mouth, mirth sparkled in her eyes and she giggled. "*Señor* Tommy!" "Everyone knows you are always sleeping in the hammock behind *Señor* Duffy's bar, under the mangrove trees, being lazy."

Tommy turned to Antonio. "Is that true?"

After a shrug, the boy tugged at Tommy's right hand.

"Politically savvy answer. Okay, I'll help you earn your wages."

Flora continued to grin and pulled on the other hand. It had been a few years since the last of the discomfort trickled away, and now his grip was at full strength. Anticipating a stab of pain in his right leg when he stood, he smiled at its absence.

A hundred percent. Life moves on. He ran his fingers through a shaggy black beard. It was a mangy disguise and getting silly in the tropical heat. For the ten days, he'd considered heading half a mile south of the marina to visit to the town barber. And an irrelevant disguise, too. Self-imposed paranoia about assassins and boogeymen in every shadow had long withered, swapped out for a life of indolence.

They had barely taken a step when Duffy popped into view from the front of the bar and beckoned him with a broad wave of his hand. A thick Irishman with a wild crop of curly red hair, he wore an expression reserved for moments of confusion and panic.

Tommy kept a pace comfortable for Flora and Antonio Gutierrez and called out to Duffy. "Why is Antonio only getting fifty cents?"

Duffy switched to a puzzled look and his jaw dropped. "Hah?"

"You're paying Flora a dollar but only fifty cents for Antonio."

"Aw, Tommy, 'twas just a number! Look, lad, that bloody Russian's back in town and he's by-damn intoxicated. You know how Yenchenko gets when he's three to the wind, you being mates and all."

Tommy glanced at Antonio and Flora, as if to seek counsel. "Uh-huh. So why'd you keep pouring shots of vodka?"

Duffy reared back and placed the palm of his right hand firmly on his chest. "For crissakes, Tommy, a bloke's got to make a living!" Indignity gave way to persuasive reasoning. "So now you've got to come in and help the proprietor, who pays you a fair and decent wage."

"I'm the cook, not the bouncer."

The large brown eyes of the children shifted back and forth, learning street English.

Duffy shook off the objection. "Speaking of which, I already gave Sergei the conch chowder to take an edge off that hundred proof potato juice he likes."

Tommy, Antonio and Flora reached the sandy, narrow lane known as Middle Street. "That was my supper, Duff. I made it for myself."

Flora's reaction suggested Tommy had overplayed anger in an effort to annoy Duffy and strengthen his bargaining position. A flock of passing tourists included several attractive woman and distracted Duffy. When they all reconnected, Flora had switched to a child-like look of non-committal boredom. Probably had a brilliant future in sales.

O'Neal quickly waved off the objection. "It was that or half a case of crisps." He sighed. "Tommy, I had to give the fellow something, and seeing as the cook's been sleeping at the rear of the establishment. You can always make more, can't you now?"

To buy time, Tommy concentrated on a Tropic Air commuter flight completing its descent to the runway on the south side of town. He brightened and said, "Normally, our fee from rescuing a pub from imminent destruction by Sergei Yenchenko is three dollars, Belize. But since you gave away my chowder and I have to face him on an empty stomach, I think *each* of the kids should get two dollars – U.S."

Antonio and Flora beamed approval.

Duffy's jaw dropped. "Hah?"

"Yes," Tommy said in a considered tone. "Two dollars *each* for Flora and Antonio. I think that's fair."

Duffy stuffed meaty fists into the tire of fat lurking under his barman's apron. "Two dollars! Each?" He cocked his head and squinted. And old pirate couldn't have done it better. "Ah, I'm thinking extortion, Tommy Kane. By-damn extortion it is for sure."

Tommy shrugged. "I can go in and say something nasty to Sergei and let nature take its course." He winked first at Flora and then Antonio, both of whom turned their heads to glare defiance with Tommy toward Duffy O'Neal. "C'mon, Duff.

Get it up. It's only four dollars altogether."

Duffy bit the corner of his lower lip and then waggled a finger. "A god damn thief you are, Tommy. You'd pick a man's purse clean for a moment's pleasure, that's true enough."

Tommy, Flora and Antonio crossed their arms and stood their ground.

"Aw, bloody hell." Duffy dug into his pocket and produced money for the children. They raced forward to snatch it. "Be off, then, and don't be spending it all on sweets, eh?"

The children scampered across the sand road to their mother, a woman named Lucetta, a housekeeper for a hotel on the waterfront. She gathered them into a full skirt that flowed from her waist and pulled them close. They rewarded her with broad smiles and loving eyes and shared with her news of their day's adventures.

For Tommy, the gesture revived the memory of his own mother, modest and shy like Lucetta, but strong. She gathered him and his younger brother in a long swirl exactly the same way. Her hair and eyes were as dark as Lucetta's, always warm no matter how exhausted she was from daily chores. When she swept her skirts around him, the warm security stronger than even the thick coverlet on his bed. The tiny room at the rear of an unpainted shack. Two beds, a chest of drawers, a handful of toys, forgotten.

The tiny room of terror, the night of the tornadoes, when the screaming roar of wind painted fear on her face, pushing in to find her sons and shelter them. The crackling and cracking of the walls, the roof, being torn apart, the bed dancing around on the floor, everyone holding on. Her grip failing, her floating for a moment and then his brother's eyes, pleading, begging. Gone into the blackness of the night, sucked into a nightmare.

And the following day, numb and mute and very small, in the front hall of Aunt Jen. His father, broken by grief, run off, gone. The front hall of a grand house, antebellum to the nines, rich with history, a landmark in Saint Tammany Parish. But strict and cold. His grandfather, his paw-paw, his hero and idol, was not welcome. When he told her his name was Sonnier, she scowled and said no more; he was now a Kane. Her words, as matter-of-fact as if she reviewed a grocery list, a list that pretended Saint Martin on the Teche did not exist at all.

And so Lucetta drifted away with Flora and Antonio, laughing, smiling and happy. Tommy followed Duffy onto the wooden porch and into the shade of a veranda. Crudely painted wooden signs tacked to posts and beams advertised the fare of Duffy's bar. He patted Duffy's shoulder. "Good man, Duffy. That's why I work for you. No matter what everyone else says, you're a fair and decent guy." He peered through a large picture window, combed windblown hair with the fingers of his right hand and stroked his beard twice. "Yep, that's Sergei all right. Sure looks like he's in a dangerous mood, too. I once saw a fellow in Lafayette, looked just like that before he – "

"Please, Tommy, just no trouble in me chipper. I can't afford any more damages this month."

"How much has he had?"

"At least a fifth."

"Hundred proof?"

"Aye. And no, I didn't water it down. He'd know straight away."

Tommy said, "I'm probably going to have to drink with him a bit to calm him down. He'll need to talk it out."

Suspicion narrowed Duffy's eyes. "Just how much might that be?"

"Couple of beers, at least." He paused for effect, then nodded. "Yep, that ought to do it."

The Irishman scratched the side of his jaw and shifted his weight. "And I'd wager it'd be that Brazilian stuff you favor."

"Yeah, Xingu Black. Good idea."

"Expensive beer, Tommy." Duffy cocked a hopeful eyebrow. "Perhaps you'd be willing to make do with a pint of plain?"

Another look through the window. "Well, Duffy, if you insist, but it's a delicate situation in there and I wouldn't want to be distracted."

O'Neal sighed. "Xingu then. But no more than two, eh?" Satisfied he was back in charge, he waggled a finger in front of a stern look. "And no trouble now, or there'll be wigs on the green."

Tommy rolled his eyes. A dusty road to obscurity. From a profession in which recognition was a sin carelessness could get you killed to a bargain for a beer on a porch in a tourist trap. *Oh, yeah, but true.* Anger faded somewhere in El Salvador. Too much time alone. Too much introspection about vengeance. Too much simple time in the sunshine. A paradise life with too few expectations.

Weeks became months and months became years and even the annoyance that the CIA was no longer looking for him was gone on the tide. Maybe the latest wars, on the other side of the world, had done him a favor. Maybe no one cared any more. Maybe it was time for a trip to the barbershop for a shave and a haircut and a civilized look again.

The Alden had been gone a long time, too. It took more and more effort to bring it into focus in the makeshift hammock, behind a bar, snoozing away summertime. Soon it'd be winter and Ambergis Caye would be stuffed with sailors and tourists bored with cruises and all inclusives. The people with Aldens would be roaming at sea, while he'd be flipping burgers and deep frying fish and chips in a dinky little bar run by an ex-pat Irishman who wanted to be pals with everybody.

And now Yenchenko was in town, boozed up on vodka and probably could care less about conch chowder.

Tommy stepped into the pub. Four tables clung to the street side of Duffy's. The bar occupied the rear, guarded the entrance to the tiny kitchen where Tommy worked for wages that would never grow into an Alden yawl.

He approached a huge body that leaned into the bar and, when close enough, he spoke gently, softly, calmly, as anyone approaching a wounded bear might do.

CHAPTER SEVEN

"Comrade Sergei, *kak pozhivaesh?*"

Yenchenko turned, his eyes glassy and slow to focus and invited Tommy to perch on an adjacent stool. The sly grin slithered onto Sergei's jaw. "*Zaebis*, Koshka. It goes well."

Tommy's personal dossier on Sergei Yenchenko was thick with experience and warm with fondness. A soldier's dialect of idiomatic profanity and covert sentimentality. A couple of years older, half a foot taller and at least a hundred pounds heavier. Unapologetic about his politics. His frequent declaration, "I am good communist still!" probably made him useful in the cynical final days of the KGB, but shot out of favor with the secret services that followed the collapse of the Soviet Union. He was abruptly shoved out, into the cold. Yenchenko always insisted his dalliance with a supervisor's wife was irrelevant, perhaps a matter of counterintelligence but at the most merely a young spy's indiscretion.

A deep passion for social justice incubated in Cuba. There he came to fondle revolution as a temptress, then aged from naiveté into stirring up trouble simply out of love for combat. A global view: Africa simply beyond control, Islamic nations too culturally extreme and Europe too mired in comfort and bureaucracy. The Americas, below the Rio Grande, offered endless opportunity. So despite a good network in Europe that he freely shared with Tommy – he actually plugged Tommy into an old network of Stasi operatives headed by Dieter Kreutzer near Munich – Yenchenko migrated to the western hemisphere and a perpetual quest for revolution. He would till this fertile garden, plant socialist revolutions and harvest a new communist order. And the CIA was an unwelcome intruder on his private turf.

Sergei took another drink directly from the bottle. He

belched, unashamed, loud and deep from within his chest, then brightened. "Is good to see you again, Koshka, despite foolish beard. Your wounds: they heal well, *tovarich?*"

An odd question at first. Only a gallery of scars illustrated his own fall from grace. But he guessed Yenchenko spoke of the psychology of damage, and became wary as he took the bottle from Yenchenko's paw to sample the vodka. The heat of hundred-proof Stolichnaya in his throat caused a wince, but he avoided a cough, and he wheezed through the sting of alcohol. "I'm doing okay." Tommy glanced over his shoulder and spoke confidentially in Russian, "Duffy's a little nervous that you might wreck his bar."

Yenchenko solemnly nodded while his tired, pale blue eyes ran an appraisal on Tommy's condition. At last he muttered in a slurry of Russian and English. "*Nyet*, Koshka. Today Sergei is not in mood. What does he pay you to prevent disaster?"

"A couple of Xingus. It's fair, I think." Tommy gestured toward the empty bowl on the bar and grumbled. "Duffy's already given you my supper."

"*Da, da*, of course. After food in jungle, is good to return to fine meal. You are good cook, Koshka. Poor shot, but good cook." He belched again, this as if to clear his throat, then donned a thief's grin. "You of course have given money for bar bill?" He scowled at the blank expression and answered his own question. "*Nyet*. You are always *zhmot*, a miser, a stingy person. It is not in your nature to help peasants find their justice."

"Which peasants?"

Near the border of intoxication and about to cross a frontier into substantial stupor, Sergei poured vodka into his mouth, swallowed and wiped his lips with the back of his hand. "Peasants. Where is no matter. They are all the same. I don't give damn." His eyes narrowed and he stabbed the air with one of his massive paws. "Sergei Yenchenko has made good career from Americans. To you, the whole world is, how you say, '*bardak*'?"

"Brothel, a whorehouse."

"*Da, da!*" Yenchenko lurched into exclamation as though he had discovered some profound truth. "The world is for *Amerikancy* a whorehouse, and you come with few small coins and take what you will, eh?"

Tommy accepted the bottle from Yenchenko and pretended to sip. One taste was more than enough. "I'm not going to argue politics with you, Serge. I'd lose anyway."

Yenchenko raised his finger as if giving a lecture to an errant schoolboy. "Koshka, Koshka, I am as usual superior. I have ear to ground, hear many things. It is Russian manner. Please. You must sit. We will drink together and remember better times and tell lies as good men should do. Then we sleep whole next day!" He belly-laughed at his own joke and gestured for the bottle, which Tommy passed with neither complaint or additional sample.

In a lifestyle dedicated to indolent complacency, Yenchenko's boisterous bravado had grown stale. But it was time to get to the point to earn the promised Xingus, so Tommy spoke in uneasy Russian, "You've been out of town quite a while. It did not go well?" He concurrently surveyed the field of breakable glassware in the vicinity of the bar and suggested they move to a table. Maybe Duffy would reward him with a third beer.

As they settled into chairs, Sergei became melancholy. It was a delicate moment, for few men were as unpredictable as Yenchenko when morose and to an unknown extent intoxicated. Three workmen entered in quest of a pint to cap the day, so Tommy and Yenchenko relied on the privacy of Russian, slowly, because it had been a while for Tommy.

Sergei confessed his latest failure to ignite a socialist revolution, this time in Guatemala. "Yes, Koshka, you correctly observe most recent operation is major failure. I had formed unit, good men, not so good soldier, but brave, and we are caught in trap. There is firefight. Nearly all die. I escape only because I carry two men from jungle, take them home to family. Perhaps to die there anyway."

Tommy nodded sympathy. Yenchenko loved combat and would probably die in battle. It was reasonable that he was depressed, because he had fled rather than making a good account of himself. Probably stuck with a crew that was longer on brave talk than military skill, typical of the young and angry radicals who flirted with danger in sleepy towns throughout Latin America. As a military leader, Sergei sounded retreat not to fight another day, but to honor the brave. Probably a minor skirmish, for nothing had appeared in the local newspapers. Tommy stayed silent to allow Yenchenko to unload anger and adrenalin and wander off somewhere to sleep for a week.

Yenchenko continued in Russian, with greater pace as he settled on efficiency. "Intelligence: fair, perhaps good, Koshka. We did not expect people from private company to be CIA, however. They were waiting for us, well armed and well financed."

No surprise. The CIA was fond of front companies for covert operations, especially to nurture a relationship with a two-bit local right-winger who played soldier by day and ran death squads by night. The region was stuffed with second stringers working as "advisers," because all the best were on the other side of the world to cope with Islamic politicians, corrupt or radical or both. Early on, it was easy to avoid CIA trainees more interested in deals with local despots. As the pages of the calendar next to Duffy's dart board turned, Tommy began to believe he was off the action list, modestly comfortable, and perhaps had a future in obscurity.

Tommy raised a hand to interrupt. "I know you enjoy vodka, comrade, but I really need a Xingu Black." He poured a plaintive look on Duffy, who set his jaw but fetched a chilled bottle of Xingu and a reasonably clean lager glass. When Duffy arrived at the table, Yenchenko growled a sloppy obscenity to keep the ruse alive and the barman scampered away.

Tommy filled his glass in the smoky golden light of late afternoon sun, filtering through a dusty window.

Sergei's shoulders drooped and he sighed. "Koshka, there is old saying, the cake is dough. Paramilitaries do business with drug people and everyone make business with CIA."

Tommy shrugged and sipped. Central Intelligence was known for spreading a lot of money around and anyone with political ambition could toss a bucket into the well, arm themselves to the teeth and travel in a motorcade.

"Your CIA, Koshka."

"Not any more, Serge. I'm out, a long time, quits. They tried to kill me, you know."

Yenchenko grunted. "You learn nothing from Sergei, who take pity on poor beginner, teach all he know from time with KGB and SVR. What is reward? You make careless mistake. How you say *besporadok?*"

"A mess." *An easy confession. Serge takes pleasure in teasing, and I'm immune from embarrassment. Patience.* There was no need to remind Yenchenko that both were agency outcasts, expats in San Pedro and refugees from reality. *Play along, see where it goes. There's a scheme in this someplace.* At a minimum, it would be a way to pass some good time and enjoy a couple of free beers before the supper crowd arrived and he would return to the grill in the kitchen.

"Da, konechno." Sergei chided. "You make mess." He paused for the usual long moment to set up the point. At last his eyes came up and locked with Tommy's. "But perhaps this bomb mess is part of plan, yes? Perhaps CIA make elaborate plan to gain trust of Sergei Yenchenko."

Amazing. "You still think I'm a double?"

Yenchenko looked away but rippled a soft shrug as he did so.

Tommy sighed. "I'm really disappointed, Serge. We've known each other for fifteen years and tried to kill each other most of them."

"So. You must now speak only truth to Yenchenko. You have no more relationship with CIA?"

"For true. We both know about the legendary ops from the late sixties and seventies, the way Company would black flag in spectacular ways to make a point. The Brits did it too. And some managed to defect to the East and settle into a comfy intelligence nest with both the KGB and the Stasi."

Yenchenko shrugged.

Tommy raised the bottle to his lips. "Like Dieter Kreutzer, who devoted the better part of his career as an East German agent hunting a mole code-named Blackbird."

Memories of a fateful day flickered in, a day of warm spring sunshine, the kind that dissolves an alpine winter and ricochets off the pale yellow stucco wall of a *pension* that bore Dieter's last name and some traditional Bavarian designs to charm tourists. And there was Dieter, who leaned back from the tiny chess table outside the *bierstube* and wore a look of immense satisfaction. His laced fingers rested on his equally immense belly. Tommy himself was about to part with a rook around which a sturdy defense had been constructed. Now and then a small car hummed past. Dieter had reminisced about the hunt for Blackbird, which Tommy deliberately tried to ignore because he thought it part of the psychology of the game of chess.

That's when Myra Fielding showed up. And it all went sideways.

The memory began to wither. Once more, Tommy mentally scanned the perimeter of the German bar. *Something was never quite right. Something was out of place. Something I missed. Argh. Let it go. Once again..*

The Xingu had crossed his palate practically unnoticed. He returned the bottle to the table. With luck, Sergei had not sensed that moment when a target's mind goes somewhere else and betrays him.

"It is not good to lie to Sergei Yenchenko, Koshka. Men

die for less than this." Yenchenko wrapped his huge paw around the bottle and slid it to the side. After a moment of contemplation, he decided. "Is good, I think. You have spoken truth, and so now I share with you most interesting information."

Yenchenko glanced to either side, then leaned forward and spoke in Russian. "CIA pays for black operations in region through clever scheme to launder money from drug dealers and for cash that cannot be traced."

"That's nothing new."

Yenchenko leaned back and tossed the vodka down his throat as if it were water. "Yes, of course. Do I speak too quickly for you?"

"A little. Take it slower." Covert ops were always off the books and usually financed in creative ways. The CIA tended to be long on expediency and short on morality, so he shrugged.

Yenchenko began to reach for the bottle but paused and shifted his tone from one of melancholy to chilly clarity in measured Russian. "I tell you this, *tovarich:* now *Amerikancy* make alliance with Cuba. It is most true. Cuban military is in drug business and has made partnership with CIA. You are surprised?"

"Surprised? Sure. Astonished? No." The Xingu from Brazil had gone down way too fast and he motioned for reinforcements from Duffy O'Neal. The Company would have set up business fronts in Latin America to collaborate with Cuban army leaders and finance right-wingers. That in turn would keep Castro's regime in check while the ringleaders simply had to wait for the old Communist to die. A simple coup would follow and all the key players in the western hemisphere would be happy. It was plausible and reasonably brilliant.

Tommy accepted his second free beer from Duffy and used his expression to report progress on the temper of Sergei Yenchenko. Visibly relieved, O'Neal retreated to the bar and customers with currency. But there would not be a complimentary third round.

"And of course, the *staryj volk* has a plan?" Yenchenko admired wolves more than any other creature and had an old wolf proverb for every circumstance.

The Russian beamed. He rubbed his hands together and a faint twinkle danced in his eyes. "*Da*, it is so. Sergei Yenchenko comes to good bar, drinks well, makes owner believe he will cause most serious damage. Owner goes to find Tommy Kane. And so we meet and now we form team."

"The wolf may be old, but he is cunning."

Yenchenko chuckled and feigned embarrassment. "To pretend to be drunk to fool Duffy is good tactic, *da?*"

Tommy hoisted his glass in salute. "Good strategy. But are you sure you haven't been to one *pupuseria* too many?"

Sergei's voice filled with confidence and authority, and he ignored Tommy's remark. "So. Perhaps we become team and attack these companies. Together we go out and shoot them all into small pieces. You will take your revenge and I myself keep Communist cause alive. I think you are almost as good as myself, Koshka. Together, we make success of small war." Yenchenko spoke with earnest reasoning as if he were utterly serious about declaring war on the United States and Cuba at the same time. He began to outline aggressive tactics, ideas born in jungle nights when it was too hot to sleep and too cold to go home

Tommy's attention and concentration drifted while, like a Viking on a quest for Valhalla, Yenchenko laid out strategies, alternatives to strategies, and alternatives to alternatives. Typical Sergei, floating through a smorgasbord of military tactical options in search of something to tantalize a snoozing cat named Tommy Kane. Complacency was good and boredom not half bad. *Nine out of ten ex-spies recommend it.* He'd become soft and didn't mind. He'd let his hair grow way too long and cultivated a shaggy beard, mostly because it meant he didn't

have to bother with shaving. Or any of the routine maintenance. On his body, the clothes of a peasant.

Yesterday were mostly troubled, like Moses Clay had
summed up. Todays were indifferent. Sure, out of habit, he'd
taken up the cause of a little fellow suffering at the hands of a
uniformed bureaucrat. And inevitably, he'd have to move to
the next town along a string of hamlets, connecting the dots to
create a jagged line down the west coast of Mexico and into
the smaller countries that clung to its belly. Downscale, one
step, one town, one run-in after the other, and, yeah, the legend of *El Gato* became increasingly scruffy.

Now *El Gato* was back in an English-speaking country and
real estate was thin. Just a couple of hundred yards remained
between tortured yesterdays and the Caribbean, where Alden
yawls roamed in dreams every now and then. The inevitable.
On hold. Just postponed, really. *Right but Yenchenko is here and
there's adventure again, a chance to march right up to Death and
spit in its eye.*

It was addiction, all right. Addiction to danger. *Maybe it's
time to just say –*

A petite and deeply tanned woman bounded into the bar.
Much younger than either of them, she arrived like a sand
bunny, in tiny shorts and a thin top, and pounced on Tommy.
An exuberant embrace. A lusty greeting that included kissing
his ear. Her golden pixie hair shimmered in the dusky light,
her sky-blue eyes carried the sparkle of Caribbean sunshine
and her body caused every man to sigh.

CHAPTER EIGHT

Everyone in San Pedro knew her only as Sandy, owner and skipper of a forty-eight foot Morgan sloop called *Freckles II*. She squared her shoulders and parked her hands on her hips to tease Tommy. "Buy a girl a drink?"

Yenchenko waved his hand toward his knee. "Come, Sandy, sit, and Uncle Sergei will pay for all you order."

She beamed, kissed him lightly on the cheek and welcomed him back to town. "That would be a lot of rum, Serge."

Tommy chuckled and pointed to an empty chair. "Long day on the dock?"

"I don't even want to tell you, Tommy. Trying to get diesel engine blowback solved in this port is such a pain!"

He motioned to Duffy a promise of payment. "Ernie and Carl?"

She sighed "Ernie and Carl. Those guys think anyone with boobs is dumb, so we spent half the day getting past the bullshit and into recognition that they were in a bit over their heads. Got it fixed, though." She held her hands aloft to display the remnants of grease, cleaned with gasoline, etched in every line on her palms.

Duffy arrived with a tall glass of straight Mount Gay rum. Her laugh was one that all knew well: a throaty chuckle not quite a giggle, sultry and charming all at once. Rewarded with a bawdy smile that caused his cheeks to redden, Duffy mumbled something and withdrew to compose himself.

Tommy spoke. "Taking *Freckles* out? A charter?"

"Nope, still no charters. Business sucks. I'm shoving off tomorrow for maybe the Virgins or Jamaica, see if I can find some action up there. The friggin' bank is getting a bit tense about payments on the boat." Sandy took a deep drink and closed her eyes to savor it. When the troubles of her day washed out with the ninety-proof tide, she drifted back to reality. "Ah, that's better. So. What are you guys plotting?"

"We were sketching out some ideas on how to wage combat against the local governments, the CIA, and maybe even the Cuban army. That about sum it up, Sergei?"

Yenchenko poured himself another vodka.

"Cool. Is this one of those paramilitary things with a gunfight or a *coup d'etat* or something?"

Tommy and Yenchenko exchanged uneasy glances. Tommy said, "Well, probably some occasional, but intense, combat."

Her eyes widened in mock astonishment. "With like machine guns and stuff? Where they actually try to kill you?"

"For true."

"*Da, da,*" Yenchenko added. "They would squash us like small mosquito." He smacked his own arm for effect.

Duffy spun around to see if war had broken out, frowned, and returned his attention to pulling a draft for a cash customer.

Sandy went for mock empathy. "Ah. I see. Uh-huh."

Not yet thirty, but already a legend across half the Caribbean. Steel nerves. A master's skill. And a love of adventure. She'd taught him the basics of sailing and tested him in scary weather, where he found her sense of assurance so calm that it bordered on the unsettling. And now she was about to pull their chain, big time.

"Hm. Is this like one of those covert things you guys used to do?"

Run with it. So he replied in the affirmative and echoed some of Sergei's concepts with reckless abandon. Sandy listened with attentive patience. When enough beans had been spilled, he leaned back and turned the empty glass in front of him nearly a half dozen times. "So, what do you think? Is it worth it?"

"I have a vote?"

Yenchenko nodded. "All present may vote. It is democrat way."

"You sure? I get awful honest after a few belts of rum." Her expression drifted from thoughtful consideration to an exaggerated display of concentration, complete with furrowed brow and a couple of chin rubs for effect. After several seconds of silence, she spoke first to her glass, but then Tommy and finally to Sergei. "I think you guys just might have an outside shot at it. You'd be famous, and you could really stick those bastards for doing the kind of shit they do. Justice with a capital J."

Patronization with a capital P. Should've expected it.

Yenchenko shifted his weight in his chair.

Sandy went to a placid, almost maternal smile. "That's just what I thought. You guys sit in Duffy's day after day, well, except when Sergei goes off to rob a stagecoach or a train or whatever, and you get drunk and tell all these stories about what hot shit you did in other places and other times. Hey, I mean, like you argue over which one of you was the best in the whole world."

Tommy and Yenchenko winced.

Sandy swirled the remaining rum in her glass before she tossed it into her throat. "Anyway, it's boring. Neither of you has much more than a couple of changes of clothes and a couple of guns you never use except to shoot cans and bottles by the packing plant when you're snockered and arguing about the 'good old days.' Maybe instead of talk, you really ought to do something worthwhile. Something that people will talk about for a long time."

Tommy invited her to continue. "Such as – ?"

Her blue eyes came up as steady as the easterly trades and

just as brisk. "Gosh, Tommy, I'd think that's something you grownups would be able to figure out for yourself." She parked her glass on the table, stood, and put her hands on her hips. "You used to talk about buying an old Alden racer, a yawl, and refitting her and cruising the world in search of adventure. 'Course, you'd be better off with a ketch. So, silly me, I came by to find out if you're interested in crewing for a couple of months or so. Pay's crap, but you'll get a nice tan. But, anyway. Your whole life is short-order cooking for meals and a bed in this dump. Me? I've got a quarter-million-dollar yacht that needs some maintenance before I cast off at first light and go roaming. Have fun, fellas and thanks for the drink. I've gotta get back to work."

She wheeled and marched out of the pub.

Sergei Yenchenko studied the nearly empty bottle in front of him and chuckled. "*Dat' pizdy*," he murmured. "Sergei thinks foolish Koshka has boot put hard on his ass."

"Oh, yeah. Where I come from, there's a saying: tell the truth, ruin the party."

Yenchenko nodded and switched the conversation back into Russian. "And where Sergei is from, there is also saying: if you have fear of wolf, do not go into forest. Tell me, *tovarich* Kane. You are afraid of wolf?"

"We're not kids any more, Serge."

A look of astonishment raced across Yenchenko's face. "Such statement is out of character from Tommy Kane of old days. You were almost as reckless as myself. Perhaps more, eh? You are crazy, person of adventure, man who makes own rule. Not this little *El Gato*," he sneered. He paused to allow his voice to fill with awe. "But *El Zorrero*, the fox who steals and shits on floor when he make departure. You have favorite expression about life, I remember."

Tommy reverted to English. "Live fast, eat well."

"And now you live slow, eat poor."

Tommy cocked an eyebrow. The Alden yawl drifted into

focus. "Perhaps."

Sergei sighed, reached into a deep pocket and withdrew a thin sheaf of paper that somehow had survived jungle combat, unfolded it and laid it on the table before him. "Perhaps, perhaps not, Koshka."

It was a secret CIA cable to Perry Foster, station chief in El Salvador. Foster. Arrogant. Fond of experimental interrogation techniques. Girls under the age of sixteen. The cable, smeared with dirt and dried blood, should have been shredded upon receipt. Just six days old, it ordered Perry and others to Nassau in four weeks to support an op directed by "Lomax/C-213." The cable was signed, "Fielding." He tugged paper money from his shirt pocket, waved it toward Duffy and ordered another beer. "Where'd this come from?"

Sergei replied with indifference. "From corpse of American called Perry." His eyes narrowed and his voice fell to an intense whisper: "Who is Fielding?"

"My last case officer. I'd like to think that she wasn't behind the black flagging, but I've never been quite sure. She mentioned 'two-thirteen' without the 'C,' and a source of mine, an ex-DEA guy, had heard of a 'C-213' narcotics op but they could never pursue it."

A sly grin slithered across Yenchenko's face. "Perhaps we can. The American Perry, he dies poorly. After he tells Sergei what he knows, he becomes of no value. No trip to Nassau for pleasant holiday." He shrugged and shook his head in sadness and his tone became wistful. "It is most unfortunate, I think."

Most unfortunate is probably an understatement.

Yenchenko leaned back and with great deliberation poured a splash of vodka into his glass. "Time marches like seasons on Steppes," he declared. "With new spring, old misunderstandings are forgotten, old rivalries become memories, eh? One must always look forward, Koshka. I tell you this for your own good." He looked up. "CIA must need security detail for important matter. I believe money, much money is to be exchanged with Cubans. Perhaps we make team, eh? We steal money, even shares, make new future. For you, perhaps it is *parusnye lodki*, a sailing boat?"

"How much money?"

"I learn between six million and ten million, American."

Tommy lifted an eyebrow. "And for you, comrade? Another war?"

"*Nyet*. The game becomes old, and perhaps I will retire to nice villa with much vodka and pretty women. For us to get good life, we make robbery from bad people who should lose money anyway. This seems to be reasonable."

Tommy rubbed his chin. "Your intel on the money laundering. It's solid?"

Sergei laid a thick hand on the upper part of the chest and tilted his head backward so he could look down his nose at Tommy. "*Da, da*, of course."

"You sure?"

"There is brothel in El Socorro – "

"Near Matagalpa and Cerro Apante?"

"*Da*, the Cubans have Nicaragua base nearby. Whores are friend of Yenchenko. I collect much honey in trap. They are like small bird – how you say – *lastochka?*"

It was a reference to Russian female agents who use sex to gather intelligence. "Swallow."

"*Da*, like swallow. They do this not so much for money as for political, so I believe them." Yenchenko tapped the side of his nose. "It is scent of money that has dirt, da? Much money that we need only to take and no one can make complaint." He paused for a moment to allow his persuasion to settle into Tommy's mind. "You and I, Koshka, are two of same, yes?"

"Yes, *bzdenok*."

Yenchenko roared with laughter. Heads turned in the bar and angry glares tumbled in a squall line across the room, but Sergei paid no attention. "How you say in English?"

"Little old man who farts frequently. Look, Serge, we're

probably going to need some help."

Yenchenko leaned back, a look of astonishment on his face. "What can be wrong with plan?"

"First, they've got all the toys —surveillance, communications, analysis: state of the art gear, stuff so good that they've got mikes the size of a speck of dust. We've got zip. Second, they have resources of intel from most of the western nations in the world, not to mention FBI, DIA, NSA, and probably outfits that use up the rest of the alphabet. We're out of the loop. Third, they own most of the government people down here, and those they don't own they control. If it comes right down to it, they'll turn us in and not feel bad about it. Fourth, even if you got close, they're not the kind of people who are going take kindly to people pinching cash from their cookie jar. They *will* come after us, and they *will* kill us."

Yenchenko drummed his fingers. "Some small obstacles, of course. With no obstacle, task is boring. You have plan?"

Bits. Pieces. Scraps. Snippets. Ideas, free-floating. Coming together. Pure folly. *Totally insane. Just can't touch the doggone brake.* "I haven't gotten that far yet. But I'll figure something out."

Yenchenko scowled. "Idea is like bread that is not long enough in the oven. What is expression?"

"Half-baked." *Another understatement. The day's getting out of hand.*

"So. We bake bread a little more. We make arrangement. Form team. Do it anyway."

Tommy retreated to silence, his arms crossed over his chest while Yenchenko toyed with his empty glass, clearly respectful as a colleague considered options. *At last. Yeah. Might work.* He stood and tugged a ten-dollar bill from his pocket and dropped it on the table.

"You depart so soon?" Yenchenko wondered. "Come, Koshka, sit. We make good drunk, tell good story, make laughter. No? Where do you go?"

"You heard Sandy. She's sailing east, to the Virgins maybe. That's where I'll find the Major." He ignored a scowl from Sergei and explained, "I'm going to have to talk him into this crazy scheme if we have half a chance."

"Poor idea. Idea, Koshka, but poor idea. He is man not to be trusted."

"And we're better?"

"On worst day of most excellent life, Sergei Yenchenko can be more trusted than Major, who is person with no name and very bad habit of leaving many body behind."

Tommy shook his head. "You and I both know this is the kind of job that will require at least three. Somebody's got to have our back. Someone really good. Can you get us anyone better? Or as qualified? He's just like us Serge. Out in the cold."

Sergei scratched his jaw and reached for the bottle, then pulled back, studied Tommy's eyes for what seemed forever and then faintly nodded.

"Where can I find you? In, say, four weeks?"

Yenchenko paused for a moment of contemplation. Then he sighed and said, "Nassau. The usual place, Paradise Island."

CHAPTER NINE

St. Thomas, United States Virgin Islands

The halo around Sandy's head was an accident of dawn. Sunrise skipped across her always windblown hair and glowed through vapor that rose from mugs of coffee in her hands, fresh and hearty and strong to launch a fine day, the last leg of a two-week journey.

It had been a half hour since Tommy sighted land while at the helm on first watch, grey dust on a purple pre-dawn horizon. Now, fuzzy, soft green at sunrise. With the Caribbean open for breakfast, hopeful terns cruised for surface garbage while more purposeful brown pelicans dive-bombed careless fish. *Freckles II* very much sailed herself in ten-knot aft air, but hands on the wheel guided him into the fantasy of the Alden yawl, a fifty-footer, knifing through groundswells under clouds lounging like cotton balls in an endless sea of fair weather.

She said, "This is a good spot to remember. Off the starboard bow is St. Thomas itself, and– "

"Specifically, Target Point. And to port are the Brass Islands. Charlotte Amalie is thataway."

"You've memorized the damn chart."

Tommy accepted coffee from the skipper. "I've been here before."

Sandy cocked an eyebrow and clutched the mug tight and close to her chin, warming her hands in the still-cool ocean air. She wrapped herself in a thick denim shirt she'd discard within an hour to unveil scanty patches of lime green swim-wear to mark critical spots on a deeply bronzed hide. They'd make port by midday, have lunch ashore, and there she would abandon coffee for the first tumbler of Mount Gay rum.

"Okay, Mister Smarty, what's the best course to Road Town?"

Tommy looked to the top of the mast to gauge apparent wind. "We could fall off to a beam reach and really pick up some speed, but maybe hit erratic air coming off the island, maybe not. Even then, we'd still have to shoot that little gap between Cabrita Point and St. James to cross Pillsbury Sound."

"Okay. This is for not just a test score, but also dinner in the BVI tonight, so get it right. If not the beam reach, then?"

Too easy. "We could take the north side past Magan's Bay and pick up the leeward passage inside Thatch, Crass and Mango Cay, take advantage of this air and shoot across the top of St. John, down past Soper's Hole and around to Road Town." He peeked at Sandy to see her mouth agape over a coffee mug stalled in mid-delivery to her lips. Tommy chuckled, plopped aviator sunglasses on his nose and slightly adjusted course.

A long-ago memory from Louisiana came into view. Eight, maybe nine, standing in the stern of Paw-paw's john boat, working the pole to propel the craft through a bayou. Paw-paw preferred the john-boat to the more traditional bayou pirogue, mostly because he won it in a bet with a tourist from Georgia and loved to show it off. The old-man lingered for a very long time between Cajun tales true and tall to determine if Tommy was old enough for deeper wisdom. "If yo' gonna lie, boy," he growled, "don't do it half-assed. Make 'er a whopper, and if that ain't gonna do, then tell 'em the truth, cuz they ain't gonna believe it no how."

A good philosophy for gator poachers. Even better on a ride from San Pedro to Road Town to enlist a professional killer in a scheme that would underscore the definition of *felony*. It didn't matter if the heist would be called robbery or piracy or perhaps even a bit of poaching, but his grandfather would surely have been proud of him at the helm of the big Morgan yacht on a Caribbean cruise. True enough, it was Sandy's yacht, but she was gracious about chain of command. The Alden was securely moored to his tomorrows, allowing him to visit yesterdays for clues missed half a dozen years earlier.

Tommy rubbed the bare skin on his jaw. A week earlier they'd made port near Kingston to resupply. Moored in quiet water, almost glass, under the magic of the pyramid of standing rigging, it was time to ditch the beard. The *El Gato* disguise was okay for Central America, but that was a week and many miles ago. Sandy had reasoned that a spy should be a bit more polished, even without consensus about what a polished spy should look like, and she volunteered to cut his hair.

Within an hour, Tommy's newly-exposed jaw was chewed by the relentless Caribbean sun and he paid for vanity over the next three days. Meanwhile, he cooked and shared duty at the wheel to keep the Morgan on a steady point of sail along the bellies of Haiti, the Dominican Republic and Puerto Rico. The boom and headstay converged with the bright white deck to the forward pulpit to point due east at the turquoise sea and a flat horizon line. Adventure beckoned on every heading, but Tommy remained true to the compass at the wheel and the one within himself. It was time to settle some accounts.

Sandy recovered from amazement. "Okay, you get an A. Just don't let it go to your head. You're sure you didn't memorize the charts?"

"I'm sure."

"So how do you know the Virgins so well?" she asked.

"No big deal. I used to be a really kick-ass secret agent, like said before." The image of the Alden evaporated, replaced by the meeting in Bavaria, playing out again. Sandy would have found Dieter Kreutzer lecherous, but Myra paid no attention that day, not even when Dieter's eyes roamed across her body when she interrupted their chess game.

"*Guten tag, mein Fräulein*," Kreutzer had drooled while he gestured to an open table near the door.

Myra had answered in a crisp voice, "*Das wird nicht notwendig sein.*"

That won't be necessary. A nearly perfect Westphalian inflection, the kind that suggests she lived there for a while rather than learning her German in a language school. *Not like Mather. His accent was different. Maybe Eastern?*

Then Myra had said, "I'm here to meet Mister Kane. And you are?"

An odd question. She should have known. And Dieter replied, "*Bitte, ich bin Dieter Kreutzer, der Eigentümer dieses Gasthaus.*" He sounded deferential, but his grin and eyes looked as though he was measuring a tasty sausage. Then she marched around the table to plant both feet firmly on the granite cobblestone and crossed her arms. *I pretended to study the board, the fate of my rook.* She had barked something about he was supposed to be in Amsterdam. Dieter took the hint and moved away. *Dumb mistake. I should have been looking around.*

Brief sparring, ending when she snuffed some time off he'd rewarded himself. It had probably upset the latest control in Langley. She snapped back. "Not any more. You're being loaned out for a black bag op." *First a cold approach, absolutely out of place in the field, and then the decisive announcement, like a command to a trainee.* Tommy squeezed the scene for as much detail as he could, but returned to reality empty-handed.

Amusement washed across Sandy's face, leading a wave of unrestrained laughter.

"Well, of course! How could I forget? Tommy Kane, master spy and rambling gourmet, rousted from his hideout in the backwater pubs of Belize, sneaking across the Caribbean to exchange secret handshakes with – who was the guy?"

"He's called the Major. No one knows his real name."

"You're joking. The guy from the British Secret Service, wasn't it?"

"*Formerly* from the Secret Intelligence Service."

"Oh, *that* secret service. I can never keep all these secret agent things straight. I'm terrible with acronyms and stuff. So if you don't know his name, how are you going to find him? Do you like Google him or something?"

"Or something."

"Uh-huh. So was he as good as you and Sergei?"

She teased with so much artificial sincerity that it spilled onto the deck as facetiousness and pooled into mild derision. *Ignore the puddle of sarcasm. Play it straight.* "Certainly better than me, but I think Sergei had the edge on the Major."

Maybe so. Pros, anyway. Not like Bavaria, where the whole nasty business started. How annoyed he'd been at the prospect of another dirty job designed to give everyone deniability except for himself. Not to mention Myra, who seemed too patronizing. Other control officers would have *proposed* an assignment. She matter-of-factly announced he was being loaned out for a black bag, a pawn on a playing field of bishops, rooks and knights.

Should have demanded to know whose op it was. Instead, a glance at Dieter Kreutzer wondering at the time if it was a good moment to get out of the trade. Dieter seemed to have gained wisdom with age and respectability with a corpulent brew of humility and *richtige ordnung*, content to banter about local football with pensioners nursing thick gray steins of warm beer at a miniscule bar. When the weather was fair, the business oozed out onto cobblestones as it had for centuries, even though the town was reborn only a few decades ago. Kreutzer had quit spying for the East when the wall came down and clung to the Bavarian hamlet to which he was posted to observe the sloppy American military divisions that hovered nearby. The Americans remained good friends and loyal customers, but now they were allies.

The little inn had always been a good cover, respected by Tommy as well as Yenchenko, both of whom admired professionalism above national politics and philosophy. Dieter kept everyone happy with scraps of information discreetly passed over a solid game of chess on balmy spring afternoons. The cool scent of the pine forests whispered down into the broad valleys and the rich air of productive farmland drifted into town and everyone was motivated to disciplined optimism. Dieter, the one target that the Major missed.

Sandy cast a mournful glance into her empty mug and her taunt eased into curiosity. "So, really, were you any good? At being a spy, I mean. It must have been glamorous and exciting."

He took the last sip of his coffee and said, "Glamorous and exciting? Not really. It's a dirty little business with dirty little people doing dirty little things, sometimes for dirty little reasons they don't even know."

"And so you're off on a dirty little stickup to get some dirty little revenge?"

He grunted. "Not really. Just some dirty little money."

Sandy cocked her head. "So you didn't miss the action, being a world-class secret agent?"

"Nah." After a respectable pause, he shrugged and offered a faint smile. "Well, except for the fast cars, fancy women, good scotch and first-class air travel."

She laughed, more than a giggle but less than a guffaw. "But you gotta tell me: who was the best, the best in the whole wide world?"

Tommy smiled. "Sergei. No question."

"Funny. He once said the same thing about you."

"Sergei lies a lot."

"He said that about you, too."

Tommy retreated to a smug smile, handed her his empty mug and adjusted course, working the wind toward St.

Thomas.

For a long time she stood still and the only sound between them was the air on the mainsheet. At last she laughed, a knowing laugh on reflection of a punch line. "Oh, gosh, Tommy, you and Sergei really are too much. Too much! But I absolutely want to tag along, to see just what you guys are *really* into. You're a swell guy and a great sailor and you can crew with me any time, but really, just too much. You want another cup of coffee?"

Tommy nodded and then declared, with all the soft assurance that his grandfather ended a tale, "And it's all for true."

"What *ever.* And I'm betting you memorized the charts."

Chapter Ten

Road Town, Tortola, British Virgin Islands

Tommy was doomed. An elegant trap sprung. Confidence flopped around in a bucket of despair. *Don't sweat. Look thoughtful, remain calm. Then surrender.*

Across a small and weathered wooden table, Percy Hill chattered in staccato pidgin with Old Stanley about a local club's prospect in a major cricket test, scheduled for Barbados in two weeks time. The cricket club's best batsman had run afoul of the law, something to do with a woman, a bottle of rum and a knife, and was presently lodged in the local jail to await a chat with the town magistrate. Meanwhile, frantic sports books recalculated odds and Percy Hill urged Old Stanley to put a few dollars on the latest line.

Sunlight flickered through a tamarind canopy on the landscape of combat. A path of dominos meandered across a table fashioned from three weary planks of lumber, a couple of feet square, that might have once been painted green.

Percy ignored Tommy's misery the way all masters do, after a decisive and fatal blow planned with patience and delivered with grace.

Stanley and Percy slammed dominoes in the Road Town market for more years than Tommy had known, filling balmy afternoons with soft wagers among old friends. And sly hustle of tourists snared in a net woven by two elderly black men who seemed just a bit confused but charmed visitors with

overdone pidgin, tired eyes and toothy smiles. Stereotype to
the hilt. They harvested a couple of hundred dollars on a fair
day.

And so the wily Percy welcomed Tommy back to Tortola
with the full tourist treatment with the same hospitality that a
spider offers an unsuspecting fly. Having sucked Tommy in to
a trap, Percy blocked him and left him with a double five in
hand After a respectable pair of minutes drifted out with the
tide, Tommy yielded and passed ten dollars across the table.

It was all right. The loss was fair payment for the stories
they'd shared over the years of a lifetime in the Caribbean, of
the legends of Western Africa, and the sea itself. But mostly
for occasional floater work in the Caribbean intelligence
community, filled with whispers the Major was based somewhere in the Leewards. Reliable guys with a rum shop tab requiring constant tending, they were Tommy's first logical step
in the methodical groundwork to connect with the Major.
Even if it meant blowing ten bucks at the domino table.

Beyond the domino table, cruise ship tourists swirled in a
frenzied search for souvenirs at the open air market where
shrewd locals rewarded them with everything from knockoff
postcards to exquisite local crafts. A steady offshore breeze still
lulled visitors into a complacency that lubricated wallets and
caused currency to swim freely across the palms and counters.
A placid, unhurried, bustling scene, it made a good cover for
penetrating the Major's layered ring of security. Tommy had
already patronized a stand for a pair of brightly hand-painted
scarves to soften the palm of Percy's niece, Margaret, who sold
vegetables at the market and reliable intelligence to those who
correctly introduced themselves.

He yawned and stretched and conceded the domino game.
Percy invited Tommy to return sometime for a match with
Old Stanley. "Maybe, Mister Tommy, you have the good luck
next time. Maybe you notice Old Stanley loses his memory.
Might be the soft touch."

Tommy looked into the eyes of Old Stanley. The hustler's twinkle. "Maybe, we'll see. Say, either of you gents know a fella known as the Major?"

"A white man?" Stanley asked.

"Yes."

They exchanged shrugs and puzzled looks. "Don't know many white man," Old Stanley told Tommy. "You maybe do better talkin' with Margaret. She maybe know."

Tommy stood to offered a warm smile and appreciation, but before he could take a step, Stanley asked for twenty dollars.

"For what?"

"For the answer to the question you make.".

"But you said you didn't know."

Old Stanley smiled and nodded and held out his hand.

Percy said, "I think, Mister Tommy, that Old Stanley gave you answer. That you didn't fancy it don't make no nevermind."

Welcome to the logic of Tortola.

He dug into his shorts and tugged out what he claimed was the last ten dollar bill he owned, then laid it into Old Stanley's weathered palm. Stanley examined the bill with disdain.

"It's all I have, Stanley. It'll have to do. Which way to Margaret's stand? No, don't answer that." He waved farewell and and fell into the slow current of Americans roaming aisles in quest of a bargain and a memory. Tommy glanced over his shoulder. Old Stanley tucked the bill into a shirt pocket and awaited his next mark.

The moment she saw him, Margaret squealed with delight and buried him in an overwhelming embrace. She took a step back to survey his body from head to toe. "My, my, Tommy Kane. Aren't you still the handsome one. I knew you come today."

"And how do you know that, Mamma Margaret?"

"Oh, my, Tommy, I be walking down the street and see the

old tomcat and so I make the spell and here you are."

"Ah, of course."

Margaret pulled two bashful, pigtailed girls in pink school uniforms forward.

"This is Prudence," she gestured to the eldest, "and the little one is Emily. They've much grown in what is it now, five years?"

It was closer to seven. He squatted to shake tentative hands and reached into the shopping bag for the silk scarves, a gift for girls who were infants when he last saw them and would certainly would not remember him.

Margaret cooed. "Now children. Mister Tommy is a very dear friend for many years and you know what? He can jerk pork and chicken with the best of cooks from Jamaica to Trinidad, isn't that so, Tommy Kane?"

Tommy grinned. "Prudence and Emily are lovely. You must be very proud." Their large soft eyes followed him upward and struggled to capture the trust that their mother so lavishly laid on the strange white man who'd just come from seemingly nowhere. "Ah, well, it's only because Margaret shares all her culinary secrets. I plan to make pelau for supper."

Margaret succumbed to silent appeals and released the children to join classmates in the audience of a steel pan group twenty yards away, serenading with familiar tunes in quest of CD sales and tips. She waved a thick arm toward her stand. "Oh, yes. Pelau. Well, Tommy, you have come to the right place, I must tell you."

Within moments she began to fill a sack with produce. "Onion, garlic not too much, and pigeon peas and a good Congo pepper. This one is perfect." She held it aloft for a brief moment for approval and slipped it gently into the bag before his nod was evident. "Oh, yes, and a nice Hubbard squash and some carrots. You chop them very fine. And parsley. And scallions, too."

As she advised Tommy to get the chicken and sweet coconut milk from Bobby's Supermarket, Sandy was cutting through a herd of tourists moving like cattle headed for the barn. Margaret's grin broadened further. Sandy carried a grocery store sack that probably contained the chicken and milk plus probably couple of bottles of Mount Gay rum to help wash down the fiery Congo peppers in the pelau. When she was near enough, she called out, "Hey, Tommy! I wondered where you went. But now I see you're at the right place for supplies."

Margaret's eyes narrowed. "Child, what you be doin' with this man?"

Sandy said, "Hi, Momma Margaret! No worries. I hired him on to crew my boat from Belize. It's just business."

Margaret scowled. "Humph. All the worse, Mister Tommy. You not be draggin' this child into your world of the clandestine, are you?"

Tommy tossed up his hands to proclaim innocence. "Absolutely not."

Sandy asked, "Clandestine what?"

Nice. Nicely done. Tommy changed the subject. "About that pelau?"

"Ah, yes." Margaret appeared to realize she may have spoken out of turn. She put on a smile for tourists and waggled a finger at Tommy. "I tell you, but only because you are the American with no arrogance. Because when you come to call, you remember the names, and ask about the children and the old ones."

"And lose every time to Old Stanley and Percy Hill."

Margaret laughed. "You toss bones with them boys, you part with plenty dollar."

Sandy chuckled. "How much?"

"Ten to Percy. He left me with double fives twice in a row. And ten to Stanley because I asked a question."

Margaret sighed and reviewed the proper way to prepare

pelau.

Sandy added, "Be sure there's plenty of bun-bun."

Oh, yeah. The tasty brown layer left in the pot.

Margaret nodded with delight. "Yes, yes! The bun-bun will speak to you, to tell you that the pelau is nice. You shouldn't worry now, just cook and eat well!"

Sandy accepted the paper sacks of supplies from Margaret, who leaned toward Tommy and lowered her voice. "What question do you have for Old Stanley?"

Sandy allowed her eyes to catch sight of another market stand, smothered in souvenirs, and drifted a few paces away to browse.

When they were alone, Tommy said. "The Major?"

"Oh, my, yes," Margaret replied. "There be an English fellow who paint the pretty pictures. I think people round here call him Mister Wells, maybe Ian for a first name? They say he has a house somewhere along Ridge Road, but I don't know it. Sometime he come down to town. Maybe you visit the shop called Agile Rabbit Gallery, halfway up Main Street. People say the lady who own it sell pictures by this man. His work, it be more abstract than most."

Tommy smiled. The Major often portrayed himself as an artist, although most in the trade believed he had little talent. But skill was not the point. A useful and potentially imaginative cover was and so he reached into his pocket and drew twenty dollars.

"Mmm-hmm," Margaret answered while she casually tucked the money into a deep pocket of her apron. "You always pay Stanley, but never all you got, Tommy. You don't feel so bad 'bout that?"

Tommy's eyes twinkled. "If I didn't cheat Old Stanley, how would I ever be able to pay you?"

Margaret's broad grin collapsed into free laughter from deep within her ample belly, and Tommy waved goodbye.

Sandy tagged along, but after fifty yards was told to return to *Freckles II*. She frowned disappointment. "Aw, c'mon. I always wanted to see you guys actually work."

"Not today. The last thing I want to attract is attention. Besides, this won't take long. The Major won't be there. Just someone who'll tell me where we meet."

She pouted. "I'm liable to stop at one of those marina bars for a couple of stiff belts of rum."

"If you want, but you'll probably miss out on the flavor of the pelau."

"Okay. But there'd better be a kick-ass party out of it. I've been at sea for two weeks and that's a long time for me to behave."

Twenty minutes later, Tommy had more than paid the price for sea legs, climbing a steep hillside on a thin snake of a road that twisted through the bowl-shaped landscape forming Road Town Harbor. Below, a safe haven for trading vessels, pirates, recreational sailors. All around, tiny shops blanketed in bougainvillea, cacti, small palms. Wildly saturated colors and quaint names of upscale boutiques on hand-painted signs.

At last. The Agile Rabbit Gallery was on the downhill side of the street, tucked behind a small manicured garden and a low picket fence. Inside, cooler air and softer light. Less than a thousand square feet, an airy feel with white stucco walls and soft grey tile floor. Immaculate. A faint scent of artist paints and thinner blended with raw woods of framing materials oozed from a workroom and storage area beyond the counter.

Between two large racks of postcards, a bin of unframed prints and matted watercolors under cellophane wrapping sparkled in sunlight sneaking through two tiny windows. A small collection of work by varied artists crowded walls and a display of picture frame materials filled the wall behind the counter, which also displayed a limited selection of painting gear. Staffing the counter, a delicate young woman had dark brown, almost black, hair, tied tightly back and into a bun, away from pale skin. Not much beach time. No identity, either on a desk sign or lapel pin. No makeup; maybe indifferent to the bar scene and comfortable with isolation.

She spoke in a high English accent when she greeted him and wondered how she might be of assistance.

Tommy laid out a broad smile and beefed up a southern accent perhaps a bit long on Texas twang. "I'm in the market for art. Something a bit more than a souvenir. Name's Tommy Kane."

"Well, Mister Kane, there are several artists represented in the gallery," she said with a restrained gesture of her right hand. "Did you have anyone in mind? Of course, if they're a bit strong for your budget, we have some fine numbered prints and a few watercolors as well."

Keeping the grin alive, he nodded and stepped forward, his eyes skimming across paintings ranging widely in realism, hunting signatures in the lower corners of each. "Any work by a fella named of Ian Wells? Been a fan for a lotta years."

"Indeed. Just over here..."

Before she could offer additional detail, Tommy found Ian's signature in an oil, mostly swirls of color that looked like an attempt at impressionism. "Well ain't this my lucky day?" He pulled a smaller painting from the flock and studied it closely in the light of the window and door. "This here's a nice one. Oughta look right nice over that li'l ol' table aside the closet door. How much will you take for it?"

The clerk swept forward and plucked the painting from Tommy's hands and returned it to the wall as if it were a baby bird that had fallen from the nest. "It's twenty-five hundred, I'm afraid, and he doesn't negotiate for his work." She adjusted the painting to perfect horizontal.

"Is that right? Dang, he's sure gone up in price since I bought my last picture from him. You sure he won't come down a trifle?"

"I think not." She stepped around Tommy and closed the shop door. Her gaze was direct and without emotion. "My uncle often spoke of an American friend. Maybe you're him. What did you say your name was?"

He leaned forward as if his eyes could not let go of a landscape that looked like Josiah's Bay. "Thomas Kane, but most folks call me Tommy."

"Interesting name, *Mister* Kane."

"Tommy. Call me Tommy. Not half as interesting as The Agile Rabbit."

She cocked an eyebrow. "You're familiar with it?"

"Oh, yes *m'am*. That's the English translation of a restaurant in Paris me and ol' Ian used to hang out. Did you say he was your uncle?"

Her smile seemed forced. "Where in Paris?"

Pull back a bit. Easy. "Montmartre. It's up at the top of a hill, sort of off by itself. Nice little place, great food, good place to hang out." Tommy clasped his hands behind his back and leaned in to his task of studying paintings that were clearly landscapes from around Tortola, but about which he could not judge artistic merit.

"Yes," she said. "South of Sacre Coeur. With the sign of a dancing bunny."

Ah, nice little test. "No, northwest, on Rue des Saules, and the rabbit is leaping out of a saucepan. At least, that's how Andre Gill painted it in 1875."

Old times. At Au Lapin Agile meeting with the Major to sort out an op running just on the edge of control. At the time, the Major used the name Gideon Lewis. Pints of ale on a noisy Thursday night at one of the old wooden tables into which many a set of initials had been carved. The waiter lived up to Lapin Agile's reputation for indifference that bordered on rudeness. Understandable. When a style works for a hundred years or more, you keep it going. The Major was growly. Pride in a contract fulfilled is lost when a sniper rifle misfires. The contract. An op. Blackbird. And SIS wanted Dieter Kreutzer silenced for an unknown reason. By the time the

Major could reload, Dieter had slipped into a taxi and, unaware of his good fortune, left Munich and a stakeout in which
the Major had invested several weeks' time.

Dieter. Corpulent. Content. The day they played chess in
front of his little hotel. Dieter, unabashedly studying the body
of Myra Fielding, his imagination running flat out. She appeared out of nowhere. After two – *no, three* – cars passed in
quick succession. Pedestrians on the other side of the street.
Faces. Blurs. Blurs because Ian's niece, the clerk at the gallery,
smiled and asked yet another question to validate his credentials.

"Of course. Do you recall the street number?"

"Twenty-two."

She nodded. "You seem very sure of yourself, the way you
answered so quickly."

He shrugged. The cabaret was such a popular place to
make unofficial contacts with all sides that the code name
"Twenty-two" meant only one place in the world. *Try for a
little mischief in the smile, ease the tension in the room.* "It was a
very popular place to meet old friends."

She remained very businesslike and asked, "Now, you also
have a Russian nickname, do you not?"

Tommy sighed and confessed. "Koshka."

The woman cocked an eyebrow. "What does it mean?"

"Kitten." *Maybe it'll charm her into a smile. Yeah, maybe not.*

"Interesting. Well, that sounds correct. Uncle Ian wonders
if you're traveling with anyone?"

*The Major already knows I'm in town. May as well be upfront
all the way.* "Yes, on a Morgan sloop. A friend named Sandy."

She retreated to restraint. "Honesty makes it your lucky
day, Mister Kane. You get to take your friend to Carrot Bay.
There's a beach bar there."

"Tulu's."

"Yes. You know it?"

"Oh, yeah." Sandy would be pleased.

CHAPTER ELEVEN

Carrot Bay, British Virgin Islands

Tommy's pelau won quiet applause under a pastel sky pocked with clouds that dazzled in orange, then pink, and finally lavender as the sun slipped into the sea. Along the shore, orange mercury-vapor street lights twinkled among mangroves and palms.

When Sandy emerged through the companionway after galley chores, she wore an expression of frustration and little else. The searing colors of her bikini glowed like neon in the dwindling light of day and she carried two glasses of dark rum. "So, okay. When does your guy show up? There's a great little bar just beyond the point."

"Tulu's?"

"Yup." She perched above the cockpit, legs carelessly askew, and teased him with a litany of distant ports: Jamaica, Greece, Tahiti, the Windwards. Her words were slurred and "Venezuela" betrayed her. "Back in San Pedro, you came off like some sand bum out of maybe Florida or California, just passing through life, no cares, no ambitions. So now I'm beginning to really believe this story about you being a big time spy guy."

"And?"

"I can't resist the feeling we could take off and probably do some interesting things."

Tommy chuckled. "How many of those have you had?"

Sandy studied her glass, tossed the remainder in her throat and said, "Not enough." Then she seemed more focused. "I, uh, well... oh, hell, it's a stupid idea."

"What?"

"Just taking off. We could be a good team, I think. I mean, nothing romantic or anything." She seemed to struggle with candor. "Chartering a bunch of whining tourists isn't all that great." She looked away. "Look, I'm probably not your type and you probably think I'm just a kid." After a pause, Sandy sighed and muttered an epithet to her empty glass. "I should have brought the bottle topside."

Tommy reached for a pair of light denim shirts and tossed one to Sandy. "Tulu's," he declared. "You deserve to pass some good time."

Her spirits soared like a glorious skyrocket. "Really? That place is legendary, a regular magnet for hedonism. Cruising set, the naughty locals – "

"Really."

She beamed. "Ah, what a guy. And here I was beginning to think spy work was sitting around being bored." She shrugged at the shirt but slipped into it anyway and tied the tails around her waist. Within seconds, she pulled the trailing dinghy close and hopped aboard.

The big silver inflatable had entirely too many horses on its tail, but not enough for Sandy. As Tommy cast off the painter, she brought the outboard to life and the takeoff lurch nearly dumped him overboard. The dinghy skipped across the waves like a flat stone cast by a child into a bayou and made a direct course for the frontier that separates civilization from decadence and a beach bar named Tulu's.

"It's like a frontier, Tommy. Civilization on this side – "

"Yeah, I know. Decadence and Tulu's on the other."

"Hah! You got it!" She stood at the stern, straddled the tiller with her thighs and swayed her hips. The dinghy zigged and zagged and somehow managed to avoid hitting any of the anchored yachts.

Tulu's. A haven for sassy music. Spicy food. Shameless in-toxication. Sort of dead ahead.

Over the noise of the outboard, she said, "Clients used to tell me that guests at that plush resort further down hoof it across a mile of sand, just to be astonished and shocked and gather stories for many a barbeque back home."

The dinghy had zoomed within an eighth of a mile when a soca band ignited a fresh round of raucous tunes. She whooped approval and fist-pumped the air with both arms, still steering with her thighs, and somehow managed to opened the throttle all the way. Her hair danced wildly in the wind. "Betcha I could run it fifty feet onto the beach," she yelled.

Stay calm. Hang on to the gunwale. "Not even a doubt in my mind but why wreck a great outboard?"

She rolled her eyes, kept the grin, and attacked a small dock. Just as Tommy's knuckles whitened, she came sharply to port and the starboard gunwale softly kissed the pier. She instantly cut the motor and was above him to command, "Tie it up smartly, then meet me in the bar and buy me a drink."

"Aye, aye," he muttered, while Sandy floated away.

Open air on three sides, Tulu's had a fleet of stools without backs, which forced well-lubricated patrons to lean in to the bar and keep a steady grip on glasses in front of them. From the slurred and boisterous speech, Tommy suspected some of them had been aboard since mid-afternoon. Off to one side, Big Marie stoked a 55-gallon grill laden with chicken and red snapper. On a rough plank stage, a soca band from Tobago held court.

Tommy settled onto a perch at the very end of the bar. Tulu hustled through several drink orders, turned and a huge grin widened even further on his face.

Some said Tulu blew in from the Windwards, others straight from the west coast of Africa. Never spoke of his past and blended well into the easy soul of the Caribbean, where privacy is respected and it's too much effort to stir up trouble anyway. Now he ignored pleas for refills to welcome Tommy. "So what you think, man? All fixed up and very pretty, eh?"

"You've gone commercial."

Tulu laughed from the belly. "That we have, Tommy. Got to make a dollar, maybe two or three, keep the womens happy. You still taking the Macallan? Cube on the side?"

"Absolutely."

"Hah! Tulu never forgets. So where's your foxy little mate, man?" Tommy began to protest, but before he could say anything, Tulu wiggled a forefinger. "Don't be givin' me the innocent look now. Word get around, man."

Dispelling rumors would have to wait for the proper ritual. Tommy accepted a single malt and suspended an ice cube above the glass until a single drop splashed into the whisky. *Perfect.* Behind him the band launched a limbo. He gestured with a nod of his head toward the probable location of Sandy.

Tulu looked over his guest's shoulder. "Ah. Lookin' very fine, my friend."

The band was a cocky crew. Exuberant brass affirmed each line of the lead singer, all backed up by an assortment of percussion and a bass player with a mind in another world. There wasn't a steel pan in sight, and Sandy was right at home. She bounced out onto the sand to organize a limbo line.

"Oh, man, we in for big trouble tonight." He ignored the bays of drunken patrons further down the bar and his face went solemn. He leaned in close while wiping the narrow bar separating and tilted his head toward a stretch of dark beach west of the bar. In a tone usually reserved for sighting large sharks, he said. "The Major be around."

Tommy nodded, finished his scotch and waved off a refill. "So am I."

Tulu made a subtle but unmistakable gesture.

"No, I don't need a piece." The voice of Moses Clay

whispered in his ear. *You don't need a gun; you need redemption. Yeah, right. With guys like the Major, being armed made no difference. You'd be dead before your finger found the trigger.*

Tulu stuffed the bar towel into his back pocket and leaned on the bar, his hands spread wide. "I know some fellas, 'round here, close by."

Tommy shook his head. "The last thing I want to do is give him even a hint of provocation. He's sensitive about that sort of thing."

Tulu scowled. "The Major, he be living in yesterdays, man. Got the brain of the overripe mango. You be careful 'round him, Tommy. Ain't no tellin' with a man like that."

It was time to venture into the shadows where the Major, a.k.a. Ian Wells, lurked and either do business or get shot. "No worries. I'll be back for another round."

Sandy had enlisted a dozen or so tourists in a hand-clapping dance limbo line to a party song called "More Fete." They had the bar high enough for everyone to walk under, and then the band changed key. She lowered the limbo bar, pranced past a group of three college-aged men, returned with a tall glass of rum and led the line on another limbo bar attack. He wondered how long they would last, then how long he would last, and then he slipped away toward the dark.

The golden glow of the party faded into monochrome. White coral sand swept toward the right and slowly dissipated into darkness. To the left, palms in silhouette and their bushy tops periodically shivered in the evening breeze. The Atlantic Ocean snuck across a dozen feet of sand and then retreated in a steady, unhurried rhythm. Tommy clung to water's edge, wet and firm beneath his feet, and peered into the darkness under the trees. An easy target for a sniper against the faint light of the sky. And maddening. For the next two hundred yards he paused several times to create a defiant profile. The only sound now was the waves lapping the beach and the rustle of palm leaves in puffs of offshore wind. Good air, air that carried a fine salt scent and comfortable warmth and beckoned him, as does a lovely and mysterious lover, to adventure and unknown.

The Major. A guy who changed names and persona like most people change clothes. A guy renowned for precise plans and an incredible sense of surroundings. A guy who once gave him good advice. *Don't focus on the conversation. Focus on the perimeter, the background, the faces in the crowd.*

Faces in the crowd. On the soft breeze his mind floated back to Dieter's inn. The images of Myra and Dieter and the chess game. Scan the perimeter. At first, vague blurs of color. Three objects that had to be small cars passing, left to right. Again. *Three cars, two people, one standing still, one walking past.*

Again, start earlier. A man standing still. Small sign on a post. Lamp post. City bus. Cars. One, two, three. Silver, silver, blue. All sedans. Man walks past.

Dammit, again. I sat down. We play chess. City buses stop and go. It's a bus stop.

Run it again. This time, very slow motion. A man, clearly American, who leaning against a lamp post. At a bus stop. Reading a newspaper. Several buses stop, pick up, discharge passengers. But the man remained.

Mather. Three cars speed past, but no details on the drivers. A second man walks past Mather. *Who was he?*

An abrupt gust of wind evaporated the memory. Surveillance. *Go ahead. Shoot. Just make sure you kill me on the first shot.* He had gone nearly another hundred yards. Movement to his left.

From a dense stand of palms, from the blue shadows of a Caribbean beach, from memories of years past. The distinct silhouette of the Major.

CHAPTER TWELVE

The Major marched toward Tommy with all the confidence of a commander about to inspect a regiment. Khaki shorts and shirt, pressed and without wrinkle, lacking only an epaulet crown and leather accessories. Shoulders drawn back, head held high, arms swinging freely above bold, long strides. He fell in with Tommy, but set the pace for both

After fifty wordless yards, he spoke with a soft, assured English gentleman's accent, free of regional dialect and inflection. "You appear fit, Thomas. I gather you've recovered well from your unfortunate demise?" An expression of concern crossed his face as he shook his head in supportive dismay. "Messy business, bombs and what not. I rather hope you didn't think I had anything to do with it? No? Excellent." His tone shifted again, this time to confidentiality. "It was the talk of the community for nearly a year and then I regret to report that you vanished into obscurity."

"Resurrection agrees with me. As does obscurity. Ian Wells, is it? And the notion you were involved never crossed my mind, although it probably should have." After a shared handshake, Tommy started to put his hands in his pockets.

"Steady, mate, steady. The lads haven't had a kill in a while and, I'm afraid, are a bit edgy."

Tommy lifted his hands into the air to demonstrate they were empty.

"Thank you. And yes, Wells it is. Wells, Ian Wells. It's as good a name as any, wouldn't you think? I know, all his cloak and dagger rubbish is a bit tiresome, but the only real way to know what's coming from behind is to look over one's shoulder from time to time and exercise a smidge of caution."

"I'm disappointed in your lack of trust, Ian. I really am."

The insolence prompted a brief, stern glare before Wells relented and extended his right arm to make a deliberate downward motion. "Right. Can't you just *feel* the crosshairs slithering away from your skull? You know, Thomas, trust is a precious commodity for those in our vocation. SIS cut me adrift, and all my sources insist they've dispatched a wet team to finish me off. So a bit of due diligence, then."

"I've got to wonder if that's really true, and whether there's even snipers in the shadows to protect you."

"Valid speculation. And rather brave, too, calling a bluff. You haven't by chance a torch on your person do you? No? I happen to have one myself." He produced a pen-sized LED flashlight and blinked it twice to demonstrate it functioned. Then he took a step past Tommy and stuck it in the sand with the lit end on top, and withdrew. "You might want to have a step or two back, mate."

Tommy rolled his eyes, but followed instructions. The light evaporated into a shower of tiny bits of plastic that stung him in a dozen places at once. A moment later, the soft pop from the rifle arrived, barely audible over the gentle surf. *So okay, there were crosshairs.*

With a smug grin, Wells said, "Splendid! That's 200 meters, Thomas, with infrared and exceptional noise suppression. A field trial for an experimental weapon. Two-twenty three cartridge." He extended his arms wide. "I've always fancied this spot, you know. On two separate occasions I've walked a target to just about here. The lads were posted there and there with H&K PSG1's and infrared scopes. The precision is exceptional, I daresay. Fifty rounds of match ammo inside an eighty-millimeter circle at three hundred meters."

Tommy nodded. *Fifty rounds, nothing. Just one would be*

enough to tear off half the guy's head. "And the body?"

"Well, that was the beauty of it. We'd bring a dinghy in from just beyond the point to your left front. It's a rather large ocean, isn't it? You get off the reef and you'll discover quite a variety of feeding fish."

"Let's walk a bit, okay?"

"Of course." Wells motioned a direction with a wave of his hand, a path that would take them further from Tulu's and deeper into darkness. "Fine evening for a stroll, eh? Old colleagues out for a breath of fine salt air, eh?"

"For true. By the way, I enjoyed your paintings."

Ian countered with a cynical chuckle. "They're dreadful, Thomas. An old man's recreation. Frightfully inadequate. However, they encourage my niece to believe in redemption."

The words of Moses Clay again echoed in Tommy's mind. "Redemption or retirement?"

Wells took a moment to consider the question. "I wonder: perhaps one leads to the other? And you? Have you been redeemed? Or retired?"

"Somewhere in between."

Wells seemed intrigued. "So it's true then? You really are off the reservation, not establishing some form of deep cover? I believe it was four – or good Lord, could it be five? – years ago some of the lads were gathered round a few pints at a charming little pub, you know, one of those warm shelters from the noise where they don't have a telly. A proper pub where friends gather to share the news over a pint or two and afterward everyone can walk home. So we'd all heard about that bombing and everyone agreed it was you who gave the slip and headed south. There was some talk that it was a CIA cover op to go after that damned Russian."

"Yenchenko."

"Indeed. However, I saw it a bit differently, knowing you and Yenchenko are mates. I suspected all along that you'd gotten the sack like the rest of us and were simply low-profiling it for a bit to see who might be on your tail. We'd heard some stories, mind you, something about this *El Gato* character and a horse in Vera Cruz." He paused for a moment. "So you really were black-flagged?"

Tommy sighed. "Everybody asks the same question. One more time: yes, I was black-flagged, and yes, it was a bombing and yes it took the better part of eight months to heal up, and no, I didn't win a racehorse in Vera Cruz, it was a piss-ant motorcycle with a bad carburetor and only a quarter tank of gas."

Wells rubbed his chin. "Everyone says it was a bay mare, about fourteen hands."

"Yeah, well, all I saw was a red Suzuki. Which I sold for fifty dollars in Oaxaca. Walking was faster. All of which proves just how legends get completely out of hand."

Wells went silent as if to digest the remark, then brightened and took a new tack. "As you wish. Well, then. You've recovered, you're outlaw, and you're ready for some action. You appear somewhat fit. Ever consider counter-terrorism work? It pays well and it's quite fashionable. I'm forming a team. I'd run you in the field, just like old times."

The last time Wells formed a team was probably a pickup game of soccer in elementary school. And the community is stuffed with every nut-case soldier of fortune doing contract work for State, CIA, Defense and Homeland Security. "Thanks, Ian, I really appreciate that. But I'm getting a bit old for combat work. It's dirty, noisy and the food is terrible."

Wells stiffened. "Quite so. Well, then, you've made your way from some backwater Central American hamlet and you've come to put forward a project of your own?"

Patience. Relax. The easy soft accent usually reserved for a first-class lie. "A straightforward armed robbery, a quick hit and run."

"Armed robbery? Really, Thomas, I'm rather disappointed at how low you've gone."

"Shares are two, maybe three million. It's drug money, Ian, dirty as it gets."

"Carlos Medina or that C-213 rabble from the CIA?"

Dang. Who doesn't know about this? On the other hand, thanks for confirming Yenchenko's intel. "Well, both, actually."

"Hm. You're quite certain you'd rather not spend a few happy and likely less dangerous months in Afghanistan?"

"No thanks. Just a quick hit and run. That's it."

Wells crossed his arms and stared toward the sea. "It's that bloody Russian, isn't it? You've partnered with Yenchenko and gone pirate. I misjudged you, Thomas. You've already tumbled below the lowest of the low. You're certain this isn't some sort of clever trap?"

Try a lie. "No idea. Just looking for a little fun."

"Still the master of understatement, eh? Who else have you recruited? Communications, logistics, intel?"

"Just us."

Ian's eyes widened. "A bit modest with the depth of your plan, don't you think? And you're willing to split three ways for an old sniper? Really, Thomas, that's ordinary contract work. You could farm it out to any cowboy." Ian rattled off half a dozen names of respected freelance snipers, then waited through several seconds of silence and unflinching gaze. He sighed. "Right. Well, unless of course you fancy the very best.... Hm. You'll need first rate taps and hacks, secure communication and support people, on the ground.... Thomas, tell me you're not serious about Yenchenko. The fellow's got a five quid ego and a two bob mind."

Every fishing hook needs a hunk of bait. "Technically, it's his op. I'm lending a hand for a share. But I told him we'd need a first rate perimeter man. For a third of the take."

Wells shook his head. "I daresay. You've thrown in with that jungle rat and you expect me to watch your back? You must be daft. That bastard can't be trusted. And you of all people should know that you just don't stick up the CIA *and* the Cubans, hop on a plane and go off to hoist a pint. These people *never* forget and *never* stop. Probably what got Dieter killed."

"What? Dieter? When?"

Wells cocked an eyebrow. "You didn't know?"

Tommy shook his head. With luck the anguish didn't show in the faint light.

"Where've you been, Thomas, a monastery?"

"San Pedro."

"Same difference. Right. Well, it was a couple of years ago. Made to look like one of those Mossad strikes on old Nazi-types. The newspapers said it was some sort of gas explosion, but the chatter had it involving some sort of bomb in that old safe Dieter kept in his office that triggered a larger device. We all believed it was CIA. Poor old chap likely had something on somebody and got careless. It happens, Thomas."

Press hard. "Something like Blackbird?"

Wells took a moment to consider the possibility rather than dismiss it out of hand. "I really have no idea. Dieter was obsessed with Blackbird, a mole in East German intelligence, but when the wall came down and I got the sack, it was an issue that evaporated."

"Why was there a contract on Dieter? *Your* contract?"

Wells offered a weak smile. "I don't evaluate the *reason* of a contract, Thomas. I merely *fulfill* a contract."

The answer seemed plausible but also odd. He spoke in present tense rather than past of an occupation of ephemeral alliances and fluid relationships. How many dots Wells himself had connected in just the past few minutes? *Press on.* "Was the contract from inside or outside SIS?"

Ian's voice had an edge to it. "Once again, I have no idea. Our section was tightly controlled and very restricted. No freelance work, no exceptions."

Back off. "I rather liked Dieter. He played a nice game of chess."

Wells seemed amused. "He played a few CIA people nicely, as well."

"How so?"

"That, Thomas, is something you'd have to put to your partner, Yenchenko. Kreutzer and that damned Russian were tight as a pair of Scottish pub mates with barely a fiver between them. All I know is they'd drive their control officers barmy because they spent too much time on that Blackbird business. Spent years on it, and all they came up with was an East German mole named Matthias. From Dresden, I think. Anyway. then the wall came down and nobody cared about Blackbird or Matthias. Yenchenko banged his case officer's wife, got the sack. I was dispatched to Munich to terminate Kreutzer."

Tommy remembered. "And you misfired. Dieter got away. You got canned."

"And Dieter wound up fat and happy in Bavaria, only to get blown up after your little adventure. And so here we are, Thomas, taking a stroll on a warm beach, wondering which direction the bullet will come from."

"If there is a bullet."

At last Wells managed a slight grin. "Oh, dear boy, there most certainly is. It's only a question of when."

For nearly a minute the only sound came from soft waves of the Atlantic on the beach. Then Wells abruptly switched subjects to the proposed robbery. "You'll understand of course, there are upfront expenses. I trust you have financing?"

"Just the score. We have to stand our own tabs."

"Ah, I see. Thomas, it's not like you to consider armed robbery. I always thought better of you. You must have a larger objective."

Tommy surprised himself with candor. "The truth. That always seems a good idea."

Wells chuckled. "Oh, good heavens. For that you need a *church*. You must have some sort of plan, then?"

Tommy outlined the rough sketch he had in mind, and hoped that Yenchenko would agree with it. "That's why I need you. No matter which way you look at it, it's a three-man job. Look at it this way, Ian. It's your chance to get a bit of revenge for yourself, bankroll a serious crew and equipment, and about the worst that can happen is that you'll get killed."

Wells cracked a wry smile. "And here I thought you were suggesting there might be a touch of difficulty attached to this. But really, old boy. Consider logistics, contemporary versus old school. Our time has likely passed, and I'm not keen on all this new electronic rubbish. But I do fancy a bit of comfort in my grey years."

"So you'll do it?"

Wells became quiet for half a dozen paces, then proposed some tradecraft techniques to communicate the old-school way, should he agree. Good ideas, too. Yenchenko would concur. Because modern intelligence work relied on technology and by staying off the grid, they would be difficult to track.

Wells asked, "Where would we meet?"

"Nassau. The usual place."

Ian sighed. "Wretched village. I suppose you're opting for the cover of tacky tourist? No? The target itself? Enlighten me with particulars."

"Night of the fifteenth, supermarket loading dock at Village Road. CIA-Cuban military cash exchange. Probably eight or ten guys."

Now within a hundred yards of Tulu's, the shadows were probably too thin for Ian's comfort.

"I'll think about it, Thomas. If by chance I join, I'll meet you in Nassau on the fourteenth. But no promises, especially if I sense something's amiss. And I'm not keen on working with that bloody Yenchenko. Just don't trust him." He abruptly peeled away, but before he vanished into the night he turned and softly waved. "And thank you, Kane, for the courtesy of consideration."

Tommy returned the salute, glanced toward the bar and when he looked back, Wells was gone. He sighed and returned to the cheer of Tulu's and the empty stool at the end of the bar. Tulu looked up from the opposite end. His eyes hinted disappointment and he stepped down the line with the bottle of Macallan in hand.

Sandy's party approached a climax. Bar patrons watched the women in the contest fail with delight and leering eyes. Each time someone collapsed and sprawled on the sand, the audience erupted in a bawdy cheer. Sandy skipped forward again and tugged at Tommy's arm with lusty exuberance. Only five contestants remained, so others along the bar exhorted him to join the game. The band poured enthusiasm into a circle of fifty onlookers who clapped in time with the popular song, "Hot, Hot, Hot." The next round proved fatal to the three college men and Sandy again pushed Tommy into the arena. Met with a renewed cheer of encouragement, he inhaled the scotch and tossed the glass aside. He made his approach. Maybe relative sobriety was an advantage. The limbo bar was very close to the sand. He pulled his shoulders back and arched as much as he could bear.

"Go, go, go!" the crowd yelled.

Tommy bit his lower lip. *C'mon. Concentrate.* Legs first, then belly. But the bar brushed his chest. *Lean back a little further. Tuck the chin into neck.* Not enough. The bar wiggled and popped loose. Tommy tossed his head back to regain balance. A desperate move. He collapsed in the sand. The crowd groaned.

Sandy was the sole survivor and hopped around to stay limber. Fire danced in her eyes.

Tommy said, "A hundred dollars says you can't make it."

"You're a cheap bastard, you know that?"

"It's a way of life."

"Hah! You're just trying to psych me out!"

"You're absolutely right."

She pranced past him. Amid a wanton laugh, she peeled off her shirt in a seductive swirl to further arouse the male patrons, then slithered up to the lead singer's microphone. With a giggle in her voice, she informed the audience of Tommy's wager and heard a roar of approval while eyes wallowed on her bright green string bikini.

"Sorry, Tommy. It's not going to work!" She shoved her empty glass at him. "Fill it!"

The kid on conga hammered so madly that he probably risked cardiac arrest. The audience cheered again while he approached three male losers. "The bottle, gentlemen."

"Yessir," the amused owner said.

Tommy returned to Sandy, filled the glass with exaggerated flourish to another excited cheer and handed it to her. The band switched key and cranked it up another notch. Sandy glided to the bar and leaned further and further back until her body was nearly parallel with the ground. Then she planted the glass of rum on her belly, allowed her shoulders to sway gently and eased even further back. The muscles in her thighs tightened, tightened, so taut that they looked like they might actually shatter. She ignored the limbo bar. Closed her eyes. Leaned her head further and further back.

Then she inched forward.

Everyone focused on the glass. As her hips passed the bar, she reached even deeper into herself and pulled the glass and her belly down. The rum sparkled in the light and her hair brushed the sand. The glass sank lower. Lower. Lower. Ever lower.

Oh yeah, the moment. Sandy slipped ahead three inches. *Clear.* Everyone mesmerized. The rest of her body wriggled under the bar. Not a drop left the glass.

The band collapsed. A huge round of cheers, whistles and applause. Sandy hoisted the glass and poured it all into her throat. The gesture closed the evening. Some lingered for a final round but, Tommy and Sandy glided across the bay in a near-silent dinghy and found *Freckles II* in calm water. The gentle movement, aft to stern, promised rocking chair slumber.

They were quiet in the cabin below and she became pensive with a fresh glass of rum. "Tommy, how come we never made it?" she asked in a distant voice, as the alcohol took effect. "I mean, we've crossed the Caribbean together, but you never hit up on me. Like, don't I, well, you know, appeal to you?"

Not in the way you'd like to think just now. "I didn't sense an invitation."

"Oh." There was a very long pause. "What sort of invitation do you need?" she murmured and drifted into a soft snore.

Not a shabby question. He collected the glass from her hand, gathered up her legs and guided them onto the bench. Her body curled up a bit. He found a blanket from the aft cabin, covered her and doused the small cabin lights. Her sun-bleached hair glowed around her tanned and pretty face. The dancing blue eyes had retired for the night.

CHAPTER THIRTEEN

Near Andros Island, The Bahamas

Low clouds, bands of faint drizzle and wisps of wind blanketed a sea lacking horizon. Everything ahead was a dismal gray and even Andros Island had faded into a sad silhouette.

With field glasses, Tommy scanned the shoreline, then studied a worn chart in his hand.

Sandy explained. "That'll be Cistern Point on the starboard bow. We can go up the eastern side of Andros and be in Nassau in just a matter of hours. It all depends on how lucky you feel about the weather."

Tommy scratched his jaw with light fingertips. The run to the Bahamas had been under constant threat of an aimless tropical depression in the western Atlantic. It might crank itself up into a small hurricane. It might fizzle into a few unhappy days for tourists, eventually dusted off by a Bermuda high. The windward side of Andros could be choppy, with groundswells running several feet, but on a beam reach, *Freckles II* would heel into a swift pace and Sandy's estimate of a "matter of hours" might be an understatement.

But timing matters. "What day is it?"

"Thursday, ever since this morning."

"We're early."

In a tone suggesting she was about to declare some sort of a record, she said, "Yup, we made great time. Thirty-six hours better than I ever expected for this time of year."

Tommy smiled. "Too early. Let's take the leeward side of Andros and pass some good time."

"Aw, Tommy, the last thing you're ever going to find on the back side of Andros is a good time. What's so crucial about ETA in New Providence?"

Tommy folded the chart. The very flat line of Andros Island as *Freckles II* drew closer. "Sergei won't be expecting us until tomorrow."

Sandy's shoulders drooped. "We're down to our last bottle of rum. There's a great bar near the marina that's a better place to wait than this creepy island."

Tommy said nothing.

"Okay," she sighed, and made a slight course adjustment to capture a faint shift in the wind as it ricocheted off Andros Island. "It's now your charter. Want to reset the main and jib? Just be aware that we probably won't be able to approach the island because the shoals are really treacherous. Not that anyone would want to hang out on Andros anyway. Once we get around Williams Island, we'll have to be careful. The whole area around Bimini is stuffed with drug runners and narcotics enforcement people."

Tommy nodded. In the old days, rum runners hauled the best from Caribbean – especially Cuban – distilleries on a fast path to backwater ports in Florida. Paw-paw Sonnier mostly made do with the local bootleg from nearby bayou stills but had a fondness for what he called "The Genuine" and would share tales about good ol' boys with fast trucks and speedy cars that met the hot boats in Florida sloughs and spread cheer far and wide. *Oh, yeah.* The old timers on the porch of the Crossroads Store, sometimes with whiskey but more often with a Regal or Jax beer, telling the tales, sharing the lore. Mostly lies or rubber-band truth. But he listened close. Fingers tight around an icy-cold soft drink, drawn from a big chest just inside the door. One day, no particular reason, the boys decided young Tommy was old enough for the real brew. *T-Tommy, you get yo'self a Regal. You too old for that kid shit.* Graduation. Into that secret world of rural folks who kept their own moral code and their mouths mostly shut about it.

It was a long way from Andros Island, a long way from piracy pure and simple. And a very long way from an Alden yacht. Leaning against a post, a reasonable imitation of a young man's slouch, comfortable with a beer in hand. But still tacking a "sir" on the end of every reply. Then one day, looking up.... Instead of rugged swamp rascals and gator poachers, he saw tired, weary men near the end of a long, hard life. "You got two choices: forget your dreams, or pay for 'em," Paw-paw said. In the eyes of the men at Crossroads, the truth about poverty and hopelessness and despair. And the romance of it all was crushed in summer air thick with melancholy.

Now he'd aged, too. Sea breeze ruffled his hair and his nostrils flared at the rich and slightly cooler scent of salt air that refreshed him. Tommy eased the main sheet from the blocks and *Freckles II* lurched ahead on a broader reach.

So, Tommy, what's new? Oh, not much, just on my way to an armed robbery. By yourself? Nah, it'll be me, a crazy Russian and a psychotic Englishman who may or may not even show up. We're going to stick up some Cuban army guys who happen to be major league gangsters and also a crew from the Central Intelligence Agency. It's just a casual kind of thing. It's just a way to pay for dreams.

Tommy punctuated the imaginary dialogue with an audible sigh. The culprit probably ten days at sea. Better to seek rational conversation with Sandy. He opened his mouth to speak but just as quickly closed it. A deep sound crept into his ears, not like an animal growl. More like a soft puff on a tuba. A look toward Andros. *Nothing.* He shook his head to to dismiss what was surely overactive imagination. *Back to the notion of the yawl. Time for Sandy to put on her broker's hat.* "Do you think you might be able to find an Alden?"

She yawned and rubbed her eyes. For a minute, only the sound of the wind in the rigging took the edge off a silence luffing anxiety. Then she said, "There's a lot of boats for sale in the Caribbean, Tommy. Why not pick out a nice sassy little ketch and be happy?"

"It has to be an Alden yawl. A racer, fifty feet or so." Once again, the sound, echoing across the relatively calm sea. Again he turned to scan the horizon. The thin line of mangrove tree drifted past in near silence. The methodical sound of a deep drum came and went once more, fading from one ear to another. Maybe it was something he'd eaten, maybe the fish they'd caught just an hour earlier. *Okay, pal. Just be cool about this.*

She nodded, wearing an expression of understanding and patience. "Probably you saw a picture of an Alden when you were a kid and it's haunted you. Why not a nice, sturdy Morgan, like *Freckles*?"

Getting nowhere. "So how much does one of these cost?"

Sandy shifted professional gears and the imaginary part-time broker hat settled onto her head. "I'm up on the market, Tommy. I could put you in a Morgan sloop for maybe two-twenty five, give or take. They're good boats, would do the job. But stick with the newer technology. Believe me, I've been there. *Freckles* – *Freckles I* – was an older boat, a yawl, as a matter of fact."

"What happened to *Freckles I*?" he asked.

She took a breath. Friendship fortified with a little rum always led to candor, but this time it took her a little longer to organize her thoughts. "Dismasted in a squall during a trans-Atlantic solo race. What was left of her broke up on the rocks in the Cape Verde Islands after ten days adrift." Her voice lowered and she stared straight into his eyes. "You know anything about force ten wind?"

"Over fifty knots," Tommy answered.

She nodded. "Thirty-foot waves. There's so much crest

overhanging the waves that the sea looks white. It laid the yacht flat on its side and when she came back up she took a lightning hit. Fried all the instruments. Blew both masts and booms right off the deck."

"Which sort of knocked you right out of the race. Sorry to hear about your misfortune."

"Yeah, but I won it this year. Not much frightens me any-more, and I'm only twenty-seven. You ever been so close to the edge that you've looked death right in they eye, Tommy?"

The fingertips of his right hand glided across this jaw, a habit from when he had his beard. *If you win, you live*, he thought. *If you lose, you die. But if you die, the score doesn't matter much, does it?* A philosophy shared by Wells and Yenchenko. A means to sustain the courage – or madness – to do what they did. When the score became important, it was time to quit.

Or was it? Paw-paw Sonnier, briefly in financial straights because of a fondness for an illegal slot machine at a dance hall a dozen miles out of town, said, "On the day you win, you ain't gonna be tired no more."

The vision of twin spreaders on the Alden's main mast re-turned. Scanning downward, toward the boom. The standing rigging, a pyramid of wire. At anchor in quiet water in the late afternoon. The sea along her hull, almost glass. Like the day in Jamaica when he discarded his beard and with it the face of *El Gato*. Now his cheeks had healed and were tanned into the leathery texture of a different place and different time, when there was no scorecard and he didn't think much about look-ing death in the eye because he didn't think much about death in the first place.

"I've been in a couple of spots." Maybe Paw-paw spoke more about death than his wallet. Maybe he was on the lee-ward side of life. Now the promise of a quiet sea on the lee-ward side of Andros was disturbed with that strange sound. Got to be something bad with the food. A forced chuckle, an upfront apology for about to be asking something stupid. "But I wonder, are you feeling all right?"

Sandy shrugged. "Yes, sure, why?"

"No reason." Maybe it was a sonic boom. As jets went, Guantanamo was only a short hop away.

She cocked her head and her blue eyes eased into a steady gaze. "You really were a spy, weren't you?"

"Yes."

"Be straight with me. Were you any good at it?"

Tommy studied the shoreline as Andros Island crept past. "I did okay."

"And Sergei and that other guy, that major guy?"

"They were very good. Probably still are."

She fell into silence for a few minutes and only the gentle creaks and groans of the rigging found their ears. "So what happened?"

Tommy turned and told her about the bomb, and the combat in Arizona, of the trek across Mexico and the hunt for obscurity. No need to mention Dieter Kreutzer and the image of Mather. *Mather. Mather who said* "Are you from the valley of the clueless?" *The accent is eastern all right. The phrase in German is "Tal der Ahnungslosen." near Dresden, the only place in East Germany that could not get radio from the West.*

Similarities. Mather and Matthias, the Matthias that Dieter Kreutzer hunted. The Matthias who was a mole in the Stasi. The Mather who stood and read a newspaper at the bus stop across the street that day. How old was Matthias? Who was the man who walked past Mather on the street? *I should have paid more attention. Like an idiot, all I wanted to do was annoy Myra Fielding. But Mather's dead, so what difference does it make?* Sandy's eyes, filled with curiosity. "It's a young man's game. After a while you get old and start looking foolish."

She scrunched up her nose at his escape into a cliché. "You're not that old. Oops. That came out kind of wrong."

"It's okay." Tommy returned his attention to the gray,

dense forest that hugged the island shoreline.

"Uh-huh. Okay, um, I suppose you have a different passport for every day of the week, right?"

"None that I should be using any more."

"Sorta makes it a bit difficult to go through immigration and customs. Which is why you didn't do something simple and obvious like hijack an airplane and just fly up to Nassau from St. Thomas."

"Aircraft hijacking is currently out of fashion." *Again.* The sound of a deep, slowly beaten drum as if carried on the wind, drifting in and out of focus. With the field glasses he scanned shoreline once more.

She laughed. "Oh, yes. For sure. Especially this day and age. I don't know who'd blast you into pieces first, the Navy or the Air Force. What are you looking for, anyway?"

"Did you hear anything just now? Some deep murky sounds, maybe a drum?"

She offered a patient smile. "A drum?"

"Or maybe like a tuba. Deep, rolling, left to right."

"Like thunder?"

"No, deeper than that. More like it's inside you than outside. I dunno. Okay, it sounds crazy, too much time at sea, not enough rum."

Sandy's laughter fled and her smile withered. "It's not crazy, Tommy."

"That's a relief."

"Maybe. Maybe not. It's the Breath of Andros. Chickcharneys. Little red-eyed elves who live in the forest. Some people say it's just a trick of the wind, and some people say it's just overactive imagination. You should feel flattered. Not everyone hears it."

"Okay, and what do you say?"

The pink of embarrassment oozed through her tan. She furrowed her brow and seemed to resist even a momentary glance at the shoreline just a couple of hundred yards off the starboard beam. "There's a lot of superstitions that hang around the Caribbean, Tommy. A lot of stories, legends, weird tales. Look, we'll be around Williams Island by late afternoon and..." Sandy's voice trailed off and she stole a glance at him. "Ever hear about Obeah?"

Once more. *The Breath of Andros.* Tommy turned as the song had faded again. "West African religion. Shango, Santeria, Umbanda, Voodoo. All off the same boats."

"*Slave boats.* Obeah is the most mysterious of all. There are a lot of believers, true believers, in the Bahamas."

"So you're saying Andros is enchanted or something like that?"

Sandy focused the course of the yacht. "No. Well, not as much as Cat Island. That's where you find the real shamans. Obi-men."

Intriguing. "So if it's not enchanted, and not many people hear the music, then how would you interpret the experience?"

Sandy bit her lower lip, then drew a deep breath of courage. "Okay. This is what some people say. If you hear the breath of Andros – the chickcharneys are disturbed by a more powerful spirit force – you are being called by an Obi master."

"On Andros?"

"No. On Cat Island."

"But that's, what, a hundred miles. Pretty powerful signal, eh?"

Her voice was firm, almost curt. "One fifty or so, east northeast. Look, Tommy, that's just what some people say, all right?"

Again his attention was drawn to the shoreline. "And you?"

"Never underestimate the power of Obeah, Tommy. It's witchcraft with a capital 'W'." She shrugged and glanced at the shoreline. "Let's just work our way up to Williams Island, hang a right, and find a nice Nassau pub. Even if it's full of tourists."

The sea had become almost calm and the wind in the shadow of the island only faint. *Freckles II* slowed to a crawl and after a few minutes Sandy spoke again. "So this espionage stuff. Is it really a nasty business?"

"Yes. And it's dirty, most of the time boring, all of the time anxious, always looking over your shoulder, always wondering who's watching, always nervous about making a mistake."

She was quiet for several long moments. "Did you, um, make a mistake?"

Tommy looked past her, toward the grey wall that was the sea and the sky and where there was no discernible horizon line between them. *Yeah, for sure. I should have been paying attention to the second guy, the one who passed Mather – or was it Matthias?*

"Sorry," she replied. "I shouldn't have asked. You know, it's a big ocean. All seven of them. We could go anywhere. Maybe circumnavigate the globe. That'd be fun."

Tommy grinned. "We?"

Her voice tumbled into a soft murmur. "I've got nothing better to do."

"It'll always be *your* boat. As it should be. Besides, I want an Alden, a yawl. So it's one last job for a fat fee, and then I'll make a clean break. You can help me find that yawl. For that, you've got to stay out of harm's way."

"Am I in danger? I mean, could I get killed or something?"

"Once we get to Nassau, maybe you'll just want to shove off."

Her eyebrows lifted and then her rigid jaw thrust slightly forward, and her nose went high in the air. Maybe she was angry. Maybe proud.

"So I really *am* in danger, just kicking around with you?"

To toss casual reassurance toward would be wrong. She'd see through it as easily as the clear water beneath *Freckles II*, where objects at four or five fathoms appeared within a finger length's reach. "It's possible. But not yet, I think."

"But I will be, like in Nassau?"

"Maybe."

Sandy adjusted the course to match the almost impercept-ible change in wind coming off the island to their starboard beam. A sly grin crept across her face. "Cool."

CHAPTER FOURTEEN

Paradise Island, Nassau, The Bahamas

Tommy put ashore in bright afternoon sunshine and tested sea legs on a gentle hill that rose to the usual place, the best rendezvous in the hemisphere, tall and pink and welcoming. Atlantis. A beacon of respite. A haven of comfort in a business of bruises. A neutral zone in a polarized world of boundaries that could shift at a moment's notice. Everyone on the dusty path of espionage could catch a breath, take a break, stand down. Here the ground rules for all sides in the intelligence community were simple: No one got killed. No one got robbed. Everyone could be civil, deliveries made, and trade gossip exchanged.

There was no need to stuff a nine-millimeter automatic into a Speedo or string bikini.

Tommy dodged the heaviest traffic he'd experienced since Las Vegas. He found cover among elderly gamblers, bubbly honeymooners and cheery families. An embroidered polo shirt identical to that of the hotel staff cost him fifteen dollars, and for just fifty dollars more in the poolside cabana bar, he camouflaged himself with a bucket of ice, two clean shot glasses, a cocktail tray and a fifth of Stolichnaya Blue Label vodka.

Tommy drew a breath, turned and surveyed a field of flesh.

A locally popular rake 'n' scrape band was well into a long medley built around "Burma Road" to fluff up a festive atmosphere. *"Bullfrog, dressed up in soldier clothes,"* the singer crooned, *"went to the river to shoot some crows...."* A battalion of waiters flitted about with trays of cocktails and pockets full of folded tips.

Tommy checked the balance of the tray and stepped into the sunshine. The eyes of half a dozen women fondled his body, and he obliged by squaring and lifting his shoulders. *"Crows smell a fire and they all fly away... Bullfrog gets back and he cry all day."* He donned a placid smile and ran a gauntlet of several soft calls for drink orders, stalling when a very tall brunette blocked his path. Her large breasts jiggled like gelatin as they struggled to break free of a tiny string bikini, impossible not to notice much less admire, especially when she unfolded a hundred-dollar bill directly above her chest. When she leaned close, he caught the scent of jasmine in her hair.

She whispered in a seductive tone. "That's a lot of ice, but you'll need it all to cool down after we're done."

Tommy studied the vessel in his hand, then those on her body, and finally her eyes. "You think?"

"Uh-huh."

His smile slithered into a smirk. *Paw-paw flicked his wrist and pointed his thumb across the paved road in town and for the first time in my life I learned what a hooker looked like. "Them, they're whole sackfuls of temptation, Tommy, and you best think twice before droolin' too much." A hundred bucks. Should I be flattered or insulted? Steady, boy. You can play later.*

And so his smirk widened into a grin and confided, "Problem is, the ice is to cool down that big Russian guy over there."

She took a step back to appraise his body while her expression shifted from surprise to pity. "Don't tell me you're – "

Tommy offered a bashful grin.

"What a shame," she muttered and moved on.

The moment she passed, he rolled his eyes and grinned even more at the last few sets of eyes furtively tracking him over the tops of paperback books before he reached Yenchen-ko.

Sergei roasted in afternoon sun on a chaise lounge close enough to admire the women in brazen bikinis, but just outside of range from pool splashes of their innocent frolic.

Tommy used his body to cast shade upon Sergei and placed the tray on a table next to the chaise lounge. He dropped the glasses into the bucket to chill, and spoke in soft Russian. "Time to wake up, Sergei."

Startled, Yenchenko bellowed. "Koshka! You are still alive!"

Tommy glanced at the empty bottle of vodka next to Sergei. "Looks like the party's already begun. I brought reinforcements."

Yenchenko shielded his eyes from the sun and studied the new bottle while he lifted his torso and strained every seam of a ridiculous Speedo bathing suit that left none of Sergei's reputation to the imagination. "Is good. So. You have taken job as waiter. Most interesting disguise. But where is *zakuska?* We must drink without small snack? Perhaps smoked fish, black bread, some caviar? Ah, but no. *Zhmot,* Koshka. Always you are *zhmot,* stingy person."

"This little spread set me back fifty bucks."

"*Amerikancy.* You always overpay." He peered beyond Tommy's silhouette. "So. Sandy abandons you? She is very wise, I think."

Tommy pulled the chilled glasses from the ice and poured shots. "She's knocking down rum at Crocodile's We took a slip at Hurricane Hole marina. It's pricey, but convenient. Sandy wasn't too excited about the cost, so I told her you would pick up the tab from your, um, investment." He looked around as he lifted his drink in salute. "Looks like you've set yourself up well. I *do* hope you're working."

Yenchenko raised his finger as if to a lecture to an errant schoolboy and spoke in Russian. "Koshka, Koshka, I am as usual superior. I have ear to ground, hear many things. It is Russian manner. Small island is filled with agents, like fleas on sorry dog. Please. Now you must sit and we will drink together and study lovely young women as good men should do, eh?" He belly-laughed at his own joke and gestured for a refill. "Of course, hotel bill will be posted to team expense for work on project."

Tommy nodded toward the hotel on the opposite side of the pool. "What about those three guys on the sixth floor balcony just over my left shoulder watching us with a pair of military field glasses?"

Yenchenko leaned right to check, then collapsed back on the chaise lounge. "It is nothing. They are only Cubans. Castro has me followed any time I am in this part of Caribbean. They are *pedik*."

Tommy continued in Russian. "We have much to discuss."

Sergei sighed and admired a brunette passing by. "Always it is business with *Amerikancy*. But this is not a good place to speak of such things." He sat up and tapped a finger to his ear to signal they were probably being recorded. Sergei gathered his sport bag for a shirt and trousers, checked to make sure his semi-automatic pistol was handy and slung the bag over his shoulder. He started to walk away, then paused to collect the bottle of vodka and stuffed it into the bag. Tommy fell in on the walk back to toward the hotel.

When they drew close to the hotel entrance, Sergei studied a swarm of taxicabs. "We go for short ride." He held up his hand. "We wait for small moment."

Tommy obeyed and they said nothing while two gray minivans departed. The doorman beckoned the third cab in line forward. "Ah. Now we go." Although they hurried, a couple emerged from the hotel and slipped into minivan ahead of them. When the cabbie hesitated, the doorman stepped forward to tell the driver to move on. Sergei blocked him, opened the door of the taxi and asked the couple to get out.

"I beg your pardon?" the man in the back seat said.

"You please exit taxi."

The man protested. "I'm quite sure you can take the next in line."

Yenchenko growled and tossed his sport bag into the front seat. "As you wish. Driver is instructed to take most powerful bomb to parliament house, touch button, make very big explosion. *Allahu akbar!* Go with Allah!"

Eyes wide, the horrified couple scrambled out of the van and back into the hotel lobby. Sergei smiled and motioned Tommy to get in to the taxi.

A scruffy and unfazed driver asked, "Where to, man?"

Sergei slumped in the back seat and suggested the Botanic Gardens. Behind them, the three men from the balcony raced out of the hotel and got into the next cab. The scruffy driver picked up speed toward the Paradise Island bridge and in the rearview mirror watched Sergei Yenchenko light an inexpensive Cuban cigar. At a traffic circle, the other taxi drew closer.

"You travelin' with a group o'fellas, mister?" the driver asked. "Few extra dollar, I shake 'em." Sergei motioned approval and the taxi accelerated sharply onto the high arching bridge toward Nassau.

If he clears the halfway point before the pursuit car gets on the bridge, we'll be out of sight.

Yenchenko said, "Is good."

"Botanic Gardens, then?"

"*Da.* Botany interests me, but not much worthwhile blooms now."

The driver chuckled and admired Sergei's cigar.

"It is Cuban, of course. But I prefer cigarette. How close does taxi follow?"

The driver's eyes flickered across the rear view mirror. "Couple cars back. Tell you what. If you got more of them cigars, I swap you dead even for cigarettes, man."

"I only smoke Players," Sergei replied as they raced

through the light on East Bay Street. "You make left turn."

Tommy looked out the taxi window to hide a barely suppressed smile. Yenchenko never smoked cigarettes and used cigars only for signals.

"My brand exactly," the driver remarked and held an open pack aloft. The taxi swerved into position, roared through a red light and turned onto Shirley Street. Half a dozen drivers honked disapproval, but the driver remained impassive.

"Is good," Sergei responded, "we make trade." He passed the packet of remaining cigars to the waiting hand of the driver. The margins of American currency peeked from under the wrapper.

The minivan wove through the two narrow lanes of westbound traffic that began to ease only after they entered a quiet stretch of banks and government buildings. Tommy began to pick up the thread of conversation, but Yenchenko's hand fell lightly on his forearm to enforce silence.

"You make right turn toward Bay Street," he told the driver as they neared Charlotte Street.

The driver said, "Hey, man, I think we lost them fellas."

"Make turn," Yenchenko ordered. He turned to Tommy. "We take separate path for short while. Sergei Yenchenko must be certain we have small time for talk." He directed the driver to turn left onto George Street and stop. "So. You take Number Ten bus to Arawak Cay. Walk two hundred meter west to garden. You have dollar for driver?"

"No. I spent my last on that vodka."

Yenchenko sighed and tugged Bahamian currency from his shirt pocket. "And no *zakuska*. *Zhmot*, Koshka, *zhmot*."

"You take care, man," the driver said with a smile. "Enjoy your walk."

Tommy settled onto the first bus in line amid half a dozen hotel workers and six American tourists who had patronized the Straw Market to harvest souvenirs and carried stuffed bags to prove it. Ten minutes later he stood before a broad open

field at the foot of Fort Charlotte with no idea how long
Yenchenko would run the Cubans around the back streets of
Nassau. He walked away from Fish Fry and past Haynes Oval
until he recognized the tunnel entry to the botanic garden.
Several cars huddled under enormous trees and he was about
seek a discreet place to wait the taxi zoomed up and stopped.

Yenchenko paid his fare and brushed past Tommy to survey the scene inside the garden gate. A large tent filled a small
meadow where a wedding party had begun to gather. He
grunted and slowed his pace to barely a crawl, pausing often to
study small name plaques before variations on the theme of
hibiscus, palm, bougainvillea and orange Poinciana trees. Each
time he leaned over, he looked left and right, waited for other
visitors to pass, and drifted toward a haven for conversation.
As they strolled past the wedding scene, just as the bride and
groom arrived, he grinned and applauded them.

"Sergei is of course known as romantic. When will you
marry, Tommy Kane, and have many strong sons?"

Tommy chuckled. "Not this week. And you?"

Yenchenko motioned Tommy toward an ornate iron
bench. "I think never to marry. It is not future for soldier. So.
We must do quickly business. The Cubans are stupid, yet
there are many of them. And many new, young, faces are on
island also. Americans, but not tourists. We must be cautious,
Koshka."

"More than you expected?"

"*Nyet*. Small force, but only annoyance."

Kids, right out of the Farm, first op for many, probably.
"And the taxi driver?"

"He is floater who is called Sammy. He is good driver, but
I think too, too – how you say, likes very much?"

"Fond."

"*Da*, fond of rum." He slowed the pace even more and
lingered to study a plant identification plaque. "So, Koshka,
you make contact with Major?"

"Yes. He's using the name Ian Wells and may be in. It's difficult to tell for sure. If so, he should be here tomorrow, but I'm not holding my breath. We should pick a familiar dead drop to communicate, since none of us trusts telephones."

A faint expression of reticence fluttered across Sergei's jaw, then evaporated in a casual tone punctuated by a shrug. "Perhaps we have good fortune and Major stay away. Money is in two shares, not three. Is good."

Red flags luffed in Tommy's mind and so did the words of Ian Wells: *That bastard can't be trusted.* "I still think we could use a third man," Tommy said.

Yenchenko sighed. "Time is short, too short to recruit. Transfer of money is tomorrow night, Koshka. So, you see, there is no need for communication arrangement. We meet behind grocery as planned tomorrow. Few men expected at transfer, so for us, no difficulty. You have plan for escape?"

Anxiety bit hard and gnawed on nerves. *In one breath, many Cubans. Now only a few. What's he up to?* "Sandy. We lay low for a couple of days, then slide out as a charter."

Yenchenko tightened his jaw. "She is most capable. But good idea? She is friend, Koshka. She is not professional."

"Amateur in our trade, perhaps, but capable. And trustworthy. I think she'd grab at it for a couple of hundred thousand."

Yenchenko seemed reluctant. "But we must take care we do not be seen or tracked. On open sea, I think Sandy's boat is no match for CIA or for Cubans."

They lapsed again into aimless chatter in Russian while elderly tourists crept past. Two couples, dressed too formally for the modern day, but probably casual for a distant time. One of the men and one of the women struggled to move their hips, and their spouses remained gentle and patient. Despite infirmities, they took in the garden with keen and eager eyes and applauded pockets of displays as if they were midsummer fireworks in a small town. Trying for a cynical image of the four of them pumping quarter slots at the casino at Cable Beach was impossible and their innocence made him yearn for long-ago days, a hot shower and a Saturday night dance where he could flirt from the bullpen and feel the tug of infatuation.

Yenchenko watched, too, and his voice trailed off into melancholy. "*Pisdect*. You know this word?"

"Fiasco. The end. Complete. A fatal outcome."

"*Da, da*. This is price for error, Koshka."

Being lectured like a schoolboy who blew a math quiz was annoying. "Tell me about Matthias."

Sergei seemed to be caught off guard. "Matthias?"

"Yes."

Sergei pursed his lips.

"Did you know Dieter was killed?"

"There was rumor, Koshka. Most sad thing happen sometime. It is nature of our work, eh?"

"And what about Matthias?"

Sergei scowled. "Why do you look backward, Koshka? No purpose. One must always look forward, not live in yesterday."

Dig in. "Tell me about Matthias."

"Koshka – "

"Tell me about Matthias or Sandy and I sail at first light."

Yenchenko glared for a moment, then sighed. "Matthias is mole in Stasi, yes? Perhaps from CIA. Dieter spend much time on hunt. I myself assist as I can, but I have many other task, too. All we learn is Matthias comes from Dresden, in university group, and is recruited by agent code-named 'Blackbird.' I have never seen this Matthias, but he would be about our age. When Berlin wall comes down, when Soviet Union come to end, all are most curious but Matthias and his control, Blackbird, vanish, poof, all gone. Dieter is in Munich, *da?* He is most, how you say, *oderzhimyi?*"

"Obsessed."

"*Da*, obsess about Blackbird and ask many questions. We

all say to Dieter, stop, enough, it is over, no one care any more. There is story that someone make attempt on Dieter, but miss, and then it is forever done. Kreutzer goes to Bavaria, where he has small business, a small hotel, to retire."

"A *gasthaus*. I've been there."

Yenchenko paused for a long moment. The look in Sergei's eyes was distant and maybe saw memories he did not want to think about. At last he turned and his eyes seemed tired. "Perhaps he continue. Make some trouble, learn something he should not know."

"How did he die?"

Yenchenko shrugged. "I am told it was bomb, but report is from second or third person. Koshka, I pay no attention to yesterday, *da?*"

His tone abruptly shifted from reflective melancholy to assertive optimism.

"Now we must make good robbery, good escape, find new life. You buy sailing boat. I find nice island with forever supply of good vodka. To hell with Major, who may not be on team anyway. Koshka, there is only small guard at exchange, fewer than ten. They will be few so they do not capture very much attention. This is known style of Medina."

"Carlos Medina himself?"

"Of course. It is his operation. CIA unit is only small player. So. Perhaps eight or ten. Is okay for us, *da?*

Three men in park maintenance uniforms, armed with an assortment of tools, worked along the path and occasionally tidied plants or smoothed mulch. They took turns; one worked and the others watched. *A great disguise as a government worker.*

"So, Koshka, we make agreement with plan?"

With Wells a question mark, there wasn't a whole lot of options. "Yeah, okay."

"Is good plan?"

Tommy chuckled. "*Kak dva paltsa obossat.*"

Yenchenko roared laughter. His eyes sparkled. "Hah! Most excellent. How you say phrase in English?"

"A piece of cake."

Sergei repeated the expression three times to commit it to memory. The work crew drew closer. Tommy ran his fingers through his hair and Yenchenko slipped into Russian to loudly give directions to the Straw Market, his voice edgy.

Been standing in one spot for way too long. "Want to take a walk over that way?"

Yenchenko declined through the faintest gesture of his hand.

When the workers were within twenty feet, Sergei's patience expired and he clarified directions, then extended his massive paw to shake hands. "You will find straw market most interesting place to obtain souvenir. But you must bargain, eh?" he summarized. "I must now go. Enjoy city, eh?" He walked away in the opposite direction. Tommy took a look at the three workmen, all of whom offered polite smiles. He responded with a light wave and formed his own plans to fill the next thirty hours.

Chapter Fifteen

Hurricane Hole Marina, Paradise Island, The Bahamas

Tommy carried two steaming platters through the companionway.

Sandy peered over worn pages of a used paperback book in her left hand and a tumbler of rum on ice in her right. "Ah, so what's this?"

"Just grouper, sautéed in a little oil with onion and garlic, then smothered with sliced tomato and a sharp cheddar cheese. It's on a bed of fresh salad greens from that little market near Bay Street." He pulled a dark green bottle from under his arm. "I also have a pretty decent chablis."

"Fabulous. I don't care what Sergei says, Tommy. You're first class at a stove." She dog-eared the book page, kept the rum within easy reach and accepted her plate. "So. Did you have a good day spying?"

He laughed at the play on domesticity. "Interesting. How was yours?"

"I won twenty-two dollars slammin' doms at Passin' Jacks. They sell crappy rum, though. Tourist stuff, not like you get at pure local rum shops in Barbados." She attacked her food and cooed a compliment. "And... I picked up a day charter, a couple from the States, tomorrow. Still gotta make a living, Tommy."

Tommy nodded while he slipped a fork under a tender slice of grouper.

"I'll be back late afternoon. I think she wants to keep him away from the slots up at Cable Beach for a while, but he seems like a night-guy, so I think she's gonna lose out. Some squalls are forecast late, probably after happy hour, so we should be okay." She chuckled. "Just once I'd like to have some of these fat wallets out in stiff weather. Give 'em something to remember."

Tommy poured wine. "I'll be up early, make a stack of fry jacks and a good supply of johnnycake for your clients and make myself scarce for the rest of the day."

"Thanks, I really appreciate it. So. How's our little robbery shaping up? I can't say I've ever been a wheel-man with a 48-foot yacht before."

"Not sure. Sergei says it's on for tomorrow night. Maybe just the two of us."

"Really? What happened with the Major guy? I thought he was supposed to be here today or tomorrow."

"Ian Wells. And, yeah, exactly."

She cocked an eyebrow but said nothing. Instead she focused on her plate and prodded a scrap of fish in a slow circle to plow sauce.

"Sergei thinks we can do it by ourselves. I suspect he wants to cut Wells out of it."

"Won't Wells be a little pissed about that?"

Tommy curled lettuce around his fork and then savored it on his tongue. "I'm not even sure Ian will show up. But I do know Sergei does not trust Wells and Wells does not trust Sergei."

She giggled. "Nice little cozy gang you've got there, Tommy. Reminds me of a couple of girls I knew in high school."

"Ouch."

"Actually, it didn't turn out so bad. The girls, I mean. They discovered they were both lesbians and became lovers. It was the sort of thing that gives a little town in Iowa a lot to talk about at the local ice cream parlor. So have you given any thought to, um, maybe pulling the plug on the heist?"

That would be really easy. Just walk away and go back to nice, quiet obscurity. Problem is I gave my word, to Yenchenko and Wells and Sandy, too, and then there's that Alden yawl. He looked up from his plate but remained silent.

Sandy tossed the last of her wine into her throat, settled the fork on the edge of her platter, and reached for the rum. "Ah, well, Tommy, I didn't really think so. Look. If this is going sour, we can still take off. It's a big damn ocean and there's other things to do besides get killed. I'm not all that fond of Nassau anyway. Never have been. The Junkanoo season is year-round now and gone commercial. Goombay this, goombay that. Bands are already into it. All for every goddamn American with a point-and-click. Prices are up at least twenty percent since the last hurricane season ended. Personally, I think Freeport's a lot more fun, but hey, I'd rather hit the out islands, like the Turks and Caicos. That's where we'll find open-minded charters who come to the Caribbean for unspoiled beaches and none of those clowns that ought to be in Orlando."

He studied her eyes. Absolutely no fear. "That about sum it up?"

"Yeah, I think that kinda covers it. So why do it?"

"Serge says it could run into the millions. You'd get your yacht free and clear. No more payments to sweat."

"Sergei is usually full of shit. Sorry, I know he's your buddy and all, but you know it's true. You know it and I know it and if this goes bad, my bank payments will be the least of my problem."

He nodded. "If I walk, Sergei will probably go for it alone and get killed."

"And if you don't walk, and you haven't got enough guys, you could wind up just as dead as Sergei, and I'd be stuck with my own cooking. Think about that for a second, okay?"

Sandy's diet was legendary and terrible. "I get the point."

She studied her empty rum glass and leaned forward. "Do you? Do you *really*?"

"What happened to 'am-I-in-danger-cool'?"

Sandy retreated. "I dunno. Maybe it was because I spent all afternoon busting my ass for a day charter and twenty-two bucks at dominos, thinking about you guys working on this giant heist as if you're going to rob some kid's lemonade stand. The more I got thinking about the Cubans *and* the CIA, the more I thought, wow, this is getting way out of hand. Now Sergei's changing the game plan, your Major guy may or may not show but certainly won't show on time. Jeez, Tommy, you guys are so hung up on this you'd stumble over cow flop because you're not watching where you're going. Typical men, I guess."

True enough. *Cow flop*. The time, long ago, when Paw-paw was up to his ears in some difficulty. Something involving a collection of gator skins stored in a shed near the old man's shack and a new parish sheriff eager to make an example. *Yeah. I was all kinds of anxious*. But ol' Paw-paw just grinned and said, "To the worm in the cow-flop, the whole world is cow-flop." *Cow flop*. No question he'd see the job through. But the young skipper of *Freckles II* had been recruited into an increasingly problematic operation. Time to release Sandy to her nomadic life. "Look, if you want to shove off, I'll understand, no hard feelings."

She sighed and went pensive. Her voice calmed. "No, I won't. I promised you a ride out of this tourist trap. And I'm not going back on my word. And I really need another stiff belt of rum."

He softened his words. "I'm kind of in the same spot."

"There's a difference."

"Not really. You're a kick-ass sailor and I'm a kick-ass secret agent. Extra points for loyalty."

"Do you think Sergei is loyal?"

Not the sort of question to be blown off. "On the surface, hard to say. But when it comes down to it, in the crunch, when it really hits the fan, yeah, I think so."

She shook her head. "You guys are stark raving nuts. Both, well, all three of you."

"It happens to old guys. Some guys get wheelchairs and drool on their shirts and some guys sleep half the day and watch baseball the other half and some guys do an occasional stickup to pass some good time. Got to fill the day somehow."

She shrugged. "I never figured you for a drooler."

"And I hate baseball."

"I guess that sort of reduces your options. So where to, after your stickup?"

After summarizing the plan, he said, "In any event, we'll lay low and not approach the dock until just before dawn, and only if we're absolutely certain we have no tail. Plan to cast off at dawn. It helps that you've picked up a day charter. Kind of like you're coming and going. Shouldn't attract much attention."

"The weather will be crappy for a night departure anyway. There's a storm system moving in. Should be some good squalls tomorrow night."

Tommy sighed. "This op just gets more and more, well, interesting."

Sandy laughed. "Understatement of the week. Okay, I'll lay in a supply of beer and nibbles. You'll probably want snacks while you count up the loot."

"Nothing fancy. We'll probably be tired anyway. Robberies take a lot out of you."

"Really? I never knew that. Here I always thought there would be some kind of adrenalin rush."

"More like a lot of anxiety." He sipped the last of his chablis and wiped his lips with a napkin. "Waiting for the cops to show up, maybe too eager to get out of town."

"And we'll sail for where?"

"Probably back to Belize, at least for Sergei."

A wry smile rippled across her cheeks. "Yeah, he's probably eager to start another war someplace. Poor guy's been off the battlefield for at least a month. What about you?"

"Haven't decided yet."

More to the mast than Tommy, she muttered, "I know. The damn Alden." Then she found his eyes and teased, "Tommy, you really ought to consider a ketch, not a yawl."

The last taste of wine in his mouth evaporated the flavor of the grouper, and in his memory he again heard Moses Clay admonish him with the honesty that can only be shared between good friends. *Remake myself? Hardly. Just ought to get a boat and take off.* Sandy had it pretty good. Somehow they would have to keep her out of harm's way. Myra's people would not give up, and if they could find him in Belize, they could find him anywhere.

Tired. Not mentally but in attitude. Before the Rashid job, a fairly upbeat attitude. Cocky, even. The six-year layoff was supposed to be just a path to mellow out. But since approaching Wells, his effort was half-hearted, disinterested, bored. *Maybe that bomb took more out of me than a little blood. Maybe I left more than I thought back at Doc's.*

The Alden. *Yeah, the damn Alden.* A fifty footer. Thin. Sleek. Fast. Slicing through the open ocean waves, carrying him to sunshine. And obscurity. And maybe a little inner peace. Now he shrugged. "Nope. It's got to be a yawl."

She shook her head and began to gather the dishes for her turn in the galley.

CHAPTER SIXTEEN

A second cruise ship had tied up the night before and a fresh wave of Americans poured onto asphalt paths aimed directly to the souvenir stands and Straw Market. Tommy picked up a cheap hat and sunglasses from the stand of Deacon Cole and fell in with the herd. A light rucksack, dangling from a shoulder. Rumpled clothes. A loaded nine millimeter automatic. Perfectly disguised as a tourist adrift in a sea of Bay Street gift shops, Tommy set off to conduct a census of CIA field agents.

It was depressingly easy. All rookies on a first field op. Young. Fit. Obvious. A little too tidy. Like DEA people visiting for a conference. A little too bored. Like trainees itching for the kind of action they think will be glamorous but more likely make them puke. A little too arrogant. Like hot stuff that hasn't yet run into guys like Yenchenko or Wells. *Or me.*

But mostly obvious. And it was difficult to not to be tempted into having a little fun. Like the blonde babe on Bay Street hanging at a jewelry store front. *Hi, there. I'm Tommy Kane. Yeah, yeah, the one with a price on his head. Just wanted to let you know you're blown and would you mind if I copped a feel?*

He chided himself. *Don't get too casual, buddy.* What they lacked in experience, they would make up for with enthusiasm. What he could expect from a veteran, he could not anticipate from a beginner. And what he might get in professional courtesy from relaxed old-timers would be incomprehensible to excited newbies. Besides, it would be harder to pick out the experienced Cubans, who'd blend in well with dock grunts and street people who worked ports like Nassau. They'd form the outer perimeter of security for the CIA-Cuban cash exchange, prepared to drop in at the last moment. Like brown pelicans working a school of fish.

The supply of gift shops and post card displays was exhausted by late morning. Maybe he'd get an early lunch. Then maybe kill the afternoon working north toward Cable Beach, grab a Number Ten back into town, rob a Cuban drug cartel and sail off into the sunrise.

Tommy slipped into Café Skans, a Bahamian diner with a Greek flair just off the tourist track and in a lull between breakfast and lunch. Soft clatter of china from the kitchen echoed in waves across the nearly empty dining room. Two waitresses filled sugar servers and catsup bottles behind a counter drained of the usual bureaucrats bound for nearby government buildings. The plan was a quiet corner table, a steamy bowl of conch stew and a really cold bottle of Kalik beer. A surprise brought a grin to his face, and he presented himself to a woman studying classified ads in the *Nassau Guardian*.

"Hello, Adrienne. Long time."

Adrienne Tillman glanced up and over the rims of her glasses, and then her eyes swept the room beyond him while her shoulders slumped and her dark blue suit found the back of her chair. "God help us," she muttered. "As if we don't have enough troubles here already."

Tommy refused to allow his smile to whither. "Feeling kind of stupid just standing here."

A large yet graceful woman, she wore her hair in a tight bun to accentuate the fine line of expressive eyes and easy smile. Her navy suit was neatly pressed and feminine frills adorned the collar of a white blouse.

"Yeah, I'm alone."

She leaned back to exhale annoyance. "I should leave you

where you are. She motioned toward the chair opposite her. "Very well, sit. But only for a moment. I owe you that much. You are off the reservation, Tommy Kane. Some even say you're dead. I can't be any help to you." Her neatly-folded newspaper found its way to the side of what had been a plate of stewed fish and johnnycake, the late breakfast in which a CIA station chief in a quiet post can indulge.

"Not asking for help. Just passing some time."

Her eyes narrowed as she watched his rucksack slip to the floor. "What you be doing in my station, Tommy Kane?"

"Just passing through. You know, a tourist."

She snorted disbelief. "You lie smoother than the prime minister. I'm sorry, Tommy, but if you've come to cause trouble, you've chosen a very bad time."

He caught the attention of a waitress. "Coffee?"

Her jaw wriggled with indecision. "Well, perhaps."

"Bad time?"

"Well – Actually, no. But only because you are an old friend and this is not business, okay? I must tell you, New Providence is stuffed with people in the trade, many unfamiliar faces, very young, mostly ours – well, Americans – and Cubans as well."

Adrienne could never resist gossip.

An indifferent waitress, with an apron pocket stuffed with tips from a good breakfast service, arrived to take Tommy's order for two coffees.

Adrienne waited until they were alone. "But it's above my level. No one is saying anything, no one is running the affair from my office. They have a substation set up on Bay Street. Above the book shop. You know it? Yes? So, I am just hoping it won't become a mess, you see?"

Tommy nodded.

Adrienne tested for *quid pro quo*. "You know what this is about?"

"No."

"Don't you be lying to me, Tommy Kane. I've plenty of friends in the magistrate's court."

His glance toward the returning waitress paused the conversation. When the check was placed beside his cup and they were alone again, he speculated more as a courtesy than a confession. "Maybe some sort of a drug thing?"

Sadness filled her eyes. "I wouldn't be surprised. There have been leaks of State Department cables concerning that business, and some people I know who have been working with DEA have been exposed. This is just not very good. Two of them are good friends."

Tommy sipped the potent coffee. *Should have ordered the Kalik.*

Adrienne tapped the fingertips of both hands together just in front of her mouth and occasionally bounced the gesture off her lips. Her eyes were warm, but wary. "So you insist you are just a tourist, a guest in my country?"

"Yes ma'm."

"Then when you met the Russian fellow, Sergei what's-his-name, in the botanical gardens yesterday, it was just by chance?"

Tommy hoisted an eyebrow. Surprise. Surrender. "Yenchenko. You run a very good station, Adrienne."

"Better than you lie," she chuckled, but raised her hand to silence the beginning of his confession. "I don't want to know," she declared. "It makes no never-mind to me, and I'm not trying to climb the career ladder."

"Thank you. You're a good friend."

She shrugged modesty, and they both knew there would someday be a *quid pro quo* to comfort a future bump in the road for a normally quiet and relaxed CIA station. "But you know, I can't help you, Tommy. Nobody can any more." She paused. "Well, maybe the Obi-man, but no one else."

Interesting. "Why an Obi-man?"

She looked surprised. "For some, there is the power of

Obeah, even if they half-believe it. You want to open doors around here? You get yourself a proper tabeejah around your neck, that's what you do."

"What's involved?"

She laughed. "Oh, my, aren't you the innocent tourist? Tommy, I must tell you: you do not find such things at Straw Market. No, no. For that, you find a real Obi-man. Or rather, he finds you. And then he talks you into going to kumina, a ritual ceremony, and – if you come out alive – you earn a tabeejah and no door is closed to you. They say it is pretty nasty witchcraft, for sure. But trust me, except for that, the old bridges, they have been burned, okay? I'm sorry, Tommy, but I can't help you. It would be a very big problem for me, you see."

Tommy answered with a soft smile. "Moses Clay thinks I should get out, do something else. Something about finding redemption."

Adrienne beamed interest. That strange rookie year, working an op in the Grenadines that had little political significance but profoundly changed Moses Clay and Adrienne Tillman. Marriages to other people, but they became involved. The affair, the first tangle with the first of a parade of control officers. Confrontations. Divorce for Moses, suicide for Adrienne's crushed husband. If they ever needed an example of an op training officers could use to illustrate what not to do.... Moses drifted for a while and then quit. Out of sympathy, they said, an underling in operations gave Adrienne the soft post of station chief in Nassau. There she pulled her emotions back together and the word was she and Moses never spoke again. Maybe she was at peace with the entire matter, interested in the same way people ask about a high school rival at a much later reunion.

"How is Moses?" she asked.

"Bail bonds in Las Vegas."

"Ah."

A faint electronic chirp interrupted. Tommy disengaged while she harvested a cell phone from her bag. As she answered, he began to stand but she waved him back into the chair, listened for several moments, acknowledged some news and disconnected.

"You still refuse the phone, Tommy?" she asked.

"Never use one. No exceptions, ever."

Adrienne shrugged and returned the phone to her bag. "Times change. Secure lines, encryption, such marvels they have now, Tommy."

Tommy offered a polite but dismissive smile. "Eavesdropping never goes out of style. I wouldn't know how to work one of those things anyway. You poke it, you flick it, you squeeze it, and all the time NSA or DIA is eavesdropping. Give me a good dead drop any day."

Adrienne rolled her eyes and returned the conversational focus to Moses Clay.

Gossip. Warm tidbits, throwaway stuff to keep the dialog alive. But she seemed to be past emotional attachment.

"He's a wise man, Tommy. You should listen to him. Tell me, did you ever find religion?"

Tommy's attention tumbled to his nearly empty coffee cup. After Moses, she became a devout Episcopalian and probably finds high Mass on Sunday morning a means of atonement, a grasp for comfort. "No, not really. Not my thing, I'm afraid."

"Then perhaps as part of your tourist visit to the Bahamas, you should visit Cat Island. Talk a little while with an Obiman. Maybe you find a different path."

And here it is again. "What do you know about chickcharneys?"

Adrienne shook her head. "More superstition! They are supposed to be little creatures running around Andros Island, but trust me, Tommy, these are stories to excite the tourists, to make adventure for them. I think they are an invention of those who have been at sea – or rum – for much too long.

But Obeah? So many believers."

The conversation had drifted to ebb. "What can I do for you?"

Adrienne smiled. "Oh, my, you are such a very kind person to someone who just said she cannot help you. Hm. Well, then, just don't make too much of a mess for me. I prefer uneventful days." She glanced at her watch. "Look at the time! I must go! I'll be late to the office."

They rose together from the table. Adrienne extended her hand to shake his, bid farewell and walked away. Tommy dug into his pocket for money. Rather than leave it on the table, he decided to linger and find a cashier and separate them even more.

Adrienne unexpectedly turned. "Perhaps there is one thing you might do for me, Tommy. The Atlantis people just called to say they think Lester Finn is in New Providence."

The name hit Tommy like an overdose of Tabasco. *Lester Finn. The other guy at the bus stop n Bavaria.. Stay calm, stay calm.* "They'd prefer him to move along?"

Her dark eyes twinkled in the mid-morning light that poured through a side window. "No, they just prefer he not visit *their* casino. Cable Beach is fine with them – they are competitors, you see – but I'd rather not have problems come up with Cable, either."

"If I see him, I might make a recommendation to catch a flight out?"

Adrienne replied with a knowing smile. "Have a nice visit to our little country, Mister Kane. Please treat her gently, for she is such a deserving lady." She turned and strode away.

Ten o'clock. At least a chore to occupy the hours before the robbery. Lester Finn was easy prey, a diversion to pass some time. Maybe get some answers about Dieter, too. After lunch, maybe a snooze on a hotel lounge chair somewhere, grab a bite at Johnny Canoe's or Señor Frog's then rendezvous with Sergei for a nice little multi-million dollar stickup. In the rain. Without a backup. Two against ten, twelve, maybe more.

You need redemption, Moses had told him. *No. I really need a first-class po-boy, dressed, or maybe a big platter of andouilles and a bowl of gumbo.* Again. The low growl from a place between his ears. Deep in his brain. The call of the Obi-man.

CHAPTER SEVENTEEN

Cable Beach, New Providence Island

Lester Finn was everyone's image of a weasel. A thin, wiry body topped off by a face that looks like a bullet on the way to something important. A large nose, weak chin, sloping forehead and dark, expressionless eyes. He combs his hair straight back and leans a bit forward into his step. Usually wears rumpled suits drooping over rounded shoulders. When Tommy spotted him this time, he was in a sports jacket and slacks over a polo shirt. All of which were rumpled and drooped over rounded shoulders.

Tommy drifted close through off-the-shelf casino decor that could be anywhere in the western hemisphere. Room illumination oozed from an army of temptation, ranks of all denominations. Harmonic electronic slot tones to hammer brains into submission. Only a few machines were in use, mostly by tourists with grim faces, gray hair and round bellies and never the glamorous folks from the travel brochures. In his own little world, Lester ripped through five or ten dollars on multiple lines.

From less than twenty-four inches away, Tommy said, "Hello, Lester."

The rumpled player flinched. The reels stopped. No winner. "Jeez, Tommy, you scared the shit out of me."

"Folks say have that effect lately."

Lester scowled and scanned the dim gaming area beyond

Tommy's shoulders. "You alone? Yeah, you always flew solo. You don't got no crew. Just that damn shit-eatin' grin. Which don't mean nothin'. So yeah, you're just messin' with my concentration, that's all, catchin' me off guard like that."

"You want to tell me how this takes concentration? I thought you just had to let your brain sauce up on Tabasco and go numb."

"Yeah, yeah. Hey, I heard you was dead, man." His eyes measured Tommy's torso. "Maybe you are. Where'd you get the duds, an undertaker?"

"Best the casino security people could do for me. Not quite my size, but I like the color. I thought it was decent for on-the-fly."

Lester's eyes shifted repeatedly from side to side. "Yeah, well, you gotta do something about standards, pal."

A nervous twitch around the corner of Lester's mouth hinted there was another twitch in Lester's knees, a fight-flight reaction that couldn't figure out what to do. The security blazer sent a message of unwelcome authority.

Tommy softened his voice to calm his target. "Long time, Lester, long time."

"No shit, man." Lester bit the corner of his lip and reached for the machine button to give the reels another punch.

Tommy's fingers got there first.

Lester's shoulders slumped even more. Defiance rose in his voice. "You ain't packing are you? Nah, didn't think so. That jacket's a half size too small and it would show."

"Waistband, in back."

"Shit. How the hell'd you find me anyways?"

"First I paid the security guy to take a walk. Second, I didn't see your name on the ban list. Then I charmed a nice young lady into letting me peek at the comps list and, wow, gee whiz, there you were. They've got you down for slots, which I thought strange, so I wasted a bunch of time in the sports parlor and at the tables, but no Lester Finn to be seen."

"Real shame," Lester grumbled. His attitude brightened when a slots attendant approach the supervisor, whispered something and nodded toward Tommy. "Yeah, real shame. You been busted, pal."

The supervisor's expression hardened and he began to walk toward them. Lester cracked a smile, but it evaporated within seconds. The casino host intercepted the supervisor. After a brief but intense conversation, the supervisor stalked off. The casino host drifted on as if nothing happened.

Lester muttered an epithet. "A guy can't catch a break."

Pretending not to notice, Tommy filled his voice with satisfaction and the soft, soothing, assured cadence of younger days. "But now here we are, nice and cozy, in a quarter slots carousel, just you and me and the guy way over there. We really need to have a talk, Lester."

Beads of perspiration formed on Lester's forehead. He rubbed his nose with the back of his left hand. "Jeez, Tommy, you gotta know I had nothin' to do with that business in Germany, okay?"

Huh? Tommy replayed the Bavaria scene again. *I look up at Myra, past Myra. Mather leans against a lamp post. City buses come and go. Three cars go by, silver, silver and blue. A man walks past, a man wearing a rumpled suit with drooping shoulders, a guy in a hurry. Lester Finn. He slows momentarily and, yes, there, he nods toward us. Then he moves away. Myra speaks. I speak. We go back and forth. Dieter is off to the side, trying to be discreet, not paying attention. Myra finally leaves. Mather is no longer there.*

Play it out with Lester. "Strange coincidence. I mean, what kind of odds would you lay that Myra and Mather and you and Dieter and I would wind up on the same street corner in a little out of the way burg in Bavaria?"

Lester offered a shrug of admission. Tommy's index finger tapped the button. The reels spun. Lester's card in the slot was rewarded with fifty dollars. The machine burbled a happy little salute, but no one paid attention.

"Jeez, Tommy. Always with the luck."

A tense pause.

"Aw, c'mon, Tommy, it was, you know, just business. Mather had me over a barrel."

"He needed you to track me?"

Lester's jaw dropped and his eyes widened. "No, no, he wanted Dieter. I swear on my mother, Tommy, it was Dieter."

Tommy hoisted an eyebrow to mask an interrogation mistake. *Just been way too long. Fake it.* "What reason did you get?"

Lester's anxiety level climbed another notch. "I got no idea, man, none. It was just a finger job, that's all. I swear to God, Tommy, just a point and walk."

Lester's confession seemed credible. *If Myra turned up to assign me to the op in California, then it was a black-flag job and I was already a target. Or maybe they were smudging Rashid and I became a target of opportunity because of meeting Dieter in Bavaria? Nah. They could have used anyone for that.*

Panic in Lester's eyes grew.

He's about to do something really dumb. Change the subject, go for a more jocular tone. "I didn't have you down as a slots kind of guy."

Lester's voice became expansive, relaxed. "It's relaxation, that's all. Sports action is slow this time of year, and the dealers? They look like fuckin' zombies. Anyway, this here's just a quarter box, and I'm guessing it's probably running with a hold of maybe seven, seven and a half for the house. So for the hundred I'm working with, I'll take around ninety-two fifty if I stick for an hour, do a couple hundred hits or so. Passes the time."

Tommy grunted. Lester's summary sounded too superficial. *Nobody in Lester's league plays to lose just to kill time. There's a reason Adrienne got the call from the casino people to quietly get Finn out of town. Gently, Tommy, gently.* "Not like the old nickel machines at Slow Marty's back home, I guess."

"What can I say, it's business, right?" Lester answered. Confidence in his words lifted and the sweat on his forehead eased. "Your shyster bar guy in the swamp probably had a hold of over ten, maybe fifteen, and the suckers would stand there in a line figurin' the jack's comin' on their first spin. These guys, they're more legit, entertainment for mom and pop and the honeymooners. You know you're gonna lose a bit, but not too much, and that's about all. More honest game," he continued. "In the old days, the rummies would try slugs. You had to be a real artist to use a monkey paw, but even then you'd lift a coupla hundred. These are all electronic, no mechanics, just a chip doing RNG."

"RNG?"

"Random number generator. Only it's not really random and that's how the house gets the hold." Lester tapped the button a couple of times but won nothing on a five reeler with way too many icons to count.

"Maybe the computer whizzes might tamper with that RNG thing?"

Finn spoke with even more authority. "Learning how to count cards would be more profitable, unless..." His voice dissipated into silence.

"Unless what?"

Lester focused on the screen. "Unless nothin'. Look, Tommy, I don't know nothin' about nothin' and maybe that's the way we oughta leave it, okay?"

Find an soft spot. Push some buttons. "Lot of collateral damage came out of that business in Germany, Lester. Some people might think about retribution and stuff. Not that I'm saying I would, but..."

The deliberate silence was too much for Lester. Again he paused in his game. "But what, Tommy?"

"My ol' paw-paw used to say, bones don't float. Unless..."

"Jeez, Tommy, you could get a guy killed."

"Absolutely, Lester."

"You'd take it out on me?"

"Dieter's dead. So are a bunch of other people. Somebody's got to pay the tab."

Lester squirmed, then brightened. "Maybe Mather could pay?"

He doesn't know? Interesting. "Mather's already paid his share. He's dead."

Lester's eyes darted left and right. "No shit? Oh, yeah, that's right, I heard something about that. You did him? That's good, Tommy. You was always the best." His voice sank into submission and he muttered to the machine. "No wonder they're still looking for you." He tapped the button and came up a loser.

"Who, Lester?"

"Aw, Tommy..."

Tommy took a turn at the slot machine's button, and won a few dollars. "You're doing good, Lester. You're racking up some points, improving the spread. Keep going. Maybe you'll get off the hook."

Lester rubbed his jaw and again look around for eavesdroppers. He whispered in confidentiality. "Guy by the name of Lomax. With a crew. Lot of rookies, but still a crew. I hear it's gonna get pretty messy. They got a bunch of them Cuban assholes running point, but the main pack is CIA. Word is they're looking to take out some Russian that went off the reservation, a guy whose clipped the big dogs a couple of times, you know, pain in the ass."

"So where do I fit in?"

"No idea. Tommy, it's true. I got no idea. But they been asking around. If I was you, I'd get the hell off the island. And soon."

"Okay, so what's the bait?"

Lester explained while he hit the machine for another twenty dollars on a lucky spin. "Some whacked-out colonel or something from Cuba, a drug guy. Supposed to be some kinda big money transfer. Only it's a hit." He turned to face Tommy and his eyes were hopeful for a reprieve.

"Let's get back to putting the fix on a machine. Earlier, you finished a sentence with 'unless'."

"Jeez, Tommy, you gotta press, don'tcha? You just can't leave it."

Thoughtful expression. Stand silent for enough moments to crank up Lester's anxiety one more time. "Look, Lester, I'm standing here trying to think of a single reason to leave it, but doggone it, I just can't come up with anything."

"Yeah?"

"Yeah, so you're going to have to explain that 'unless' or we can slide on over to the security office and discuss, well, stuff."

"You'd do that?"

"I never bluff, Lester. Just couldn't get the hang of controlling tells."

"For crissakes, why, Tommy? I mean, a guy's gotta make a living."

"Let's just say I'm doing you a favor."

"Yeah?"

"Yeah, Lester. There's some people on the island that would rather see ol' Lester kind of move on. Catch a flight to anywhere. No fuss, no trouble."

"Casino people?"

"Yep. I'm sort of doing them a favor."

Lester shook his head. "Looks like everybody's doing everyone a favor. Only, I'm the guy gettin' screwed."

"Like they say, Lester, it rolls – "

"Yeah, yeah, down hill." Lester sighed and again scanned the perimeter for anyone out of place. "Jeez, Tommy, I'm not here to scam the joint. I'm here on a job." He paused. "Look, Tommy – "

"I know, I know. You don't want to die."

"Well, yeah."

"So you tell me what it is, and I'll do you a favor."

"Yeah?"

"For true."

Lester rubbed his chin again, then pulled a black object, about the size of a jeweler's case for a ring, from his pocket. He flipped a lid open to expose a tiny button. "I'm doing a little offshore research. Stuff the sleazy stateside casinos don't need to know ,if you catch my meaning."

"You're doing good Lester. So what does it do?"

"Jackpots. Any machine. Just point and click, like one of those TV remotes. Some kinda transmitter or something. Makes the machine pay the jackpot. Whatever it might be. For whatever player."

"Yeah? Only it's the kind of thing you can use only once in a year, otherwise the casinos get wise. But interesting. Who's work is that? I don't think it's yours."

Lester's voice fluffed admiration, like a spinnaker filling with aft air. "Nyx, man, the best hacker of all time."

"Nyx? This hacker guy got an actual name?"

Finn cocked an eyebrow as if puzzled, but then relaxed and said, "Gal, Tommy, gal. You remember Bug?"

Bug. Probably still best wiretapper, ever.

"Had a daughter, twenty something now. Lucy Tramani-an."

"That's not Bug's last name."

Lester chuckled and hit the machine a few more times, but lost all three. "Heh, they don't exactly see eye to eye, Tommy. She really pissed off Bug when she took her mother's maiden name."

"Okay, got it. So show me how it works."

"Here? Now?"

"Yeah, show me." Tommy waved toward Lester's machine. "Do a jackpot."

"Not on the machine I'm using. I don't want to get busted." He looked around. "There. See that schmuck way over there? He's working a five-dollar box, end of the aisle. Everybody thinks they're better machines because they get more play and pay more often. Crock of shit. Anyway, the guy's probably desperate to cut his losses. Seems like a nice fella."

Lester's hand wrapped around the strange black object. The slots player slumped back in his stool and his shoulders drooped. He rubbed his eyes, stared at the machine, and reached for his player card. Lester mumbled a curse.

C'mon, buddy. Go for one last shot.

The player flexed his hands to loosen weary fingers. Maybe mid-fifties, worn down by addiction, maybe a bit angry with himself for a wasted morning and perhaps certain he would catch the devil from a spouse settled in a sad chaise lounge by the pool. Twice he raised his hand, twice he retreated.

Change of mind. Maybe the guy'll quit, find some strength, walk away. But maybe if he got one really good moment of luck, he could make a clean break and quit the gambling for good. Or maybe not. The player raised his arm slightly, hesitated once more. Then touched the button.

Lester Finn's hand tightened around the mysterious black box.

The reels flashed an endless range of combinations, then froze. The machine erupted with pulsing lights and electronic shrieks and the word "Jackpot!" blinked in a million colors on the screen. The player looked stunned. Casino chaos exploded. Every head on the floor turned. Other players drifted near to grab a look. Three attendants and the slots boss swarmed to verify the happy moment.

Lester and Tommy together turned to slip away.

Lester said with pride, "Half a million, the guy won."

"You did the right thing, Lester." *Maybe, maybe not. No matter. Better find Yenchenko, tip him off, before he gets killed.*

CHAPTER EIGHTEEN

The first fat raindrops dissolved the last of Tommy's cover as a tourist. Even the most dedicated Bay Street shoppers fled the squall line, mostly toward the cruise ships lounging at Prince George's Wharf. Sergei and the CIA people, apparently all gone to ground. Dead drops empty. Contact points vacant. A gloomy blend of exhaustion and melancholy from too many miles on pavement, sunshine-seared eyes, dust, and thousands of unrecognizable faces. Sandy's forecast was dead on and it was going to be a long, wet, unhappy night.

Each crack of lightning caused him to flinch and the blackened skies stoked unease. Old wounds, never healed. *Take a break. Get it together.* A decent margarita. A platter of conch fritters. And a moment of shelter at Señor Frog's. There were two possibilities. Maybe Yenchenko picked up the same intel and was holed up somewhere nearby, wondering the same stuff. Or Serge didn't know, and was about to walk into a trap.

Tommy dipped a chunk of conch into a fiery sauce and speculated what Sergei would do if he had learned of a trap but could not contact Tommy. Ian's warning. *That bastard can't be trusted.* Dark thoughts, billowing up like storm clouds. *Maybe ol' Serge'd cut and run, leave me to take his place. Maybe he set the whole thing up for Myra and the C-213 group, to finally settle the score.* The margarita was almost gone. He could have another, make the best of a refuge from the sheets of rain. On the other side of the coin. Sergei always displayed loyalty to his team, even if it meant shame on the field. *Yeah. Yenchenko would show up early, warn me off, and we'd sort things out later.*

Tommy put the empty glass on the table. The words of Myra Fielding, from way back at Doc's shack. *You're a pain in the ass, but you're loyal.* It was time. The rain on the roof was like someone dumped a ton of ball bearings, then another. Sergei and his great ideas. If it just wasn't for all the lightning...

A big, nasty crack made everyone jump and look up. More flashes, flickering through heaps of clouds.

So turn up your collar and take your lumps. It's a helluva night to die. Out into the storm, out into the bush. At Meadow Street, to zig-zag across to Blue Hill Road, any effort to hurry was lost. Sheets of rain lingered only for a moment in his clothes before forging paths of icy chill. Sandy. Dry, warm and cozy in the cabin of *Freckles II*. Smug in being right about the weather. A tumbler of Mount Gay rum in hand. Thinking about guys wandering around in the storm looking to get killed. Her life uncomplicated, receptive to unexpected possibilities.

The Alden yawl. Maybe down toward Barbados in January, where the tropics were bright and sunny and hot as hell. Rob the drug guys, buy the boat. Incentive. *There are times when a squall like this is a welcome relief, like that little storm just off the Dominican Republic, taking the edge off the heat and washing off all the salt at the same time.*

Along the long curve of Wulff Road, cold and miserable and hoping the storm would pass before the supermarket rendezvous. Maybe Sergei'd have a few snorts of hundred proof vodka. Just open a vein, plug in an I-V. Village Road. The supermarket, already closed for the day, looming in the eerie darkness that chases a storm. It'd be nice to wring out clothes. Instead, the Beretta, from the waistband of his trousers, in his hand, chambering a round.

Yenchenko was nowhere to be seen. His simple instructions. *You take small roadway to rear of building. There you find area where trucks deliver goods to store. This is where we meet.*

Icy fabric, plastered to his skin. A lighter step passing the darkened storefront. The service drive, marked by a low concrete retaining wall. Along the building, close, cautious sideways steps. Both hands clutching the Beretta to his chest.

Where's Yenchenko? I'd sure hate to be shot by my own partner.

The corner of the building. Voices. The grip on the pistol tightened. *Cubans. Spanish, with a Cuban accent.*

Count voices. *Three. Four. Okay, four. No, five. Easy, easy. You've done this before, just keep the breathing steady.*

A sixth voice. Yenchenko, who could speak better Spanish than English, but still did it with a clipped accent. *"Chingate tu madre, carbon!"*

A Cuban replied in a soft and calm voice. "Again."

A terrific smack on skin. Yenchenko grunted.

The soft voice had a cold edge. "Why do you come to this place?"

"I tell you. I steal fruit. I am thief."

"Don't insult my intelligence. Again."

Another sharp smack. Louder. *That's gotta hurt.* Yenchenko's growl. *Yeah, working through the pain. It hurt. A lot.*

The soft voice again. "You want fruit? I'll give you some fruit. You see this? You know what this is?"

Sergei's voice was a slurred mumble. "Mango."

"Si, si. If you don't tell me the truth, I take my little friend here, and I shove him right down your fucking throat, eh? You will gag and choke and want to puke so very badly. You want to die eating a mango, *muchacho?"*

Time for a better look, a prone position on the wet pavement. Shimmy a bit left, forward. Dim light from a single loading dock security bulb behind a flock of shadows. Yenchenko's enormous body was tightly secured to a tiny chair in an elbow of the building. One Cuban used a fistful of Sergei's hair to pull his head back. Blood oozed from a dozen wounds. Hard to guess how severe the damage was. Two more

Cubans, dressed in black combat fatigues and gloves to protect their knuckles, stood on either side of Sergei, while two more flanked the guy in charge. The backs of the hitter and the soft-spoken man were be easy targets. A seventh man stood watch, a few paces away. Tricky range of fire, ringed with a saggy chain link fence, with thick brush on the outside and an assortment of trash inside. No way to improve his cover

The interrogation continued. "You are pathetic. Perhaps you think you are smart, attacking my boats, killing my people, taking my money. You know something, *muchacho?* I have many boats. I have many people. And money? It is just paper."

The posture, the tone. *Medina. Major Carlos Medina, the big guy himself.*

"But I tell you something, *asqueroso*, you don't fuck with my pride. So. You have two choices. You can talk and tell me about the American and I promise a quick death, or you can be a *pajero* and die very slowly. You are very wet, eh? I have a car battery and you have very tiny balls."

Yenchenko mustered a snarl. *"Vali otsuyda!"*

Russian curse. Time's up. Sergei's exhausted. Target Medina. A little to the right, arms extended, bracing elbows on the pavement. The barrel of the Beretta lined up on Medina's torso, a spot just under his right arm where the lungs should be. Finger tightening on the trigger. Medina turned slightly. Adjust aim.

From somewhere between his ears came the call of the Obi-man.

Dammit, not now.

From somewhere in his memory came the words of Moses Clay.

Sorry, Mo, no redemption today.

Medina turned again and began to push Yenchenko's head back. The mango was in his right hand.

Okay, go for the center of his back. Now.

From somewhere above, a white flash, a muffled crack, the clatter of a cartridge being ejected. Medina's head vanished in a burst of red spray and his body collapsed onto the pavement. The other men turned as one to look up and reached for weapons.

The guy on the left. Tommy pulled the trigger and the Beretta barked. As the target spun and fell, he went for the second hitter and got off shot number two.

Yenchenko came alive and rolled away. He crushed the chair under his weight, but before he could stand, the Cuban who held his hand started to raise his arms and then fell straight back when another round from above crashed into his forehead. Then another.

The seventh man began to retreat. Tommy fired again. The last targets went down in a flurry of shots and were still. Tommy rushed forward. Bodies sprawled around like discarded rag dolls. The metallic scent of blood, pushing out with the rank stench of the pavement and whatever the rain had stirred.

Yenchenko struggled helplessly with rope that bound his body. "Koshka! Hello! You are alive still! Sergei is most pleased to see this." He paused and glared at the rope and sighed while Tommy unravelled it. "You are early. You have no chance for a military career, Koshka. You lack discipline."

"Nice to see you, too."

"So. You are – how you say? *Poryvistyi.* Ah, of course: impetuous. I was naturally ready to break loose of shabby western rope and kill all with bare hand. You have spoiled it for me, *da*?"

Never a shortage of audacity with Sergei. The roof. "Sorry, Serge. But someone from up there fired first." Along the top edge of the building, concrete block rose perhaps two feet above the flat roof and would have provided excellent cover.

Ian Wells stepped from the shadows. A sleek sniper's rifle

was slung butt end up across his right shoulder, and he carried a thin wooden case in his left. The varnish and brass corner guards glowed in the faint light from the bare bulb over the loading dock. "That would be me," Wells announced. "Rather fine shooting, Kane. Still using that old Beretta?"

"Yeah. Looks like we both helped Sergei stay alive."

"*Da, da.* Alive still," Yenchenko reached down to tear a shirt off one of the bodies and used it to wipe blood that spattered his face. "You have lucky shot, eh? What is weapon?"

"Heckler and Koch PSG1. The precision is exceptional," Wells cheerfully reported while he eagerly turned his attention to the carnage.

To nobody in particular, Tommy muttered, "Fifty rounds of match ammo inside an eighty-millimeter circle at 300 meters."

Yenchenko grunted. "Perhaps you take much time with aim. Perhaps you are old and your eyes feeble."

Not likely. "You look like hell, Sergei."

The Russian shrugged. "I have felt worse pain. It is of no consequence. I heal most quickly."

"Yeah, well, you probably want to thank Ian for having your back, even if you had the situation in hand.

Yenchenko's eyes looked high above Ian's shoulder and he sighed. "*Spasibo,*" he muttered.

"You can do better than that, pal."

Sergei shrugged away reluctance as if yielding a toy to a playmate that he no longer desired. With forced enthusiasm, he said, "*Bol'shoe spasibo!*"

Ian scowled. "Filthy bugger." Then an acid smile. "Very well, then. you're welcome. Right. Let's have a look at the bodies." He approached the first and used his toe to prod the corpse. "This looks like your kill, Thomas. Bit off the mark, but adequate, considering the circumstances."

The body was sprawled on its back, two bullet holes on the chest, legs tangled and twisted. A pool of blood from the underside oozed onto the dark pavement. A face he did not recognize from earlier in the day. Young, twenties maybe. A kid with a family and a girlfriend and no more tomorrows. A soldier, a casualty. Collateral damage. Dead. No adrenalin rush this time. No sense of victory, achievement, a mission completed and a report to file. Just tired. Very tired.

Wells used a thin flashlight to examine the remains of Carlos Medina, whose upper right quarter of his skull was gone. In a cheery voice, Ian admired his handiwork and concluded, "Not your everyday drug pusher. Someone's got a big gap in the supply line, I'd say."

This is nuts. Wells is treating it like a dessert buffet and Yenchenko, just like Sandy said, is full of it.

While Wells continued his survey, Tommy spoke to Sergei. "You weren't kidding when you said the Cubans were tailing you. Care to fill in some of the blanks?"

Yenchenko wiped the remaining blood from his hands with the torn shirt and tossed it aside. "We make meeting to do some small business. It is of no importance."

"It is now. Dammit, Serge, this was supposed to be a simple robbery, not a slaughter."

From behind them, Wells interrupted. "Got a bloody Yank over here."

Yenchenko seemed unrepentant. "I am loyal comrade, Koshka. I am captured, but do not speak name of good friend. The cake, *tovarich*, remains as dough, eh? All goes badly. Such things happen."

Ian's barked in a more insistent tone. "Got the bloody CIA over here." He held a credentials wallet up in the air while he searched for a wire. "Anyone know a bloke named McGrath?"

"No," Tommy and Yenchenko said in unison.

Wells sighed. "I thought you said the local station chief was a friend, Thomas. This is not going to sit well with the local embassy people. You didn't warn her?"

"She is, and no, I didn't."

Movement caught Yenchenko's attention. He stepped over a corpse to approach the body of the third Cuban, a stocky man of perhaps thirty-five and Tommy's second target. Massive bleeding from an abdominal wound, probably close to death. Without hesitation, Yenchenko reached down and pulled a sidearm from the man's holster. Sergei stood over the sprawled body and took an executioner's aim. He curled his lip, hissed "*svoloch*" and shot the Cuban in the head.

Wells continued to sift through the corpses and discovered a small black travel bag. He tested the weight of it in his hand. "Ah, this feels like money," he announced. The Major unzipped the bag and nodded. "Indeed. Looks like two-fifty all right."

Two-fifty?

The scent of the carnage again. Sharper, heavier than before. Ian's words became hollow and distant and the building began to blur and the naked light bulb over the loading dock began to sway. Same scent as Rashid's front yard and burning metal at Doc's. Not a good sign. *Steady. Take a – No. This is nuts. This is just totally nuts.*

From the edge of the kill zone, a weak groan. All three men turned. The seventh man, wounded, maybe briefly unconscious, stirred in the faint light from the security lamp.

Yenchenko grunted and marched forward, a rhino on a rampage. The wounded man looked up. Sergei in a shooter's stance. The Cuban's legs fought for traction to push away. In his eyes, panic, fear, resignation. Sergei paused, probably to savor revenge.

"Sergei, wait."

Yenchenko took aim and growled in Russian, "Fuck off, Tommy."

The Beretta in Tommy's hand rose and was trained Sergei's massive torso. His voice lowered into calm, assured command. "Hold it. Or I'll shoot you where you stand."

CHAPTER NINETEEN

The faint splash of a drop of water into a puddle. Soft thunder, fleeing northward. The rustle of shadowed leaves stirred by a puff of salt air.

Ian Wells, frozen in a half-bent position, his eyes fixed on Tommy's pistol, his expression partway between surprise and uncertainty. "Steady, mate. Steady."

Sergei Yenchenko, half turned to face Tommy. He ignored the pistol and stared instead into Tommy's eyes. On his face, neither anger or fear or frustration. Puzzlement. Evaluation. Calculation. A quiet, even voice. "*Da*, it is so, my friend. You make expression of man prepared to take life of another. You make posture that is threat. Not so good, Koshka."

"Indeed, Thomas, it's bloody – "

"Stand down, Serge."

Yenchenko continued to lock eyes, unflinching, showing precisely why he was so dangerous.

"Koshka, with you it is always too much caution. This bastard is in small moment dead and we all find nice warm bar to drink much and make long conversation to find answer to puzzle, eh?"

"I mean it. Step aside."

Sergei shrugged and lowered his weapon. He moved a few paces away and gestured for Tommy to have the honor of execution. Wells exhaled relief and zipped the bag of cash.

Tommy squatted next to the wounded man. Thin, middle aged, perhaps forty or forty-five years old, with skin weathered by a hard life. Eyes wide with anxiety and misty with fear. His mouth moved but seemed unable to form words. The words of Doc's neighbor, Miguel echoed in memory. *"Please señor, I do not wish to die."*

After a gentle examination of the shoulder wound he had inflicted, Tommy spoke to the man in Spanish. "It's serious, but you'll live. Medina and the others are dead. My friend believes you should also die. What's your name?" Tommy hunted for a weapon of any kind, but found none.

The man winced at Tommy's touch and nodded acknowledgement. A tear escaped from his closed eyelids and wandered across his high cheekbones. He whispered, "Cesar Hernandez. I am the pilot of the aircraft of Colonel Medina. I am unarmed. Please – "

Hernandez made no effort to resist. Live or die. Admirable courage.

To Yenchenko, deliberately in Spanish, he said, "Let's let this one go. To kill him means nothing to us."

Sergei grunted. "There is old Russian proverb: the sandpiper is small, but bird just the same, *da?*"

"I concur, Thomas. It's poor form to leave unfinished business on the field."

Tommy again spoke to the pilot in Spanish. " Cesar, now both of them want you shot. Perhaps you can help me persuade my friends not to kill you, okay?"

He nodded, but kept his eyes on the gun hand of Sergei Yenchenko.

"So. Why did Medina come after the Russian?"

In a raspy voice, Cesar explained about the piracy and Medina's pride. "But also the men from the CIA are afraid of a *yanqui*, the one who is called *El Gato*. They made a deal with Major Medina to find this American and kill him."

Tommy nodded encouragement for the pilot to continue. "How many men?"

Cesar's eyes surveyed Tommy's face. "There were two, but

maybe more. Perhaps, *señor*, you are this *yanqui*, the one they call *El Gato*, the cat. The black cat."

Yenchenko sighed and muttered to no one in particular, "All cats are black at night."

Cesar said, "Please, *señor*. I do not wish to die. I wish to defect."

There's a twist. "Defect?"

"*Si, señor*. I have no family. They are all dead. I have only two weeks ago been assigned to Major Medina by the army. The usual pilot, he is injured. I knew nothing of his business in drugs."

"So that's how you're connected with these guys?"

"*Si*. Not many in Cuba can fly such an aircraft as the Major has. I am trying to escape Cuba. I seek only asylum. I have nothing to offer but my word, *señor*."

Wells groaned disbelief. "Look, Kane, he's a Cuban. When was the last time you ever heard a Cuban tell the truth?"

Yenchenko nodded and aimed his weapon directly Cesar's head. The pilot did not flinch. Instead, the look of resignation, a man preparing himself to die.

"Dammit, Sergei, wait! Look, Cesar, you need to help me now *Ahora mismo*."

Cesar bit his lower lip and seemed to struggle with the hot pain of the gunshot wound. "I heard them say they will not allow *El Gato* to leave the island alive. They have many people watching."

Wells shook his head. "So much for a commercial flight out of Nassau."

Cesar's eyes widened into hope. "Colonel Medina has – had – a private jet at the airport. A Gulfstream, a four-fifty."

"A Gulfstream?" Tommy asked. "That takes a crew of two."

"The copilot is – was – an Army officer. He is just over there." Cesar gestured toward one of the bodies.

Wells rolled his eyes. "This is dragging on too long,

Thomas. Let's get on with it. I'll shoot the bloke myself."

Kane looked down at Cesar. "Kind of a half-baked plan to escape."

"*Si, señor*," Hernandez said. "I had hoped to run away at the airport, but they brought me here with them. But if you wish to kill me, then I know I will die a free man."

It made sense. *If your pilot was shaky and you were on Western soil, you'd keep him close.* The words of Moses Clay whispered in his mind: *You need redemption.* He spoke to Cesar in soft Spanish. "There is a clinic nearby that is open all night long. I cannot take you there. But if you make haste, you'll be able to get help and maybe they'll grant you asylum."

Yenchenko shot a glance toward Wells, who pursed his lips and shook his head. "Not a chance, Thomas. They'll ship the fellow back to Cuba after a few happy weeks in Her Majesty's Prison. We'd be doing him a favor to put him down right here."

"No. Not this time. Give me your hand, Cesar. Let's get you on your feet. Good. Take this, hold it on the wound."

Yenchenko muttered a sigh and a Russian obscenity while he stuffed the pistol under his belt and assisted Tommy support of the wounded Cuban.

Wells shook his head. "An old ladies aid society, that's what it is. Look lads, we can't waltz this chap into the emergency service at Princess Margaret's or we'll all have a bit of a go with the local constables."

"Got any suggestions, Ian?"

"I know a veterinarian nearby. An old friend. Discreet."

"A vet?"

"Well, look, Thomas, he's only a Cuban."

Yenchenko exhaled a sound of annoyance. "He is soldier, like us."

Ian scowled as the skies opened a second time and sheets of rain poured over them. "He's a *disaster*, Sergei. Like us." The hiss of rain pelting leaves and pavement jumped several notches. Water splashing on Yenchenko's head caused oozed blood to streak into pale pink rivers meandering across his face. "Bloody perfect. Just bloody perfect. Five quid on this man to haunt you, Thomas. You lads can rescue puppies if you'd like, but I'm off to find a dry pub and a glass of Macallan."

Yenchenko began to take a step but paused when Tommy's stood still.

"We go together, Ian." Tommy raised his free arm and the Beretta in his hand came with it. The eyes of Ian Wells and Sergei Yenchenko followed Tommy's free arm, rising with the Beretta in his hand. From a short distance away, thunder rumbled in the dark sky. *Amazing. No urge to flinch.*

Yenchenko stared at Wells and cocked an eyebrow.

Wells shook his head in dismay. "Very well. We can drop off the Cuban and *then* I know a pub, decent food, drink. Not too far. Come, come, Thomas. I'm being reasonable. Especially considering how much money there is."

Yenchenko turned to study Tommy across the semi-conscious body between them. "What has changed, Koshka? You are not same man, I think, as person in botanic garden."

"Same old me."

The rain intensified and Wells pleaded, "I daresay, Thomas."

Yenchenko shrugged as they began to ferry the Cuban pilot to sanctuary. "I think not, Koshka. You were good adversary in old days, almost as good as Yenchenko, eh? But now? Now I think you are dangerous man."

Chapter Twenty

The Pig's Eye Pub was the sort of bar guys in the trade prefer. Dark and smoky. Too noisy to be bugged. Too hazy and crowded for surveillance. Transient clientele, these the crews from yachts of substance. The masters favored black tie, closed casino rooms and private dining. The crew needed a den to unwind, tell tales, drink with abandon.

As Ian promised, it was a short walk from the veterinary clinic where a buddy would patch up a gunshot wound and not trouble the cops with it. On the road from the supermarket gunfight, passers-by probably thought Tommy and Sergei were helping a totally snockered pal to the dock. No one paid attention. Now the were just a trio of wet rats in soaked clothes and tattered adrenalin.

Under a post-and-beam canopy that held fast against many a rampage of weather, the Pig's Eye was all too familiar, welcoming working men and wanton women to a proper pub cluttered with thick glasses of ale and stout, stained paper coasters, smoldering ashtrays and crumbs of currency. Like Duffy's, but a bit more upscale. And a lot more upscale than village cantinas between San Pedro and the American border. Like Duffy's, but with entertainment. On a tiny triangular stage, barely 18 inches above the stone floor, two sturdy Celtic fiddlers and a demure guitar player tossed forth a stream of traditional Irish tunes about green valleys and distant shores for perhaps thirty or so patrons who marched on a path toward inebriation, melancholy and empty wallets.

Yeah, perfect. Barely noticed amid taunts and laughter and tales from liars' tongues. The exception –   a grey-whiskered, angular guy who watched close as they trooped past his post near the middle of the bar. Khaki shorts and shirt hung wrinkled and loose on a wiry frame, and a cap with an extra long fisherman's bill perched on the back of his head. The old man returned his attention to a hefty barmaid with red hair curled into reckless abandon. The guy must have had a certain charm. She laughed, then giggled, then laughed again at the old man's words.

Wells led the way to an empty, rough wood booth blackened with age and nicotine. *Like any boys who'd been out in the rain for maybe a month, setting there with water dripping off, trying to be casual about it.*

The old man rose from his stool, strode toward them, and presented himself. He pulled his shoulders back in confidence, stuffed his fists into his waist and thrust his jaw forward, his eyes clear and his expression bemused. His voice was confident, firm and slightly slurred. "Looks like you fellows have run into a bit of weather." After he looked at Yenchenko's face he added, "and maybe a bit worse."

Uneasy glances circled the booth. Tommy said, "Might be."

"Well, sir, I'd very much like to buy you gents a round," the old said. He motioned for the barmaid, and when she began to move toward them called out, "And bring the boys a few dry towels, too."

The barmaid nodded and grabbed a handful of white from under the bar.

"Yessir," the old man, "that was a fair little squall that came through tonight, a fair little squall. I believe it's passed now, though. Moving on out to sea. Northeast, I suspect." The barmaid arrived and the old man helped distribute towels to the soaked trio, then said, "Now, whatever these gents are drinking tonight, Maureen, it's on me. Just put it on my tab, all right?"

Maureen giggled again. "Whatever you say, Walter."

"Ah, that's a good girl. It's a splendid pub, gentlemen. I come by now and then for the companionship. And the music, of course." He cocked his head toward the stage and cupped a hand around his ear. "They're playing the 'Cuffolda Reel' and 'Stone in the Field,' you know. Smartly done and proper." He passed at least two twenties to Maureen and asked her to pay the band if they'd play 'Robbie Hannan's Jigs.'

"Absolutely, honey."

An unabashed grin spread from ear to ear. "Ah, that's grand. Just grand."

Sergei and Tommy swapped uncertain glances to ask each other who the old man might be and both replied with faint shrugs. Wells ignored them while he and Yenchenko mopped excess water from their chests and shoulders and traded towels for drink orders. Wells fancied Macallan, while Yenchenko decided on two pints of Guinness for himself. Tommy used his towel to pat down his shoulders and arms and then voted for Macallan, neat, with an ice cube on the side.

"So, fellas, mind if I join you?" Walter immediately answered his own question and began to settle into the empty space next to Tommy and opposite Yenchenko. "'Course you don't mind. Nobody minds the fellow who buys the booze, do they?"

Tommy said, "Sorry. I didn't catch your name."

Walter chuckled. "That's probably because I didn't give it. Poor manners. An old man's failing." He extended his right hand. "Campos, son, Walter Campos. And you'd be Mister Thomas Kane, o'course, and you're Mister Yenchenko, Sergei, I believe. And you, sir, are Mister Ian Wells, but known in the trade as the Major."

Yenchenko's eyes narrowed. Wells studied his folded hands on the table.

I wonder which one will kill the old guy first. Probably Sergei.

His hands are under the table and he's probably already aimed. "You're very well informed. I hope you're just as cautious."

Campos beamed in false modesty. "I am. And thank you, Mister Kane."

"Tommy."

"Very well. Tommy it is. Yes sir, it's a fact. I like to be well informed. Man in my position needs that more than just about anything. Money, power, prestige, all things most men want: it's about being well informed. Wouldn't you agree Mister, uh, Tommy?"

Maureen returned with a round of drinks for the band of three and bandages seasoned with admonition for Yenchenko. "Lads your age should call the bloody police rather than engage in street fights. Tsk. What a bleedin' mess you are."

Sergei leered at her body and she leaned way forward to allow him a better view before she retreated to the bar with an extra sway in her hips.

While Tommy suspended the ice cube over the glass until a single drop splashed into it, he said. "Being well informed can sometimes get a man killed."

Campos beamed. "Exactly so, Kane, exactly! Now take for example that little shootout you boys had with those Cubans tonight. They were by any man's mark pretty well informed. But here you are, alive and well, except perhaps for Mister Yenchenko, none the worse for wear, and if they haven't found the bodies already, the police soon will, and there'll be lots of questions that they won't have answers for, and that's because they're not as well informed as you boys, or even myself, you see."

Yenchenko shifted his weight and inhaled his second drink and spoke in Russian. "*Tovarich* Kane, he is old man but young problem. I take this *vanka* behind building and kill him quickly, then we find a good meal, eh?"

Wells continued to study his hands. No reaction.

Odd. Very odd. And then there was the bag with the money.

"No," he replied in Russian, "Let's see how this plays out."

Wells took a sip from his glass and stared at the beverage.

Tommy spoke in English. "I'd like to hear how well informed the Major is."

Ian's jaw tensed, but he remained silent.

Campos watched the byplay with obvious amusement. "Allow me to fill in the blanks, Mister Kane."

"Tommy."

"'Course. Tommy. I'm afraid I'm responsible for your difficulties tonight, you see. There never was to be an exchange of cash, clean for dirty. I wanted to bring the three of you together and, well, test your mettle."

Yenchenko cocked an eyebrow. "So all is set up, like trap?"

"Afraid so, Mister Yenchenko. Afraid so. Regrettable, but necessary."

"The cable, the order for CIA?"

"Counterfeit. Astonishing, the work they can do these days. Astonishing."

"The whore in El Socorro?"

Campos looked satisfied. "Bought and paid for. Not too expensive, mind you. Affordable."

Yenchenko nodded. "Old fool, you should prepare for death. Because you are old man, I make you die most quickly. But you die in next few moments."

Yeah, because six guys got killed and one shot wounded and Yenchenko took a whipping. For nothing. Because we were had. Tommy said, "Serge doesn't like being deceived. He probably won't give killing you a second thought. I don't like being sucked into this sort of thing either, so that makes two guys who'll kill you. And Ian? He used to do that sort of thing for a living, maybe still does."

Campos raised his hands in mock submission. "No need for undue excitement, boys, I'm not interested in causing a problem here. And you did, in fact, make a huge improvement in narcotics trafficking. But I have a, well, interesting proposition I'd like to share over another round of drinks."

Yenchenko hissed, "I kill this *pizd'uk* in next moment, Koshka. Unless you let another escape with soft attitude."

Sergei's eyes were ice cold. Yenchenko was more than capable killing Campos or anyone else that got between him and the door. Wells had to be the point man for Campos, and this was no chance encounter. And Campos was probably the kind of guy a person didn't gun down without serious consequences.

Campos sighed annoyance. "Look, Kane, you're the only reasonable fellow at the table. You play golf, don't you? Surely you do. Lyford Cay, back nine, Thursday afternoon. We can discuss things a bit more, shall we say, reasonably."

"Golf? It's not my – "

"Please don't patronize me with ignorance, Mister Kane. I know all about you. As I said, I'm a man who likes to be well informed. And Mister Yenchenko, you'd do well to stick with guerrilla activity in Central America. You're rather good at it, but you're an inept diplomat and a rather poor negotiator."

In the eyes of Yenchenko and even Wells, the expression a predator wears when cornered and prepared to throw caution to the wind. And attack. The music, the bar banter, the sound of glassware all muted, as if it submerged into the water on a coral reef, in that place where little fish like to hide, unaware that in an instant, they will be eaten alive. *Walter Campos is about to die. And these guys aren't going to wait around for the cops to show up with handcuffs and be politely led away. This could become a real mess, real quick.*

The muscles in Sergei's arm tightened. Ian seemed oddly relaxed. *Maybe that's why Wells is so dangerous.*

Tim to defuse the confrontation with a more jovial tone. "Well, I for one wouldn't mind a pleasant round of golf. And I'm thinking that Mister Campos here doesn't necessarily want to do business in a public place. And maybe understands that we might want to sort things out a bit among ourselves."

But he also wants to deal with me, and not the others. A trap? Maybe. But we're already blown.

Sergei's arm relaxed a bit. Wells took a drink.

"Ah!" Campos beamed. "I'm most gratified, Mister Kane. Most gratified. That you understand, o'course."

And probably gratified that he didn't get shot. Wonder if he knew how far he pushed it, how close he came. I bet he did.

Campos slid from the bench and stood. "Well, I'm off to bed. Got a seven o'clock tee time. I'm an old man, you see, need my rest. The balance of your drinking tonight is on my tab. Good night, gentlemen." With a broad and jolly grin just a half step away from easy laughter, he turned and marched toward the door. As he passed Maureen, gave brief instructions and gestured toward the three soggy spies. Then he patted a few shoulders and slipped away into the night.

Yenchenko's expression slid into embarrassment and he sighed. "Perhaps Sergei becomes too old, becomes town fool, like *vanka*, and make dream from intelligence that is shit from donkey, eh? I make too much drink after we meet, sleep poorly but for long time, and hear there is not exchange of money, but most clever trap. So I go early to supermarket to make warning of you, but Cubans make capture and rest you know."

He drank deep from his second pint of Guinness and motioned for Maureen. Vodka would be probably be the next beverage on the table. After a long moment of reflection, Yenchenko looked up, his expression melancholy. "I most seriously regret difficulty I make for you, *tovarich* Tommy Kane. I make depart in morning, and take nothing from share."

"Not at all. We were all in it together. " He turned to face Ian. "The one thing I'd like to know, is how Walter Campos managed to be in this particular bar *before* we arrived. And how you knew how much money was in the bag."

Wells continued to stare at his glass. "Hm. Yes. Well, mates, it appears I owe something of an explanation."

CHAPTER TWENTY ONE

A stubby glass turned round and round in Tommy's hand, swirling the last of his whisky. Ian's demeanor and the cold approach by Walter Campos was unsettling, rekindling a frustration fighting a losing battle with patience. *Okay, so we're really all second rate and we're basically just trying to make our way. But it's time for Wells to come clean. I want Sergei to react to it. I want the both of them to come back to reality.*

"Go ahead, Ian. Explain."

Sergei cocked an eyebrow and his expression dissipated into an icy glare. "*Da, da.* You explain. I am most nearly killed this night. Worse, I am made to look, how you say, *glupyi?*"

Tommy translated. "Silly, foolish. Goes for me, too."

When the barmaid arrived, Yenchenko ordered an entire bottle of vodka. Wells opted for a second scotch. She turned to Tommy. "Would you be wanting another single malt?"

"Yes."

"And a bit of ice?"

"On the side." She nodded, gathered empties, and departed.

Attention turned to Wells, who looked at Tommy with neither defiance nor indifference but rather the glum relief that follows the completion of an unpleasant task. "It was just a contract, Thomas. Nothing personal."

Yenchenko was less charitable. "You make explanation. Or you die. I do not care which."

Wells shrugged. "Campos made an approach in Tortola,

after you left. I was giving serious thought to not participating, Thomas, but when he explained matters to my niece, well, I thought it best to join the group, pick up a few quid on the side."

"So you sold us out?"

In an even tone, Wells justified his subterfuge. "My contract was to deliver you to this pub on this date. *Undamaged.* I don't know the reason why, but only that the contract is properly fulfilled."

"And so your arrangement with this Walter Campos is complete?"

"Of course," Wells replied. "And as something of a perk, we've got $250,000 to share, which I believe was the upfront payment the CIA gave Medina to kill you and Yenchenko. After all, you chaps *were* planning to steal all *their* money."

Yenchenko raised a finger. "You mean, of course, only *deposit* for assassination."

"Sorry, Sergei, *payment.* That's all you're worth to them. One twenty-five each."

Yenchenko sighed disappointment. "*Zhmot.* All world is becoming *zhmot.*"

"Who tipped the Cubans?"

"My guess, Thomas, would be Campos. But you lads were traipsing all over New Providence, so who knows for certain."

"Why Campos?"

"He's the sort of fellow who likes to pit all sides against each other and see who wins. I'd wager he did it as a test."

"What about the CIA, C-213?"

"From my perspective. It was most certainly their little show. I'm quite certain they're not done, either." Well paused and shifted to a thin smile. "I didn't know you played golf."

"Long time ago. Played some in college. And not all that great. Not great enough to have any sort of reputation."

Yenchenko scowled and poured vodka into his throat. "Most silly game. Hit tiny white ball all over big field for no purpose. But old man has made good research."

Wells rebuked him. "Excellent research. And it's a game for gentlemen, Sergei. A recreational excuse for deals and schemes among businessmen, politicians, people with class and breeding. Something you quite understandably fail to comprehend." He turned to Tommy. "Especially at Lyford Cay. I'm afraid you're up against it, Thomas."

"How so?"

"It's about as exclusive, private and gated as you can get. Not at all keen about casuals mucking about their course. Unless you're a member, you shan't even reach the clubhouse. It appears Campos is putting you to another test."

"Thinking that if I even show up, I've got what it takes for something."

"Indeed. Rather sophisticated work, for which you will be handsomely rewarded. He's a chap with a lot of money and even more pull. One of those gents whose name is never in the press but has substantial influence and power."

"Any thoughts about what he has in mind?"

"Afraid not. Sorry, old chum, about all this. However, he specifically wanted you and paid me handsomely for the privilege of an introduction. I don't think it's a trap. Not that sort of bloke, if you ask me."

Some introduction. I've got to jump a set of hurdles just to hear what the old guy has to say. There were alternatives. All three could slip away on *Freckles II*, before dawn, disappear again. There was no need to get involved in field work again. Sergei would just have to cut his losses, and Ian was paid well for the scam that suckered both of them. On the other hand, revenge would be nice. The C-213 business, relegated to just a bad memory, was back on the front burner. *What had Sandy said about doing something memorable?*

Halfway through a relaxing breath, the call of the Obiman returned. A new alternative began to form, fuzzy and vague at first, but on a straight line to clarity. The others were waiting for some sort of direction.

"We could make the CIA wish it hadn't messed with us."

Quiet words, like the smoke of a twenty-dollar cigar, hung above the table and lingered long enough for everyone to study its many whispers.

Ian rolled his empty glass in his hand. "This can't be personal, Thomas. Make it personal and we'll all be killed."

"I understand."

"I mean it, Thomas. We may be the stray cats of the community, but I'm keen on being a live cat than some sort of road kill."

Yenchenko's eyes narrowed. "This is interesting idea, but surely not practical. CIA people most certainly outnumber us, have many resource. But, hah! It is good you think well enough of comrades to make offer." He lifted his glass, offered a profane toast in Russian and then changed course. "You are loyal soldier, Tommy Kane. I have made you disappoint, but still you think well of old friend. I volunteer, personal or no."

Wells shifted his weight in his chair. "Right. Well, it *was* a bit cheeky to put you lads in harm's way. No hard feelings, Thomas?"

"None."

Wells seemed satisfied. "Nevertheless, Thomas, this remains a really delicate – " Ian paused when the others slumped in dismay. "– Well, actually, potentially plausible idea."

Tommy opened his arms. "What's that phrase? The mutt's nuts?"

Wells rolled his eyes. "I wouldn't venture quite *that* far into sarcasm, but if nothing else it would get them off our backs for a bit. But Thomas, the odds are nevertheless a bit of a challenge."

Leaning into the table, his plan to evolved. "I wasn't thinking about a frontal assault. More along the line of picking them off one at a time and ransoming captured assets."

Wells sighed. "You're out of your mind, Thomas. They'll simply send reinforcements. How long would you keep this nonsense going?"

"Until they send the big dog, and when we bag him, we'll make a deal."

Wells furrowed his brow. "Kidnapping is a dodgy endeavor, Thomas. Surely the CIA are going to know they've been nicked by three old poachers who fancy a bit of the crown's venison."

Yenchenko nodded. "Major is correct. You kill all, you walk away. You capture all, and they have made capture of you. It is nightmare of logistics to hide asset, feed it, make security."

Ian nodded. "I count only three of us and the first thing hostages organize is an escape plan. But good show in trying to rescue a blown op, Thomas. Energetic thinking, and certainly thoughtful to recruit us."

"It was just a thought." *There's truth lurking in the shadows here, and maybe it's time to face it.*

An uneasy silence, with each of the three guarding candor. Yenchenko had an unlimited supply of vodka. Only a drop of Tommy's Macallan remained. Wells finished his scotch.

"Need another round?"

"Indeed, Thomas. Another might be splendid."

Slowly, patiently. Try an end run. "You know what? We probably ought to just pack it up, get out of town, go home with our tails properly between our legs."

Wells began to protest.

"No, I mean it, Ian. The plain truth is that I'm just not all that great. Got into the agency, did some field work, blew a few ops, wasn't too good at playing the game. On a scale of one to ten, I'm maybe a two or three, but definitely not a big leaguer."

Yenchenko burped. "I make better score for you, Koshka. But if you wish truth, the FSB discard me for poor performance. Some operation, I get too many men killed."

"Plus there was the matter of your boss's wife."

Sergei chuckled. "*Da*, of course, but she is slut. Useful for sex only. Sergei is like *El Zorrero*, the fox who steals and shit on floor when he make depart, eh?"

The chuckle became infectious and sly grins formed all around.

"*Da, da*, it is so! There is expression in Russia. She play nice tune on leather flute, eh?"

Wells laughed harder. "Poor bitch must have bloody choked."

Yenchenko's reply was pious and lofty, casually said. "Of course. I am legend."

The laughter went full throttle and challenging to motion for Maureen to fetch another round, doubles this time. When it settled, Yenchenko muttered to Wells, "And it is you, of course, who cannot shoot Dieter Kreutzer."

Mirth tumbled into loud sighs. Wells looked into his empty glass. "It wasn't a misfire. I simply couldn't shoot the poor bastard. Too much history. Fell into a slump, went a bit daft, got ball-sacked."

Intriguing response. Time to ask again. "Who wanted him killed?"

"Nice try. As I said before, no idea. I'd like to think CIA, but I was never quite certain. So I quite simply lost my edge. Just went soft as an old man's dick. Until tonight anyway."

Trust. Candor. Now. "It happens. It's happened to me."

Yenchenko looked puzzled. "You have gun to misfire also? Most strange, for you have such small caliber dick."

Laughter exploded again. Maureen delivered heavier doses of scotch and a smile for Sergei, to which Tommy and Ian could not resist an opportunity to tease.

As hilarity began to fade, Yenchenko grunted and lowered his voice. "There is expression, *khui pinat'*. You know this?"

Tommy sipped scotch. "Yeah. Kick dicks all around."

"Perhaps alone we are not so good, but together can *khui pinat'*." His expression hardened.

Wells muttered to his whisky, rising to meet his lips. "You're still out of your bleeding mind."

Sergei drummed his fingertips on the table and cocked an eyebrow. "Perhaps. What you think, Koshka?"

Besides the absolute certainty that Wells was still hiding something? Let it go for now. Come up with something. Anything to get us started. His glass pushed aside and his forearms parked on the table, leaning in. "All you need is a speedy boat and any one of dozens of deserted cays less than a couple of hours away. Tranquilize them, sniper style, and lug them, drunken sailor style. Did either of you notice where they're headquartered on Bay Street?"

Sergei and Wells looked to each other.

Wells said, "Second floor, above a book shop. Too many antennas up there."

"Plus, operation center most vulnerable when teams trade shift. Early morning strike make target easy capture."

It was working.

Wells pressed his tongue against his cheek and rolled it across his bottom teeth. "Staff of no more than four or five, but soft and perhaps not even armed. A flash grenade, bit of tear gas and they'd fold in seconds."

There we go.

Sergei rubbed his jaw. "We require small truck to take equipment away. Then we have means to communicate with CIA. Small police truck. We make it appear to be raid, arrest of some minor hooligan."

It was hard not to grin.

Wells nodded at Sergei. "If the field people have no communications to direct them, they're blind mice, helpless."

"We pick them off, use police truck to take to very fast motor power boat."

"Right. Like one of those adventure outfits. I know a lad

who has a Pantera Thirty-six he hires out when the season is high. Knows the cays down in the Exumas, all three-hundred-and-some-odd. The bloke can be trusted. We could hire a warehouse near customs to stash hostages until we move them in small groups."

Tommy asked, "How do you know?"

"He's a cousin of mine, Thomas, and prefers to avoid going back to jail."

Yenchenko nursed from his vodka bottle. "What is crime?"

"Assault with a deadly weapon. His bare hands, actually. One of those karate or judo or what-not enthusiasts."

A good plan coming together. *Got to get away from conventional guns.* "Speaking of weapons, there's our veterinarian here on New Providence. For the right fee, you'll be well armed with tranquilizer rounds."

Wells said, "Fentanil. Large animal tranks can be a bit dodgy on humans. Wouldn't want them to die on us. Hm. Perhaps I can work on something of a modification. Lighter load, faster acting."

Yenchenko kept nodding. "It work well in terrorist matter many year ago. If not available, we perhaps can find supply from police."

"Anticholinergics?"

"But no pepper spray or taser. Too messy."

The turn of the conversation was pleasing and it was time to step back and let them collaborate. "I'll leave it to you guys to work out the details."

Ian's eyes narrowed into distrust and uncertainty. "And you, Thomas?"

"Something I've been meaning to do. And then I'll deal with Campos, see what he wants."

Yenchenko said, "Perhaps is again trap. As Major observe, this is most difficult test."

Wells patted the bag next to him. "Well, at least we have seed money."

Not exactly. "No. In fact, Ian, you can hand it over right now and kiss it goodbye."

"Kane, that's not how proper colleagues behave."

"I'll leave you with twenty-five thousand for expenses, but the rest goes with me. That's the price of messing with me and Sergei. You forfeit your share."

Yenchenko objected too.

"And you, Serge, with all your slick whorehouse intelligence, you have already given up your share."

Wells sulked. "This is very poor form, Thomas. Very poor form indeed."

Yenchenko cocked his head and glared at Tommy. After several seconds, his expression softened and his eyebrows rose. "*Nyet*," he said to Wells. "I realize *Tovarich* Kane has good plan. He is permitted to take money. You sit in good position on roof while Sergei Yenchenko take many blow from Cuban *pedik*. I take your share and I give to good friend Tommy Kane. You don't like? I break your neck with bare hand."

Wells bit his lower lip. "I'm not the sort who works on the cheap, Kane. Well, just amongst us, it was quite a lovely sight, Medina's head vaporizing. An utterly precision kill. God, how I've missed it. Here's the money. The moment was worth it."

That's why it took a while for him to shoot. It had nothing to do with Yenchenko being punished, but only getting back in the saddle.

He accepted the bag from Wells. "Not to worry, I'm putting it to good use."

Sergei asked, "Sandy?"

"Yeah. She's earned it."

"You tell truth?"

"You'll just have to trust me. And each other."

CHAPTER TWENTY TWO

Cat Island, The Bahamas

The dock underfoot was rough, sun-bleached, narrow and barely serviceable. Beyond, *Freckles II* retreated from anchorage. The mainsail filled on a beam reach and Sandy was away on a fair wind, a fine dream and fresh adventure. She had accepted a change of plan and without objection. Not to mention $225,000 in cash with minor protest, payment for weeks at sea and good fortune for her trouble.

A new and warm memory. The way she gasped at the sight of the bundles of currency in her hands. How she tried to push it back to him. For once, at a loss for words, before she stammered, "It's just way, way over the top. I can't accept it."

"It's time you caught a break," he had told her. "Pay off your loan, be as free as the trade winds, chart your own course, take that trip around the world you were talking about."

"Tommy, I just can't."

"Yes. You can."

She had looked into his eyes for a long time. "You're about to do something really, really scary, aren't you? You're looking for the Obi-man. You and Sergei and that Major guy are going to kick some serious ass."

When he pressed the bag back toward her, he said, "And you're getting safely out of the way."

"I should help."

One last time, she tried to return the money, but with less

force.

"You are. By getting out of the way."

The canvas bag crept closer and closer to her, until she at last she clutched it tight against her body and her eyes misted over. "You're not going to get killed or something, are you? I mean, I'd hate to go running around looking for that Alden if you were dead."

"I'll be all right."

"You're sure?"

"Take the money, Sandy. It's time."

A good memory, standing alone on the dock, watching *Freckles II* slip away, toward the Caymans, where a patient banker held the paper on Sandy's yacht. When the Morgan became just a spot among the reflections of sunlight on the turquoise water, it was time for a long, melancholy breath, taking comfort her departure drew no attention and satisfaction it was best for her to be free, not mired in the muck of intelligence work. *All the best to you, good sport, fine friend, young lady. I hope we'll meet again.*

Time to face an emotional void, to turn to face the village of Arthur's Town, the legacy of Arthur Catt, a professional pirate from a different time. All he owned, all he possessed were the clothes on his back. Shorts, a faded denim shirt, sandals. And a rucksack with a change of clothes, the loaded Beretta and two extra clips of ammunition. And the weapon had become excess baggage, yet difficult to abandon.

Time to lift the chin, close the eyes, drink deeply the scent of the salt air. Time for guidance, from somewhere deep in the mind, especially the call of the Obi-man heard off and on ever since Andros. *Nothing.* Just the sea slapping a land's edge, the wind whispering past. *Pull it together. Find a bar with no tourists and a cold beer.*

A local rum shop would do. The table conversation of several men in the comfort of shade evaporated. Only the sharp clack of dominoes fractured an uneasy silence. The barman stood in a faint fog created by American-made cigarettes simmering like incense in two little trays shared by the domino players in an airless corner of the nameless pub. Tommy ordered a Dragon Stout

The barkeep presented a cold bottle. "So where you stayin', man?"

"Don't know yet. Had a bit of a row with the lady on the boat. Any recommendations?"

The bartender shrugged. Bald, wrinkled teeth, squinty eyes. Solid, like an aging middle linebacker. Beefy arms. Probably a baseball bat at the ready under the bar. "Maybe she calm down, come back, take you on your way."

Tommy lifted the sweating bottle. "I don't think so. She was plenty pissed and it's her yacht."

"Too bad, man. Women, they always be causin' troubles for the man."

"Yeah, well, screw 'em." The empty bottle returned to the bar. "Let's have another round, eh? And pour one for yourself."

"Sure thing, man. But you know, there be no cuttin' here. And this be a cash bar."

"Don't worry about a thing. I can pay."

The barkeeper stood his ground.

In the verbal disguise of a naïve and boisterous American, a bum down on his luck, Tommy brightened as if epiphany had just arrived. With his hand thrust in his pocket, he said, "Oh, sure, of course! You want to see the money." *Now pause, grin, look hopeful.* "Say, maybe you need a cook? I can cook pretty good, pay for my bar bill."

The barman replied with a look of disdain garnished with suspicion. "Don't need no cook. Most fellas, they come here not to eat, but to drink. Cold beer, cheap rum, that be our stock and trade."

A fifty ought to do it. A nice wrinkled one, gently unfurled on the bar, nicely smooth out, with the tips of fingers anchoring it. "Maybe you know some place that needs a cook?"

The bartender's eyes widened and his hand crept forward across the bar. "Maybe. You go down the road a little way, you see a picket fence needing fresh paint. The sister there, she do some restaurant trade sometime. Maybe she need the cook."

The bartender's tone was suspect. The and fifty slid a fraction of an inch toward the barman, an invitation for truth. "Maybe you know some other places?"

The bartender's hand retreated. "Not many people on Cat Island. And fewer like you, tourists with some money to spend. Maybe you go down to Moss Town, maybe try your luck down there."

Enthusiastic ignorance always worked. "How far is it?"

"Pretty good walk, maybe thirty miles."

"No chance of buying a ride? I saw an old Jeep parked outside."

The bartender shook his head. "That old Jeep, she not running. You probably won't find a ride, not even with all your American dollar. You take the road out there south, past the airport. Just keep on walkin', man, 'til the road come to the town."

Shake the tree, see what might fall out. "Say, do you think I might run into any trouble?"

"Maybe. Maybe not. Folks 'round here, you never can tell, though. Best keep off the roads at night. Not a good place for the white man, you see?" He looked down at the fifty on the bar. Tommy's hand was no longer on it. "You want another drink?"

"Sure, why not?" A glance at his watch. *I'm not the only one watching.* "Wow! Look at the time! I'd better get moving if I want to get a good start before dark."

The fifty had vanished. The empty bottle was replaced with a full one, perspiring in the heat.

The bartender's eyes narrowed. "What you really want on the island? Why you come here?"

The disguise was probably overplayed. "Hey, nothing sinister, pal. I'm just sort of stranded and I've got some time to kill before the mail boat heads back up to Nassau."

"The mail boat, she shove off from the dock out there on Thursdays. It cost you forty-five one way to Nassau. Meantime, you take care, don't be causin' no trouble."

Try a chuckle to show anxiety. "Pirates still around, eh?"

"Yeah, maybe so."

Tommy picked up the beer bottle. "Change for his fifty?"

The bartender frowned. "Fifty? I don't see no fifty. You gimme ten dollars American. Dragon Stout, they be five each. So we square, man, we square."

"Ah, of course. I get it."

"Do ya?"

"I'll, uh, just check out the domino game."

At the table three steps away, the old men ignored all but the bones in play. Probably table stakes of points and pride. The fellow closest to the wall was probably ahead. Stepping around, he placed the bottle next to the leader.

The old man studied the bottle for a moment, then looked up without expression. Again he examined the bottle, before returning his attention to the dominoes.

Yeah, this feels right. Time to go. Out into the light, caught between the white of day and gold of sunset. The road went only one way, south, past a pharmacy that carried a good brand of mosquito repellant and confirmation of directions. And several young guys, lounging near a soft drink machine, watching with sullen interest. *Part of the game. Play along.*

The single-runway airport forced the road from Arthur's Town to make a wide circle with an embankment that was as good a spot as any. The tie-down and maintenance area was filled with taildraggers, trikes and a few multi-engine piston aircraft, all frozen in a dusk that crept in cold on prevailing wind from the east. Without a tower, the field used pilot-controlled lighting. Hopefully, everyone was on the ground for the night. While changing clothes in favor of darker shades and long sleeves, the first onslaught of mosquitoes pounced on his neck and legs. About to lather himself with the repellant, but headlights interrupted, bouncing along the road on the far end of the curve. Several mosquitoes bored into his neck, Time out to slap on some of the icy liquid. His legs were on their own. At an obvious spot near the road, the day's shirt spread out to form a blanket, and the rucksack became a makeshift pillow. The Beretta was tucked into the back of his waistband, safety off and with a round in the chamber.

The growl of low gear and four wheel drive that tested rotted pavement with trepidation, added up to an older Jeep, like the one outside the bar. Flashlights scanned the roadside. Time to settle back, pretend to be asleep. *The boys from town. If they're just passing by, no harm done. If they're from the Obi-man, be careful. If they're out for a nice little mugging, this could get interesting.*

At last came whispered voices and soft steps on gravel and fractured asphalt. A group of three or four. Closer, closer. Distant chatter, hard to make out. But closer... The glare of lantern flashlights stabbed his eyes.

"On your feet, man," a voice demanded. "We come for what you got in your pockets."

Show confusion, as if just awakened. His left hand up, waving, trying to brush the light away, a frightened civilian alone in a bad place. Baseball bats, tapping on strong hands.

"On your feet, white boy."

A shame. The local kids, simply out to rob him. *Kind of like what the three of us were doing in Nassau.*

Another man, younger, spoke from behind a barrage of light that blinded him and sheltered them. "Let's see what you got."

"Hey. Hey. Hey, what's going on?"

Soft laughter was the answer. The pattern of legs and feet organized his shot group. *About ten or twelve feet away. A bit nervous about stepping into the brush. Four of them, all with bats. Maybe the one on the left has a knife behind his right thigh. Can't be sure.*

"C'mon, fellas. I've only got a couple of dollars and I'm gonna need that for my fare back to Nassau. Gimme a break, okay? Look you can have the watch if you want." He held up the back of his left wrist and hoped it sparkled in the spotlights while his right hand reached behind his back for the comfort of the pistol grip.

"We take it all, Yank."

No question. The bartender. "Okay, okay. You'll let me go afterward?"

The second hand snickered. "We see about that."

The bartender said, "Hand over the wallet."

"Yeah, yeah, no trouble." Left hand waving surrender. Right hand, reaching back, where wallets and nine mil automatics share space. The flashlights in front drifted back and forth like machetes in a cane field. Hand on the Beretta grip, closing around it.

The bartender barked, a nervous edge in his voice. "You be hurryin', man."

The barrel of the gun slide free of the waistband. Warm reassurance along the skin of his back. Several mosquitoes punctured calves and thighs. Ready. Steady. And – A strange sound rumbled down the hillside. *Not quite animal, not quite human, certainly not machine.* Louder, wider, to a shriek, pounding his skull, crushing his hearing. Forehead grinding, squeezing, like an orange being juiced. Hot pain, ear to ear. Grip weakening, fading, no strength... *Hang on to the weapon. Open your eyes. Look. Look....*

Flashlights on the ground. In the glow, the jaws of the four men stretched in agony, but they made no sound. The robbers stepped back, their hands over their ears, staggering toward the Jeep. One by one, their flashlights expired. Two stumbled and fell, yowled on the pavement, scrambled to catch up to the others. The driver fumbled with the ignition, but the Jeep failed to start.

The shrieking sound withered and drifted away on an icy north breeze. The Jeep's engine came to life and it lurched into gear and sped off into the darkness and Arthur's Town. The Beretta in his waistband no longer comforting, but icy, wet.

The flashlights glowered for a moment and came back to full shine.

The old man. The domino champion. The man he'd given the cold Dragon Stout. Taking slow steps, as if afraid to fall, steadying himself with a long walking stick in his right hand, a stick as gnarled and worn as his face. His eyes were buried deep within the creases of many years and the tufts of white hair on his head shone in the faint evening light. He wore a faded polo shirt scarred by several stains and light-colored shorts that were tattered along the bottom edges. His feet were sheltered by worn sandals. At the edge of the road, he studied the flashlights with the bemusement of a magician teasing a gullible audience. He nodded, grunted, and softly waved the walking stick.

All four lights went dark again.

In silence, the old man measured Tommy with care. He sighed. "You be one crazy fella, invitin' the quashies to come for you that way, turnin' them into rude boys." The old man closed his eyes, as if to listen to something and nodded in meditation. When his eyes opened, he spoke. "You be the Wanderer."

Tommy's eyebrow rose and he heard his voice say. "And you are the Obi-man. Not just an Obeah master, but *the* Obi-man of this Island."

"I am Joseph. Joseph Akintunde. But many call me Babu."

"Grandfather," Tommy said. *How do I know this? My words are running on autopilot.*

Joseph seemed pleased. "Yes, yes, I be the Obi-man. You are not afraid?"

"No."

Joseph sighed. "You have no children?"

"No, I don't."

"I have a son. But we are separated by time and culture. There was a daughter, too, but she died."

"I'm sorry."

"It be okay. Her spirit come round now and then, and we talk." He paused, then spoke with firmness. "My grandsons, the children of my daughter, they say I should wear the fancy clothes like the television preacher man, get the proper haircut, buy the fancy walking stick. Then people will have the fear. But, Wanderer, I say to do these things, it would cost plenty dollar."

Joseph gestured that they should walk along the road away from Arthur's Town and into the darkness, deeper into the mysterious island, away from the outposts where white men lived, past little houses and shanties and silent eyes and grim faces. Joseph's pace was slow, but without infirmity. His sandaled feet momentarily tested each patch of ground for firm footing.

"Tough times being an Obi-man?"

"Oh, my, yes. Nobody respect the Obi-man anymore. Everyone gets their religion from the Internet with the click-click. You sure you are not afraid?"

"Sorry, but no."

"You should be. I call you many times, but you don't come, you go to Nassau instead. It is no wonder, Wanderer, that many people try to kill you. I am not very happy with you at all."

"I see. Please do not view my lack of fear as lack of respect,. How did you know I went to Nassau first? Some sort of spell?" Maybe like the science of voodoo, scraps of reminiscence from the strange rituals of an ancient Creole woman he and his boyhood friends called The Old Hag, who reviled them all with as many curses and spells as she had wrinkles on her cheeks and he had heard stories of scientists who could conjure images from a distance.

Joseph shook his head. "I have a nephew called Sammy, who drive the taxi for the Russian spy in Nassau. We both use the telephone, latest generation. Tell me, Mister Tommy Kane, why do you seek the Obi-man?"

Uncontrolled candor, like blurting honesty when just drunk enough to let the tongue wag freely. "The Obi-man already knows the answer."

"Revenge, she be tricky business. You betray to avenge a betrayal and are in turn betrayed. The circle has no end. You been betrayed, Wanderer. Why you wish to live in such a circle?"

A rhetorical trap. *Any debate about the circle will go nowhere. I could try punishment and justice, but not to any man whose people progressed from political slavery to social slavery to economic slavery in just a few generations.* The air freshened as the road wound down to a path along the sea. The mosquitoes that plagued him earlier had vanished. *There's some advantages to being an Obi-man. Bet the mosquitoes never bite him.*

Joseph said, "No, they do not."

Heat rose in Tommy's cheeks and ears. "You're very good at reading minds," he heard himself say.

Joseph rolled his eyes and scowled. "Babu cannot read the mind. Many mind, they should not be heard anyway. No, Wanderer, the spirits come, whisper in the ear. You have come for something, Wanderer. You wish to use the science, perhaps." Before Tommy could duel with a lie, Joseph continued. "Perhaps you wish for the tabeejah, so you can make believers fear you and help you."

Talk about embarrassing...

The Obi-man sighed again. "Everyone uses religion for what they desire, Wanderer. But sometime, you get more than you expect." Joseph set his jaw for a moment of reflection and nodded as they walked along the dark road. "Some people, they say Obeah is a science. Some say it is foolishness. And some say it is religion. What you think 'bout religion, Wanderer?"

Resist the urge for an easy, impulsive answer. It was a test. Even if Joseph owed Tommy his life, he wouldn't part with a first class spell in exchange for a casual comment. "It doesn't matter what a man *thinks*. It depends on what he *believes*. What he believes in the middle of the night, when he's all alone."

Joseph nodded. "Many people, they are afraid of Obeah. It is all evil, they say, about the spells and the hatreds and the superstition. But they do not know Obeah. Back there, in Arthur's Town, I was thirsty but had no money. I call out, to the spirits in the other world. They visit you, and you give me drink. You see? Something good."

Charming. Amusing, even. "That beer cost me forty-five dollars."

Joseph scoffed. "What is money? Only paper and metal, only the path to evil, I think. Take away all the money, and there be less evil in these parts, maybe further away, too." He fell silent for several paces, then apparently made up his mind. "You be plenty fucked up, Wanderer. Maybe you come to the kumina tonight, where the spirits come from all around. You come. We make your head straight."

Babu stopped and leaned into his walking stick. His ancient eyes, from deep within a landscape of wrinkles and countless visits with generations of the dead, settled into an even, patient stare at Tommy.

Tommy set his jaw tight, but it quivered anyway and the stars blurred in his eyes.

"Yes, Wanderer," the Obi-man whispered. "And to once again touch the skirts of your mother."

CHAPTER TWENTY THREE

South of Moss Town, Cat Island, The Bahamas

Daylight. Through fluttering eyelids. One eyelid. The right one. Through a wince, bright light, skipping across the beach and pouncing on revival. Sand. Why the left eye was closed. Buried in the sand. Sand trickling into a mouth on a slack jaw.

Every inch stiff, exhausted. The pillow of sand was immediately unwelcome and Tommy rolled onto back, his forearm warding off sunshine. Well into morning. His head stopped moving, but a sense of elasticity stretched it further, then yanked it back. Like an old cartoon. Fine coral sand clung to exposed skin and all his hair. A stretch. A groan when battered muscles objected.

Just like the day years ago. Awaking in a gravel parking lot after Fat Tuesday food, drink and dance at Dup's Lounge. Near Eunice. Four college buddies, drinking their way through a forest of bottles of Turbo Dog and Dixie beer. Consciousness returning near Johnson's Grocery. Four miles and six hours still could not unaccounted for. The cure. Staggering into Johnson's for the hottest boudin in the meat case. Knocking down a pound of it, right on the front steps. Plus a po-boy laced with onions. Stern glares of disapproval from the genteel crowd that usually hung out at Savoy's. Too bad, folks. Revived, but with a brain working like a bowl of maque choux. Hitching a ride to Opelousas. Finding the guys passing some good time tossing back shots of bourbon in Slim's Y-Ki-Ki while the owner auditioned new zydeco talent. The following day, back in class at LSU, revived and refreshed for the final push toward semester exams.

No boudin or po-boy today. Just the sensation of fried gristle deep inside and a hollow space in his head. The smell of swamp gas, even though there was no swamp within hundreds of miles. Maybe twelve, fifteen feet beyond his toes, the Caribbean caressing a ribbon of wet sand. Single sit-up. Half of another. Arms drooping limp across knees drawn up to take the edge off the hangover, everything.

The rucksack. Within arm's reach, half buried in the sand. Reeling it in. *Something's not right. Feels like it's full of sand. Darn zipper's stuck.* Air gushed from his lungs in a gasp. The bag stuffed with bundled currency, a blend of Bahamian and American cash. *Where's my piece?*

Inflating anxiety. Small of back, sides of the bag. pockets of his shorts. *Dammit...* The rucksack upended, bundles tumbling to the beach. Empty. Dropping the bag onto a pile of paper money, slumping back into the sand. *Well, Moses, if this is your idea of redemption, it's a first-rate way to get started.*

The pale pink beach was deserted in all directions. A gentle breeze ruffled the edges of the bundled cash. A rough count while repacking the bag, methodical, organized. *What is money? Only paper and metal*, Joseph had said. *Only the path to evil.* The count stopped. The packing turned efficient. The bag, zipped, closed.

Sunlight, maybe two hour or so into the day, tossed a million diamonds on the tiny wavelets of a peaceful sea. The beach could be anywhere. A braided string around his neck. On the string, a tabeejah. The kumina the night before – well, maybe the night before – was not a dream. The charm looked like a cat's paw, decorated with bits of feather, a few beads. *Time to be alive again.*

He gently placed the tabeejah atop the rucksack, stripped

off his clothes and entered the shallow water for a sea bath.

After, a strange sense of ease. Peace. Comfort. Sitting in the sand, the tabeejah around his neck, waiting for what fortune it might bring. Recollection. The kumina had been lubricated with an strange bitter cocktail of home brew: mangos and mystical herbs. *Probably a hefty dose of DMT, judging from the stages of the experience.*

It began with the intense throb of many hands slapping drum skins in perfect unison. They'd made a fire from shipping pallets and marked their faces with the warm ashes, drank the brew without gagging, and began to dance. Faster and faster they circled the fire in a step of reckless abandon, discarding reality to welcome the spirits invoked for reasons held captive in very private places of their minds.

After thirty minutes came the pale green glow and the swirl of fuzzy forms in his eyes, then behind his eyes, then deep from within him. From blackness, awful monsters of the bayou pounced upon him and chewed his flesh until his skin was afire. Joseph waved a rattle toward each to chase the demons away. Forms on the sand writhed and quivered and swayed in a slow, methodical rhythm and began to circle the fire again, again and, yes, they actually floated in the air. One by one, the monsters were washed away on the night wind and the dancers were rewarded with ecstasy, atonement, consolation.

And an eternity of comfort when he beheld the serenity of his mother's face. Babu, the Obi-man, had fulfilled his promise. His mother's voice, her scent, the warm security of her skirts, just as the children had enjoyed in San Pedro, and his eyes filled with tears of joy.

When the dancers lay spent and exhausted in the twilight, they smoked narcotics and drank the last of Babu's potion. Ghostly voices came, echoing even now in the morning sunshine. Voices blurred together, like a room full of people who spoke all at once, not so loud as a party, but...

And then all the voices seemed to separate for a moment. His grandfather, who muttered as much to himself as to the boy who scampered along on a dirt road that led to home. Paw-paw carried a big pail of crayfish in one hand and all the wisdom of the ages in the other. "You got to help the little guy sometime," he began. "The world don't give a shit about the fella who look out only for hisself."

All the other voices folded back in, like a tide that rose on both sides at once. *No! I want to hear the rest of what he said that day. The day before the tornados.* Cursing himself for inattention, tears flooding his eyes. No pardon for inattention. Just a scrap of memory without the context to define a path for himself.

Open your eyes. Time to stop bawling.

A skiff, nineteen or twenty feet at the waterline, propelled by a spritsail and guided by a centerboard. But a hefty outboard motor at the ready, on the stern. Two teenage boys dropped the sail and pulled the centerboard and the skiff gently came aground in the sand just three feet from water's edge. They wore shorts two sizes too large, cinched at the waist, and tank shirts at least a size too small, stretched tight across muscular torsos. Neither face was familiar from the kumina.

"Hello, mister!" the helmsman called. "You be lookin' for transport to Nassau, maybe?"

Up and at 'em. "Yeah, that'd be great."

The second boy disembarked and took charge of the painter while the helmsman stood well balanced with a swelled chest and a broad grin.

"I am Addo," the helmsman announced, "and here is my brother Sule."

"I can pay."

Addo pointed toward Tommy's neck. "No matter, mister. You wear the tabeejah of Babu. We are fishing since dawn but have caught nothing. Sea spirits say to take the white man where he wishes to go, then the fish will find our hooks. That is what Sule says, anyway."

Sule was clearly the more reserved of the two boys. "I'm sure Babu will reward your kindness. But I carry no magic."

Sule shrugged and gestured for Tommy to step into the skiff. The expression in his eyes was the same as Pokey Jarrett on that hung-over Ash Wednesday when Tommy insisted he had weathered the night of Mardi Gras in a virtuous manner. Sule said nothing, but Pokey cracked a smirk and firmly declared in an accent more Texas than Louisiana, "Every time I step into what Tommy says, I hear something go squish under my boots and horseshit comes to mind."

The sail remained furled. The outboard ran for about fifteen minutes, when a small town appeared to starboard. The buildings seemed different.

"Arthur's Town?"

"No, Mistah. That be Moss Town. We got a long way to go."

Moss Town? That's a good thirty miles south of Arthur's Town. Just be content in being alive. They'd follow the coast of Cat Island, cross the channel to Eleuthera and then make their way a good fifty miles across Governor's Harbor. A long trip. Plenty of time to get it together, enjoy the air rushing past, seated in a bow running high in the water. "What day is it?"

Addo shrugged. "It is today. You are too late for yesterday and too early for tomorrow."

By the time they passed Arthur's Town, the bashful Sule and the polite but distant Addo. opened up and for the next couple of hours told their stories and some of the legends of Cat Island on a rising tide of exuberance. Most of the stories connected to Babu in manners direct and oblique. Stories told well, reminders of the folklore of his native Louisiana. Kids, wide-eyed and skittish in the mystical theater created by his paw-paw, a first-rate tale spinner, who shared soft and spooky accounts of gator hunts, swamp bogeymen, moonshine and Huey Long. Before long, he himself stood in the center of a wide arc of older boys in coveralls, arms crossed and somber in silent testimony, while young children sat near and shuddered as stories about swamp monsters and the Loup Garou marched to a scary climax. Always with the calm assurance it was all "for true."

Addo was more nonchalant about bended truth, but Sule disguised the absurd into believability with great skill. The impromptu spells casually cast by Obi-men ranged from the simple to the ornate. Like an Obi-man who was thirsty and therefore brought rain that incidentally saved a crop of beans, and the story of how Babu's power even altered a vehicle registration to prove that a poor man had not stolen a truck. When Tommy's eyes found Addo after hearing the tale from Sule, the cheery brother shrugged. "What is a piece of paper to a master who can make it rain?"

And they seemed to assume Tommy's tabeejah had significance, explaining that for reasons known only to the Obi-man, a long tradition that excluded whites from Obeah had been modified. It was the white man, they reasoned, that struggled for more than two centuries to demolish the mystical religions of Western Africa, included anti-Obeah laws and grave punishment on a number of the old colonies.

"But I think," Addo asserted with some pride, "that Obeah is stronger than the white man. What the white man does, it does not matter. Obeah survives."

Sule held a harsher view. "The white man, he be weak because his belief is based on a dead man who does not return. Obeah brings all the spirits 'round, to watch over us, keep us safe."

Yet the conversation danced around the superficial; none of them were truly on the inside, but it would probably be Sule's destination. Addo had the makings of a fine charter captain not only because he could handle a boat with expertise but also because he had the gift of chatter essential to comfort the wealthy American fishermen in quest of trophies. And after a time the incessant drone of the motor numbed the dialogue into the silent companionship of three men with private thoughts and perspectives.

The Alden yawl. A struggle to bring it into focus, drifting instead to the image of his mother from the night before, and the words of his grandfather in his ear. The sea settled into an eerie stillness of broad undulations of blue-grey water that evaporated into a blue-grey sky at a horizon line sometimes punctuated with the olive tufts of a nameless cay in the long string of the Exumas. The Alden blurred, but only for a little while.

Sifting reminiscences. The chess game in Bavaria. The plan of Yenchenko that turned out to be the plan of Walter Campos. *Are you from the Valley of the Clueless? Yes, Mather – or is it Matthias – but now I possess a clue. A clue to what?* The words of Myra Fielding and those of Moses Clay. *She found me at Dieter's hotel, at the same time Mather did. Moses found me in a toilet, puking my guts out. Mather. Matthias.* Missions, mayhem and moments of suppressed panic floated by like flotsam from too much past and too little future. Reminiscences. Free association. The lyrics of "Burma Road." *Crows smell a fire and they all fly away, bullfrog come back and he cry all day. Crows. Black men, the black men of 1942. Black man. Carter Blackmann, the deputy director of operations. Blackbirds. Blackbird. Crows. Over the Hill. Into the bush. Burma Road. The Alden.*

Solomon's Lighthouse grew on the western horizon and conversation revived. When the skiff touched shore just above East End Point, Sule and Addo again refused payment. After a shove off and a wish for good fortune and a safe journey home, Tommy stood on the same kind of sand as the beach that morning, witnessing the same kind of departure as the day before.

Addo and Sule waved and were barely a hundred yards offshore before they hoisted the spritsail to conserve what little fuel they probably had left on board. Maybe the magic would provide a decent catch and a fine meal. But under the seat on the skiff, they'd find a bundle of cash.

Tucked under his shirt, the tabeejah was soft and provided a chest-filling warmth, somewhere along Eastern Road. He soon stretched out in the bed of a scruffy pickup truck laden with vegetables for market. No apparent reason, but the truck squealed to a halt on the narrow road and the driver and his son seemed grateful that he didn't seek admission to the front seat. It was Wednesday, they said, and dropped him off near the yacht club, to dissolve into a flock of tourists.

CHAPTER TWENTY FOUR

New Providence Island, The Bahamas

Dead drop number one, nothing. Ditto number two. And now, near the Straw Market, drop number three was empty. Nothing left but a dismal hike to Arawak Cay and maybe an overdose of introspection. *Where was everybody?*

A gray minivan, a taxi, swooping into a U-turn and touching off a lot of angry horn honking. Settling at the edge of West Bay, with a window rolling down. Sammy. Yenchenko's street guy.

"Hey, Mistah Cat-man, I come to take you to Cable Beach, where your friends be eatin' the nice evenin' meal at Johnny Canoe's."

A smile of relief, appreciation for the lift, a break for the legs. *If they're having dinner in a very public place, they're working a surveillance target.* As the taxi zoomed away from Nassau onto West Bay Street, Sammy's eyes in the rear view mirror took long look at the tabeejah.

"You been to see the Obi-man," the driver said. "You been to kumina."

"You are Sammy, the nephew of Babu."

Sammy's laugh seemed to mask anxiety. "That be one first-class tabeejah, to know such things."

"Not hardly. Joseph said you talk on the telephone."

Sammy rolled his eyes in embarrassment. "Please Mistah Cat-man, you don't tell the Russian fellow, okay? He pay plenty dollar for driving service when in Nassau."

They roared around a parked bus and cut off another taxi

"Mum's the word. And it's Tommy."

"Babu say anything about Daniel?"

"Who's Daniel?"

Sammy sighed. "Daniel be his son, but there be some bad feeling between them."

"What's the problem?"

Sammy chuckled. "Well, right now he be in Her Majesty's Prison in Fox Hill, awaiting trial on some matter involving the computer. Him with all his high and mighty education, now he be takin' a shit on the five-gallon pail in a tiny cell. Bad place for any man to be, I tell you."

"He stole a computer?"

Sammy shook his head. "No, man, they say he steal *with* the computer. He work at the airport, but with the police charges, he lose his job. His father, the Obi-man, he be plenty pissed about this matter, and not be liftin' a finger to help poor Daniel."

Intriguing thoughts fled when the taxi came to a halt directly in front of Café Johnny Canoe's, a few paces from the Nassau Beach hotel casino where Lester Finn had given some lucky guy a break. *Or was he just a shill? I've got to get out of a business built on constant suspicion.*

A hundred dollars settled into Sammy's hand.

"Sorry about your cousin. Does he need money for bail?"

Sammy answered with sad eyes. "There be no bail for him, I think. Only escape. You take care, Mistah, uh, Tommy. You watch where you sit tonight, okay?" He quickly put the taxi back into gear and flitted away into the noisy traffic on West Bay.

The hostess looked up from her station at the portal of a packed house.

"Table for one."

She studied her chart. Behind her, just a collection of

tourists, people normal-sized. No standouts like Yenchenko. That left –

"Outside on the terrace would be nice."

She looked up to see a twenty dollar bill in his hand. "Of course, sir. Right this way."

A corner location, near the entry to the indoor section of the restaurant. The parade of waitstaff would bother any other patron, but the view of all the tables was perfect. Thin shrubbery bordered the terrace on three sides, and on the line nearest the street, Yenchenko and Wells dined on seafood with a white table wine and appeared to be involved in a pleasant conversation. When the waitress offered a menu, Wells caught sight of him but registered no reaction.

They're working a tail all right. He scanned the tables, one by one, left to right, front to back. A couple halfway between Tommy and his friends. *Late twenties, modestly dressed in American sportswear, and they speak softly but not directly to each other.* Her back was to him and she had curly hair. Like Myra Fielding. Her left hand made frequent, slight adjustments to her purse. *Wait. Why is her purse on the table?* Other women's purses. Hanging on the chair. On the floor, next to her feet. One on the table, but small, a clutch. No bigger bags on the table.

Yeah, that's the target alright. A platter of conch fritters and an ice cold Kalik beer to celebrate successful deduction. Ian and Sergei took a pass on dessert, coffee and after-dinner drinks. Wells appeared to use a napkin to calculate a tip, then stuffed currency into the waiter's check folder and rose to leave just as Tommy's order arrived.

As they passed, they spoke meaningless chatter about evening activities. From Ian's right hand a folded scrap of napkin dropped near Tommy's plate. *Gather it in.* The American couple with the bag stood. She spent a lot of time with her hand in the purse while he studied the check. She hissed an order at him and Tommy took a guess: *Don't worry about the damn tip. Let's get going.* As they passed by, relief that it wasn't Myra Fielding and he wasn't blown.

Through the shrubbery terrace veil, the couple departed. Ian's note unfolded in his hand. It read, "NW corner, Fish Fry, 30 Min."

So it goes. Half the beer down his throat, a couple of fritters into his belly. A pair of twenties on the table. A casual search for the Number Ten bus on Bay Street. A small group of hotel workers huddled at the stop, creating a good cover. Together they clambered aboard a thirty-two seat jitney with dollar bills and quarters in hand. *The others took taxis, but the question is whether Wells and Yenchenko will run them around town a little so I can catch up or whether I'm supposed to arrive later.* He stood when the bus approached Arawak and decided. *Earlier.*

He got off about two hundred feet south of Goldie's Conch House and drifted north into an arena of authentic Bahamian restaurants ringing an open area At the menu board on the front railing of Goldie's he pause. The building was painted in huge blocks of saturated blue, green, pink and yellow. A big sign on the roof promised this was Arawak's specialist in conch salads and a proud purveyor of Sands beer. Inside a dark-paneled bar, a second shot at supper, the house specialty and a cold Sands. With the moist bottle in hand, a retreat to the front porch and a comfortable point of surveillance behind the menu board.

Wells and Yenchenko arrived from the same intersection, but separated fifty feet into the area and faded into a thin collection of pedestrians clinging to the various restaurant fronts. Right behind, the couple from Johnny Canoe's. With a few hand gestures they also separated and began to track Sergei and Ian one-on-one.

This should be fun. Mark the time. Five minutes and they'll be running around completely dumfounded. He sipped beer for four minutes. The salad arrived. When he looked up a minute later, the man and woman met in the middle of the narrow street, gesturing futility and looking hard in all directions. *Yep, they've lost 'em. Nice job, guys. All, well, all four of you.*

The man said something to his lapel and pressed a hand to his ear while the woman crossed her arms and slowly turned a full circle.

Tommy peered over a big sign attached to the railing that warned "No Loafing!" *Wow, can they really make it more obvious? All they need are blue nylon windbreakers with "CIA" in big white letters on the back. They're utterly confused, and it looks like someone's giving them the business for losing their targets.* Both Sergei and Ian probably in position for their next move. To the charming waitress, "Yep, another beer. How's the seafood platter? Nice? Good. I'll take one. Please hurry, I'm starved. The only meal I've had all day. Yeah, yeah, it happens. Here's a twenty for you because you're so darn nice. Thanks..."

The couple briefly discussed radioed instructions from their control and then each other. One more look around. They walked at a brisk pace south along the edge of the street and toward a small park at the far end of the cay.

An early evening breeze billowed in from between Crystal and Long Cay to take the heat off the asphalt and sandy dirt. A platter of redfish, shrimp and the inevitable conch arrived. Twenty pleasant minutes of dining.

Then, the drums.

Distant. Somewhere south.

At first, just two or three, hunting for unison. Now four, five and more, then a dozen at least that pulsed, throbbed and chattered at a frantic pace. The glow of small fires and the scent of burned pallets, creeping across the cay, along with dusk. Boys, all ages, working the skins as they tightened from the fires. Practicing for Junkanoo. The same intense rhythm of kumina, only here, on the cay.

Yeah. That'll work. Wells and Yenchenko, laying a trap for their targets. Another Sands and a question for the waitress, whether the musicians were strays or part of one of Nassau's collection of bands.

She scowled at his ignorance while she cleared the empty platter and bottle. "That be Roots. Here is their practice ground, every week, 'bout this time." Resignation filled her voice.

It must get old after a while. Better slow down on the beer. The light of day shrank and as it did, an audience magically appeared. A few, a dozen, a hundred, then just a sea of humanity, swarming an almost-deserted street and sidewalk. As the pavement was carpeted with people, the crispness of the drums dulled a bit, but continued to multiply. The tempo was relentless.

And then the parade began.

Horns of all kinds, cowbells, whistles and African shaker rattles exploded in song, way down the Cay. Countless drum skins thundered under countless hands. An immense mob of young people surged around the corner from the staging ground of the park and oozed up the curved street toward the bar. Some tee shirts declared "Roots" while others declared they were proud fans of Kalik.

Several unit directors flitted about to keep the group as organized as a weekly rush can be.

On your feet. Park the beer.

While the band roared enthusiasm and every member strutted back and forth, round and round, fans along the street swayed with the rhythm of a sound so intense he could feel it on his skin. A thousand people or more packed the little square solid across sidewalks and the street itself.

There's Yenchenko.

Tall enough to be seen and white enough to be noticed, a polite and deferential Sergei worked his way through a gauntlet of Junkanoo fans, past Twin Brothers and Andros restaurants.

He's flushing the quarry. Ignore him and pick a spot. Andros Restaurant. That'll do.

The young couple appeared, she along the buildings behind the fan line and he on the edge of the street in the thin
area that divided admirers from participants.

Sit tight. He's bringing them to me.

Tommy glanced left. Yenchenko had vanished like a rabbit
into brush.

Okay, here we go.

The couple pulled up at the corner, about twenty yards, as
the enormous Roots contingent choked the street. Horns of
all shapes blared a simple but harmonic tune, over and over.
And then there were the drums, the endless lines of drums, the
drums that celebrated the rhythm of another continent, another time, in one joyous voice.

The couple turned, looked, turned and looked again.
*Rookies, barely off The Farm. They've lost our guy again. Control
has got to be going nuts. It's getting darker. The street is packed.
They're blind as...*

The woman grabbed her right shoulder with her left arm.
Her legs wobbled. The man didn't see the hit until he turned
and saw anguish on her face. He reached out for her but she
dropped to her knees.

Go. Right now. Off the porch at Goldie's, just as the woman
completely collapsed. Her partner leaned over her, arms wide
as if to ward off spectators. Panic all over his face. *Push through
the crowd.* The man turned to look at him and opened his
mouth to say something, but couldn't be heard amid the noise
of the band.

Yell, loud as you can. "It's okay! I'm a doctor!"

The man began to nod. The dart hit him high on his back,
into his shoulder. *An inch to the right and I would have been the
victim.*

Damn, Ian, that's really tight shooting.

The man's face went limp and down he went. Kneeling
over both bodies to recover darts. *Flashing lights. Red lights.
White van, orange stripe. Ambulance. Local EMS.*

Gripping the pair of darts in his hand. Options. Stuff them into pockets and risk being stabbed? Or toss them and leave evidence?

Okay, guys, what's going on?

An empty paper cup from a bystander's hand dropped to the pavement. *Phew. Nick of time.* The darts into the cup. While standing to direct the ambulance, crushing it with a foot, grinding it into irrelevant street litter.

The Ministry of Health ambulance backed into the corner with care, but only a handful of Junkanoo fans in the immediate vicinity paid any attention. The white truck stopped. Just fade away or stick with his newfound patients? A second later he knew. Yenchenko, in an Emergency Medical Services jumpsuit, stepped out of the ambulance to take charge. The band front gyrated less than fifteen feet away and a platoon of trombones and trumpets seared ears.

To Sergei and everyone else gathered round, he said, "I believe they've taken ill."

Yenchenko yelled. "No problem! Help has arrived!"

"Do you think anyone can hear us?"

"*Nyet*," Sergei said in a voice that could not be heard over the thunder of the drums. "It is useless to make cover talk."

As the woman was on a litter and strapped to it, the interest of onlookers drifted back to the exuberant practice of Roots. Yenchenko tugged a second litter from the truck as Wells appeared. He also wore an EMS jumpsuit and tended the second patient and then whisked the unconscious man into the ambulance followed by the three kidnappers.

Sergei banged on the side of the truck and from the driver's seat, Sammy the taxi driver turned to wave. He put the van into gear and gave two short siren blasts. The van crept toward Bay Street, lights flashed and traffic paused to allow the ambulance to pass.

In silence, Wells and Yenchenko searched the two bodies. As they found transmitters and homing devices, they held them aloft for inspection. Wells grabbed a fistful of towels and used it to wrap the video camera in the woman's purse. Sammy made frequent turns, and with each they slowed just enough to allow the kidnappers to discard communications gear onto the pavement of Nassau. By the time they cruised past Princess Margaret Hospital, their captives were secure. Sammy killed the red lights and they paused long enough at an intersection for Wells to plant the camera on the back of a horse-drawn sightseeing carriage.

As they pulled away, normal conversation replaced panto-mime. Yenchenko passed CIA identity cards for inspection.

"How many more?"

Wells said, "Six. An abandoned warehouse on Arawak."

"What's left?"

Yenchenko grunted and grinned. "Estimate for control is three.".

"That's a good count?"

"*Da, da*. Of course. I make brief talk with one captive, who seems credible."

"He's not damaged, is he?"

"*Nyet. She* is unharmed. Perhaps a small bit frightened, but most helpful in brief interrogation."

Wells shrugged. "Yenchenko seems to have a way with women."

Tommy leaned back for the ride to the warehouse. "I'm sure. I really like your ambulance. Looks very professional."

Yenchenko wiped his brow. "Is *most* professional. It is real ambulance, stolen yesterday."

"No kidding? The real deal?"

"*Da*. Comfortable, good emergency aid supply, but most poor on gas mileage. We borrow from repair service, some small difficulty with leaking rear seal. We make temporary re-pair." He studied the unconscious pair. "Happy couple will make nice dream together."

Wells chuckled. "I expect they'll feel utterly wretched in

the morning. Considerable amount of vomiting, I'd wager."

"Nice shot, by the way, Ian." *No sense in complaining about how tight he works.*

Sergei shook his head. "Is poor shot. Off mark by five centimeter."

Ian's eyes narrowed in anger. "More like two, two point five. It's a vet's rifle at eighteen meters. It needs to be resighted."

Yenchenko tugged at latex gloves on his hands. "You say same yesterday at bus station. In Russia, there is old saying: is one thing to promise, another to perform."

Wells fired right back. "In the U-K, there's an old saying: oh, bugger off, you stupid prat." Then he leaned back and advised Tommy, "Sorry, we're a bit unresolved on teamwork issues."

"But you're making progress?"

Yenchenko shrugged, but the impatient Wells replied, "See here, Thomas, I accept the fact that I owe you a favor for setting you chaps up with Medina, but Yenchenko's insolence drives me barmy. My only consolation is knowing that if I shot the bastard in the head, the bullet would exit the other side unscathed."

Sammy navigated narrow streets and came to a stop outside a darkened customs warehouse on the cay. To the north, the Roots show continued unabated and it echoed across the landscape. "Let's just get unloaded," he said.

Inside the warehouse, a row of large crates labeled "Machine Parts" in both English and Spanish stood in the center of an otherwise empty room. Each crate was just big enough to serve as a jail cell.

Tommy asked, "Machine parts?"

"No originality from Russians. *Ever.*"

Yenchenko was indifferent. "Is good disguise for sending arms to Cuba. So it is good disguise for sending CIA people to small island."

Ian handed the remaining identity cards to Tommy. "You'll likely want these, mate. When do you want to hit their control?"

"Not until we get the first string down here. These are just kids up from the training. What about transport?"

"Laid on, first light."

"I see. Six plus these two. Eight prisoners. Big load."

"Three runs, Thomas. Dave's boat does ninety, so there's time to get it done in one day if we don't go too far."

"I'd prefer one, longer run."

"As you wish. A bit cramped, but workable. You still plan to meet Campos at Lyford?"

"Yep."

"Right. Hm. Crew of three, eight prisoners. I should think we'll be all right." Wells provided directions to Nassau Dave's dock and it became time to split up.

A dozen yards distant, Cesar Hernandez slept on a worn metal cot. His thin body was barely evident under an even thinner blanket and a makeshift table nearby was covered with medical supplies.

Tommy turned to Yenchenko, "How's he doing?"

"Fair, Koshka. I make new dressing on wound two times each day as animal doctor recommend. I give drug to make him sleep. It is better this way, I think. Of course, he is most lucky person that you are poor shot. Damage to body is small, so he make a good recovery."

"Okay, okay. Poor shot. Guard duty?"

Ian raised a hand. "I'll take the first watch. Yenchenko has the second and will run the truck. We'll meet at dawn."

Yenchenko followed Tommy into the darkness. His appearance was tense and perspiration flowed across his head.

"Serge, I don't want to hear any bitching. Work it out."

Yenchenko crossed his arms and his eyes narrowed. He glared for a long moment. "*Da, da.* Of course. You are boss. *For now.*"

CHAPTER TWENTY FIVE

Across the street from the shuttered office of Nassau Dave's Adventures, in the rosy glow of daybreak, Tommy leaned against a stucco wall in a shop doorway. He sipped unremarkable coffee through a slit in the plastic lid of a foam cup, taking comfort in the absence of traffic and the ability to yawn without shame. A few feet away, Ian paced in a tight circle of annoyance.

Nassau Dave was late.

Ian sneered. "Probably in a bed somewhere nearby with the catch of the day. Usually tourists, the sort enchanted by his bloody Aussie-rules-football body. Deep tan. Blue eyes and long, windblown blond hair, of course."

"Of course. Not to mention the charming down-under accent."

"And *a lot* of teeth."

"What they call a regular cheeky tosser, eh?"

"Don't patronize me, Thomas."

"You can't possibly be jealous."

Wells scowled. "I am *not* jealous, damn it."

Tommy leaned back to encourage the last of the coffee out of the cup and into his mouth. "Ah, okay."

Just as the first stab of sunlight slithered across the channel and under the Paradise Island Bridge, Nassau Dave shuffled across Bay Street from somewhere about a hundred and fifty feet north of the doorway.

Dave jammed his hands into pockets of khaki shorts, and

sunglasses dangled from a string around his neck. He sported a pale blue sweatshirt that zipped up the front, just high enough to display a bit of chest fur and declare virility. While Dave concentrated on a padlock at the gate of his shop, Tommy peeked around the edge of the doorway. A woman exited a nearby building, on the same path Dave took. She wore baggy sweats, dark glasses and a dour expression and had dark hair pulled into a ponytail. She crossed the street. Her gait suggested she was late thirties or early forties. Her expression hinted she was unhappy with the hour of day, a possible hangover, the reality of Nassau Dave. Or all the above.

Wells turned to watch the woman pass. Her eyes were fixed straight ahead. Dave opened his office and slipped inside.

Ian's shoulders slumped in disappointment on the same breath that expressed relief. "Filthy bugger."

"Which one? Him, her or us?"

"Damn it, Kane..."

Tommy grinned, tossed the cup into a trash can, and stepped toward the street. "Oh, c'mon, Ian. Yenchenko will be here any minute with the hostages."

Dave's thin office was dominated by a scruffy glass display case, the shelves of which mostly offered sunglasses and sun block at inflated prices, along with the assorted souvenirs to suggest the participants had just conquered "Jaws." To port, a pegboard stuffed with life jackets and rescue equipment reinforced the notion that "Jaws" might not be easy to subdue. A passage under a hand-lettered sign directed patrons to a bathroom shrouded by a drab curtain.

After the introductions, Ian began to admonish Nassau Dave for tardiness. Tommy stepped away to study the shelves in the case, pretending to ignore family issues. Although Ian tried to pull rank on his younger cousin, Dave wouldn't enlist. Wells insisted on discipline, but the Aussie clearly chose chaos. Ian preferred dignified propriety, but Nassau Dave seemed thrived on a casual *joie de vivre* reminiscent of the Mardi Gras maxim, *laissez les bons temps rouler.*

Recalling the words of Myra Fielding at Doc's shack, Tommy smiled. *Insubordinate. Reckless. Irresponsible. Failure to follow protocols. Ignores regulations. Many reports incomplete. Loose cannon. Violates policies. On and on...*

Ian Wells, by any alias, might never imagine Nassau Dave as a sniper, but to Tommy. Dave might have been his kind of field agent. The internal mute button switched off and the dialog crystallized

Ian said, "Good lord, man, the woman certainly seemed grumpy to me!"

Tommy turned to see Dave shrug.

"Of course she's grumpy. She's middle aged, a tad overweight and an American. Look mates, I did me best to brighten the Sheila's day, but I had to toss her just to take on a job for you blokes. Which, I'm beginning to think, might not be such a grand idea."

The argument had gone from a family table matter that was none of his business to a team issue demanding intervention. "Maybe this is the sort of thing you boys ought to resolve over a few cold ones. We've got work to do and Yenchenko will be here any minute."

Dave asked, "Who's Yenchenko?"

Wells sighed. "Another bloke who's got a way with women."

After an uneasy silence, Ian turned to Tommy. "You're quite certain that you want to maroon these chaps? It's a simple matter of weighting the bodies and tossing them just off the reef, you know. Save us all bother, and we'd return before lunch."

"Sorry, that's the plan. We don't need any more bodies. We're doing a kidnapping, not a military operation. We got everyone in town excited for a day or two and now it's time to stay under the radar. Dave, we've got some, well, goods to move from Nassau to a nice, deserted cay. One with trees, but away from popular traffic."

Nassau Dave appeared relieved that he would not be an accessory to one of his cousin's murders. He pulled some large rolled charts from a bin behind his cluttered desk, unfurled them on the counter and pointed to several small cays well to the south. "Well, guv, at full throttle the Thirty-six could be there and back in maybe six hours. These little ones, here, here, and here, are ideal. But sometimes used by bare boaters to drop anchor with their Sheilas, grab a couple coldies and root about."

"Not quite. I'm looking for something isolated, with lots of sharks and rays to keep them out of the water."

Dave brightened. "Nice sand sharks, is it then?" His fingers found a collection of spits of land that looked like they were out of the mainstream of recreational traffic. "They run five or six feet down here, nasty looking but harmless, unless you're chumming."

"You're certain?"

Nassau Dave spoke with all the eagerness of someone who wanted to be one of the group but had no real chance. "Oh, absolutely!"

Tommy studied the chart and agreed.

Dave rubbed his hands together. "Right. Anyone care to crack a tinnie or two before we shove off? No? Okay. Tell you what, mates, I'll just wait for you lads on the boat if that's good?"

Tommy smiled and Dave departed.

Ian started an assessment, half apology, half explanation, all condemnation.

"He's an asset, Ian. A floater maybe, but our asset. Deal with it."

Wells lifted an eyebrow. His gun hand found the countertop and he began to tap his fingers, in that nervous gesture just before he killed someone.

"I'm telling you as a friend, Ian, that you've got to let go of whatever issues you have. This is a job, requiring teamwork. No time for personal matters, old rivalries. We're on the same side, like it or not."

Ian's frown collapsed into a dispassionate and icy mask, the kind men wear when they don't really care who dies. "I certainly grasp the concept of professionalism, Thomas, and this has nothing to do with it."

"Want to tell me about it?"

Wells leaned back and his eyes narrowed. "My private life is my own concern, Kane. I'm not some schoolboy giving it a go for the first time you know. I can manage quite well, thank you very much."

It's got something to do with a woman. The spirit of his grandfather whispered in his ear: *Every man wears gloves for his own reasons. But I wonder what he's doin', wearin' those gloves.*

"Very well, then, Thomas. She was just an amusement I picked up on a flight from Kiev. A passing attachment for a man who hasn't had any in a while. Look, Kane, if I fancy a bit of recreation, it's my business I should think. That damned Yenchenko ought to quit peeping and..." His voice faded into embarrassed silence.

Just as Tommy guessed the cautious Wells had become mired in a honey trap with one of Yenchenko's swallows, a growl erupted from behind them. "And what, *tovarich?*"

Ian whirled and a nine mil Glock materialized in his hand.

Yenchenko looked down the barrel with indifference and Tommy's eyes followed the line of Sergei's left arm down to a beefy paw that barely concealed a throwing knife. Ian's only hope would be to strike first; if he hesitated, the blade would puncture his torso, dead center, and he'd bleed out in a few minutes.

The sounds of the room fled and left an eerie silence in their wake. Neither Wells or Yenchenko paid any attention to Tommy, who eased past Wells, out of the line of fire. *If I make the wrong move, it'll be like tossing a lit match into a pond of gasol-*

ine. Tommy's arms crept upward and to both men he displayed an outstretched palm to incubate a truce.

The sound of a doorknob and the rush of salt air fractured the tableau. Wells took a quick step sideways to create a line of fire for all three men. Yenchenko began to react, but Tommy used a hand to block his arm.

Nassau Dave's eyes widened. "What the bloody hell...?" His words trailed off and he raised an arm in self defense. "Crikey, lads!"

Wells again raised his gun to aim at Yenchenko's chest, but the Russian had already holstered the knife and answered with a dismissive sneer. Ian stood down.

Dave exhaled relief. "Look, mates, you can have a go anywhere but here, all right? The last thing I need to attract is Old Jack, eh?"

"Dave's right," Tommy said, mostly to Sergei. "Let's all just get back to work, okay?"

Yenchenko shrugged agreement, but Ian seemed to struggled to contain anger. Tommy stepped in front of Wells and softly said, "We're going to have a chat about Russian birds."

Ian's eyes were ice cold, but he faintly nodded to accept a sliver of breathing room to save face.

Dave heard none of it and smacked his hands together in a single loud clap, rubbed with vigor, and tried to brighten the atmosphere. "Okay, mates, I've got provisions aboard the Pantera and we can shove off anytime you're ready for a bit of a spin on the fastest bloody craft outside of Miami."

Tommy turned away from Ian and toward Yenchenko, half a step behind. "Do you have the cargo, Sergei?"

His reply was casual, as if he spoke about an order of sandwiches. "*Da, da,* of course. In small truck, tied and hooded. However, there is already some traffic on street, yes? Where can we load where there are not so many eyes to watch?"

Nassau Dave said, "There's a little-used dock two miles south, private, out of public view."

Tommy said, "Works for me. Ian, you go with Dave and I'll ride shotgun with Serge on the truck."

Another uneasy moment of silence.

"*Nyet, Tovarich* Kane. Sergei will make delivery alone. It is good that you will have some time to visit with old friend, I think."

Tommy sighed. It was time to confront Ian and Yenchenko wanted no part of it, probably to avoid being shot. As they separated, he was left in the mental stench of a foul mood. *Three experienced agents. Too much ego. Scrapping like kids over a playground toy. We're vulnerable to third stringers from the CIA. The best will be in town in a day, maybe sooner, and they'll have crosshairs dancing on our necks. That hammock at Duffy's sure is appealing.*

Ten minutes later, Tommy helped cast off the lines on the dock, the tabeejah dangling from his neck, catching Dave's attention.

"That's some souvenir you've got mate. Fancy a bit o' that native magic, do you? "

"It's no souvenir."

"From Cat Island? The real deal is it?"

"Yes, the real thing."

Dave cocked an eyebrow but his expression became one of awe. To Ian, Nassau Dave offered the confidence of an insider to an ignorant tourist. "You'd do well to belt up, mate. The yank's a right boomer and'll likely stomp the bollocks off a no-hoper the likes of you. He's got the bleedin' obi-folks on his side."

Wells looked astonished. "You don't really believe that rubbish, do you?"

Nassau Dave brought the engines to life. "You're aboard my boat now, sport, and I'm the god damn captain." He lowered his voice to that of a stern warning. "You give me one more ounce of shit and I'll gut you throat to nuts and feed you to the god damn sharks."

Tommy found a faint smile and a sigh. *I guess all pirate crews have their ups and downs.*

A massive array of engines propelled the long, thin power boat and Dave struggled to stay under the channel limit. Tommy tidied the lines and met Ian halfway. They settled into vinyl cushions and watched the passing scene not so much for its tourist memories as for anyone using spotting scopes or binoculars watching them. The growl of the engines masked their voices and assured privacy while Tommy spoke and Wells listened. Eventually Ian nodded. They shook hands just as Nassau Dave came to starboard and cut his engines to idle.

Dave aligned the bow of the Pantera with the empty dock adjacent to a deserted stretch of narrow beach. Tommy and Wells wrapped lines around cleats, and as the noise level diminished to just the wavelets tapping on the hull, Wells whispered, "On your honor as a gentleman, Thomas, not a word."

"Agreed." The three men stood silently to await the appearance of Yenchenko and his captives.

Even if he's the only trooper on the parade ground, Sergei loves precision. Exactly as promised and right on time, he backed a small box truck into the dusty path that served as a boat launch and exited the vehicle with an AK-47 in his hand.

Wells shook his head. "That bastard could stroll into a church and come out armed to the teeth."

Tommy said, "Oh, I don't know. He'd blow up half a town to take out a sentry. You'd bring that H&K and be a hundred miles to sea before they figured out where the shot came from."

Wells dusted off the compliment with a scowl. "And you, Thomas?"

"I'd cheat."

"Of course. I should have guessed."

Sergei grunted a coarse command in English toward bound and hooded hostages in the truck. As each tumbled to the ground, Yenchenko prodded them to their knees in a neat row. One by one, they were loaded aboard the boat. As they prepared to cast off, Tommy turned to Nassau Dave. "Need a bit of advice from a local expert," he said.

Dave's eyes drifted across the tabeejah and he offered a weak salute but an eager smile. "At your service, guv."

"Best place to be properly outfitted for a round of golf?"

Dave rubbed his chin. "High or low?"

"Lyford Cay," Wells said.

"Try Wallace and Speers on East Bay, but mind you, they're a bit pricey."

Ian sighed. "Don't fret, mate. He cheats."

Chapter Twenty Six

Lyford Cay, New Providence Island, The Bahamas

Tommy approached the tenth green with all the aplomb of a second-round leader at The Master's and tugged a soft glove onto his right hand. He had a putter tucked under his arm and a ball in his pocket.

Tall and lean and weathered by a lifetime of sunshine, Walter Campos leaned on his putter and wore a smug smile. He called out in a voice filled with all the self-assurance that a multi-billionaire could muster on a Thursday. "Splendid of you to join us, Mister Kane! We're each lying three, and I'm afraid you've missed the first four hundred yards."

Tommy tapped the brim of his cap in salute and presented an easy smile. "Sorry, sir. Traffic, you know."

Walter's aged eyes twinkled. "That's all right, son, that's all right." He waved to his companion. "You know Max Siegel, I'm sure. Max produces all those action films, major studios, and he's trying to persuade me to go in on a new project for thirty million. Max, this young fellow is a friend of mine, Mister Tommy Kane, from Louisiana. I'm sure you know the Kane family. Good stock. Well established."

Tommy and Max shook hands as if they were at an LSU alumni reunion. Both said "Of course" and "Good to see you," even though they had never met. Max looked stout but not flabby and on the sad side of sixty-five. He gave Tommy a fast once over through thick, dark-rimmed glasses while his smallish mouth wrapped itself around an immense cigar. He wore a floppy hat in contrast to the long-billed khaki baseball cap that crowned the white mantle of Campos.

Oblivious to the artificiality of the moment, Walter cruised onward to declare that Max might put the arm on Tommy for a few million and loaded up key words with an extended bass drawl as if to admire his own speech. "It's going to be one of those *spy* movies with a lot of *car chases* and *gun* battles. What do *you* think, Tommy?"

"Wow, I don't know much about the movie business. Sounds a bit scary to me."

Walter laughed and spoke with confidentiality that rose into fanfare, each word drawn out a bit longer than normal and injected with astonishment. "You know, Tommy, if you ever want to get into the movie business, Max is the man to see. Film. Television. Distribution, those places that people rent movies from. It's a god damn *entertainment empire.*"

Max turned his focus back to his ball. "But no fucking porn We make family features, nothing more than PG-13. Well, a few R-rated, but only when the money's right. You interested in the business, Mister Crane?"

"Kane. Sorry, but I'll probably take a pass."

Siegel drew a deep breath and exhaled annoyance. "Yeah. Yeah, you would. You young money guys today got no balls. In my business, you got balls or you got nothing. Isn't that right, Walter?"

Campos grinned. "That's an *uphill lie*, Max. You can make a fortune on one of your movies, and you can screw a starlet like no tomorrow. But you can't putt down hill worth a shit."

Siegel crouched to study the twenty feet of tightly cropped lawn between his ball and the pin. He stood, stepped left, then right, crouched and stood again.

Indecision. Tommy recalled the words of his college coach, a fair player who never quite made the tour. *Indecision's a grave sin for a serious golfer. A second of doubt and you blow the putt.*

Max circled the line between his ball and the pin and paused before he began a second circuit to tap ash from the cigar. Out on the fairway, four men hovered in a tight group about 150 yards away, near the consequences of soft tee shots. Beyond them, the clubhouse and scattered estate rooftops peeked above the tree line. To the left and right, lush fairways and soft greens, guarded by generous but tricky traps, created the 18 holes of a very private playground for the very wealthy and very powerful.

Walter cooed advice. "It might go left, Max. But not too much, I think, not too much. Green's fast, too. O'course, it's an *uphill lie*."

Max dropped the cigar just off the green and approached his ball.

Walter turned to Tommy. "We're playing a round for a hundred. So it's understandable that Max is taking his time on a tricky *uphill lie*."

Siegel nodded, turned and squinted toward Tommy. "What do you think, Mister Kane?"

Tommy smiled. *Campos is working on Max's mind, and doing a good job, too. He's probably going to win that hundred bucks. Maybe.* "I think it's a makeable putt. But it might run a bit right. Just a bit."

Walter studied the turf under his feet, then lifted his head to show a broad grin and twinkling eye. "It's an *uphill lie*, Max. Be a good fellow and take your shot."

Max scowled and turned to see the lie from a fresh perspective. "Twenty says I drop it."

"Twenty bucks?"

Max stepped up to the ball and muttered, "Twenty thousand."

Heat rose in Tommy's cheeks and curled through his ears. *They're playing for a hundred grand, not a hundred bucks.*

Walter Campos ignored Tommy's raised eyebrows. "All right, Max. Twenty's fair. If it takes twenty for you to finally get over your jinx on an *uphill lie*, so be it."

Max again stepped away from the ball, his concentration shattered. "Goddammit."

Walter was unperturbed. "Let's sweeten the pot. If you miss, you'll have to donate fifty or so to Warren Sterling's senate campaign."

"And if I drop it?"

"Why, Max, you have to think of the future of the country. All those endless possibilities that made us the men we are."

Max had recovered his cigar and stoked it back to full cloud generation. The conversation continued as though Tommy was not there. "Sterling's a Republican. I hate goddamn Republicans."

Campos sighed. "Max, Max. You have to get past that union mentality. It doesn't really make any difference whether he's a Republican or a Democrat or an Episcopalian. He'll be *our* senator, looking out for *our* interests. I believe that's how the game is played, Max. Even from an *uphill lie*."

Max remained unconvinced. "Episcopalian matters, already. My late mother, whom I loved dearly, hated goddamn Episcopalians."

Campos slowly shook his head. "All right, Max. He's not an Episcopalian. Take your shot. But remember, it's an *uphill lie*."

Max rubbed his chin, grabbed his club and stepped up to the ball. "Fuck it."

Walter leaned into his putter and studied a cloud high overhead.

Max practiced a backswing that was too short and would leave him at least six feet from the pin. *He's going with a break to the left. He's doomed.*

From somewhere, a cell phone chirped to demand attention.

Max cursed, stepped away from the ball, and dug into his pocket to take a call.

Campos whistled a gentle tune and continued to study the cloud while Siegel poured epithets on whoever was on the other end of the call.

Every second, his face got redder, and his hands began to shudder. *The putt's no longer makeable.* Out on the fairway, the next group paced about in frustrated circles. A bit of offshore air picked up and the scent of the sea filled Tommy's nostrils. The image of the Alden drifted into his mind and the freedom that went with it tugged at his soul.

Siegel completed his call. "Look, I gotta get my pilot, get to New York. Fucking money guys are hung up on some financial shit, which I gotta settle or I'm out a fucking bundle. Like fucking now. God damn sons of bitches – "

Walter put on the worst artificial expression of surprise and sympathy Tommy had ever seen. He cooed in a voice that would calm a wounded bear. "Aw, too bad. Max, it's just not your day. But that's all right. No harm done. We'll let the wager go, o'course. Try again another day."

Max seemed to be lost in the business problem and recovered his cigar and stalked off toward the golf cart. "Yeah, yeah. Another time."

In a voice that blended compassion with encouragement, Walter called out, "Just leave my clubs on the ground. I'm sure Mister Kane will share his cart."

"Yep," Tommy said. "No problem." *Wow, Max must be in a real jam. Didn't even pick up his ball.*

Max Siegel half scampered, half stomped toward the cart. Campos cocked his head and found his grin, dripping with way too much innocence. "Shame about our round. I would have liked to clip Max for that hundred. But I also thought we might chat a bit about, well, something of a proposition. If you're interested, o'course. If you're interested. Care to play a few holes, get some air, Mister Kane?"

Just something strange going on here. "That call Max got. It was no coincidence, was it?"

Walter began to organize protest, but knew he looked away and relented. "Very perceptive, Mister Kane. It wasn't. But if you had been just a bit later, I might have won a bit on that putt." He used the shaft of his club to point at Siegel's untouched ball.

"It's a makeable putt," Tommy contended.

"It's an uphill lie. Twenty feet. Wicked break to the left."

"Nineteen and a half and it's going to break right."

"You're pretty sure of yourself, Mister Kane. I like that trait in a fellow. A fine trait it is."

Tommy heard his grandfather's words. *I may not be right, but I am sure.* He wanted to shake his head to banish stray thoughts and keep his mind clear, but couldn't because it would be a tell of indecision. So he shrugged to gesture certainty in his words but indifference at the prospect of proof.

Walter seemed amused. "Well, then, son, give it a try. Fifty says it breaks left."

"Sorry, I don't have that kind of money."

"I'd be glad to take your marker."

"No, thanks. I don't owe anybody and I don't plan to start today."

Campos studied the head of his putter but said nothing.

Tommy glanced at Max Siegel's ball and a relatively simple lie. *Now he's stuck with indecision. Be prepared to walk away. Sergei and Ian and I can run our little op, make a few dollars, and get out of town. I don't need this. Or do I?* The breeze that might have disturbed Siegel's putt faded into calm. The tabeejah around his neck on a line of leather seemed to pull on his neck. Walter's putter head rolled back and forth on the green. "But I'll do it for fifty dollars."

Campos looked up. A twinkle of sunlight danced in his eyes and he cocked his head. "You've got yourself a wager, Mister Kane."

Tommy tugged the putter from under his arm and tested the weight of it with his right arm. He smiled and approached

Max's ball. "Tommy. Friends call me Tommy," he said.

"I'm not sure we're friends. Yet. But it's still – "

"A makeable putt. Chatter all you want."

"I'm not going to get into your head, am I?"

"No. No, sir, not at all."

Campos beamed satisfaction. "I didn't think so. Well, then, son, show me what you've got."

Tommy walked up to pull the flag, then returned to Siegel's ball. He squatted to check the grade of the green and picked up a scrap of litter as a cover to feel the grass for its speed. After he verified his guess on distance, he picked a spot just over a foot beyond the cup as a target. Tommy took a pair of practice swings, the first too long, the second about right, and put the sweet spot right on the ball.

Eye on the ball, he told himself, *nice even stroke.*

Campos cleared his throat. Terns called to each other a short distance away, where the sea caressed a narrow beach.

Concentrate. Eye on the ball, he told himself again and, as he went completely deaf, *nice even stroke. Nice and even.*

The putter swung like a perfect pendulum. The shot was launched into a gentle curve. As predicted, it broke right, not left. The ball skittered a bit on the tips of turf, then rolled smooth. It clattered dead center into the cup.

Campos nodded approval. "You're a very resourceful man, Mister Kane."

Tommy reached into the hole to retrieve the ball. "Why would you say that?"

"Because you're here to play a little golf, in one of the most securely gated communities in the western Hemisphere. I suspect that tabeejah helped?"

"Yes, I suspect it did. The security guys at the gate appeared deferential."

Campos stepped up to his marker, placed his ball and fondled his putter. "So, you've been out to Cat Island to see that obi-fellow, Joseph something-or-other."

"Joseph Akintunde. The Obi-man."

Walter took a short practice swing. "And you went to his kumina. Got your initiation. And now you've got a *key*. I wanted to do that once. Offered the fellow a small fortune for the chance. But he said he didn't want to deal with the devil. Do you think I'm the devil, Mister Kane?"

The Obi-man's words. *What is money but paper and metal? Only the path to evil. Joseph didn't want to deal with money. Campos misunderstood.* "I think I have a tabeejah, and you don't."

Campos took his stroke, a bit too firm. The ball careened off the outside corner of the cup and came to a stop two feet left of the hole. He accepted his fate without complaint, and tapped it in.

"I would have given you that two-footer."

Campos used his club shaft to balance himself while he pulled the ball from the cup. "There's no gimme's in my world, Mister Kane."

"Tommy."

"As I said, Mister Kane, a very resourceful man. I like that in a fellow, resourcefulness. It suggests you might be helpful to a man like myself."

"I'm not looking for a job."

"I didn't say *work* for me," Campos replied in a patient tone. "I said *helpful*. A man, a cautious man, a resourceful man, who might do someone a favor. At my level, Mister, well, Tommy, fellows do favors for friends. There's always a bit of a *quid pro quo*, o'course. *Always*."

"Of course."

With a wave of his arm, Campos directed Tommy to the cart and motioned the impatient group still in the fairway to proceed with their second shots. "We might have a common interest, Tommy." He paused for a moment. "Do you mind if I call you Tom?"

"You can call me anything you like. But friends call me Tommy."

Walter chuckled. "Of course, son. Of course. Anyway, I believe we might have a common interest. And I rather suspect collaboration might be, well, mutually beneficial."

The worst that will come of this is a relaxing eight holes of golf with some wacky old billionaire. Maybe I'll get an Alden out of it. Just hear the old guy out. "Always willing to listen."

Walter Campos grinned broadly. "Splendid! Let's play some golf. No wagers. Just for fun. A couple of fellows out for a nice afternoon's amusement. And a proposal that I believe you'll find difficult to pass by."

CHAPTER TWENTY SEVEN

As they approached the eleventh tee, Tommy's feet savored the kind of soft and luxurious carpet he had forsaken years ago for the rough realities of a troubled world. Even the sea, with all its possibilities, had a certain firmness. Sandy's well-mannered yacht could hammer a wave and everyone aboard would have to absorb the texture of a living ocean in their ankles, knees and sometimes hips.

But Lyford Cay was an oasis of pampered and gentle accommodation that the very wealthy arrange for themselves, within a sanctuary of comfort secured by sturdy walls and staffed gates, a bastion that defined civilized insiders as much as it precluded troublesome peasants, a shrouded community in which people were still people and sometimes behaved poorly, but unnoticed.

With each step, he ticked off a list of names of private pockets of vast wealth and substantial influence on half a dozen continents he discovered after he was orphaned in circumstances that most of the residents of Lyford Cay could not begin to grasp. As much as Lyford Cay reminded him of all the reasons he had abandoned Louisiana society, the soft grass underfoot, the soft pop of tennis balls on club hard courts, the soft air from Old Fort Bay conspired to cause soothe and relax him in touchpoints of serenity.

A generous tee ground displayed gold, blue and white markers for players of varied strength, barely scuffed by pop-up hitters.

"Par three," Walter Campos declared with all the gusto of a man eager to conquer a mountain. "I'm an old man, playing the blue today at 153 yards. But if you'd prefer gold, it's one-sixty-two." He paused, then added, "Or maybe white at one-forty-seven." Campos drew a five iron to gamble on a perfect swing.

Two decades ago and with the wind at his back, Tommy would have shown off and pulled a seven iron and taken wagers for at least a pitcher of beer. He was wiser now, out of practice and the breeze erratic. He would have preferred a six iron to unleash emotions and really clobber the ball, but had gone cheap at Wallace & Speer's and carried a light bag. A restrained five iron would have to do. He opted for the gold tee box.

With a broad wave of his arm and an easy grin, Walter said, "I'll give you the honor. Go ahead and punch that puppy. Right at the pin."

Tommy tested the balance of the shaft in his hand, set his ball and took a pair of practice swings to rediscover the game. He sought encouragement from the memory of his grandfather, but only heard the old man warn, *"That boy, he been feedin' that gator, hopin' it'll eat him last."* Thanks, Paw-paw. With a puff of air, his mind found the eager face of Sergei Yenchenko. *"To live with wolves, you have to howl like a wolf."* *Yeah yeah, a little adjustment. Show the old guy a really nice draw.*

Campos followed the flight of the ball. "Oh, poor luck. You hooked – "

The puff of air found the ball and first-rate backspin stuck it ten feet high of the pin before it rolled a good foot and a half back toward the cup.

" – I guess not. Well played, Tommy."

"This is a really nice course. Play here often?"

"Fellow by the name of Rees Jones designed it. And, yes, I do."

"I've heard the name, but never had the pleasure."

Campos grinned and took a nice swing that put him comfortably on the green. "I'm a great admirer of Jones' work. I was always partial to Congressional, the Blue Course. Thought it was his best. His courses prove he understands the game, not just how it's played. Drives us old duffers crazy, o'course, but this is not intended to be sport for wimps and wussies."

They tucked clubs in their bags and set off toward the green.

Walter continued. "He once said, 'All successful people need to be mindful of what got them there.' What do you think about that?"

"I think I'd agree with Mister Jones that you have to build a few golf courses before you design them. You're very well informed, sir."

"I make it a point to be informed, well, the best I can anyway. Take, for instance, that little gunfight the other day out at the supermarket. *The Nassau Guardian* was all a-twitter about it for a day or so, but as usual the tourist industry stepped in, tamped things back down to a smile. They didn't say a word about Medina's boys, o'course. Not a word. That's for fellows like us to know."

"Or experience."

"Ah, well, experience can be obsolete, Tommy, *obsolete*. For example, an experienced fellow in your trade would logically expect money to be laundered in an exchange of big, black bags. That's not how it's done any more. All electronic transfers, you see, just one computer talking to another for a couple of seconds. Much more efficient, wouldn't you agree? And safer, too. Fellows like your little team can't just stroll in with guns to take it."

"I could lie and say we were just playing along to see how things would unfold."

Campos rummaged in his bag for his putter. "You could, son, you could indeed. But you won't."

"Point made." He tugged the putter from his bag and hoped concentration tagged along. Each man found reward for a shrewd tee shot with easy par and the discussion continued on twelve, which at five hundred yards almost made Tommy regret his commitment to the longer distances.

"But o'course, Tommy, I don't know which of you three actually killed Medina, or that idiot from the CIA. I find it frustrating to be out of the old loop, you see."

"Does it matter?"

"Not at all. Carlos Medina was a foul fellow. Just pond scum, really. No loss and only a temporary setback for all the players. However, a man in my position is willing to pay to satisfy curiosity. It passes the time. Makes for good conversation over a round of first-rate single malt."

Tommy was on uneasy ground with a man who could pull a lot of strings but who nonetheless was an unknown. Because Campos had used Wells to set up the entire thing, he said, "Ian. He got Medina just as I was taking aim."

Campos nodded. "The Major – that is, Ian Wells I believe it is now – he's a good man. Damn fine shot. Knows his business. Reliable. But unfortunately, I believe he's got some issues. Good trooper in the squad. But not the sergeant."

It was impossible to guess how much Campos knew about Ian's circumstances, so he said nothing while he played his second shot from the center of a manicured fairway, about ten yards behind Campos.

Walter chose patience and laid up short of a series of deep bunkers. Tommy pushed too hard on the next shot and was mired in sand with only the rescue of a wedge to keep things even.

"Are you a sergeant, Mister Kane? Wait. Before you say no, maybe out of humility, maybe out of caution, allow me to put it this way: I think you're fine sergeant material, Mister Kane. May we speak candidly?"

That's why I'm here, playing a bad lie with an iron that I can't quite grip properly. "Of course."

Campos easily won the hole. As they strolled to the four-teenth, he said, "You're quite right that I'm well informed. For example, I know a great deal about you. Understandable if that makes you just a bit uneasy. People like ourselves, well, we kind of cherish privacy, staying out of the spotlight, not calling attention to ourselves, wouldn't you say?"

"This looks like an uncomplicated fairway. About 400 yards?"

After a tremendous drive, Tommy had the better lie and a clear approach to the pin. Walter tried a fade, wound up mired in second cut and winced, but kept a curse in check.

My turn to tease. "I'd say you ought to draw your second shot a bit and lay up opposite that big bunker."

Campos paid no attention. "And of course, like all men we have flaws, perhaps an indiscretion or two in our younger days. Something we'd prefer others to overlook. Ignore maybe. Or not be troubled with if they don't know."

"How about forgive?"

Testosterone had begun to bubble. Campos pushed his next shot too hard and left himself with a very long putt. Tommy held back and was short of the pin by fifteen feet. Walter's grin was absent on the long walk across the green. A bogie or worse was imminent. At the first opportunity, Tommy deliberately used too much club toe and blew a shot well right, then fluffed a tap-in while Campos renewed his concentration and they finished the hole with unhappy scores, but even.

Campos chuckled. "Forgive, Tommy? Forgiveness is for dedicated lovers and genuine Catholics, but rare for men such as we."

"People change."

"Leopards never change their spots, and tigers never change their stripes."

And a wolf will always howl. What Yenchenko said on a spring day at Duffy's in San Pedro, when Sergei prepared for another paramilitary adventure and justified his addiction to combat. Now self-doubt flickered momentarily before a puff of air from an unfamiliar place extinguished it.

Campos sailed on. "But it would be fun, wouldn't you agree, to erase it all and start fresh? Maybe we'd not make the same mistakes."

"I wonder. But mistakes, indiscretions, what we regret, they're not going away, are they? And there's really no way to back up, start over, erase anything is there?"

Campos turned. His expression blended patience with a twinge of anxiety as he stepped into candor that he would usually shroud. "Perhaps not all, Tommy, perhaps not all. Some things that cannot be rectified can be *repaired*. I'm an old man. I'd very much like to be remembered in a positive way."

Where's he going with this?

Campos said, "You're a careful man, Mister Kane. Capable and careful. Good combination. But, o'course, you weren't always that way, were you? You *became* capable and careful with *experience*. You *grew* into competence. Not all men do, o'course. Certainly not all men from your background. O'course, I knew your father."

You come from tall cotton, Moses Clay had erroneously said. *My daddy was too poor to paint and too proud to whitewash.* "You probably mean my uncle." Tommy approached a simple six-foot putt and knew he shouldn't have begun the stroke while thinking about it.

"No, I mean your *father.* Jake Sonnier."

But the club face was in motion. *I should have stepped back. But didn't. Too late.*

"Oh, bad luck. Your putt went well off the mark."

Two feet wide and four feet long. Anger rose under the tabeejah. *This guy's got the golf manners of a gorilla.* "How did you know him?" He tapped the bogie putt with too much indifference and left it an inch short and his spirits sank even more.

Walter's words were filled with casual reminiscence. "We roughnecked awhile in West Texas, then worked rigs in the Gulf. Years ago. He's gone, now, o'course, got careless with some heavy equipment. Nice fellow, hard drinker, a bit reckless, I'm afraid."

Had to be after he ran off, went drifter. Well, at least I know how it turned out. Or am I just being played by Campos? Why would he make up a story like that?

Campos looked sincere, even a bit sad to be the bearer of news that would cause a reaction in most men, but not Tommy.

Walter brightened the conversation with a change of topic. "Tell me, when was the last time you wore a suit? I don't have to get gussied up very often, but do so from time to time, you see. You strike me as the sort of fellow that might not even own one. The kind of fellow who travels light. Efficient. Simple and unfettered seems to be your style, your fashion."

The last time I wore a suit was in Germany. Not even a suit, really. It was a blue sport jacket with grey slacks, a dress shirt with no tie. My favorite loafers. Didn't even notice them while I played chess with Dieter and Myra walked up. Buses went by, then the cars. There's Mather and Lester and it all went to dust and dirt and grime from there.

"It's been a while. Can't say that I miss it."

"But you could wear one if you had to?"

Tommy shrugged. "Depends on the circumstance, Walter." *I'm getting impatient. What's the old fox want? How do I ask? Push and he'll dust me off. Beg and he'll use me like a Costa Rican whore. Leave it, and so will he. This way.* "Perhaps I can do you a favor."

Campos seemed relieved. "Perhaps you can. A person with your range of talent and skill could help set some things to right. And I'd be grateful, very grateful."

The conversation lapsed into intermission on the fifteenth. A par four of charm and comfort, it allowed both men to relax into casual play that carded bogies for both, but without anxiety. And it gave Walter Campos time to organize his thoughts before he stepped onto the tee of the 429-yard sixteenth hole, which Tommy would play at 455 from the gold markers. No disappointment, no anxiety. Just a certain freedom when he pulled the driver from his bag and launched a tremendous shot that, once aloft, hitched a ride on a fair wind.

Walter applauded. "Magnificent shot. Magnificent. A touring pro could not have done it better. Did you know, Mister Kane that we have, well, had, a mutual acquaintance? Fellow who ran a little hotel outside of Augsburg."

Dieter Kreutzer. He's not gathering his thoughts. He's nervous, oddly vague. Maybe long range surveillance? Keep moving, don't get specific. "Played a great game of chess."

"Something of an ornithologist, too. But not very good at bird-watching, I'm afraid."

Blackbird. And he got killed because he made a mistake, pushed the wrong button, asked the indiscreet question. "I'm familiar with his interests."

"He was a good friend, a colleague in fact. We did some business many years ago. There are some records, a file."

"There's usually a record of business transactions. Often stored in safe places."

Walter's second shot was forty yards shorter than Tommy's, and Walter laid up to avoid a nest of bunkers. By the time the golf cart caught up with Tommy's ball, he had already decided to gamble on a bump and run to attack a narrow gap and a low rise to the apron of the green. Just before he addressed the ball, he took a casual practice swing and looked around for eavesdroppers who toted technical gear rather than golf clubs. A shortage of good cover, but Campos was clearly off his game. The view would be better just above the pin and smiled when his gamble paid off and the ball obeyed, skipping across the fringe into safety on the green.

Walter nodded, but seemed tired and again reached for an

abrupt change of subject. "I'd like to invite you to an event Saturday evening, Mister Kane. It's here at the club, one of those charity things to save something or other, where all the up-and-comers overdress and fellows like me go to enjoy the game. Black tie. I understand some important people will be there. Carter Blackmann, for example."

Black tie. Black flag. Blackbird. Blackmann. "Never actually had the pleasure."

Campos opted for a pitching wedge and dropped his third shot to within four feet of the pin with a much better lie than Tommy. "Really? I would have thought – well, not important I suppose. Sometimes prudence is just as remarkable as a fortunate gamble, don't you think?"

Tommy's laughed was too artificial. "Maybe Mr. Blackmann has your records tucked away in a file cabinet in Langley."

"No, I don't believe so. We've already looked into that. I have some well-placed people working on it, and they assure me the files I'd very much like to recover are elsewhere."

Tommy opted for a safe first putt and the consequential tap-in. "Certainly the assets you have at hand are capable of resolving this matter?"

"Oh, I'm sure. But I'd prefer to outsource this project." Walter took his time, and produced a par.

"How come?"

"Why, deniability, Mister Kane, deniability." He lowered his voice. His eyes twinkled and the grin on his face was pure arrogance. "If my people fail, it only compounds my problem. If you fellows fail, well, Mister Kane, you simply die."

CHAPTER TWENTY EIGHT

Near Her Majesty's Prison, New Providence, The Bahamas

On a pole halfway into the Straw Market, within the stand of Deacon Cole, the chalk marks of Wells and Yenchenko proved Tommy was the last to arrive, and that the mission to the outlying cay with the captured agents had gone well. Plus, his partners had not killed each other.

As a dead drop, it was ideal. A sea of tourists flowed slowly through the aisles, oblivious to espionage activities, in quest of the sort of souvenir bargains Cole offered: phony native handbags and African print scarves mostly smuggled in from China by way of Panama, free of duty and comfortable in profit.

Sammy the Taxi Driver had been hired by Sergei to periodically drift past. Each mark was a signal to find the maker on the dock; when the total reached three, he was to wipe them all clean and hand Cole sixty dollars.

Tommy waited for Sammy in the shadow of an enormous cruise ship, watched tourists come and go and considered possibilities. Blackbird. Blackmann. Carter Blackmann. Deputy director of operations. An unsettling concept that conjured a wide range of speculation. The preferred version was that Blackmann was then, as now, CIA, and had successfully infiltrated the East German Ministry for State Security, the Stasi. But the problem was why would he come after Dieter long after the Wall came down? Long after Germany reunited? And after all, for the most part, was forgiven? The German government had swooped up all the Stasi files before the Americans or Russians could get to them and presumably wouldn't have been surprised if the CIA's expected activity was in the net. They'd probably just turn it over to their pals in Langley anyway. So why kill Dieter, even if the old East German spy was still obsessed with it? What was he going to do with it? Write a letter to the editor of the Augsburger Allgemeine?

That was the preferred concept.

But Dieter had once said something odd about Blackbird.

Tommy put himself back at least a dozen years to the Fünfgratturm Tower, an ancient security structure mostly closed to tourists. Something about the stairs. The stairs were rotted out, something like that. They were going to fix the stairs, but Dieter didn't know when. The meeting had been set up with some difficulty after a rendezvous at Dom Saint Maria. Just an exchange of envelopes, something having to do with a diplomatic problem.

The Ring of Mercy. Dieter had a great sense of humor even then. But it didn't work out. He said Blackbird screwed it up. Dieter almost walked away. A terrible time setting up a new meeting. If Blackbird was a ally, why would he screw it up?

And so they met for only a minute or so, at Fünfgratturm. Dieter was in a foul mood. He was sweating. In April, on a chilly day, just before a rain. He looked like he had been running, but he was not a runner, not even then. He muttered something, almost a growl, but just sort of out of frustration: Verdammte you-something. Was Blackbird was working for someone else? Had that someone else had infiltrated the leadership of the CIA?

Tommy sighed when Sammy's taxi pulled up by the dock.

I think I'd like to ask Carter Blackmann why he had Dieter Kreutzer killed. I think I'd like to ask him about C-213. I'd like to know why I got black flagged. I'd love to know what he has on Wal-

ter Campos.

Tommy climbed into the taxi. "Where to?"

Sammy chuckled. "I find you fellas some nice place to kick back and have your talk. Over the hill. Into the bush. To a place where the white man does not go."

The cab took an unhurried and varied path through the narrow streets of eastern New Providence Island, further and ever further from the coastal rim of the tourists and the wealth. When certain he was without a tail, Sammy's route became more direct and the taxi came to a stop near a liquor store with a sign next to it that said Kirki Bar.

"You carryin', Mister Cat-man?"

"No."

"Then you be plenty certain to let that tabeejah show." Sammy advised. "Your friends, they be in the back, outside. Don't be hangin' inside, tabeejah or no. I'll park the taxicab, come back in a while."

Wells and Yenchenko were in a sheltered patio behind the bar, fifteen miles and worlds apart from the luxury of Lyford Cay. Through an open window, the very deep bass of a locally popular radio favorite thudded into the sunshine and masked domino game table talk and masculine banter of a ghetto rum shop.

Sergei and Ian took turns recounting the tale of the high-speed run in Nassau Dave's craft, of how they stripped the hostages of outer wear to encourage them to stay sheltered from the sun, and how they tossed them into shallow water while the sand sharks, properly primed with chum, swarmed nearby. Yenchenko's eyes twinkled while he described the breasts of the women as being too small for his taste. Wells scowled annoyance, then changed the subject to the extent of provisions and supplies they had left for the captives. Sammy arrived with a second round of beer and stood patiently to the side while Tommy reported on his activities at Lyford Cay. Like the head of cold beer too quickly poured into a warm glass, apprehension grew.

Tommy concluded, "So the bottom line is that he wants us to steal some sort of file with his name on it from the CIA, then either destroy the file or deliver it, whichever is easiest."

A half-empty bottle of Kalik turned in the thick and calloused right hand of Sergei Yenchenko, propelled by his thumb into a counter-clockwise direction. He had listened with the close attention of a skilled debriefing officer and was settled back as comfortably as he could be in a metal frame chair on the verge of collapse.

"Well?" Ian prodded Yenchenko. "Say something to discourage this idiotic endeavor."

Sergei leaned back again and rubbed his chin. He stared long and hard into Tommy's eyes, who found the faintest of smiles and refused to flinch.

"So, Koshka, how much does this Campos pay for file?"

"Good heavens," Wells cried. "You can't be serious!"

Yenchenko raised a hand to silence the Englishman. "We take small moment to listen to *Tovarich* Kane."

"Have you lost your mind?" Wells asked in an exasperated tone that faded into resignation. He looked first at Sergei, then Tommy's implacable expression.

"Small moment," Yenchenko repeated in a soft voice. He looked to Tommy, and the eyes of Ian Wells followed.

The light breeze withered and muggy heat descended with silence onto the table. Somewhere a dog barked and a motorbike sputtered past on the street. Even the radio music vanished and light laughter from the domino game escaped through the window behind Wells. Sammy leaned in a bit to hear a conversation that had withdrawn into whispers.

Tommy began to reach for his beer, but changed his mind and leaned forward instead. "There's a front company, probably just on paper, where the laundering takes place. The C-213 group apparently got hold of it when it was legitimate. Campos believes they reduced it to an office and then just closed it up. The only assets left are, of course, the cash. Campos was a quiet investor, got pushed out. Not too happy about it and would like to have it back. But he's willing to give it up in exchange for that file."

Ian's eyes narrowed. "Give it up to whom? Us? What would we do with it?"

"Strip it. Split it. Three ways, walk away."

Yenchenko cocked his head. "What is value of asset?"

"Campos says it's nearly a billion dollars U-S."

Ian muttered, "And he would know this how?"

"He's got someone on the inside. He says, anyway."

Wells reached for his bottle. "Oh, right. I've heard better lies a dozen times daily. And I've got a bridge over the Thames for sale." He took a sip but looked like his head had already left the island.

Yenchenko shrugged. "*Da, da*, Koshka. And I have uncle in Kiev."

"Serge, you were the one with the solid intel, from a brothel, about actual cash changing hands at that supermarket loading dock. Ian, you were the one who channeled that intel to Sergei on instructions from Campos, and showed up half hoping it might actually be true. And guys, it was Campos who told me that we should have known better, that money in that volume doesn't travel in a suitcase. It's all done electronically, wire transfers and computers."

Wells and Yenchenko looked at each other, then back at Tommy, who paused in his story to take a sip from his own and not very cold bottle.

Yenchenko pursed his lips and muttered an obscenity in Russian.

"Thomas, For once Sergei and I agree. We're hardly surprised, Thomas. The old Yank is out for a bit of cheap freelance because he's been sloppy and left a paper trail. I'd wager a tenner that the CIA are perfectly justifiable in holding the codger's marker. Sorry, mate, I'm not so keen on the idea either. Whilst Campos is trying to make us drool, we're having a go at our own nice little operation, from which we might actually have a bit of fortune and get off the island with a bit of cash. And our lives."

Yenchenko leaned forward and folded his hands on the tiny wood-plank table, barely large enough for a couple of drinks and a light game of dominoes. "Koshka, Koshka," he said in a tone designed to soothe rather than challenge. "You must hear own word, *da?* We make simple operation, and..." He turned to Wells first, then Tommy. "Please: how does one say *vykup?*"

"Ransom," Tommy and Ian answered in unison.

"*Da, da*, of course. We make simple operation and *ransom* CIA hostage, make depart. Like old wolf, we return to safe den in forest. This Campos proposal, Koshka, I think chance for success become most small. Outcome is most poor. *Pisdect.*"

Ian sat with arms crossed while he leaned back so far that the front legs of his chair rose and fell to the ground. He rocked in cadence with a soft wind that crept over a rusted corrugated metal privacy screen attached to the weary chain link, often topped with barbed wire, that lined the edge of the road and scarred the bright, saturated and various hues of paint on small bungalows and cottages. "It's that damned Blackbird business, isn't it, Thomas? You simply can't let go of it. A trifle sad, I think."

Sergei gave Tommy a look of pity. "Koshka, we do not give fuck about this most ancient history." He hoisted his empty bottle to signal Sammy for another round.

"Look, Thomas, we're respectful colleagues and alive and some of us have moved on. I cautioned you about making this personal. Your loyalty is admirable. But Dieter's dead. Mather, or Matthias or whoever he was, is dead. The blokes that came after you in the black flag incident are dead. You're out of the CIA. So what if this Carter Blackmann is Blackbird? So what if he's got paper on Walter Campos? Serves the old bastard right. I'm beginning to regret —well, I actually *do* regret — having done a simple errand for him. Got us all into a bit of a bother, I'm afraid. My view is that we cut our losses and retire from the field."

Tommy said, "I'm not so sure. They'll send reinforcements. I'm guessing Blackmann himself is the case officer on this op and he's coming to town. Even if we don't take on this missing file thing, we're going to see some action. We could up the score at the very least."

Wells appealed to Yenchenko for support. "Poor fellow's gone daft, Sergei. Utterly daft. Say something, damn it."

Sergei spoke in a firm, but soothing tone. "Task is most difficult, Koshka. We must use all new technologies for such a plan. These are skills we do not have."

"Precisely, Thomas. That rather leaves us out in the rain without a mack. We're old school and avoid that sort of rubbish. For a good reason, I might add."

Yenchenko nodded. "*Da, da.* All at table know what make journey over air or wire may be heard by *sogliadatai*, person who – "

Tommy interrupted. "Eavesdroppers, I know. But in our line of work, it's getting to be a bit difficult."

Wells said, "It's kept us alive thus far." But his eyes drifted downward and settled on the neck of the empty bottle before him. "Although it's likely true that we'd best consider retirement. I myself am becoming less keen about field work with the odds increasingly stacked against me."

Yenchenko seemed less convinced. "I am old soldier. A small bit tired, perhaps, but make comfort in manner that is familiar. Old wolves hunt in such a manner. What is American expression about dog?"

The expression used every time he and Yenchenko spoke about new technologies in the field of espionage. "You can't teach an old dog new tricks."

"*Da*," Yenchenko said as poured beer into his mouth. "It is so."

While the three men sat in silent reflection, Sammy had quietly retreated to fetch another round of Kaliks, and fractured the reverie when he parked new bottles on the table.

"How did you say that front company was worth? In cash?"

"Not quite a billion. U-S."

"Hm. Just for the sake of conversation, let's have a look at the proposal, which from my perspective has two facets. First, we must trust Campos and retrieve his file, which may or may not be *inside* the Central Intelligence Agency in Langley or *some secret location* that is most certainly secured by the CIA. Second, we must somehow break into the CIA's internal system *without being detected*, and then *without any accounting skills whatever* electronically transfer nearly a billion dollars, also presumably well guarded, to some sort of location where we can harvest it."

Yenchenko said, "And unless CIA become most sloppy in recent time, network cannot be breached from outside America border. Soviet and Russian intelligence try without success many time. So I am informed. So. We must now make travel from here to within U.S. with no document. Any document make trail, yes? New border security can easily track, then turn many agent loose to find us, capture, throw into American prison. Perhaps detention camp at Guantanamo Bay? This place us in Cuba, where we have poor fate, I think."

Ian took a turn. "And, of course, a great deal seems to rely on the good will of Walter Campos. What makes you think that he's being entirely truthful? We could snag his file only to discover that this billion dollars is just smoke and mirrors, or, worse, merely smoke."

Tommy enjoyed a sip of really cold beer. *They've talked it out. Now it's my turn.* He leaned forward to set the bottle on the table, but left enough room for his forearms to park on the surface and he folded his hands together. "We get the money first. He's agreed to that. I think they're sort of blackmailing him."

Wells tossed up his hands. "Oh, well, then, we'd simply steal it and be off on our merry way?"

"A contract is a contract." Turning to Yenchenko, Tommy said, "Remember what you said at Duffy's? *Some small obstacles, of course. With no obstacle, task is boring.*"

Yenchenko took a chug of beer and belched. "So you have plan?" He allowed the silence that followed to start squashing the idea.

Can't lose the initiative without some sort of reply. "Kind of, but I've got to work out some details. Cesar said Medina had a private jet at the airport."

"A Gulfstream, a four-fifty," Wells agreed. "Lovely aircraft, but...?"

"I'm trying to figure out how to steal it, re-register it, and manage to fly into U.S. airspace as if it was just a routine corporate flight."

Ian chuckled. "You might have a pilot, Thomas, but we hardly need another partner, especially a Cuban we don't know. Besides, you'll most certainly require a sophisticated computer for that little bit of magic."

Sammy spoke up. "I know a fellow who can help you."

Tommy said, "Daniel? How is he? I'm sorry I forgot to ask."

"Not so well, I think. He not be strong enough for the jail."

Yenchenko asked. "Who is Daniel? What is this about jail?"

Tommy explained the circumstances.

Wells sighed. "Oh, right. In addition to multiple counts of hostage-taking, and negotiating a ransom, now we're going to break a fellow out of jail, who *may or may not* assist us in stealing a forty million dollar aircraft with a wounded chap with *no bona fides* in the cockpit and that *none of us* can fly, forge a complicated set of documents and *manage* to travel into the States, where we'll *rob them* of one of their more secret files and nick a *billion dollars*, and then discreetly vanish to a life of comfort and leisure, and no one will mind terribly."

"Plus we solve the Blackbird puzzle."

"Oh yes, quite right. Almost forgot about that. This project is getting a bit out of hand."

Yenchenko leaned back, suppressed a burp and then heaved a loud sigh. "*El Zorrero*," he recalled. "The fox who steal all your money, then make shit on floor when he depart."

He gets it. Tommy turned to Ian. "We're going to need some paper."

Wells shrugged while he sipped from the bottle.

Then Yenchenko, who shifted his weight in the little chair and looked at his beer bottle for a moment. When he looked up, he rubbed his thumb and forefinger together.

"How much? We're not talking serious stuff here, just enough to work the prison."

Wells interrupted. "Passports, visas, other travel documents? Conning a couple of jail bureaucrats is indeed not complicated, but we do have to clear American customs at some point."

Tommy nodded. "You guys would be more comfortable with the whole package at once?"

Sergei and Ian shook their heads in agreement.

"How much, Serge?"

"For three, within day? Perhaps one-fifty, two hundred. *Thousands*."

Tommy rolled his eyes. "Can't do it. Way out of our budget."

Yenchenko began to argue the case for quality work from a cobbler of substantial stature, one of the old KGB's top men, who had fled to a comfortable but underground existence in Freeport.

"I can go seventy-five for the lot. That's about it."

When Sergei protested, Wells cut him off. "Tell you what, Thomas. Dave and I will pay a call on the man in Freeport, and I'll give him twenty-five. Plus five for Dave."

"Most crazy! What make you believe such foolishness?"

Ian cocked his head, took another sip and smiled. "Because when Thomas and I stroll into that prison, you and your forger will still be alive."

Sergei turned to appealed Tommy, who bumped the ante a fraction. "Tell your guy that I'll owe him a favor. Kind of sweetens the offer wouldn't you say?"

Yenchenko shook his head, then capitulated. "*Da, da*. It is agreed. You are dangerous man, Koshka, most dangerous man." He studied his empty bottle. "But Sergei Yenchenko has nothing else to do today."

CHAPTER TWENTY NINE

Her Majesty's Prison, Nassau, The Bahamas

Tommy drifted through a slow circle near the intersection of Yamacraw Hill and Fox Hill roads. *C'mon guys. This is the fourth time I've crossed this corner. I'm the wrong skin color and somebody's going to get suspicious pretty soon.*

When Sammy's taxi at last swept in from the north, it paused just long enough for Tommy to climb aboard.

Sammy said, "The main gate is just down here. I wait a bit, then make a pass, oh, 'bout every five minutes or so?"

Wells passed a manila envelope with a variety of identification documents. Passports and visas had a good feel to them and would probably clear U.S. immigration without challenge. Unfamiliar with the sort of documents an upscale solicitor from a major firm in Nassau might carry and with no idea about the Ministry of Health, Tommy shared the local documents with Sammy.

It marked the end of a very long night. While Ian and Nassau Dave made the run to Freeport, Tommy gathered props for his own role, and it was close to dawn when the taxi found him near Shirley Street to begin delivery runs. Now the sun shone brightly into the taxi and his eyes suffered in the glare.

Sammy spent some time for a careful look and returned the forged identifications. "Very nice, gents, very nice. You look like you're walk into the magistrate's court, Mister Cat-man, all blue suit and fancy tie. The Major lookin' pretty scary, too, like he about to shut down the business with no license."

Tommy could barely resist a smile at the documents. "Charles Vane? Wasn't he a pirate?"

"Indeed he was, Thomas. Er, Mister Vane. Indeed."

"And you are?

"Bellamy, Samuel. *Doctor* Samuel Bellamy, but most folks call me Sam."

"I'll keep it formal. And our Russian friend?"

"Why Jack Rackham, of course. Yenchenko is still working on pronouncing it properly. He's working the streets to see what new CIA people are in town."

"And here I thought SAS snipers had no sense of humor."

"Subtle, perhaps, Mister Vane, but a proper English gentleman knows when to smile."

Sammy looked puzzled. Tommy explained. "Wells has outfitted us with identities of famous pirates. They set up shop in Nassau a couple of hundred years ago and even formed their own government."

"You be crazy fellas, that's for sure. Here come the main gate." He explained the route to reception and advised them to follow the signs to the Remand Centre. He picked up a thick envelope from the passenger seat and handed it to Tommy. "My solicitor friend, he make the documents as we said last night. He give me these old bags to make you look official. Cost me two bottle of rum, man, but it be worth it if you spring Daniel."

Tommy studied the petition and the magistrate's order while Ian looked over his shoulder to familiarize himself with the scheme. Sammy passed two worn brown leather briefcases to Wells, one for each and both stuffed with an assortment of papers that seemed official. Tommy slipped two packages into his.

"I hope the lines are short today. The shift change is supposed to be at seven, but you never can tell. You be lookin' for an officer named Felix, new fella, tall, kind of thin. He wears glasses, with the gold metal frame, okay?"

Tommy answered with a patient smile. "Got it."

"Okay, so Felix, he be a bit uncertain and will call the supervisor, who is named Dobbin, and he be the believer. He get you what you want. You gents packin'? If so, I hold your guns for you. Otherwise, out you go. Now."

The taxicab slowed to a stop at the prison gate, a sort of tan stucco that curved inward to the jail.

Don't let the façade fool you. When everyone says it's in real need of reform, it's a scary place. The government doesn't want to coddle criminals, and the families of the criminals know full well they're not being coddled.

As Ian and Tommy strode with confidence toward the first hurdle, Ian leaned in to say in a soft voice, "Just keep that filthy animal scrap handy, Thomas. I don't want to stay any longer than necessary."

"That makes two of us."

The deferential but indifferent gate guard pointed to the visitor reception area. When they stepped in, both took a forced breath to remain calm. Benches were packed with dozens of visitors who could wait for hours until the sluggish procedure of the prison might let them actually see the relative behind bars. It was a path that Sammy had followed several times.

Tommy produced a business card and Wells an identification badge, which the reception official studied with an expressionless face. Tommy pulled the envelope from his jacket pocket. "I have a magistrate's order to see my client," he explained, "and Doctor Bellamy is here to make sure the client is all right."

The reception officer began to reach for the envelope, but Tommy pulled it away and stuffed it back into his jacket pocket.

Wells squared his shoulders and stepped forward. "Well, man, look lively, won't you? The Ministry of Health is not to be kept waiting." His eyes narrowed and he leaned a bit forward and pointed. "What's this? A button on your tunic is missing. I daresay, this is something that should be brought to the attention of the proper authority in the Ministry of National Security. I'm quite certain that the Prison Service and the superintendent – "

"Please go ahead," the anxious reception officer stammered. "Remand Centre is just that way there."

Wells lingered. "And do something with that bloody button, eh? This may be a prison, my good man, but we nevertheless have *some* standards, don't we?"

By now the reception officer was on his feet and struggled to form a posture similar to attention. "Yes, sir," he answered with a slight salute.

"Very good, officer. Carry on, then." Wells turned to set the pace at a proper march.

They were halfway to remand when Tommy hissed, "You don't have to make a show of it, Ian."

"The fellow is a disgrace to his uniform. If we weren't committing a fraud, I'd turn the fellow in, have him suspended."

"Yeah, well, we *are* committing a fraud, so take it easy. Sammy says prisoners are packed 30 to a cell, share a slop bucket to relieve themselves, get one bucket of water for bathing, have to sleep on cardboard or concrete, lousy medical care if at all. Not my idea of a place to get stuck in."

"Compared to a couple of places I've seen, this is paradise, Thomas. Remember that secret prison the CIA ran in Romania?"

"Oh, yeah, sure."

"Sammy didn't say anything about car batteries, those big alligator clips, cattle prods, nail pliers, water boards or icy cells, did he?"

"No."

"Then these prisoners have got it soft, don't they? Let's find our man and get on with it."

As Sammy had predicted, the tall, thin officer who wore glasses occupied a small desk under a large sign that said "Remand Centre." The name on his tunic said he was Albert Felix and the crisp creases in his uniform and his polished brass and leather suggested he took his post seriously. A flutter of courtesy crossed his face when he looked up and used a lifted eyebrow to open the conversation.

Tommy offered deference, presented a card and said he and Doctor Bellamy from Ministry of Health were there to find Mister Daniel Akintunde. "Say, you must be new, Albert. I don't recall seeing you before."

Wells seemed surprised at the unexpected tactic, but Tommy had already passed a point of no return. Ian looked relieved when Albert admitted that he'd been on the job for less than a month.

Tommy casually rolled on. "You must be the fellow they hired from that posting. Passed all the requirements, got in your training?"

"Provisionally, Mister Vane. I am serving the probation period for a few months."

"Well, Albert, bravo for you and well done."

"Thank you, sir. Thank you very much."

Tommy began to pull the envelope from his pocket, but Felix was allowed only a brief glance. "So, Albert, I've got a magistrate's order from the Prerogative Board of Mercy for his release."

Confusion swept across Albert's face. "Sorry, sir. I know of no such thing."

"Happens all the time. The superintendent doesn't let the working stiffs know what's going on, eh?"

"If you say so, sir."

Ian produced his credentials. "It's quite all right, Felix. I'll vouch for Mister Vane. Can you at least round up the prisoner and we'll move this right along?"

Albert Felix remained reticent.

At least someone around here is a professional. If this wasn't an op, I'd buy him a beer.

Tommy asked, "Perhaps a supervisor might be of assistance? Is Mister Dobbin available?"

Albert Felix shifted to an expression of relief and reached for the phone parked on the corner of his tiny wooden desk.

He can pass the buck and not make a mistake. Right or wrong, Dobbin will tell him he did the proper thing, might even pat him on the back with a note in his personnel file.

A minute later, a round and soft supervisor stepped into the room and displayed indifference that builds arrogance. Tommy pounced with an eager smile and extended hand, this time sharing the petition and order from his pocket.

Dobbin looked dubious. While three women who sought another prisoner entered the Remand Centre office, he did what all good bureaucrats did: retreat to his lair and hope to guess a solution enroute. "This way, if you please," he said.

Wells followed Dobbin into the supervisor's office and Tommy brought up the rear. As he crossed the threshold, he tugged the tabeejah from under his shirt.

This had better work or we're going to be sharing Daniel's cell with about two dozen other thugs and it ain't gonna be pretty.

Dobbin motioned both visitors to chairs opposite his desk, which was three times the size of the one Albert Felix used. He studied the papers in silence, somewhere between bored and annoyed.

Maybe he's going to simply take a bribe and help us out. Sammy said some do but wasn't sure how much it would take. Some didn't. They were simply enamored with power. Tommy's hand felt the leather briefcase in his lap for the first bundle, wads of Bahamian bills that totaled ten thousand dollars, U-S.

Dobbin extended his hand toward Wells and wriggled his

fingers, demanding credentials.

He wonders whether he's about to be bagged by the guys downtown. He's going to make absolutely sure this isn't a sting.

Dobbin drummed his fingers on his desk and turned again to the documents forged by Sammy and Yenchenko the night before.

Naw, he's going to make some calls. He's not going to take our word for it. He's going to call our bluff.

When Dobbin looked up to speak to Tommy, his eyes froze on the tabeejah hanging from Tommy's neck.

I've got to make sure this is utterly believable.

Tommy reached for campfire memories, when the older boys took to a flickering stage of spooky tales, when younger boys perched on fallen logs, wide-eyed and terrified of creatures that lurked in shadows nearby, when a soft voice of assurance shaped the most outrageous lie into bone-chilling gospel. And from the mists of memory came the cadence of The Old Hag, the Creole voodoo practitioner who lived alone in a cluttered shack eight miles from town on a murky road and cast spells on everyone, including Tommy's grandfather, on many occasions.

In an instant, he discarded the mantle of an attorney and slipped into the cloak of a flim-flam man. He reached into the scruffy brown briefcase and produced a leather pouch, created the night before in a Bay Street novelty store that sold make-your-own-voodoo-charms from a cheery display rack. He weathered the trinkets in an Arawak rum shop, and now delivered a moaning fanfare to a sweating man named Dobbin.

Tommy's eyelids drooped to ease his entire mind into a mystic reverie. The remand supervisor pushed back from the desk. Tommy leaned closer. Dobbin's chair ran out of floor and he pressed hard against the wall, his eyes wide with terror.

From the memory of kumina, Tommy floated into Ashanti chant. *"Obayifo kum wadi-wamma-me, na onkum wama me-na-esua."* He repeated it three times, each slower than the past.

From the bag, a collection of ordinary souvenirs, scuffed and treated to venerable authenticity, appeared in Tommy's hand. One by one, he arranged the collection on the desk. A cat's foot. A dried toad. A pig's tail. Goat kid skin, with cryptic symbols in dried blood. And at last came the goat's horn, a centerpiece from which Dobbin could not look away.

"It – it – it be filled?" the supervisor stammered. His facial skin twitched.

"Yes, Dobbin." Tommy's soft voice descended into a slow hiss. "*Yes.*"

Sweat trickled across Dobbin's forehead. His chest puffed brief, shallow breaths and his hands gripped the edge of the desk but could not escape.

Tommy found the soft voice and inflection of Joseph Akintunde. "Ashes. The blood of the black cat. Human fat. And *dirt from the grave.* These things, they fill the horn."

Wells looked nervous and eased away from the performance. Dobbin gasped for air.

Tommy lowered his trance voice even further and growled to all the walls at once. "*I am Babu.*"

The supervisor began to choke up and whimpered, "Yes. Yes, master. You be the Obi-man."

Tommy pressed on as if he hadn't heard. "*I have taken your shadow.*"

Terror contorted Dobbin's face to the point of tears. "No, no! Please, master! No!" His voice trailed away into a faint moan. Ian shifted in his chair and leaned even further away from Tommy.

"*Obayifo kum wadi-wamma-me, na onkum wama me-na-esua.* I am the Obi-man, the sorcerer who kills with the magic. I be the one who kill the man who eats, but gives the Obi-man nothing. I be the one who does not kill the man who eats, but give the scientist a little piece."

Dobbin gulped for air. "Please, please, master. What... what... what must I do?"

Tommy pulled back a bit as if he were about to abandon the soul of Dobbin the supervisor, and his hand hovered above the goat horn.

Dobbin gasped and a gurgling sound bubbled up from his throat. His shirt was soaked with sweat.

Tommy opened his eyes and sighed. His voice was mechanical, from far back in his throat, as if under the control of some distant and evil force. "It is such a bad thing," he said, "to take the son of Babu, to lock him away in the jail house, to make the child suffer so. He is called Daniel. He is *my* child."

"Yes, master, I... I... I understand."

Tommy's hands, with fingers outstretched, fondled the objects on the desk and Dobbin's eyes obeyed as they followed each movement.

"You are a believer. You know the path of Babu, the way of the Obi-man. You honor him by sharing a small piece of the meal you enjoy, the *suman* that the hunter share with the stranger. Perhaps you give this boy Daniel to these men. Perhaps your shadow will return. Perhaps you will avoid the Obi-water, the water that make you waste away. *And die.*"

A heavy silence hung for an eternity in the small office. Tommy released a breath of exhaustion. With great reverence, he gathered the items, one by one, from the desk and returned them to the leather pouch. When he finished, he took a small cloth and dusted away any magic that might have lingered.

Dobbin bit his trembling lower lip, wiped his brow, and picked up the telephone to order the release of Daniel Akintunde. In his best barrister tone, Tommy agreed that Daniel would be taken not to the remand court at Fox Hill, but downtown, to Nassau. There he would be properly freed by the Prerogative Board of Mercy, for he was no longer a threat to national security.

Ten minutes later Wells and Tommy stood in the courtyard waiting for Daniel. Ian spoke at last. "First rate performance, Thomas. You even had me believing that rubbish."

Daniel stepped into the sunshine, away from the prison guards, free of red and white striped remand uniform and in the rumpled civilian clothes from the day of his arrest.

Tommy turned to Ian. "What makes you think it was just a performance? And what makes you think it was rubbish?"

Wells struggled to harvest some sort of reply, but ran out of time when Daniel drew close to greet them.

Tommy guessed he was in his early thirties, unmarried but not unattached, and in just a few dozen paces had managed to dismiss any emotional trauma from Her Majesty's Prison. His hand stretched out and introductions were exchanged.

"My father sent you, didn't he?"

"No." Tommy wave of his arm to direct him toward the exit from the prison complex. "Why do you ask?"

"You're wearing one of his tabeejahs, Mister Kane. Just as Sammy said yesterday. One of the better ones, too. He does have favorites when he creates them. You've been to Babu's kumina, and he's got you interested in the science." Daniel glanced over his shoulder as they walked away. "They said something about Remand Court?"

"No court. You're a free man."

Daniel grunted and anger flashed in his eyes. "I'm a person of color on an island in the Caribbean, Mister Kane. That's an oxymoron. You seem surprised. A black man in the Bahamas who is educated. It sometimes happens, you know. And now I assume there's some sort of *quid pro quo.*"

Wells hoisted an eyebrow, but said nothing.

Got me. The stereotype of the simple island native who was not properly grateful. I oughta be ashamed. "You're perceptive, Mister Akintunde. And correct. My apologies."

Daniel smiled at both the confession and the sight of his cousin's taxi. Wells opened the door of the minivan and stood to the side. Just before he boarded, Daniel looked directly at Tommy and said, "I have a bachelor's degree in mathematics and a master's in computer science from Stanford University,

Mister Kane. I graduated *summa cum laude* and went to Stanford on a full ride. I am a recognized expert in software engineering and systems analysis. I am very good at gaining entry into mainframes and data manipulation. I'm not at all impressed with island superstitions. Please don't patronize me."

Ian Wells blocked his path to the taxi. His voice lowered to a soft, intense snarl. "Thomas and I did our bit in a couple of no-name schools, mostly paid our own way, did our tours with government work straight from hell. We lie. We cheat. We steal for a living. I'm a professional killer and, trust me, very, very good at it. You got pinched, mate, so you're not exactly the mutt's nuts. I don't particularly give a fuck whether your cousin, your old man, or some West African mumbo-jumbo sprung you from this two-bit shithole. The fact is that this bloke is making a spot for you on a premium league squad. Or maybe you'd prefer to do a ten-to-fifteen in that bleeding dump over there?"

Daniel Akintunde glanced at Sammy, whose reunion joy had faded into a hard stare. Daniel wilted as he took a seat in the cab, and took comfort in Sammy's quick and easy forgiveness.

Ian turned to face Tommy and muttered, "Sergei's quite correct, you know. You're a very, very dangerous man indeed, Thomas."

CHAPTER THIRTY

The Botanical Gardens, New Providence, The Bahamas

In long shadows of late afternoon, drifted among botanical specimens and heard long-ago words from Moses Clay: *Young men have dreams, middle-aged men have ambition, old men have gardens.*

Amusing. Moses had no garden, had forfeited ambition, and had sacrificed dreams. Dreams. No chance for a garden on a yawl. If there ever will be a yawl. Paw-paw *had counseled, You got two choices, boy. Forget your dreams, or pay for them.*

Tommy bent low to examine the Latin name on a plaque, a name which he struggled to form into a sound, a name that meant little other than the recognition that some people must have thought it important enough to plant it, nurture it and give it an identity. Maybe it was time to settle down, own more than a rucksack with a change of clothes, a wad of cash and a gun. Stroll about in the sunshine unconcerned about anyone lurking in the shadows, with a gun. *What's the yardstick for ambition?*

Tommy studied the map from a wire rack just inside the gate. *Being an innocent tourist would be fun. Boring, but fun. Instead, I'm waiting for Wells and then Yenchenko to run a fox-and-hound with an ambush to tie up this crazy game.*

The night before Yenchenko thankfully volunteered to be the fox and bait the trap. Sergei made the rounds of bars popular with off-duty CIA people where he feigned intoxication, spoke a bit too loudly and attracted the desired attention.

The trap was organized on a deserted beach after midnight and launched at Deacon Cole's when the Straw Market opened. As the last man to arrive, Tommy counted two chalk marks on the post and bought a bright yellow silk scarf for ten dollars U.S., saw the cryptic "all clear" message on the receipt, and departed with the scarf in a paper sack in his left hand.

A botanic garden workman, twenty yards distant, raked with deliberation and remained focused on his task. A lot different than the last time, when they stood around. *Ah, okay, there's another one over there and, yep, right behind that little tree, a third. Everyone's working much too hard for this time of day. Yenchenko said there were four.*

Ian appeared from an adjacent path. He studied the same map with a furrowed brow and as he examined the exhibits, inched ever closer to Tommy and said, "Pardon me, sir. Are you at all familiar with the facility? I'm having a bit of a challenge with this frightfully inadequate map."

"You're not alone. Perhaps we can work it out together."

"Well, you're a good fellow! I'm most indebted."

They snuck glances at the workmen on the perimeter and reached the same conclusion.

Tommy tapped his right ear. "Kind of ridiculous."

"Sorry, Thomas, force of habit and all that. We're *supposed* to be burned. Where's Yenchenko?"

"He said there's a fourth guy. Probably reeling him in." Tommy pointed to a feature on his map and they drifted through a slow loop into a wooded area. As soon as they were outside the visual range of the three workmen, Wells handed Tommy a tranquilizer handgun that resembled a toy Lugar and pointed to the safety. They separated and took up cover near immense, dense shrubs.

Ian had a better view of the garden entrance and signaled Tommy when Yenchenko stepped in. Then Sergei's fourth target. The pack formed behind Yenchenko. Two hung back to block the exit. The others trailed him, moving individually, separated by a dozen yards.

Sergei browsed tourist-style, drifting toward the shrubbery. Tommy and Ian took cover on opposite ends of a loop in the path. Yenchenko strolled for a few paces, studied a plant, consulted the guide map, and moved forward at a pace testing the patience of everyone in the tableau. He unexpectedly picked up the pace and hurried into the hidden portion of the path.

The first workman abandoned his rake and wheelbarrow and ran to catch up.

Yenchenko nearly brushed Tommy as he passed and marched a dozen paces forward. Tommy moved deeper into the shrub and froze. Yenchenko turned, put his hands on his hips and produced a grin.

The workman nearly ran around the corner, saw Sergei and pulled up short.

Yenchenko gave a soft wave.

Tommy lifted the dart gun and shot the workman in the back.

Sergei hoisted his fist with a thumb in the air, stepped forward and disconnected a thin wire that ran from the collar of the workman's shirt to his ear. He dragged the body to a bench and deposited the tranquilized agent into a seated position, like the man had simply fallen into an enjoyable nap.

Sergei pointed a finger to the right and stepped back into the path. Wells nodded and faded into the cover while the second agent hurried up the several steps and rounded the corner to find Yenchenko in the same pose. The agent's eyes went to Yenchenko, to the body on the bench and then rolled when Ian put a dart into his neck. As the man crumpled to the ground, Ian disconnected his earpiece in one fluid motion.

Sergei grunted when he parked the second body on the bench. "*Der'mo!* I become too old for such foolishness."

Tommy asked, "You okay?"

Yenchenko waved dismissal. "Most excellent, very good, of course. So. You now reload to capture remaining two flea. Quickly. Sergei becomes bored with game." He pointed toward the direction he would take and used a finger to draw a small circle in the air. As he passed Tommy, he pulled the scarf from the souvenir sack, stepped out into the clearing and waved it high and bold, retreating to an empty bench while Tommy and Ian reloaded. Within ten minutes, the team lined up four unconscious bodies, stripped of identification cards and electronic equipment.

When the last transmitters had been destroyed, Yenchenko was the first to speak. "Sammy come in small moment with utility vehicle, remove these *piz'duk.*"

Tommy stuffed the badges into his pocket. "To the warehouse? That's where we have Daniel and Cesar stashed."

"Not this lot," Ian answered. "To Dave's, straightaway. He's expecting a bonus, Thomas."

"Understood. He'll get a good share."

Sergei grumbled. "And what of Sergei Yenchenko? He is for all day bait, *da?* Where is bonus for Yenchenko?"

Tommy and Ian stared in disbelief.

The Russian shrugged. "I spend much of day to set trap. For me, it would be easier to simply break neck. But I am good team member. Bring them to you alive."

Wells dismissed the complaint with a shake of his head. "Only one really dumb Russian would volunteer to be down range during a live fire exercise."

Yenchenko produced an expression of shock and used it to appeal to Tommy. "So. You see? I must make tolerate of such, such – how you say, *plokhoe otnoshenie?*"

"Attitude."

"*Da*, of course. Such miserable attitude."

"I'll buy you a drink." To an icy Russian glare of annoyance, he added, "Okay, a bottle."

"*Zhmot*, Koshka, always *zhmot*, a stingy person." He stood and produced a paper packet of photographs from his pocket. "Some snapshot. Time pass us by, Koshka. All photos today made from camera with no film. Only one shop in city have camera with film, and make photo from film. Most sad."

Wells leaned in to examine the image in Tommy's hand. Taken in the baggage claim area at the Nassau airport, four of the faces from an afternoon commercial flight matched the unconscious hostages on the bench. Two remaining photos lingered Tommy's hand, an action not lost on Yenchenko.

"So, *tovarich*, you see also, eh? These four arrive as tourist, but when they go to get suitcase, take none, but remain. Not very good, I think. So they become easy target."

"And these two blokes?"

Tommy said, "The younger one was part of the black flag crew in California, the fourth man on the wet team that nearly killed me. He wasn't on the commercial flight?"

"*Nyet*, Koshka. Four men in baggage make depart, but something seem incorrect. So Sergei Yenchenko wait, make some small inquiry. These two come on private jet, have photo taken by clever Russian – me, of course – and quickly leave with no suitcase also. It is small matter to find flight record and manifest with name."

Ian applauded. "Oh, well done!"

Yenchenko seemed astonished at the praise, but immediately cloaked it with a continuation of his report and pointed to the photograph of the younger man. "He is called Lomax. Christian Lomax. *Da, da*, Koshka, I have seen name on paper in jungle."

Tommy stared at the image. *And I heard the name from Lester Finn. The guy running the op here in Nassau. Lomax. C-213.* "And the other guy?"

Yenchenko beamed with all the joy of a man who had discovered the ultimate truth. "He is called Blackmann. Carter Blackmann." He looked directly into Tommy's eyes.

Wells gestured a desire to be let in on the secret.

"Deputy director of operations. The big dog himself. Right on time." *Blackmann. Blackbird?*

Wells cocked an eyebrow. Sammy approached with an ambulance litter.

"Is good, eh?" Sergei said. "We capture biggest fish, make trade for useful circumstance. Or we kill them, get much revenge. I leave choice to you, Koshka, but now I make assistance to Sammy and we dispose of these sloppy agent." He spoke with all the indifferent confidence of a field commander about to tidy up a battlefield and prepare for the next conflict, satisfied with a small victory, even if he hadn't actually pulled the trigger. Yenchenko and Sammy loaded two bodies on the litter for their first trek to the van parked down the hill, near the entry to the garden.

For several seconds, Wells and Tommy watched them go. Then Ian spoke in a soft and gentle tone. "He's a good soldier, Tommy. First rate, well disciplined, an eternal warrior. For a Russian, anyway. However, Thomas, I think we should have a word."

Another complaint. Not this time. The situation is getting too tough for that. "I said before, Ian, you guys have to work it out."

Wells had busied himself with storing weapons and supplies, but looked up and wore an expression of astonishment. "Oh, good heavens, Thomas. I've no professional quarrel with Yenchenko. We're colleagues, after all."

Tommy sighed impatience. "What, then, second thoughts?"

Wells shrugged. "Perhaps. The CIA are a dangerous lot and tolerate just so much annoyance from blokes like us before they become harsh in numbers and force."

"You think that's where we are?"

Wells bit his lower lip and produced a firm glare from a bowed head. "Oh, yes. We've got the deputy director himself in the game now, which means this is no longer a bit of amusement. Even if he hasn't memorized your file, he's got with him the one fellow who can identify you on sight. We've lost the advantage of secrecy. May as well lay in a supply of those citizen band radios."

Tommy pressed on. "So let's go take the com center, get the advantage. I can deal with Lomax and Blackmann. They're just targets."

Wells shook his head. "Do you hear what you're saying, Thomas? You're going to kidnap the deputy director of operations of the Central Intelligence Agency, hold him for ransom and then just flutter away?"

"Yeah, sure."

"Really?" Wells scowled. "It's no longer just about you, Tommy. It's about Yenchenko, myself, Sammy, Daniel, Cesar, your friend Sandy and God knows who else. These are people who don't leave loose ends, mate. This is a first division club and we're a pack of weekend duffers."

"But – "

Wells raised a finger to silence him. "Look here, Thomas, if it were just a raid and run, I might concur. I'm concerned about the escape. The scheme to steal the Gulfstream, fake a crash, resurface with a new registration and fly into the States may not be as simple as it sounds."

Tommy studied their perimeter and pursed his lips. "Daniel seemed to have a plan," he argued. "He's been working with Cesar on it."

"Oh, I'm quite convinced he has the talent to transfer title and do a proper FAA registration. But to fly in from a European destination, even I know you need a flight plan, oceanic clearance, follow the traffic flow and check in on a strict schedule at a series of checkpoints. It's going to require multiple flight plans, transponder changes on the fly, lord knows what else. American airspace is a bit dicey."

Wells paused. "Look, Thomas, I rather like young Daniel, and I'm the first to admit I don't know very much about all this computer rubbish. I'm a bit anxious about this Cesar fellow. We know little about him other than he was running with Medina. But I rather think I can read people fairly well, and I believe Daniel is in over his head. I can see his frustration. I think he's got a problem he's not yet come to admit."

"So your recommendation is?"

"Perhaps we should simply collect our ransom from Blackmann and make our way out of here in a more discreet fashion?"

The breeze from the bay freshened and ruffled leaves in the shrubs and trees around them. Yenchenko and Sammy began the return for the last of the bodies.

"Does Sergei feel the same as you?"

"No idea. I wanted to discuss it privately, Thomas. I've too much respect for command lines to muck about undermining the leader. Look, I'm with you. Just offering a word of counsel, that's all."

Tommy lightly tapped his fist against his lips and weighed alternatives. The deal with Campos and walking away rich beyond belief. But a deal hardly written in stone. Or swap the hostages for cash, maybe an negotiated out. No worse off than before. Or charter a boat, sneak into the States, take off for points south and west. Or hire Dave run through the thicket of druggies and DEA, flop into the East Coast, vanish.

The allure of salt air. The comfort of obscurity. The Alden yawl, floating away on the tide, but was he aboard? Ian waited with patience in a stance of parade rest. Yenchenko prodded Sammy into a quicker pace up the path. The crush of management and organization, longing for the freewheeling, independent style that had been his trademark for years. Yenchenko's words from the meeting at Duffy's: *All who are present may vote.*

"It's not my operation," Tommy told Ian. "It's *ours.* I think we should decide together."

Chapter Thirty One

Bay and Elizabeth Streets, Nassau

A light blue panel truck turned from the steady flow of traffic and backed into an open parking lot space. Tommy opened the passenger door and joined Ian. Behind them, three police uniforms and a tuxedo, hung shrouded in dry cleaner plastic. On the floor a carton of tranquilizer darts kept a box of guns company.

Tommy asked, "Any difficulties?"

"No. Sizes might run a bit large on the khakis and the penguin garb is a forty-two regular with thirty-six thirties."

"Should be perfect. Here comes Yenchenko and Sammy in that ambulance."

Wells shook his head. "They're pressing their luck with that stolen lorry."

"We wrap it up today."

For a couple of minutes, Bay Street traffic crawled from right to left, mostly because of horse-drawn carriages, some painted white, others black and red. The section of street was almost entirely discount jewelers. On the sidewalk near the target, a man paced back and forth while he displayed a diamond merchant's hand sign, and the air shimmered from bright sunshine that overwhelmed a handful of scrubby trees.

Wells sighed. "I rather wish I could go in with a proper weapon. I feel like I'm tossing darts at a girlie pub."

"We're doing okay. We'll be holstered up in a few hours."

"Quite so. You're comfortable with this? Once we hit that post, there's no turning back. Snatching a few hostages is one thing, but that's the belly of the beast up there. They're not going to be keen about a frontal assault."

Wells was correct. *This really is the last moment we can back out, walk away, not become targets.* "Why not? Got nothing better to do today."

The emergency services van backed into the space adjacent to the panel truck and blocked the view Tommy and Wells had of the two story building across the street. They took the cue and got out to rendezvous at the rear of the panel truck. As promised, Daniel was the third man in the truck.

Yenchenko rubbed his chin. "Sammy counts four in control center, but I am not certain."

Sammy said, "The fellow with the sign – Jack – says four. He counts them as they go into narrow stairway and up to the second floor."

Eyes turned to Yenchenko.

"Perhaps it is so. Perhaps it is only three."

Tommy asked, "How long have they been in there?"

Sammy said, "Couple of days. They take turns coming out for food. Jack see them gettin' the thigh snack and the sandwich from the Chicken Shack down the street a little ways. But Jack, he sometimes have trouble. He say all white people look the same."

Yenchenko shrugged.

Eyes turned to Tommy

"What do you think, Thomas?"

If Sammy was correct, the fourth man in the command center was probably Lomax and it could get messy. If Lomax wasn't there, it could really get out of hand. *But one way or the other, this is the hornet's nest and we're about to smack it with a stick. The party's tonight at Lyford Cay and there's no time to screw around.* "Okay, it's time."

When the panel truck door opened to reveal the costumes,

Sammy's eyes widened. "I get to be a constable?"

Wells took command. "No, lad, you get to be the *sergeant.* Think you can wear the uniform properly?"

"I do my best, sir. But what about the others?"

Pride filled Ian's voice as he handed the uniform to Daniel. "You're the constable. This should be proper fit."

Daniel studied the constable's uniform with obvious apprehension. "I – I, well, I don't want to be a part of no killing, man."

Wells and Yenchenko rolled their eyes, but Tommy smiled and said, "No, you're just to play a little part in the attack. Non-speaking role. No one's going to get killed except us."

"You're certain?"

"Yes. You're going to be our tech guy."

Wells reached for the third uniform, which bore three Order of the Bath stars and the authority of a chief inspector. "This one's mine. I'll brief you lads in the ambulance whilst we gear up."

Yenchenko glanced at the tuxedo. He scowled, but said nothing as he joined Tommy in loading weapons.

Ten minutes later, Sammy knocked politely on an unmarked door underneath a tiny surveillance camera. A tinny intercom voice answered and Sammy declared he was making inquiries about Daniel Akintunde, who had escaped Her Majesty's Prison and was wanted in connection with some sort of computer crime.

A terse voice said, "No such person here, buddy. It's a private office. Unless you've got a warrant, the door stays shut."

Sammy glanced with uncertainty down the hallway beyond the range of the camera. A nod of approval from Wells. Sammy and Daniel retreated partway down the stairs. All the men stood absolutely still for five minutes. Wells used a hand gesture directing Sammy to return to the door and knock again.

"Like I said before, take a hike, pal. No warrant, no entry."

"But sir, my supervisor – "

"Get lost, asshole!"

Wells nodded. Sammy and Daniel withdrew.

Again Wells clocked off five minutes. Another hand gesture. Tommy and Yenchenko pulled masks across their faces and crept forward from their respective shadows, pinned to the wall outside of the surveillance camera's field of view. Glances around. Everyone set. Wells motioned for Sammy to step forward again, following this time in an assertive march toward the door.

Wells used a riding crop to tap on the door.

Right on cue, the voice came back on the intercom. "For the third time, get the fuck out of here. You aren't – "

Ian drew a folded piece of paper from his pocket and held it aloft. "This is Chief Inspector Samuel Bellamy. I've got a warrant to enter the premises. Either comply with our instructions or we'll gain entry by force."

A pause. The voice inside said, "This is a facility of the United States government. You're going to have to contact your chief for further instructions. Get it?"

Wells glanced toward Yenchenko, just out of surveillance camera range. "Break the bloody door down. Take everyone into custody."

The voice cried out, "Just hold it!"

The the door lock clicked and the door opened just a crack. A young, chubby face peered out and began to speak.

From his waist, Wells pulled the trigger and shot a dart into the man's belly. Then he turned to the side. Yenchenko rolled into the door with a shoulder firm enough to go through a wall. The door flung wide open and Yenchenko burst in, followed by Tommy and then Wells, who had abandoned his cap and covered his face with a black mask.

Yenchenko fired almost straight ahead, then turned right and out of Tommy's line of fire. Tommy's target was still seated. Just a kind of nerdy kid, glasses, tee shirt, jaw wide open in shock. Bag of snacks near left hand. *Pick a spot. Fire. Down he goes.*

Within moments, the room fell completely silent except for the soft hum of electronic ventilation fans and a faint, repeating beep. Tommy held a finger aloft to insist on silence, then pointed to surveillance cameras. After cloaking them, the team snipped wires behind them and finally pulled plugs from wall sockets. Yellow, green and red lights went dark, and after a methodical search, the masks came off.

Wells motioned for Sammy. "Right. You lads return to the ambulance, change your uniforms. Daniel can help with the a litter, and bring Sergei's EMS uniform. Quickly."

Yenchenko looked at Tommy and cocked an eyebrow.

"Yeah. I think we're good. If not, we're busted, but nothing we can do about it."

"*Da*, is true." Sergei settled into a chair to relax.

Tommy and Wells searched bodies.

Tommy's target had slumped and rolled onto the floor. He pulled the dart, rolled the unconscious form and found a wallet. Wells handed him two more, and Tommy sifted them for identification. Feldon, Anthony R. Omaha, Nebraska. Age: 23. Brown hair, hazel eyes. Must wear glasses while driving. Organ donor. *Good for you, Tony.* University of Nebraska Alumni Association, just renewed. *Go Cornhuskers.*

Scott, Timothy J. West Caldwell, New Jersey. Age: 26. Blond hair, blue eyes. *No restrictions for glasses. Home Depot credit card, which looks like it's seen a lot of use. Timothy must be a do-it-yourselfer.*

Cohen, Marvin L. The Bronx, New York. Age: 25. Brown hair, brown eyes. *Also has to wear glasses while driving, which he had on when I shot him. Snapshot of a girlfriend? Yep, judging from the inscription on the back, which is signed "Rachel."*

Just youngsters, probably on their first field assignment out of Langley. Not even field guys. Just regular CIA communications people, doing their job. Must have been exciting to be staffed out to the Bahamas. *Wonder if Rachel minded.*

Just regular guys. Collateral damage. But still alive, and being marooned on that cay won't be a problem for them. Three bodies. Yenchenko was right. Lomax was absent. *Time is really, really up on this operation.*

After laying out the bodies for Sammy and Yenchenko to remove, Wells and Tommy turned attention to a bank of black computer monitors and keyboards. Wires led in all directions like spaghetti, and the long work table was littered with crumbs.

"Right. Bloody computer rubbish. I've half a mind to pour some chemical all over it and destroy it."

Tommy chuckled. "Yeah, problem is, we'd have no clue what we should use."

Yenchenko grunted and stood. He picked up a small toolbox and found a hammer. "Sergei Yenchenko now exhibit how to break toy into small pieces."

Tommy sighed, but Wells said, "Let the Russian have his fun. He's not happy unless he's demolishing something."

"No!" Daniel cried out. "Stop!"

All three turned to see Daniel step through the doorway and repeat his plea.

Yenchenko froze in mid-swing. "This is merely CIA computer. We destroy it, send message of our own."

Daniel dropped the litter and Yenchenko's jump suit. "That's state of the art communications equipment. You can't buy it anywhere."

Sergei tossed the hammer aside. "We cannot leave equipment here."

Wells shook his head. "This lot might be booby-trapped or something. Gives me the shakes just to be near it. Thomas, use that magic necklace of yours to kill it."

This is nuts. It's just a computer. Humor the man. Tommy held the tabeejah slightly away from his chest and muttered an artificial incantation. "That ought to do it."

Beyond them, Yenchenko looked amazed and muttered an obscenity at the foolishness of it all. "In corner, I see boxes. We put equipment in boxes, haul to warehouse. Then we destroy everything?"

Daniel said, "Oh, no. Not at all. This is valuable, very valuable. And trust me, Mister Wells, there is no magic in it."

Tommy asked, "We could add to the ransom, then?"

Daniel caressed the gear. "I'm quite certain, Mister Tommy. This is not the sort of hardware the CIA would want in enemy hands."

Yenchenko sighed loudly and shook his head. He climbed into the EMS jumpsuit and turned his attention to Sammy and the three bodies. As they loaded the first on the litter, Sergei rolled his eyes toward Tommy and then made a witchcraft sound and gesture toward Wells to mock Ian's incomprehensible fear of an array of electronic trash.

"Filthy bastard," Wells growled. "I swear, Tommy, that when we're done I'm going to put a round right in that Russian's ear."

"Steady, old friend. No harm done. Let's box this junk up. Like Daniel said, it's worth a few dollars. Personally, I'm more worried about Lomax. You boys take care getting these guys on the truck. Don't screw around, okay? Get them to Dave, get them to the island, find some cover."

Ian glared for a moment, then pursed his lips. "Damn, Thomas, I dearly hope you've got this under control."

Tommy grunted. "Yeah. So do I."

CHAPTER THIRTY TWO

Lyford Cay, New Providence Island

Tommy laid his enveloped invitation on a silver plate in the hand of a man who wore a butler's smile and a maitre d's authority. The man guided Tommy across a carpeted foyer, softly lit and tastefully furnished, toward a portal flanked by two men who looked like waiters but were more likely security guards.

At the doorway, a young woman with an expensive up-do, a long sequined teal gown, a broad, cheery smile and just a bit too much enthusiasm in facial makeup accepted the invitation. "Thank you so much for joining us, Mister Vane and welcome to Lyford Cay. I believe Mister Campos is expecting you and has already arrived. May I escort you?"

Tommy clung to a placid, faint smile. "Thank you, if not inconvenient, that would be very kind," Tommy softly replied.

"No problem, sir." She took a half step to the side and extended her arm to motion him forward. "Is it your first time with us?"

The golf course probably doesn't count. "I'm afraid so."

The answer gave the hostess the opportunity to become a tour guide. She was a marvelous docent but even a more polished security chief, the earpiece barely noticeable above a spectacular emerald earring, the light automatic nearly unobtrusive in a clutch bag. Faces, snippets of conversation, ambiance. The well-heeled charity events from long past coaching him into a mood nearly forgotten. *And frankly, not all that bad.* She made a few introductions and paused to allow for handshakes and courtesy greetings, all of which eased Tommy into a social hammock replete with fair wind and filtered sunshine. *But the hostess never introduced herself. That's why she's security.*

They passed through several layers of attractions for the evening, all sunny yellow with delicate white trim, a somewhat modernized and faux British Colonial. Light jazz from a piano trio cascaded along the hallway: a bit of Cole Porter, a bit of Sammy Cahn, a bit of Johnny Mercer, a bit of nostalgia, the tunes that everyone sort of knows and smooths unease and anxiety.

A dining room, round tables seating six each, upscale china, nice hand cut crystal and sterling silverware, floral centerpieces just a bit oversized for conversation and all under polished brass and sparkly crystal chandeliers.

A meeting room, simple chairs in rows with a podium and easel on the far side, probably for a charity auction.

A patio, paved in tiles with rich blue outdoor furniture, half of which was canopied by the building balcony and all of which was covered by younger people drinking hard.

And a reception room, also cheerful yellow, with a well-staffed bar set up on thick linen and small groups of six to eight in upscale and tasteful apparel. People lingering politely for the punch line of an old joke and then reshuffling for the next bit of banter.

The jazz trio, tucked into a corner, caressed familiar standards and whispered requests, and the tip glass on the piano was stuffed with currency of significant denominations.

Tommy's guide navigated islands of wealth and power to a group of four men. Like Tommy, they were all black tie, conservatively tailored, and everyone clung to a modest glass. Walter Campos roared with laughter, caught sight of Tommy and the nameless escort and waved them into his circle.

After an exuberant handshake, Campos began introductions. "Boys, I'd like you to shake hands with Mister Charles Vane, a fellow with a keen eye and deep wallet. Shrewd investor. The sort of fellow it's good to know. Mister Vane, here's Dave Clayton, one of those old guard New York bankers who makes derivatives sound almost honest."

"Mister Vane, a pleasure."

"And of course, Senator Warren Sterling, who's running for reelection, first rate Republican, and will be more than glad to take all your loose change."

A forced laugh. A lot of teeth. An eager hand, thrust forward, disarmingly friendly. "Every little bit helps. How are you, Charles?"

"And o'course, Mister Carter Blackmann, who's a deputy director of *the* god damn *C-I-A*. He's the fellow who's in charge of all the spies, so watch what you say!"

Carter Blackmann turned to stare deep into Tommy's eyes through a slight squint and rimless glasses and he mustered only the faintest hint of a smile. "Mister Vane," he echoed while he offered an anemic handshake that quickly dissolved, as if he'd just soiled his hand.

"Charlie," Tommy replied with an overdone Texas wheeler-dealer accent and an equally direct stare. "Everybody calls me Charlie."

"May I get you a refreshment?" the hostess asked Tommy.

"Thank you," Tommy answered. "Single malt, neat."

"Of course. Anyone else?"

"I'm good," Sterling said through a smile lecherous enough to make any woman uneasy.

Campos held a still full glass aloft and so her eyes moved to Clayton, who easily drained his own glass and then said, "I'll get my own. Gotta take a leak anyway."

As Clayton began to move away with the hostess right behind him, Tommy and the others bid polite farewells.

"So, are you interested in politics, Mister Vane?" the senator said.

Tommy beamed. "Haven't had much experience with it, sir. I try to keep an open mind, though. You gents are keeping a watchful eye on the country, I'd bet. I've heard good things about you, sir, that's a fact."

Sterling leaned a bit backward to underscore false surprise. "That so? We must have mutual acquaintances."

"Charlie here knows a lot of folks," Walter declared. "Lots of folks. Lots of *right* folks. Family's well connected."

"Walter is much too kind," Tommy said to Sterling, but out of the corner of his eyes he caught an intense glare from Blackmann and thought Campos must have seen it too because Walter took a sip from his glass and used his pinky finger to point away from the group.

Senator Sterling picked up on the cue. "Well, that's just terrific, Mister Vane."

"Charlie."

"*Charlie*. Yes, terrific." He extended his hand. "Awfully nice meeting you but I'm afraid I've got to go make the rounds, press the flesh, say hello."

"Absolutely," Tommy smiled. "And good luck with your campaign. I'll bet the best man will win the election."

"Ha, ha! We hope, well, we know so!" He somewhat anxiously bid good evening to Campos and Blackmann, dropped his glass on a passing tray carried by a club waiter, buttoned his jacket, brushed up a smile and quickly found a new shoulder to pat. His departure was barely noticed by Tommy, Campos or Blackmann.

Walter launched a conversational shift. "Charlie here's one of those razor-sharp Texas boys, always scouting around for companies to buy, restructure, sell off. Regular forty-four caliber fellow."

Blackmann stared hard at Tommy and his voice was chilly. "Is that right?"

"Walter's very enthusiastic in characterizations."

"Nonsense!" Campos almost bellowed and leaned toward

Blackmann, who pulled slightly away. "He's got an eye for *sleepers*, good track record, comes from solid *southern* stock, good stock." Walter wore a broad grin as he turned to Tommy, lifted his chin and looked down his nose. "What's that company you've been after? Oh, yes. Gulf Chemical and Gas. Wonder what it's doing price-wise. Oughta buy a couple of million shares, turn a fancy profit when Mister Vane makes his move."

Blackmann's jaw twitched. "That sounds very much like insider trading, Walter. The sort of activity that attracts the attention of the Securities and Exchange Commission." He turned an imperious gaze back toward Tommy. Reflections of chandeliers in his glasses made his eyes look like fire. "Besides, I believe that firm is privately held. I rather suspect it's not for sale."

Campos feigned astonishment. "You don't say!" He reached out and put a consoling hand on Tommy's shoulder. "Well, Charlie, looks like we're out of luck. Misinformed, son, *misinformed.*"

Tommy continued to share a stare with Blackmann. *I wonder who's going to flinch first,* he thought. "Oh, I don't know. Everything, everyone, has a price."

"Or a price to pay," Blackmann countered.

Tommy forced a slight smile and slowly blinked to acknowledge the barb. *He's good. Really good. Did Walter tip him off? Or did Lomax spot me somewhere? Maybe this, maybe that. Maybe, maybe, maybe. Keep the game going a bit longer.*

Tommy shifted to innocent conversation while he regrouped. "So what brings you to the Bahamas? Surely more than this charity event."

"You're correct, Mister Vane."

Tommy grinned. "Charlie."

"As you wish. Perhaps some sport fishing, Charlie."

Campos watched with obvious fascination. "Lots of first-rate crews in the area, Carter. Pick your trophy, and by God they'll lead you to it."

Blackmann offered a weak smile and continued to study Tommy. "I'm sure. But even little fish, bottom feeders, they'll do for amusement."

Walter grinned. "And so they will, so they will. Well, boys, I'm off to bed. I'm an old man. Got to be up early tomorrow. First light. Crack o'dawn. Flying up to Virginia, little place called Charlottesville. Looking into a little horse farm up there, place to hang my hat. Know much about the region, Carter?"

Blackmann shrugged. "Monticello. University of Virginia. Nice area. I'm sure you'll find many properties of interest."

"Have they got many blackbirds up there? I'm not too excited about blackbirds. Bad luck, some say."

"I have no idea." Blackmann extended his hand. "A pleasure seeing you again, Walter. Have a *safe* flight."

Campos chuckled. He shook hands all around and tugged a business card from his pocket. "Here's my card, Mister Vane. If you're still interested in a profitable venture, give me a call. Day or night. Got *key* staff, round the clock."

Tommy gave it a courtesy glance and tucked it into his jacket pocket while Campos strode off with all the purpose of a professional athlete taking to the field.

When they were alone, Tommy continued the ruse but Carter Blackmann immediately cut him off. "I'm not interested in your pathetic little game, Mister Kane, whatever it is. You've been a bad boy. A bit of an annoyance. An unpleasant distraction. Do you know what I think, Mister Kane?"

"What?"

"I think it's time for you to stop or be stopped. Personally, I find the latter alternative preferable to the first. That's what Mister Lomax – the gentleman standing just over there by the doorway – that's what Mister Lomax suggests. He's an earnest member of my team, Tommy. I value his counsel."

"But you're the man in charge."

"Indeed I am, Kane, indeed I am. Now I think it's time for you to tell me what this is all about, to give me a detailed briefing, to accept the consequences of your actions."

Tommy took a sip from his glass. They were no longer eye to eye. Blackmann seemed to be looking *through* Tommy and focused on a point beyond where Tommy stood, no longer intent but rather impatient while he awaited the confession of an errant schoolboy.

Maybe it was Walter's doing. The old man playing all sides against each other, like some gladiatorial contest where the local ham-and-egger gets the shot for the title against a couple of hungry lions. Or maybe Campos was helping in some obscure way.

Images of Sergei and Ian and Sandy and Sammy and Daniel and Cesar rolled through his mind. *To hell with Walter Campos.* "It's just a mess that's gotten out of hand, sir. It would be great to work out some sort of truce and we can all call it a day. No need for me to become a real problem for you."

Blackmann smiled for the first time and it blended astonishment with arrogance. "A problem for me, Mister Kane? Let me assure you that you're just a teaspoonful of static in a sea of white noise."

Tommy shrugged. "But here you are."

Blackmann sighed. "Yes, Mister Kane. Here I am. So just as an amusement, state your terms. Then I'll decide if you live or die."

"I've got a whole bunch of your people as hostages."

"Yes, yes, I'm fully aware of that. So what? I really don't care."

"And some communications gear."

"Quite so. I tell you what, Mister Kane. Return our equipment and I'll let the three of you off the island. You can retreat to your pathetic little backwater hideouts and if you promise to behave yourselves, you'll stay alive."

Tommy hoped for a bonus. "And the hostages?"

Blackmann looked directly into Tommy's eyes with an utterly passive expression. "I could care less. Not negotiable."

"Your own people?"

Blackmann shrugged. "Trainees, rookies, the cost of doing business. That's why we have the stars on the wall, Mister Kane. It should serve as a lesson to others."

Tommy could not keep his right eyebrow under control and it shot up in surprise.

"When you're prepared to return my equipment, contact Mister Lomax and he'll organize some sort of safe passage off the island to wherever you want to go. But no cash, no reward, no ransom, no nothing. You've lost, Mister Kane." With a sweeping gesture of his arm he continued, "All this? Way beyond your league, I'm afraid. You're simply not a good fit. Perhaps you should accept it and, well, just move along."

A hard knot in the belly . A burning sensation growing in his chest. His jaw betrayed him as it tightened and his eyes began to narrow. With a bit too much defiance in his tone, he said, "And what about Blackbird?"

Carter Blackmann replied with a patronizing and serene smile. "That bird," he gently declared, "has flown. Yes. Flown. Far beyond your reach. A shame for you, wouldn't you agree? Have a nice life, Mister Kane. What little value and substance it has."

Blackmann turned to walk away, and Tommy noticed Lomax pull himself away from the wall he leaned against to a position of almost attention.

The knot rose into his throat and went rancid. His ears were hot and perspiration moistened the fabric just above the skin of his torso. The room felt close and stuffy and the music from the band became muffled and far away. *Not even a drink to take the edge off. The hostess never returned. She works for Blackmann, not Lyford Cay. They knew I was coming.*

Carter Blackmann paused and turned. "Oh, and just a bit of advice, Mister Kane. Don't ever confuse audacity with skill, and don't ever confuse position with power."

Tommy lied. "I've heard that many a time. Doesn't the last part of that go *and don't ever confuse age with wisdom?*"

Blackmann cocked an eyebrow and smiled. "Good evening, Mister Kane."

The CIA deputy director marched without interruption to the doorway guarded by Lomax.

The room went in and out of focus, rolling like sailboat in a series of waves from starboard. Alone. Very small. Humiliated. The big dog had lifted his leg and marked him like a downtown lamp post. *And I let the bastard get away with it.* The wisdom of Moses Clay, the laughter of Sandy, the curses of Sergei Yenchenko, the stories of Dieter Kreutzer, the fury of Doc, the chant of the Obi-Man, floating past like flotsam in a Mississippi flood. Just out of reach. Just tough to grab.

And then the words of his grandfather, his paw-paw. *Don't leave nothin' the way you found it.*

CHAPTER THIRTY THREE

An oasis of alcohol sprawled across several narrow tables staffed by crisply uniformed bartenders. Toward the ends, ponds of pink and lime punches anchored a forest of glass that wore all the better labels. Just upslope stood a line of wines, mostly European, and an assortment of materials to create cocktails to satisfy any whim.

Or steady any nerve.

May as well knock off some of their booze before slinking out of here with my tail between my legs, Then I'll go break the news to Sergei and the Major and they'll want to saddle up armed to the teeth and prove they really are barbarians.

"Yessir?" the bartender, a slight man with a professional smile and blue-chip demeanor, asked.

"Macallan?"

"Of course, sir." His hand gathered in a bottle of 25-year-old scotch and he presented it for approval. Behind him, the jazz trio turned its attention to a medley of Sinatra standards and launched it with a cheery arrangement of "Come Fly with Me."

Calm began to flow his veins and pumped a celebratory urge to his mind. "Make it a double, with a cube of ice on the side."

"Yessir." The barman gathered up a Glencairn cut crystal glass and poured comfort. He added an ice cube on a cocktail napkin and moved on to the next patron..

Closed eyes. A moment of meditation. A moment of expectation. *Exhale.* He held the cube above the glass between his thumb and forefinger to tease a single drop loose and tumble into the glass. The jazz trio slipped into a lush version of "Witchcraft."

A sultry voice behind him said, "That's an awful lot of water going into a glass of perfectly good scotch."

A glance over the shoulder. A twist of the torso. A full turn as all the air fled his lungs and every muscle froze in awe. Confidence sparkled in her dark eyes and her lips teased him with an easy smile, softened by dimples. Cheeks with just a faint blush of amusement as she turned her eyes away from his and toward the glass in his hand. An elegant sleeveless floor-length gown, the color of sunlit claret wine, flowing perfectly across every contour of her body.

He mustered a smile as much out of admiration as embarrassment. "Old habit, to bring me luck. At least, that's what a good friend told me a long time ago. Just a drop. The scotch is excellent, but I can't say much for the ice cube."

"Well, at that rate, you may very well drown, but I rather doubt you'll become intoxicated. So has it?"

"Has it what?"

"Brought you luck." She extended her hand and widened her smile. "Hello. I'm Amanda Owens." In mock confidentiality, she added, "But friends call me Mandy. I'm sorry if I've intruded on a situation requiring an incantation with an ice cube. I do hope it's not a moment of misfortune."

Tommy took her hand into his, gently as if afraid to tarnish its softness. "Hi. I'm Tommy Kane. Well, technically Thomas, but everyone calls me Tommy. Or worse."

She laughed, easily and without nervousness. "Tommy. You know, a lot of men would shorten Thomas into plain old Tom, which immediately conjures the impression of a stray cat. Or a turkey. Tommy. It's a perfectly good nickname. A charming ring to it, don't you think? Like one of those people who play all day and party all night."

The first easy laugh of the day. "Not hardly. And yes, it has."

"Has what?"

"Brought me luck. Can I get you a drink, uh, Miss Owens?"

"Then we definitely need to celebrate. Yes, please. One of those would be nice. And I really do prefer to be called Mandy."

The jazz trio began to play "I've Got You Under My Skin," and Tommy's cheeks went hot. "Ice? Most women – "

"I'm not most women. Tell me, um, *Tommy*, are you as young as you look or as old as you think you are?"

He gestured for the barman to signal the drink order. "Jury's still out on that one." Tommy turned back to Mandy's direct, melting gaze. Same impression. *Oh, my.* She shrugged while his eyes followed the soft ripple of her shoulders all the way to her neck and beyond. "I always thought that question was the other way around."

"Not for those of us of a certain age. I've always thought men were just as vain as women, but afraid to admit it, wouldn't you agree?" She waved off the ice cube and accepted a scotch, neat. "Thank you, Jimmy," she told the bartender and returned her attention to Tommy. "But then what would I know? I'm just a simple girl from New York City."

After his nose fondled the scent of the whisky, he sipped from the glass. "That seems like a contradiction in terms."

Mandy tried an earnest expression. "Actually, it's an adjective to suggest a level of humility. Did I succeed? Were you impressed?"

Tommy pursed his lips. "Sorry, you failed miserably. At the humility part, I mean. But points for effort. Does it matter if I'm impressed?"

She smiled again and dissolved the last of his anxiety. "Oh, gosh, yes! You strike me as the kind of guy who's considerably more sophisticated than he shows, which gives you an intriguing air of mystery. That's very attractive, you know."

The trio's medley had drifted into "Call Me Irresponsible," but the music had gone soft, muted, distant. Everyone else in the room faded into dimmer light and the remaining glow bathed her face. "And you strike me as the sort of woman who's much more complicated than she appears, a quality I find rather intriguing." He took a bigger sip than he wanted, but it gave him moment to breathe, to steady himself, to recover from the unexpected.

"I'll just bet you do. *Tommy.*"

Oh, wow. How does anyone say someone's name that's halfway between teasing and fondling? His mind whisked back to a first teenage romance, when all he could think was *oh, my, she was pretty. Everywhere I looked she was pretty.* He smiled and fractured a brief but anxious pause. "That's a very nice dress, nice color. It seems to fit your style."

Her eyes stayed steady, unflinching, direct. "You've been looking at my body. Should I be flattered or call a policeman?"

"I'd prefer a vote for flattered, but don't want to presume."

She looked down at herself. "Ah, well, it's one of my favorites. By David Aire. I don't get to wear it as often as I like." She leaned in to emphasize a confidence. "They say the color is raspberry, but I never thought of myself as something destined for a pot of jam. Hm. I don't see a policeman anywhere."

Okay, that was really dumb. Fix it. "The pearls look good, too."

"They were my mother's, old favorites."

"Nice to see that class is an inherited trait."

Rewarded with an affectionate smile to mess with his emotions even more, he chased around in his brain for a sense of self control. The musicians shifted gears, to "I've Got the World on a String."

"So," he said. "What sort of work do you do? I'm sure you're not one of those do-nothing society types."

She beamed. "Thank you for that! I'm a writer, a reporter, actually."

"Covering the society scene? No comment, then."

Her expression became more serious. "No. I'm an investigative reporter."

"Definitely no comment. So what brings a reporter like you to a society function in Lyford Cay?"

Mandy chuckled. "Well, for one thing, I noticed you chatting with Carter Blackmann."

"Ah. Nothing to it, really. Well, actually, we were just introduced this very evening."

"Uh-huh. And the other man. That was Walter Campos, wasn't it?"

"Yes, it was."

"May I ask how you know him?"

"We played a round of golf the other day and he invited me to this event tonight. I suspect I'll have to buy something at the auction later."

"And what do you do?"

Discarded spy with a price on his head. Kill people sometimes. Casual kidnapper. The occasional jailbreak. Short order cook with a hammock. Sand bum. A good ol' boy who just can't stay out of trouble. A lot of trouble. "I'm just an independent investor. Nothing fancy."

She laughed. "I find that hard to believe. The 'nothing fancy' part. So... what brings you to the Bahamas?"

Tommy cocked an eyebrow.

She looked regretful. "Sorry, it's just habit. I ask a lot of questions for a living."

Tommy drew a breath, grateful for a moment to collect thoughts and a worthy lie. "I'm shopping for a yacht. Someone said there was a fifty-one-foot Alden yawl for sale and I thought I'd look into it."

"Did you have any luck?"

"No, afraid not. The current owner changed his mind and

it went off the market."

"Sorry. It's always a bit sad when things don't work out the way we planned. Was that the reason for the ice cube?"

"Sort of." An uncomfortable lapse begin to form. "Say, would you like to get some air?"

"Oh, dear. Do I appear under inflated?"

Tommy laughed aloud. "No, I meant – "

Mandy grinned. "I *know* what you meant."

He felt his cheeks redden again, and his words tumbled out in a stammer. "No, not that at all. I meant just some fresh air, a bit of a walk outside."

"Ah, well: you mean the proverbial romantic stroll along the beach, even if it's a waning moon?"

"I could conjure some. Extra moonlight, I mean."

Mandy ignored him and extended her left foot through the slit of the dress. "Uh-huh. On the beach. In the sand. In these shoes."

"You could take them off."

"I don't think so. I'm afraid I've glued them on." She laughed again, but her eyes showed sympathy. "But the patio would be nice. A little less close than in here."

"Can I refresh your drink?"

Mandy gave it only a moment's thought before she declined. "I'm fine, thank you. But I would like a couple of minutes to powder my nose if that's all right. That's what women do when they try to figure out what to do next, you know."

"Certainly." She walked away and his eyes were stuffed with awe but didn't care. Every step she took was destined for memory. The trio provided a perfect soundtrack with a silky version of "Nice 'n' Easy," and when she vanished into the hallway, he drew a deep breath, swirled the remaining scotch in his glass and poured it into his throat.

A passing accepted the empty glass. Tommy floated toward the patio door and the soft evening breeze drifting onto the cay from the glistening sea beyond. Only a handful of guests shared the pleasant air and none intruded into Tommy's anticipation at a change of plans.

Ian Wells will scowl, then put on a look of satisfaction that he was proven right. In an earlier time, he would have volunteered to join Sergei Yenchenko in executing all the hostages and then slip away to the relative comfort of his own nightmares.

Sergei Yenchenko will scowl, reach for an AK-47 and a stack of high capacity magazines and take out his frustration on the first soldiers that cross his path. He'll put on fatigues and find a camp in the jungle and set Central America on fire.

Tommy thrust his hands deep into his pockets and struggled not to pace back and forth while he sorted out what to do with the unexpected turn of events. *Walter Campos is probably in this up to his ears. I just want Carter Blackmann. I wanted that clown on a plate. But now...*

Tommy had been staring at the sea too long. He turned to await the return of Mandy Owens and all the intrigue and mystery and captivation and infatuation she carried on shoes she would not take off to walk on the sand.

When she appeared in the doorway, her eyes did not search for him. Instead, she was stopped by a young man in a jacket a size too large. The discussion looked amiable, as if they knew each other. They turned to face someone else, someone slightly hidden from view, and launched a three-way conversation. The young man dissipated into an observer's role and Mandy tapped her clutch purse lightly on her right thigh, as if impatient.

Each time Mandy turned to the young man and showed her profile, admiration grew.

She's beautiful. Drop-dead gorgeous. Amazing. She defines class. Even knew the name of the barman. Did he wear a name tag? I can't remember.

Problem was that even if she was something really special,

it was not the time or place.

How did she know the barman's name? Why was she asking about Blackmann and Campos? Why doesn't she want to walk on the beach? The problem with this line of work is paranoia. One of these days, I've got to find another line of work. Moses said I needed redemption. Hell, Moses, I need a real life.

The young man made a phone call, briefly passed the cell phone to Mandy, who listened, nodded and then passed it back. The young man put the phone away, looked around and departed.

Mandy continued to talk with the unseen person for a few more seconds and then it looked as though the dialog ended. While Mandy glanced around, the other person briefly passed through the chandelier light and then disappeared.

Dark curly hair. That walk. Myra Fielding.

Mandy looked nervous, edgy, uncertain. Tommy began to walk toward her. She saw him and waved him off. Then she shrugged, made a little wave of farewell, and turned to leave.

Why was she waving him off? Changed her mind? Was she just working him for an article? Or was she working for Myra Fielding and C-213 and Carter Blackmann or Walter Campos? Or any one of a dozen other stupid speculations?

The jazz trio, now muted, finished its Sinatra set with "One for My Baby."

Tommy sighed. *It was fun while it lasted.* He took one last look at the empty doorway, tightened his jaw and slipped away into a shadow.

CHAPTER THIRTY FOUR

Arawak Cay, New Providence Island

A dozen empty beer bottles littered a makeshift table constructed from a ragged slab of plywood atop two wooden crates. A naked light bulb cast a gloomy, low-wattage glow rather than harsh clarity in the musty, damp warehouse.

Twenty feet away, Daniel and Cesar discussed the theoreticals and implications of altered identities for a jet aircraft that might or might not be impounded by local authorities, might or might not be in the corporate hanger, and might or might not be closely guarded. The frustration of different languages and perspectives rose and fell on a tide of frustration and exasperation.

As the last to arrive at the table, Tommy got the folding chair with the bent leg. It rocked each time he shifted his weight while he told the tale of Lyford Cay to an audience that watched impassively, now and then disappointed, sometimes obviously dismayed. He left nothing out, and saw eyebrows flutter when he talked about Mandy Owens.

When Tommy finished, Wells offered a second beer and Yenchenko leaned back and rubbed his chin, then his eyes. He sighed and said, "In Russia, there is saying: *Zhizn' prozhit' – ne pole pereyti*. Life is not like crossing meadow."

"I never expected life to be easy, Sergei."

Wells tapped the side of a nearly empty bottle with his forefinger. "It's the Owens woman. She's got under your skin, hasn't she? No? Sergei, the chap's gone smitten with the honey pot they put out for him. I'd wager ten quid and take odds." He turned to Tommy. "Take it from this old friend, that's as true as the sun rises and sets. You've got to get a bit more steady on. Toughen up, lad."

"*Da, da*, it is so. Here we sit with warm beer that is shit, in sorry warehouse. I wear clothes of soldier, you wear fancy suit of rich man, but we are not so different. This is, of course, trap. I tell you this for your own good, eh?"

Wells nodded. "Precisely. There's no value to returning that computer crap from the com center because they'll nail us at the exchange. They won't send children this time. They'll put the best lads on the field."

Tommy said, "They wrote off all their own people. Didn't even care."

Yenchenko sighed again. "Perhaps. But only perhaps. This Blackmann is most shrewd. If he is Blackbird, then he will be most comfortable with lies. He say to you, well, you can kill them all or let them die, because it does not matter. If this is so, then he is not American because this is culture that go to most extreme effort to rescue one of their own."

Wells shook his head. "Dangerous generalization, Sergei. But if Blackmann wishes us to believe the lads we've captured are expendable, he gains the upper hand. I wouldn't be at all surprised if he mustered the Coast Guard to retrieve the hostages and cart them off with crisps, ale and a jolly 'well done.' They're perhaps lounging in front of the telly, watching one of those silly programs they have these days."

Yenchenko took a sip from his bottle. "Because power boat driver Nassau Dave is on American payroll?"

Ian set his jaw. "Or maybe your man, Sammy, is Blackmann's inside man? Perhaps they used us to spring young Daniel, who prevented you from demolishing the equipment?"

Tommy asked "Where is Sammy, anyway?"

Yenchenko belched. "He go for case of beer and food for

all."

Tommy smiled at Ian. "Or maybe you're still working for Campos, who's fronting the op for Blackmann?"

Wells chuckled. "Or maybe that Obi-fellow, Joseph, got you drugged up, loosened your tongue a bit, and tipped off Langley."

"Or Whitehall."

Yenchenko's eyes twinkled. "*Da, da*, and it is you, Koshka, who prevent me from shooting Cuban pilot. Oh, you say, 'let the little fish go.' Because in end game, you betray us all and fly back to your CIA and they put medal on chest."

Tommy shrugged off the slander and looked at Wells. "You just happened to know a veterinarian who provided some sort of magic concoction, and just happened to know a guy to transport hostages." He turned to Yenchenko, "And you just happened to catch a couple of company people with a set of orders that should never have left the station and you verified it with a jungle hooker hired by Walter Campos."

Sergei scowled and waved a hand of dismissal. "It is most clear. Both of you are in conspiracy to make end of Sergei Yenchenko, who is miserable leader of revolution but annoyance to those who insist on order."

Wells rolled his eyes. "Oh, get on. The lot of you drew me out into the open so that ultimately when you return the phony communications gear, they'll take me out in retribution for that little matter in Moscow that embarrassed the Americans and the Russians."

Tommy popped the cap off the last full bottle on the table. "And all along I thought it was me. When I left Lyford Cay alive I knew I wasn't the only target. What's next?" He hoisted the bottle and drew a sip.

Ian said, "We sound retreat, close up shop. We use Dave to leave at first light, make our way to the States or points south. I'd fancy points south, myself, but then I'm the only one with any sanity at all."

Yenchenko scratched the stubble from two days without a razor. "*Nyet.* Your tongue will take you as far as Kiev. Perhaps this Dave cannot be trusted. Perhaps he deliver us on plate to CIA. Perhaps we execute him, steal boat. How difficult is such a boat to drive?"

Wells lowered his voice to a confidential whisper. "Easier than a bloody Gulfstream jet. And we don't have to trust a Cuban. Why stop with Dave? Let's terminate Sammy, Daniel, Cesar, everyone we can't trust."

Tommy looked up. "Each other?"

"How do you mean, Thomas?"

"*Da, da,*" Yenchenko spoke. "With good company, even death is without sting. We are most excellent adversary. So, I think, I make worthy death, good end to good life. Who will oppose me?"

Tommy smiled. "No one, Serge."

"Ah, so it's to be me, then," Wells softly replied. "I was always rather keen on dying as an old man whilst watching the sun rise, but I – "

"No, Ian. Not today."

Wells and Yenchenko exchanged puzzled expressions, unaware that they had somehow formed a theoretical team to execute Tommy.

Tommy leaned forward. "Maybe that's what Blackmann wants us to do. Set us on each other, weaken us as a group. What we have in common is Dieter Kreutzer."

Ian said, "And our skills, as inadequate and antiquated as they are."

With the finality of a professor in a lecture hall, Yenchenko said, "Of course it is so. I make small test for both my comrades, to sharpen their mind, *da?* In Russia, it is truth that if you take wolf from different pack and put them together, they will kill each other before they make team, make new pack."

"It's the same in the States, Serge." *I was leading you to that very point.*

Sammy entered with a case of beer on his shoulder and a box of fast food under his arm.

Tommy said, "Let's organize a bigger table. Time to eat."

Wells stood and stretched. "Good idea, Thomas. I didn't really want to kill Yenchenko anyway. Or you, for that matter."

With his hands interlaced behind his head, Sergei leaned back in reflection. "We are same as *artel*, group of Russian workmen who form association to do task, make contract with shares. Equal is usual, eh? So expression mean we work as team, have better result. Now it is time for much food and more beer and story with good lies, eh?"

Tommy sighed. "I think it might be a better idea to work up some plans."

Yenchenko shrugged. "Is good. We make plan, then we drink and tell story."

Wells shook his head in dismay. "Disgraceful. Let the rascal off the hook and all he wants is to get properly pissed. Open the box, Thomas and I'll fetch the lads from their computer."

While they ate as a group, Cesar found clarity in his native Spanish and described as best he could in layman's terms the issues with North Atlantic Tracks, certification for extended range, two-engine operational performance standards, flight plan requirements, and radio checks and prescribed intervals. "Daniel amazes me with his ability to enter secured areas, but simply transferring the title on the aircraft, then registering it with the FAA is the least problem. Changing transponders in mid-flight is possible. But you cannot go anywhere without a flight plan. And for your scheme, you will need two: one from Nassau and one from any airport in Europe, which has been properly filed without anyone noticing that no such aircraft departed."

Tommy said to Daniel, "I thought you could do all this electronically."

"Oh, for sure, I can make the flight plan from Nassau. Security here is more relaxed. But getting into the computer in Heathrow, DeGaulle, even the smaller airports is much more difficult. We took a peek without calling attention and I am very sad to say that it is beyond me."

Yenchenko drummed his fingers on the table. "So. If you make good hack, scheme would work?"

Cesar answered in English. "Yes. I think so. But it would be more helpful to have some flight history already filed."

Wells swallowed a bite of chicken. "Such as?"

"The aircraft arrived from somewhere, on some date, and there would be a record of it. Perhaps someone sees something odd, checks, and finds the aircraft flew in from, maybe New York or Miami or whatever a few days earlier. It might have a record of service, maintenance, fueling, that sort of thing. All these little details are important, *señor.*"

Tommy rubbed his eyes. "Thank you, Cesar. Do you think your arm is okay to fly?"

"*Si, señor.* There is some stiffness, but I can ignore it to gain freedom."

Tommy turned to Daniel. "You've done a great job, but as you say, it's getting very complicated. What do we need?"

"You need someone who is very, very good, someone much better than me, the best of the best."

"I don't suppose we could post a notice in *The Guardian,* then?" Ian asked.

Yenchenko sighed and allowed his meaty hand to browse the box of food for a substantial refill on the plate before him.

Tommy smiled. "Know anyone like that?"

Daniel looked away and bit his lower lip.

"Daniel?"

Daniel drew a breath and turned his head to face the patient expression of Tommy. "Yes, I maybe know of such a person. They say the best in the world."

"Here in Nassau?"

"No, sir. The States, maybe New York area."

"Okay, but we're kind of running out of time here. Might be difficult to get him down here on short notice."

"Oh, heavens no! With the computer, a person can be anywhere. Location means nothing."

Ian's eyebrows rose. "Thomas, I'm not all that keen on strangers, especially one that I can't see."

"We've got to try, Daniel. Who's your guy?"

Daniel took another helping of fish and chips. "I only know the handle, the name the person uses online. This person, they shroud identity in layers, but over time I am able to arrive at some deductions." Daniel's voice filled with pride. "The person, a network actually, is known widely in the community as 'Echo.' The main person behind Echo is called 'Leto' but that is only a mask for one called 'Nyx'."

"N-I-X?" Tommy spelled out.

"No. N-Y-X."

I've heard that before. Lester Finn used it in the casino. "Nix, man, the best hacker in the world." *But not 'nix.' Nyx. Bug's daughter, Lucy.*

Wells nodded approval. "The lad's got first-rate intelligence instincts. Your hacker does, too."

Tommy agreed. "Impressive."

Daniel said, "But there is more. Nyx may be a code word for one called 'Nemesis.' I am not so certain about this, but the name has been mentioned."

Let him fill in the details. She may be Bug's daughter, but you just don't pick up the phone and cold approach. He passed another beer to Daniel. Sammy and Cesar listened while they ate chicken and conch fritters.

"But there is another in the Echo network, whose name is rarely mentioned: *Akna.* I do not know what all these names mean, just that they exist, you see?"

Ian finished chewing a piece of chicken and reached for some breaded fish. "I know." Heads turned. "Greek mythology." He looked at surprised expressions from Tommy and Sergei. "Right. I'm not uncultured, you know. I fancy a bit of history now and then. Took a class at Sandhurst."

"So, explain names." Yenchenko prodded.

Wells cleared his throat, then took a sip of Sands beer. "Well then. Echo logically refers to a network; she was a nymph who got a speech impediment from Hera and could only repeat what others had said. Leto was the mother of Apollo, I believe, and Artemis as well. Zeus was the father. Leto means hidden, or forgotten. I'd suggest hidden is the appropriate reference here, eh?"

"Agreed," Tommy said. "Go on."

"Very well. The third layer is logically Nyx, the Greek goddess of the night. Our hacker is the daughter of Khaos – rather interesting – and the wife of Erebos. Nemesis refers to retribution or righteous anger, as well as it should for Nemesis was the Greek goddess of vengeance and justice."

Tommy nodded. "All feminine." *The best hacker in the world. Lucy Tramanian.*

Wells shrugged. "But I regret to say that Akna doesn't fit the pattern."

Yenchenko grunted. "In Mayan folklore, Akna is goddess of motherhood and birth."

Tommy said, "I'm impressed. Serge. I didn't know you were into Central American mythology."

Yenchenko belched and swallowed a substantial slug of Kalik. "Such foolishness is most useful tool when army is made from locals. Good soldier, such as me, take advantage of all things. But for us, I see no advantage. This hacking person is far distant, unknown for making contact, has no motive to be of assist to group. I vote for power boat to Florida Keys."

Not necessarily.

Ian said, "Right. And a likely encounter with the Coast Guard or the American DEA."

Take a chance. "I think I'll get in touch with her."

Yenchenko laughed. "You are resourceful, Koshka, almost as good as myself. But I think we have come to end of game. We accept loss, we make depart, we forget this madness."

Tommy showed a sly smile that Ian Wells noticed but Yenchenko did not see. "And if I can work it out? Would you be in?"

Sergei looked up from another round of fish and chips and stabbed at the air with his fork. Bits of fish flew in all directions. "From time we are in Duffy's bar, you always say you make it work out. We work this out, we work that out, and now we are in trap that we make for ourself. You are good comrade, Koshka, but even that filthy object made from bits of animal and bird will not save you now."

Wells asked, "You're quite certain, Sergei?"

Yenchenko retreated to his meal. "Very well, it is so. We make wager. I join force if you get this hacking person to fix path for jet aircraft to take us to millions of American dollar."

Tommy turned to Daniel. "That phone you were using to connect to your computer: mind if I use it to make a call?"

Ian's jaw dropped. "I say, Thomas. *Are you daft?*"

"No," Tommy said as he accepted the cell phone from Daniel. "Just changing the ground rules. So, Daniel, how do you make this thing go?"

CHAPTER THIRTY FIVE

The image of Bug. A squat round man with thick black plastic rim glasses, nearly bald except for a thin line of hair around his ears, perhaps halfway through life and comfortable in coveralls with utility logos on the chest and back.

Tommy dialed a number from memory.

Bug. A foul man, foul of breath, foul of mind and foul of temper, a loner who didn't care about being alone and took every opportunity to offend anyone who offered a kindness.

The line was busy. He dialed again.

Bug. A master at wiretapping, eavesdropping, peeping, recording anyone, anywhere, anytime. The man. Only the most elite assignments for stratospheric fees and left everyone to speculate what he did with the money because on Bug, it never showed.

Still busy. Dial again.

Nice to be only one of a handful of guys who could recognize Bug on the street. Makes for a good marker in times like this.

A click. A few electronic sounds. Some static. And then Bug growled into the phone. "Yeah."

"Tommy Kane."

Bug grunted. "Yer full of shit, asshole. Tommy Kane don't never use no phone."

Tommy had persisted and recited several facts that only Bug and Tommy would know.

In a wary tone, Bug said. "Look, Tommy, I'm on a job. Nice warm van, nice pastrami sandwich from that great deli in Brooklyn, a six-pack of cold ones from a bodega up the street. Life is good, Tommy. I don't need no shit."

"One quick favor. I need to get in touch with Lester Finn."

"Lester? Jeez, Tommy – "

"Calling in a marker, Bug, that's all."

"Shit. Okay, call me back in three."

When Tommy handed the phone back to Daniel, he saw disappointment on the faces of Yenchenko and Wells, but intrigue from Daniel, so he explained. "Bug is one of the best, maybe the best if you don't count the tech teams at NSA and CIA. He works solo, off the books and for only a limited clientele."

"He does the wiretapping?"

"Yep. And he has a line on a guy named Lester Finn, who I bumped into the other day in Cable Beach. Lester made a huge mistake, the kind that can get people killed when he handed me the name of the person he was working for. He called someone 'the best hacker in the world,' and used the word 'Nyx' in the same sentence. And I got a name."

Daniel nodded. "So, this is what the secret agent really does, then?"

"Yes. Not very exciting, is it?"

Daniel shrugged. "Nyx, or Nemesis or Akna, it makes no never mind, for she wears the white hat, does only good, no evil. She's for justice for the people, the common fellow, not for the fat cats, the rich ones."

"Did you know Nyx was a woman?" *I'm not going to identify her by name. No need for anyone else to know. And certainly no need to mention she's Bug's daughter.*

"No. I only learned tonight, when you pieced together the identity."

Ian said, "And if I were you, I'd forget what you heard. Any of these players would squash you like a sand flea. As for you, Thomas, with that filthy mobile, you've ventured very far into uncertain ground. I really do hope you know what you're doing."

Yenchenko grunted. "For myself, I stand with *tovarich* Tommy. He is man who make risk, sometimes win. We live in different time, now. Even wolf must adapt to new season, winter to spring, spring to summer."

"And then comes autumn and then winter again. Let's just see if we're alive in the morning, then. Might as well turn in. Sea or air, I suspect we'll have a busy day tomorrow."

Yenchenko and Cesar finished their beers and with Ian withdrew to makeshift cots in a darkened corner of the warehouse.

Tommy called Bug again.

"Yeah. Okay, so we got a tight line. We can do some business."

"Pro bono, pal."

"Jesus, Tommy, I got expenses."

"And I know what you look like. Get a message to Lester, okay?"

"Shit. Okay, just this one time."

"Tell Lester to reach out to his jackpot friend Nyx. N-Y-X." *But where? Certainly not a cell phone.* Tommy presented a confused and harried expression to Daniel, who guessed the problem and immediately scribbled a series of digits interrupted by periods on a scrap of paper.

"That don't look like a phone number to me," Bug muttered.

Tommy read further and with a shrug said, "I-P."

"First a goddamn phone, now a goddamn P-C. You must be in deep shit, pal. Who's this N-Y-X?"

Wow, he doesn't know. Or maybe he does and is not saying it on a phone. "Sorry. buddy, need to – "

"Yeah, yeah. Okay, Tommy, got it. No guarantees, as usual."

"Thanks a bunch."

"Yeah, well, you won't be sayin' that when we settle up your next tab, buddy. I don't run no goddamn charity. You wanna get yer ass in a sling for anything else?"

"No, that's it."

The line went dead, and the wait began. Tired eyes. A yawn. A good change of course, but a path running counter to a lot of instincts. The song of the Obi-man, the whisper of witchcraft. Resistance. Seduction. Kumina. The spirits of the night, saying to let go, feel the warmth of the tabeejah. Sail fearlessly into uncertain waters.

And don't drink that much beer so fast again.

Daniel said, "You are listening to the words of Babu. But, yes, I'll stay with the computer if there's ever a reply from Nyx or Nemesis or Akna."

"You're really okay with this?"

Daniel's eyes fell for a moment and then he lifted his chin and answered in a firm voice. "Oh, I think so. I spent most of the night contemplating, thinking about life on Cat Island. The technology, she's a captivating mistress, but she's become much too sophisticated for me. I don't want to go back to prison. Not a good place for a fella such as I."

"Nyx is probably not going to be too happy with you," Tommy said.

"Oh, for sure. I've heard stories, what they say about those who cross Nemesis, or Nyx."

"I don't want to put you into any kind of a jam."

"It doesn't matter. I'm thinking about getting out of the life."

Tommy nodded and stood and found his way to a shadow. *She owes Lester, probably really angry with him, but she owes him. As for Daniel? She'll probably slice him right out of the loop. He's probably already out but doesn't know it yet.*

Tommy stretched out. On the cusp of sleep he understood the days of old-style espionage had fluttered away on the winds of technology. And he had become emotionally attached to the pursuit of Blackbird, not so much as a matter of justice, not as a contractor for a fat cat, but merely to duel with an annoying arrogance. The money promised by Walter Campos, if it was there at all, was just a bonus.

Once, when Paw-paw had run afoul of the parish authorities by some act that came down to simple defiance, he was being led to a patrol car and told young Tommy, "Sometimes a man's got to prove hisself to hisself for no good reason other than to get his chin off his chest."

Tommy slipped into a pleasant dream in which the Alden yawl cruised at a gentle pace through the Antilles, a dream that ended when Daniel shook his shoulder.

"Sorry to wake you," Daniel whispered. "There's a message."

Tommy blinked his eyes and stretched and took in the sound of soft snores from distant corners in the abandoned warehouse. He focused on the faint glow of the screen of Daniel's laptop a dozen feet away. "It's okay. What time is it?"

"Four thirty."

"Wow," he said after a yawn. "She's a night owl."

"Yes, it seems so."

Tommy pulled himself to his feet and padded toward Daniel's humble office. He winced when he stared at the monitor, which was pure white except for a blinking cursor and a single line of text: "Why are you bothering me?"

Tommy yawned and blinked hard several times to beckon full consciousness, then he dictated, "Have a problem stealing a Gulfstream Four-fifty." *That ought to work.*

Daniel shook his head, typed the message and they both stared at the blinking cursor, each lost in their own thoughts. For Tommy it was a fresh visit to a memory of long ago, when he and a friend named Packy Boudreau discovered the amusement of party line telephones and the coy and giggling conversation of a neighbor girl whose name he could not recall. They talked about boys, and sometimes with boys, and Tommy and Packy, barely on the edge of puberty, were intoxicated by a strange brew of hilarity and enchantment.

Wonder what happened to old Packy. And I know her face, but can't find her name. Probably a grandma by now, weathered and tired and a lifetime away from those simple joys that Packy and me tarnished. Dang, what jerks we were.

My old man was plenty mad about us messing with the party line. He was mighty proud of that phone, but Paw-paw snorted and said it would come to no good. So when my father caught us eavesdropping, he smacked both of us and ran Packy off. The full whipping came late that afternoon, when the storm clouds began to gather on the night of the tornados. Then my old man said he had an errand.

And left us alone.

Two minutes of silence in the warehouse passed. A fresh message arrived: "Then don't steal it. Go away."

Tommy sighed. "Tell her we're trying to catch a mole, very high in the CIA. It's really important." *Yeah, right, this is gonna work. Not.*

Daniel obeyed and tapped out the message on the keyboard.

"What part of go away don't you understand?"

Yenchenko and Wells were right. We should have used Dave's boat, even if we had to kill Dave. Okay. Personal favor time. Maybe it'll work.

Tommy dictated, "Lester Finn hit the jackpot. Nice toy."

Daniel and Tommy settled back to await a reply.

I was sitting on a fallen log and staring at the wrecked house. It looked like someone had just shoved it over with a giant hand, but the peak was still intact as if the giant hand was unable to squash it. Paw-paw come up from nowhere and called out and looked around, but there wasn't anybody left. When we walked away to his shack, the telephone pole by the road was gone.

And so was the girl down the road whose name I can't recall.

And so was her mother.

And so was my old man.

While they waited for his aunt and her husband to come, his grandfather was mostly quiet. *But he found a couple of beers and we each had one. And he gave me a sad ol' look and said, "You stay away from them god damn telephones. Ain't no good ever gonna come from them, no."*

Tommy calmed an itch on the back of his neck and his eyes turned to Daniel's laptop computer. *Sorry, Paw-paw. Times change.*

Close to five minutes passed and Tommy began to think the conversation had ended. *So, it was a long shot. They don't always come in.*

Tommy smiled. "Well, it looks like we blew our shot with Nyx."

"Be patient. It sometimes takes a moment to check routing for security. I am curious, though. May I ask why Yenchenko calls you 'Koshka'?"

"It's Russian for 'kitten.'"

"Kitten?"

"Yes. He does that to keep me from taking myself too seriously."

"Ah. I see." Daniel's eyes flitted back to a change of light from the screen.

The text said, "State your request."

Tommy rapidly and softly tapped the side of his nose with his forefinger, bit his lower lip and stared at the message. He drew a substantial breath. "Go ahead," he told Daniel, "brief her on the plan."

This time the delay was only thirty seconds.

"Not only dangerous, but stupid. Necessary rate of descent to stage realistic crash would cause GS450 to break apart. You might survive slower dive, but cause many to spend much resources in search for wreckage."

Okay, she's got access to data on the aircraft and stress capability. Probably correct about causing an expensive search/rescue, too.

Tommy directed Daniel to type, "Suggestions?"

"How important is jet?"

Tommy grinned. "Very."

"Registration?"

Tommy gave Daniel a puzzled look.

Akintunde understood and rummaged through notes on

scraps of paper next to the computer. "Cesar mentioned it... yes, here it is."

"Give it to her," Tommy said.

Daniel typed. "CU-N2468"

After a brief pause, she replied. "That's Cuban military intelligence. You guys nuts?"

Tommy chuckled. *Oh, yeah, we sure are. She's very good. Okay, professional to professional.* He dictated, "Need title transfer, FAA registration, help with flight plan."

"You have jet and crew?"

"Yes." *Just go with it. Just let this play out. Listen to the tabeejah.*

For more than a minute the cursor blinked mindlessly on the screen and Tommy resisted the temptation to organize a precise plan.

"Go to jet, prep for flight. Contact again at 0800 EST. Nemesis."

The message faded and the image of a black panther's glowering eyes replaced it on the screen.

"Oh, my," Daniel muttered as the dialog's significance sank in. "you're definitely playin' in the first division now. I'll go with you to Pindling."

"It's okay," Tommy replied. "No need to put you to any trouble. You've been a great help. We're even."

Daniel laughed. "I used to work at Pindling, so I know the layout well. I can run the computer for you. Plus, I want to see this for myself."

Tommy shrugged, shook Daniel's hand and turned to awaken the others.

The contingent was quickly operational. Ian replaced the dressing on the shoulder of Cesar Hernandez and then joined Yenchenko in opening a long wooden crate tucked unobtrusively in a shadowed area.

Sergei hoisted an AK-47 with a sawed off stock and rammed a high-capacity magazine into it. "No more toy this time," he growled.

Tommy tightened his jaw and accepted his Beretta from Wells. "Just no civilians, okay? We're escaping, not overthrowing the government."

Wells produced a 9mm Glock and a wooden case that bore his H&K .223. Three 12-gauge short-barrel tactical shotguns went into a duffel and Yenchenko helped with ammunition.

Ian paused. "I trust we're allowed some carry-on?"

"What about hostage?" Yenchenko asked.

"What about them?" Ian countered. "We're certainly not about to bring the lot back ourselves."

The Russian shrugged. "They are like us. Soldier on assignment. They follow orders. We are better, of course, but they are prisoner."

Tommy agreed and picked up the envelope with all the identification cards. He turned to Sammy. "When this is done, win or lose, I want you to go to Café Skans. You know it?"

Sammy nodded and accepted an envelope with a set of coordinates scribbled on the outside.

"You're looking for a woman named Adrienne Tillman. You hand this to her, and only her. Say nothing. Then you walk away, take off. Nothing more. Got it?"

"Yes, yes. I can do this for you."

Yenchenko took a step forward and his voice lowered to an intense threat. "Take care you do this. *Or you die.* Understand?"

Tommy pursed his lips. A moment of truth. He asked for the phone and tapped the number of the crisis center in Langley. After only the briefest pause, he said, "Flash for C-213. Com gear blue minivan, one hour, employee parking, N-A-S." He disconnected.

Daniel folded up the laptop and Cesar buttoned his shirt. Tommy took one last look around. "Okay," he said to no one and everyone. "It's time."

Sammy and Daniel gathered up two cardboard cartons of

CIA equipment, neatly closed and tied with twine, and walked toward the door behind Yenchenko and Wells, both of whom clutched duffels in their left hands and pistols in their right. On the way out, Tommy's hand found the light switch and the warehouse went black.

CHAPTER THIRTY SIX

Pindling International Airport, The Bahamas

In bold red letters, a sign on the door declared, "Authorized Personnel Only - *Personal Autorizado Sólo - Cubana de Aviación.*" Just to the right, a substantial hasp was plugged with an equally substantial padlock.

"I am sorry, *Señor* Tommy," Cesar mumbled. "Major Medina must have locked it as we left."

"No, Cesar. He only *thought* he locked it." Tommy dug into a pocket of his rucksack, produced a small leather pouch, and withdrew two delicate tools.

Wells approved. "There's a good fellow. Annoying of Medina to keep us from our appointed task. Glad I shot the bastard."

Yenchenko took half a step back to keep watch while Tommy attacked the lock. With a few seconds, it succumbed and the back door of the leased hanger swung open. He motioned the others forward while he stowed his burglary equipment. When he entered his eyes tracked across a vast, spotless painted concrete floor. Medina's private jet gleamed in golden light that trickled through dusty high windows.

It's like a sleek bird of prey. "Oh, wow."

Cesar offered an empathetic smile, but Wells and Yenchenko rolled their eyes.

Yenchenko began. "First it is sailing boat...".

Wells chimed in. "...And then the woman at Lyford Cay."

"...And now small jet airplane, nearly toy." He relieved his shoulders of duffel bags stuffed with weapons and ammunition. "Perhaps Koshka has mind of small boy, eh?"

Cesar's shrug and smile were deferential, and he was unashamed of the twinkle in his eyes when he spoke to Tommy.

"*Si, señor*, they know nothing, eh?"

Tommy followed Hernandez to the tip of wing and he could not resist a touch while his eyes followed the twin streaks of blue paint along a pure white fuselage from just behind the nose to just under the tail.

Cesar's voice filled with pride. "She is not quite ninety feet long, and the wingspan is nearly 80 feet, and about 25 feet high." They drifted to the front of the aircraft and Cesar opened the hatch to allow the steps to descend. He gestured toward the door of the aircraft and said, "Welcome to my world, *Señor* Tommy."

As he stepped aboard, Tommy looked right. Plush beige fabric, leather benches and seats, inlaid wooden tables stretching toward the rear of the craft on either side of a carpeted aisle. To the left, a cockpit stuffed with knobs, switches, buttons and computer screens. Cesar rattled off barely heard specifications. "Cruising speed, 460 knots – about 525 miles per hour – a range of 4,200 nautical miles." *Half of me wants to feel like a barbarian that just broke into the treasure box. The other half feels like I just put on the nicest suit I ever wore.*

Cesar grinned. "So, *Señor* Tommy, do you think you would like to help me fly it?"

The cockpit. Complicated. Glamorous. Tech. Himself, pure grunge, out of place. A half hour earlier he, Wells and Yenchenko had been laying belly down on a steep embankment that ran from a service road into a drainage ditch still murky with runoff from a passing squall the night before. Coarse brush beneath their bodies was cursed loudest by Ian Wells and ignored best by Sergei Yenchenko. The clothes they wore were caked with a thin mud and crumbs from the brush.

Sammy, Daniel and Cesar had been dispatched to slip through security and past the probable surveillance of Lomax's CIA unit. Their goals were casual disguises and unobtrusive transportation. At regular intervals, incoming commercial flights completed final approach just a hundred feet or so above them and had left all of them weary of noise, touchdown tire chirps and the blast of reversed thrust.

By contrast, the soft silence in the immense hanger offered a seductive respite and the interior of the jet was a cocoon of pure class and comfort.

He offered Cesar a smile that was part resignation, part relief and part mischief. "Call me Tommy."

"*Si, si*, as you wish."

From below, and with the hollow sound produced by a voice that echoed across concrete, came a call from Ian Wells. "Have you chaps reached the benediction yet? We've got work to do and Daniel has a message from Nyx."

Cesar shrugged and they disembarked, but not before Tommy's eyes fondled the interior one more time.

Daniel had set up his computer on a makeshift table near a parked tug by the main door, and Tommy strode past the nose of the Gulfstream with renewed purpose to continue with a thirty-eight million dollar felony. His eyes found the message from Nyx on the screen:

"Title transfer and FAA registration complete. Triton Air, Allentown, Pennsylvania, N226TK. Pink temp good for 90 days with FAA, radio for 5 yrs with FCC. Okay?"

Wells peered over his shoulder. "Rather fancies her Greek mythology, eh? Triton was the son and herald of Poseidon, god of the sea. I wonder if she's not a bit keen on you, Thomas. I mean, why even suggest a location in Pennsylvania unless it's an invitation?"

Tommy stared at the screen, rubbing his chin.

"Thomas?"

"The registration... My initials at the end."

"So?"

"My birthday is February 26. 2-2-6."

Yenchenko said, "Perhaps it is all random, not to call attention."

Curiosity alone makes me prefer Ian's theory. But no way am I going to admit it. "Answer yes."

"Await flight plan. 20 min."

It was 7:58 a.m.

Tommy turned to Cesar. "Okay, we're all beginners. Tell us what you need us to do."

The pilot issued instructions and uncertainty rose to command assurance as they prepared the aircraft for flight.

Daniel's call interrupted at precisely 8:20 a.m.

"Plugged into NAS systems and monitors. Where's the bad guys?"

Tommy dictated the message from the night before and in a moment Nyx replied, "Wow, four guys breaking into somebody's car. Crowbars, glass everywhere."

Daniel typed, "That's them."

"Flight plan follows. Write this down."

Tommy and Daniel watched a stream of gibberish flow onto the screen, and Daniel transcribed it, handed it to Tommy, who in turn passed it to Cesar.

Hernandez scratched the back of his head. "I do not understand."

"What?"

"This is a flight plan for Cubana 468, CU-N2468, to Caracas, *Venezuela.* There must be some mistake. But no, the track would be correct. The details seem right. But to Caracas? I do not understand."

Tommy asked Daniel, "Did we get that right?"

Daniel asked for confirmation.

"Confirm." The cursor blinked slowly at Tommy. *I know where this is going.*

"Tell her we got it."

Cesar's eyes widened.

Nyx wrote, "Parking lot plan expired. Move your guys."

Tommy motioned for the telephone and entered the number of Langley Center. Then he said, "Flash C213 Com gear, middle stall, men's restroom, departures NAS." And he disconnected. To Cesar, he said, "File the plan. How long do you think?"

"Thirty minutes," Cesar answered.

"And once we're cleared to go?"

Cesar turned to study the aircraft. "From a dark, cold flight deck? At least fifteen minutes."

"Thirty to forty would be better," Daniel suggested. "You don't want to appear as though you be departing on the sly. Most aircraft, they take a little bit of time."

Cesar nodded. "*Si, gracias.* I prefer at least ten minutes for the APU, er, auxiliary power unit, and twenty for the engines. They need to warm up. And we have an inexperienced crew. There is much to do in the cockpit, my friend. We'll also need fuel, perhaps 5,000 pounds."

Daniel nodded. "Jet-A, 750 gallons or so. There is a vendor."

"Order it," Tommy answered. "But wait twenty minutes."

"It's expensive."

Tommy grunted. "Ask Nyx to use a credit card. I'll reimburse her."

"And you'll need a co-pilot uniform. The fellow who came on the flight was a little shorter, but perhaps...?"

"We'll make do," Tommy replied. "No time to find a tailor."

While they walked toward a narrow set of lockers, Tommy called out. "Ian, Serge, Sammy? We've got to find some aircraft paint, white and black and a couple of really tall ladders."

Cesar seemed puzzled.

Tommy explained. "I'm betting she's going to change flight plans electronically once we're aloft. She's going to run two flights in the opposite direction. We're going to the States, Cesar, so we've got to get those registration numbers on the engines altered."

Hernandez looked shocked. "But Tommy, the flight plan is for Cubana. We would be breaking the law!"

Ian Wells sighed while he loaded a twelve gauge riot gun. "Cesar, that's what we do for a living."

"But we're filed for CU-N2468!"

"And we'll have to enter U-S airspace as N226TK, so I'm going to bet that the tower here will not pay attention to the number on the plane, but rather the call sign and transponder," Tommy replied. "At least, I hope that's what I think she'll want us to do."

Cesar grudgingly agreed and departed to deal with the flight plan.

Sammy had been exploring a bench stuffed with tools and supplies and called out that he'd found paint. "Don't you be worryin' none, Mister Tommy. I do the taggin' when I'm in school, pretty fancy, too."

Tommy laughed. "I don't need graffiti, Sammy. Just some plain old letters and numbers."

"Piece of cake, boss!"

Yenchenko shook his head at the preposterous remark and sighed. "I bring ladder, supervise."

Tommy nodded and turned back to Daniel. "Ask Nyx if there's any way we can find out where Carter Blackmann went. He might be the big dog in the CIA, but he's got to file a flight plan, too."

Daniel nodded and typed away. It was 8:35 a.m.

For four minutes, the only sound in the hanger was the hiss of paint sprayers. Cesar's uniform was a nearly perfect fit, but as the pilot warned, the co-pilot's shirt and trousers were an inch short. Tommy cuffed the shirt low on his forearm and ignored a bemused smile from Yenchenko when Sergei caught sight of his ankles.

"Got an answer, Tommy," Daniel called. "Left on a Citation Ten, registered to Central Intelligence at 2310 last night, destination CHO. The call sign was Raven 213."

"Charlottesville." *Raven. Blackbird. Two-thirteen. C-213.* "Thanks, Daniel, that helps." He strolled over to his newly acquired private jet to watch the Sammy's progress. "Doesn't have to be perfect. They'll be seeing it at quite a distance from the tower."

Yenchenko drifted close and spoke in a low voice. "You are good with this scheme, Koshka? It is big gamble, with high risk. Too many untested team member, most unusual technology."

"I'm thinking we don't have much choice, Serge. Ian, you and I could probably shoot our way off the island, but they'd bag all the others."

He scowled. "This may yet have some consequence. Do you make plan to take all with us on flight? How will we explain so many people without document?"

"Daniel wants to go home and this is where Sammy's life is. Besides, we need them on the ground for finishing touches."

Yenchenko crossed his arms and took a wide stance as he watched the new registration numbers grow on the side of the jet engine. "I think they are good soldier, Koshka. I am most opposed to consideration of them as expendable asset. You have plan?"

"Yup."

It was good that Sergei didn't press it, because it would be more luck than tactics for Sammy and Daniel to vanish. And work only if both of them actually wanted to. *The problem with this line of work was always when someone just couldn't leave it alone. Like Dieter. He could have just walked away from Blackbird and run his little hotel with all the pleasure that comes from being a free man.*

Off in a corner, the garbage bag that held the clothing muddied at the end of the runway. On his body, the snug fit of a shirt with co-pilot epaulets a half size and a lot of skill too small. *Yeah, Tommy, like you, too. Just can't let the gator go. This really is how guys get killed.*

They both turned at the sound of footsteps at 9:04 a.m.

Cesar marched across the floor with a packet of material in his right hand and waved it aloft. "We've got clearance."

From the other direction, Daniel called out. "We've got problems," Daniel countered from the other direction.

They gathered around the computer to read a message from Nyx.

"Bad guys gathered at restroom entry, looks like they're done."

Ian muttered. "Bugger. Now what?"

Tommy sighed. "I picked a bad one. Should have figured it wouldn't take much time to get through an airport crapper. Wanted to save the actual drop for later."

Yenchenko brightened. "What flight prepare to depart?"

Everyone looked perplexed, but Tommy acted. "Ask Nyx to identify any flight that has clearance in the next ten to fifteen minutes. Besides us."

Daniel's fingers danced across the keys and he noticed the time was 9:08 a.m.

"You guys for real?" came the reply. "A United flight to Newark and then an American Eagle to Miami."

"Then us," Cesar said.

Tommy sought the telephone again and decided the CIA's communications gear would be on the United flight, in baggage. "They'll call it back to the gate. It'll take twenty, thirty minutes," Ian warned.

"Yes. And buys us just a bit of time, too." Tommy called it in to the communications center at Langley.

Yenchenko grinned. "You have most good plan, Koshka. I have, of course, deduce. Such skill is Russian manner. You make delivery in baggage claim, eh? They are far from tower, far from departure window, far from make connection with authority. Most clever, Koshka. I myself have used such a plan, I think in '83 or perhaps '84."

The jaw of Ian Wells had slowly opened in astonishment and now it was time to speak. "Sergei, you really are quite pathetic."

"Is true!" Yenchenko cried in protest.

"Don't you *ever* grow weary of oozing bullshit? Right. Let's get this aircraft on the tarmac so we can fuel up and get the hell out of here."

Daniel took a long look at his computer, then folded the screen down and handed it to Tommy at 9:10 a.m. "Good luck to you, Mister Tommy. I'll keep my fingers crossed."

"You guys'll get out of here okay? They may have it locked down pretty tight."

Daniel replied with a faint, brave smile. "We shall see. I hear the call of the Obi-man."

Tommy nodded, then pulled the tabeejah from around his neck and offered it to Daniel. When the son of the Obi master waved it off, Tommy said, "Maybe it'll help with some of the local security guys."

"No, sir. It was for you. The tabeejah cannot be given to someone else."

Tommy grinned. "Then perhaps you'll return it. I think he'd like to have it back. I think he'd like to have you back, too."

"You think so?"

"Yes, Daniel, I do. Who knows, maybe you'll get one of these for yourself some day."

Daniel's eyes misted in a faraway look. He bit a quivering lower lip and shook Tommy's hand. Then he excused himself to help Sammy hitch up the nose gear of the Gulfstream. A set of heavy electric motors shattered the silence and bright light poured in as the huge hanger doors opened. Cesar carried a clipboard as he performed the ritual of the walk around, and within minutes, 5,130 pounds of jet fuel topped off the tanks inside long, graceful wings. The fuel crewmen paid no attention to the fuzzy edges and occasional runs of paint on the engines. Cesar signed for the fuel and they rolled on to their next errand.

Aboard, Tommy handed the computer to Ian Wells.

"What's this rubbish?" Wells asked.

"You've been elected to be the communications officer. I'm certain we're going to be chatting with Nyx."

"Thomas, I must protest – "

Tommy shrugged. "I'm going to have my hands full in the cockpit doing a lot of complicated stuff I know nothing about. And Serge – "

Ian Wells lifted a hand in resignation. "Precisely. Very well, then. But only because we're mates, and we shan't make a habit of it." He lifted the screen on the computer and saw the time: 9:25 a.m.

As Tommy settled into the cockpit, Cesar Hernandez was already focused on the task of startup and paused only to hand a card with a string of checkpoints on it. "Welcome to my office, Tommy. Let's begin."

Below on the tarmac Sammy and Daniel drove the tug away. Two cardboard boxes were behind them and they made a nearly straight path toward the baggage servicing area of the main terminal. An American Eagle jet slowly made its way toward the runway, and in the distance a much larger United jet was surrounded by an assortment of security vehicles.

Tommy gave a nervous laugh. "You do realize I have no idea what I'm doing, right?"

Cesar sighed and chuckled as he followed a checklist and flipped switches. "Why do I get saddled with all the rookies?" All the reticence in his voice had vanished, supplanted with a tone of utterly cool command.

Tommy adjusted the pressure of the headphones and tweaked the position of the thin, foam-covered mike to a point just in front of his mouth. The chatter of air traffic control and a half dozen pilots burst into his brain, along with the dry, emotionless litany from Cesar, who pointed to switches and gauges as the countdown began and smiled broadly when the tower gave him a squawk.

When he triggered the auxiliary power unit, the jet came alive, but there was no time to savor it. Electronic screens burst into a variety of colors and too many numbers to follow rambled in inexplicable patterns. Commands became ever more rapid. Growing panic at being unable to keep up. Gratitude that Cesar Hernandez, a man without a passport, a man without a country, a man with a bullet hole in his shoulder, a man who was about to enter United States airspace about as illegal as anyone could get, was still a man in love with flying and patient with a clumsy student.

The real surge began when Cesar was satisfied with data from the gauges, flipped a pair of plastic covers and touched square buttons labeled "engine start" at precisely 9:36 a.m.

Tommy watched the American Eagle flight creep onto the runway and used the moment to gather a fragment of calm. The muted roar of the engines varnished the excitement of the experience with a warning that this was a serious place to be. It was anything but the simple pleasure of an afternoon sail in gentle air. In his ears, the pilots were all business as they communicated with the tower in terse brevity. Air Traffic Control without emotion advised Cesar that Cubana 468 had been moved up in the departure order, which Cesar blithely acknowledged. They watched the American Eagle pause for a moment and then throttle up. Daniel and Sammy's tug stopped and Tommy saw two tiny spots in ground-support orange move around.

When the American Eagle was airborne, Air Traffic Control directed Cesar onto the runway at his earliest convenience. The vehicles around the United flight began to scatter. From behind them, Wells called out and Tommy tugged the headphones away from his left ear.

Ian hollered. "Nyx enquires what's next!"

"We're good to go," Cesar told Tommy. The jet rolled forward under its own power.

The controller's voice crackled in Tommy's right ear.

"Cubana 468 clear for takeoff." It was 9:54 a.m.

"468 cleared for takeoff," Cesar echoed and the aircraft picked up speed to reach the runway. In the distance, the United jet was sealed up and began to creep toward them.

"Dammit, Tommy!" Wells cried from the first seat.

Tommy watched the gauges flutter while the Gulfstream found a position on the runway and paused. "Ask Lucy if she would mind putting an announcement on the public address system."

Wells muttered a curse in a voice just above the rising noise of the jet engines. "I won't repeat her comment, but she agrees to assist."

"Make it: *Attention Mister Lomax. Please meet your party in the baggage claim area.*"

Cesar said, "We're ready for takeoff, Tommy."

"Let's wait thirty seconds for Lomax to get inside."

"Cubana 468?" the tower asked.

Cesar offered a simple excuse for the delay. Tommy pursed his lips and nodded. Seconds ticked away. A faint vibration spread through the aircraft and the gauges declared the engines fully ready.

At last Tommy nodded.

"Cubana 468, good to go," Cesar said to the microphone. His right hand grasped the throttles and eased them forward. The dashed line on the runway began to race under them. Pavement rumbled underneath. Engines reached a screaming pitch and the landscape swept past, faster, ever faster. They zoomed past the lumbering United passenger jet and then the tower and Cesar pulled back on the yoke. The rumble vanished and the nose of the Gulfstream reached for the puffy white clouds and rich blue sky.

"Gear up," Hernandez instructed Tommy. After the final heading instructions from air traffic control, Cesar bid the tower crew a good day at exactly 10:07 a.m.

CHAPTER THIRTY SEVEN

Allentown, Pennsylvania

Drop by drop, a cold drizzle crawled across his hair and slithered down the back of Tommy's neck. The weary baseball cap was saturated, the second-hand jacket damp, the baggy trousers overwhelmed in the chill of a fall afternoon.

Traffic on Fifteenth Street, at the onset of rush hour, crept through a funnel of parked cars. Tommy's ride from the airport, several miles east on Route 22, was long gone. The last of the cash had earlier been used for an overpriced rental car from an off-brand dealer who needed a bribe to disregard the lack of driver's licenses, insurance evidence or major credit cards. While Tommy and the snotty kid at the counter negotiated, Yenchenko made no secret of his desire to pull out an AK-47 and steal the best car on the lot. But Ian Wells had gently intervened. "This is America, mate. Everybody's got guns, *especially* the policemen."

Amid grumbles in the wheezing rental, Ian and Sergei had set off toward Charlottesville, Virginia.

On Fifteenth Street, almost an hour after they separated, he stood in a former parking lot thick with weeds, paper and plastic litter, broken glass and evidence of narcotics traffic, just to the north of a sad, low brick building. In the rain. A weathered painted sign stretched across the face of the structure and whispered "Tramanian Brothers Carpet and Flooring." *We just stole a thirty-eight million dollar aircraft right from under the noses of the CIA and we're flat busted in Allentown, Pennsylvania. Yeah, this is really traveling in style.*

All the windows were boarded up. Several signs said "Sorry, closed today," and others warned trespass was not only forbidden but those who ignored the order might be prosecuted to the full extent of the law. He found an unmarked door on a loading dock.

Drizzle evolved into a light shower and Tommy knocked for the third time on the door. The building had to be occupied because the satellite dish on the roof was brand new, the cables from the street recent and numerous, and the light on both security cameras was on.

From nowhere, a woman said, "We're closed, pal, sorry."

Tommy looked left, right, then up and saw a painted box with perforations in the front that must have housed a speaker.

"Looking for Lucy Tramanian. I'm Tommy Kane."

"Nobody here by that name. Go away, or we'll call the cops."

"How about Echo? Leto? Nyx? Nemesis? Akna?"

There was a longer pause this time and then the voice came back. "You don't look like Tommy Kane. You look like a bum."

"Triton Air. N226TK. Out of Nassau. Just wanted to say thanks and pay for the jet fuel."

"Okay, you're welcome. You owe nothing. Now go away."

"It's raining out here."

"So go find an umbrella."

"Look, Miss Tramanian, I'm just wet, cold, tired."

"Yeah, well, welcome to Allentown. You can leave anytime you want."

"Got nowhere to go."

"You've got a private jet. You can go wherever you want."

Tommy paced back and forth with his hands in his pockets and the chill of the late autumn rain dug in deeper. "Look, I'd really appreciate your help."

"You've already had my help. Look, fella, if you don't take off right now, I'll call the police."

Tommy mustered a smile. "No, you won't. Neither of us can afford it. But suit yourself. I really did want to express my gratitude. The registration shift and double-flight plan was a stroke of genius. Lester said you were the best. Now I believe it. Thanks again, and good luck to you."

He turned up his collar again and winced at the chill. *When you spend too much time in the tropics, you forget about places like Allentown.* Tommy looked at the street scene and decided, *I bet everyone in the neighborhood would like to forget about Allentown, too.*

Tires of passing cars hissed on wet pavement, so he barely heard the click of the lock and the voice behind him. "So why are you interested in Carter Blackmann?"

Tommy turned back to see a mousy woman with straight light brown hair and thick glasses perched on her stubby nose stare at him. She was perhaps three to four inches above five feet tall and rarely outside because her skin was so pale. And she had a small caliber revolver pointed at his chest.

"Excuse me? I was just about to leave, maybe find a cardboard box to crawl under, maybe get a bottle of cheap booze from the local liquor store."

Her eyes focused on the weapon and then rose, and her voice softened as she lowered the pistol to her side. "Maybe you should come in, get out of the rain."

Disappointment. Despair. Defiance. *Exhaustion's the culprit. Indecision is the result.*

Lucy meanwhile looked long and hard in several directions, perhaps anxious that someone watched. "Well? Do you want to dry off or not? Want something warm to drink? Or do you just want to be an asshole and a martyr to boot?"

"A towel and coffee would be good. Thanks for not shooting me."

"The day isn't over yet. But, okay. I'm burned anyway, may

as well have a goddamn open house."

That's the problem. Hackers work in secret, from obscure hideouts. Like this one. But between Lester Finn and Daniel Akintunde, a stranger like me knows who she is and what she does. If I know, who else knows? I'd react the same way.

He stepped toward the open door from which she had vanished.

While his eyes acclimated to the light, Tommy assessed the room: surprisingly vast, gloomy and completely empty. At periodic intervals, low-wattage incandescent lights hid behind masks of steel mesh and splashed ponds of light on the concrete floor.

She strode forward in firm, rapid steps and he followed in silence. "So what are you, some sort of secret agent?"

"Not any more."

"What are you now?"

"Unemployed."

She nodded. "Lot of that going around in the Lehigh Valley. Can I buy you a cup of coffee?" She motioned toward a river of black cables that snaked across the floor toward what Tommy guessed must be an office. From under a closed door, a shaft of light escaped and trickled several feet before it yielded to the gloom.

At the threshold he peered at a large array of black and beige metal and plastic boxes tethered in a web of smaller wires and gray cables. In the center of the room stood a folding table, its legs tan under a surface of dark patterned plastic that was supposed to resemble an exotic wood but nevertheless looked like a cheap surface of a cheap folding table. A cheap fluorescent light hung above and twin four-foot bulbs struggled to illuminate a room that was almost entirely metal shelving, cardboard boxes, and wastebaskets that overflowed. On the perimeter, mismatched filing cabinets stood with empty drawers partially open and large, almost opaque trash bags were stacked nearby, filled with shredded paper.

Three flat screen monitors formed an arc around a keyboard, surrounded by cellophane wrappers of snack foods of all kinds. The litter spilled down to the floor. Tommy eased through the trash and his eyes roamed the monitors. One offered displayed gibberish that scrolled ever upward. A second was full of colorful boxes that Tommy guessed were financial market activity. The third was paused in the middle of a line of some sort of code; the cursor patiently blinked as it awaited command.

"Yeah, yeah, I know," Lucy said as she dropped the gun on a table. "It kinda sucks." She studied him in the stronger but harder light of her lair and was unable suppress a smile. "But, then, wow, look at you. You really do look like shit."

"They don't have a decent tailor in this city, it seems."

"Looks more like off the giveaway rack at Salvation Army Thrift."

Tommy looked down at his shirt and trousers. "As a matter of fact – "

She poured coffee, hoisted the cup and Tommy nodded approval at black. "You're joking."

"No, the one down by – "

"I know it," Lucy said while she handed him the cup. "Donated a bunch of shit there just a few weeks ago. Never knew anyone who actually got the stuff, though."

The heat of the mug was a delight in his hands, but the hot coffee was even better in his throat. It was very strong, not quite as strong as Doc made it but stronger than Duffy's or Sandy's yacht and it was the first drink since the beer last night and the little bit of rainwater they captured at the end of the Nassau runway. Hunger pangs rippled through his belly. "Say, can I buy you supper or something?"

She looked startled. "Um, well, first of all, you look like you're dead broke. And, second, I don't go out with strange men who steal private jets." Her eyes fell away. "But mostly I don't because men don't ask me to."

Shame reddened the cheeks and ears of Tommy. "Sorry, I didn't – "

"Men never do. But hey, you've found my little Oz and met the wizard herself. You can't go away hungry." She reached over and picked up a case of credit cards. "I make these myself. Like to use numbers of politicians mostly. I think I've got half of Harrisburg here." She looked up, then nodded toward a stack of similar cartons, each about the size of a shoebox. "And there, and there. And those too. We have a lot of politicians in our capitol, Mister Kane.

"Tommy. Call me Tommy." *Phony credit cards. That's why the jet fuel didn't cost us anything.*

"Whatever. But it's a pain in the ass to have to actually turn a stolen number into an actual card they can swipe. Costs a fortune." She reached in and tugged a card at random. "Here's a nice one. Big dog from PennDOT, I think. Let's order a pizza and we'll eat in."

I'm beginning to like her style.

Thirty minutes later, Tommy accepted a steaming pie from the college-age driver who for some reason appeared anxious about delivering one pie, two big carbonated soft drinks and complimentary breadsticks to a seedy looking middle-aged man at the back door of an abandoned building with very few lights on behind him.

"I hope you gave him a nice tip," Lucy said while she tugged the first slice from the box.

"My last five bucks seemed fair." The pizza a puddle of colors, slightly warm, coated with grease and about a half inch thick. *It's been a long time. Boy, do I miss a good bowl of gumbo.* He could barely manage the soft drink, sickeningly sweet, and disregarded the bread sticks, which he looked inedible. Two slices of pizza became a fetid mass in his belly. *Welcome home to America.*

Lucy Tramanian methodically worked through the remainder of the pie, folding each slice in half along the long side as if it were a tortilla with something useful on it. She punctuated each slice with a long draw on the straw of a brown beverage in a wax cup, and as she dined, they spoke.

"So I don't understand. How can you be tapped out?"

Tommy nibbled. "Lot of expenses."

"I thought you spies had huge, unlimited expense accounts. First class all the way, no restraint. A guy I know says even the waterboards are top-of-the-line."

"Only in the movies."

"What was it like to fly the jet?"

"Scary. I was afraid I'd break it. What was it like to break into all those systems and rearrange stuff?"

She took a hard pull on the soft drink. "Scary. I was afraid I'd get caught. Gets scarier every time. The good old wild west kind of days are gone, I'm afraid. Used to be a kind of sport, you know, break in, leave your mark, brag about it. Then some went black, everything from crime to espionage. Some went white, doing a little justice, fixing some perceived wrong." She paused for a bite of pizza, chewed it briefly and continued, "Now there's professionals from all over working every system. China. Russia. Iran. Israel. Poland. India. Brazil. Not to mention, of course, our own collection of alphabet outfits. It's gotten so crowded that it's getting tough to get anything done and there's so many organized groups that us independents are getting overwhelmed. Just the other day I was doing a favor for a whistle-blower, good guy, involved with a light rail system in a city not to be named. Just your routine political corruption, an official doing a little skimming. So I get stuck in a honey pot that was just set up by a crew from China Telecom. Such a pain!"

"I didn't know. I guess I should have suspected, though."

"Exactly. I'll show you. Hand me your smart phone."

Tommy shrugged. "What's a smart phone?"

"Very funny. Gimme." She extended her hand and wiggled her fingers.

"Don't have one." The pizza was cooler and less appetizing.

"Everybody has a smart phone."

"No. At least not me."

"Some kind of phone... Wait, you had a laptop."

"That was Daniel's. Or at least it came from Daniel. We chucked it after we landed."

"No tablet, no laptop, no phone, no nothing?"

Tommy offered a placid smile.

Lucy pulled back and stared for several seconds. Her expression was one of pity and her voice softened. "Oh my God. I'm so sorry."

"Why?"

"You must have been stuck in some monastery somewhere."

"San Pedro. Belize."

Lucy tugged another slice from the box. "I knew it. No wonder. You went up to Nassau for a little excitement and stole a Cuban military jet for a change of pace. So what's your interest in Carter Blackmann?"

Tommy related all he knew and how he knew it, then finished with the unanswered questions. She listened while she ate two more slices and finished her soft drink, and when he was done she asked, "Want any more of this?"

Tommy waved it off. "I'm good, thanks."

"Yeah, me, too. I like the guys who own the parlor, but the pies are kinda shitty. Too much grease if you ask me. But they take credit cards. Maybe I'll stick it in the fridge and do the rest for breakfast." She closed the lid on the box and set it on top of equipment that appeared to be disconnected. "So. Let's start with some easy stuff. CIA is getting really pissy about letting outsiders into their system, but the public information side is wide open."

Lucy spun around in her swivel chair, tapped a few commands to clear a screen, and then paid a visit to the Central

Intelligence Agency. Tommy watched from a safe distance but without any grasp of the material she examined.

"Ah, well, your mysterious C-213 is easy enough. That's Carter Blackmann's office suite. Here's a phone number. Want to give him a call to say hello?"

So C-213 is a unit designation belonging to Carter Blackmann. What had Myra Fielding said? Barry Mather worked for Blackmann. Lomax worked for Mather. Or was it the other way around? Blackmann's people were also up to their ears in narcotics traffic, probably to fund off-the-books projects. "No, thanks. I doubt that he's in."

"Oh, yeah, something about Charlottesville. Virginia? Hm. Let's find a bio, maybe the address of his place in Virginia. Ah. Here we go. Pretty heavy resume, Tommy. Guy's a big leaguer, probably still rising." Her voice trailed off to mumbles as she read the history of Carter Blackmann. "Talk about Mister Perfect. The guy is almost too good to be true. Let's just see."

Lucy lapsed into complete silence while lines of text scrolled upward across the screen. She repeated the list twice, then shook her head. In a voice laced with intrigue, said, "This is really, really odd."

Tommy leaned forward. On her computer monitor, Lucy repeatedly scrolled up and down several more times, switched to another set of files, then another, and finally returned to the first. Tommy was left in the electronic dust as she zoomed ahead. When she stopped, she turned and with her fingertips brushed her hair back over her ear.

"What?"

She began to speak, then paused to reframe her discovery in a context that a neophyte might grasp. "When a file is stored on a computer, the computer logs the date and time it was filed or modified. All the biographical data for Carter Blackmann was not only loaded at the same time, but it was backdated, again all to the same date."

Tommy shrugged. "So maybe there was some glitch and they had to fix stuff? All I know about computers it that they're always getting fouled up."

She chuckled. "It's the users that get fouled up. Computers pretty much do just what they're told. But to answer your question, all the other directories behind these public web pages look fairly normal. Someone's been revising Blackmann's biography and made a monumental screw-up." She crossed her arms and displayed a look of smug satisfaction.

I know I'm missing something, but I have no idea what. Maybe the guys were right. It's getting out of hand and I'm getting too old to learn. Is there still time to walk away? Nah. "Sorry. I'm utterly ignorant about this stuff. Blackmann's about as political as it gets, so his public image is always going to be retouched and smoothed out. And trust me, the people in the CIA make monumental screw-ups all the time."

Like the chess game at Dieter's hotel. I'm pulling Myra's chain when I should have been paying attention to Mather. And Lester. Maybe even Blackbird or Matthias or whatever his name was. Monumental screw-up.

Lucy pressed her hands together, then used them to touch her lips. "You're really perceptive and absolutely correct."

Compliments are always nice to calm the target. Targets like myself..

"But if you're going to go to the effort to backdate, then why blow it on the load date? It doesn't make anyone guilty, Tommy, but it does create an anomaly, something just enough out of place. Ninety-nine out of a hundred people wouldn't think twice about it. But you think he's dirty. So now these things get noticed, raise a suspicion. And give us a starting point."

A queasy sensation rumbled through his body. Hopefully, just the pizza and not illness from the cold rain, the exhaustion of the day. *Or those first hints of aging, when your body starts to let you down.*

"You okay?"

"Just tired, I guess. Long day." *Now, there's an understatement.* "I'll be fine."

"So why did you steal that airplane? Really."

"Needed a ride. Why did you help?"

"Needed the thrill. I've never hacked the FAA before, and it was kind of interesting, concocting a flight plan. Airports are easy, but the network running all those jets around is really elegant. Trust me, flying is really safe and secure. What are you going to do with the plane?"

"Probably keep it. I'd like to learn how to fly it."

"What about the others?"

"The pilot's laying low, and my partners are headed for Blackmann's farm."

"To kill him?"

"Reconnaissance. They're not much into computers. Neither am I, for that matter."

Her eyes repeatedly sought the discovery on the screen. Maybe anxious, maybe distracted. She was going to pursue it with or without him. All his senses were being drawn in from the surfaces of his body and sucked into a cesspit of bad pizza, shallow sleep to often interrupted and the despair that thrives like a virus in the grim aftermath of chaos. His eyes burned and wanted to close tight.

"Maybe you ought to get some rest. You really do look like death warmed over. There's some mattresses on the other side of the warehouse. There's a bathroom, too, with a shower that sometimes works. Grab any towel."

I know she's right. I want to stay with this, but I'm out of gas. Haven't had any decent rest since, when? Yeah, since Andros Island, the day before I heard the Obi-man. The image of the Alden wouldn't come. "You're right. Thanks again for the assist. We would have been sitting ducks without your help."

"Really?"

"Really."

Lucy mustered a faint smile. "Good to know I'm going out on a positive note. You guys were supposed to be my last little adventure. Like I said, it's getting way too crowded, way too dangerous and, no offense, but if you can figure me out and track me down, well, then, I'm really burned."

"Sorry. And no offense taken."

"It's okay, Tommy. Honest. I'm tired of the game anyway. Nobody cares. I could be Joan of Arc and they'd still burn me at the stake."

"What are your plans?"

She sighed. "You know, I'm thinking maybe six months or a year off. Get a condo in Miami or someplace warm. Sit around and read library books all day, eat too much, not give a shit."

"Then what?"

"I dunno. Maybe get a job as a stock clerk at a discount store. Or a custodian in a museum. Maybe buy a farm in North Dakota."

Tommy thought of the past six years and what he had envisioned for the balance of his life. "Sounds boring. But maybe boring is good."

"Yeah, maybe so. I'll think about it tomorrow. Just one last little hack and I'll pack it up for good."

Chapter Thirty Eight

A whisper of light from a tiny, distant window, a glimmer so faint his eyes required no adjustment. Dreamy icons gathered after a dreamless sleep, welcoming him to consciousness.

The Alden. Freedom, on a course for endless horizon. Mandy Owens. Beauty and grace, in a room full of illusion. The Gulfstream, majestic power, stolen from a dead man.

When Tommy yawned a second time, the icons dissipated. *Stench.* The stench of dusty mattress, faintly moist concrete, his own clothes, the rags from Salvation Army.

At the tiny bathroom sink, he prepared to scrub dirt from the polo shirt and khaki shorts, way out of season for Allentown, but at least his own. Just as he was about to plunge the shorts into a pool of lukewarm water, he rescued a stiff card and a twenty-dollar bill from a pocket.

The business card from Walter Campos. First class card. Thick stock. Just a name and number, not even an address. A second look, a grunt of amusement. Not such a first-class card after all. Walter Campos. (217) 147-8255. Phone number can't be right. *Never heard of an exchange starting with a one.*

Looking up, toward a cracked mirror. *Welcome back to reality. There's got to be something better than this.* The sodden clothing in the sink. *Okay, pull it together. Feeling better, had a good night's sleep, like the one after Joseph's kumina. What day is it? It is today, Addo had said. You are too late for yesterday and too early for tomorrow.*

He found Lucy Tramanian lost in keyboard taps, muttered grumbles and a flow of code on her computer screen. She touched something and the flow stopped. "Aha," she said to the monitor. "Gotcha, you sonofabitch." Her posture stiffened and she leaned a bit forward, typed for a few seconds, then leaned back as if to admire a work of art.

"Morning," Tommy said. "Am I interrupting?"

Lucy spun in her chair. "More like good afternoon. Wow. Not exactly what I pictured in a spy."

"The media always gets it wrong."

On a packing crate near her chair, half a box of doughnuts kept company to a folded set of clean clothes.

"Welcome back. You've been out for sixteen, almost seventeen hours." She extended her arm and waved toward the doughnuts. "Breakfast?"

Pink frosting with colorful bits of candy had begun to fracture as it dried and the off-white filling that oozed from one of the pastries looked indecent. "No thanks."

To the folded clothing, she said, "There was a guy, about your size. I didn't remember them until after you were asleep."

"What happened to the guy?"

Her voice was melancholy. "He went away. They always did. After a while, they never showed up in the first place. How about coffee?"

"Coffee would be good." His eyes roamed the room for a pot but found only a pair of foam cups from the same store that sold the doughnuts. One was empty, the other full and probably cold.

"There's a microwave. And some actual mugs. You can warm it up. I took another chance on black."

"Perfect." His hand wrapped around the foam container and peeled off the lid.

"So, tell me about your family."

Tommy's immediate reaction was defensive, but he remembered the image in the mirror, decided he no longer really cared, but nonetheless asked "Why?"

She backed away slightly, like a kitten does when unsure of a new toy. "Sorry. Kind of a hobby. I always wanted to know how someone gets into espionage, and I bet it has to do with the way you were brought up." Her tone shifted to apology and she looked away. "I guess I spend too much time alone."

Tommy cocked an eyebrow and began his answer while he poured the coffee into a ceramic mug and brought the microwave to life. He summarized with honesty and without emotion. The coffee was stale and awful but delicious and welcome at the same time. *People who ask about your family usually want to tell you about theirs.* "What about yours?"

She looked away, toward an uncomfortable memory. "Just my father."

Bug. The guy everyone knew only as Bug. Understandable. What girl wants a dad who everyone knows as Bug?

She took a breath and sighed and a faint shrug. "He wanted me to be like him. I didn't. But I failed. Now I'm too proud to go crawling back."

Let it go, change the subject. "You sounded like you solved some sort of problem when I came in and interrupted. Like you won a round."

Lucy Tramanian's eyes lit up and an expression of satisfaction flooded her face, like sunshine when a dark cloud goes away.

"Oh, yeah. Well, not all that big a thing. There's a Ukrainian guy in Brooklyn named Alexei Krikunenko, but everyone knows him as A-Man. King of the spammers, you know, computer experts who flood everyone's email with junk. He specializes in faked internet links that go to porn sites. Gets off on putting it on monitors in school classrooms and labs."

Tommy winced. "So you figured something out."

"Not only did I lock up his computer, but his server, too."

"He sounds like the kind of guy that'll just pick up somewhere else."

Lucy grinned. "Not this time. I stuffed his hard drive with all the evidence in a big child porn ring the Justice Department has been working on. Lifted it from a P-C the feds were using as bait in their investigation, buried it in his drives, made him look like the source and tipped off the cops. They're knocking on his door right now, with a warrant."

"What about the real ringleader?"

Lucy she reached for a doughnut. "I'm nearly certain they already have him. Well, her, actually. Just haven't figured it out yet."

"And your spammer guy?"

"He got a bonus," she answered. Lucy studied the doughnut and dropped it back in the box. "Detailed plans of JFK and Newark Airports, with a lot of bomb-making stuff. Between the FBI and Homeland Security and no valid visa, he's going to have fun for a while. Think they might waterboard him?"

Tommy rubbed his chin. "Maybe, but not on U.S. soil. You'd have to rendition him to another country."

"Any suggestions?" Her hands seemed poised over the keyboard.

"Who's busting him? FBI?"

"No, just NYPD."

"Your spammer guy will be just fine in Rikers. Inmates aren't fans of terrorists, but they really despise child porn guys."

"Fantastic." A pause of satisfied reflection ended with, "So, yeah, I'm in a good mood. I was doing a favor for an old teacher of mine, and it worked out okay."

"We should celebrate. I found twenty bucks in a dirty pair of shorts. Why don't I buy you breakfast?"

Lucy bit her lower lip and looked around the room that Tommy suspected was her entire world. Finally her eyes found his and she spoke softly, but with resolve. "Sure, why not? Only more like lunch, or an early supper. I've heard of a really nice place, Pennsylvania Dutch, on the road to Emmaus."

"Fine with me. Anything but junk food and old coffee."

She gathered up a simple bag, keys, a few credit cards and a tentative smile. "First, we're going to make a couple of stops. We'll need to get you a car and some decent clothes. The nice thing about Route 22 is that you can pretty much find everything you need."

Tommy gathered folded clothing from the carton and promised a better appearance. He looked at a changing expression on her face, as if she changed her mind and made decision. He lifted his eyebrows to inquire.

She sat down and her shoulders slumped. "I'm sorry. I'm not being fair. I've got some news for you. I think I figured out the identity of your Blackbird."

CHAPTER THIRTY NINE

Lucy tapped a keyboard button and a pair of faces appeared side by side on the monitor. Although the images displayed faces of much different ages, they were the same man.

On the right, the formal CIA studio portrait of Carter Blackmann stared straight ahead, at a point beyond the camera. Stiff, uncomfortable, distant. A smile both thin and forced. An adversary even to the photographer, and an impatient one at that.

The man on the left. Impatient, but furtive, not quite making eye contact with the camera, the kind of picture they get of you when you're getting a driver's license the day after you partied too much.

Lucy leaned back, crossed her arms and presented a smug smile. "Meet Josef Rabemann. This is a photo from 1978, about the time he joined a group known as the SED."

"*Sozialistische Einheitspartei Deutschlands.* We called it the Socialist Unity Party, but everyone believed it was just a hyper-Communist front for the old USSR."

"Wow, you can say those twenty-five cent German words pretty good."

Tommy shared a smile of modesty but focused on the screen. "Spent a lot of time there." *Rabemann. Raven, raven man. Blackbird. Blackmann.* "The most fundamental mistake someone can make when faking identities in a hurry. Carter Blackman may be a big leaguer, but he made a bush-league mistake."

"Yes, well, *Rabe* is the German word for *raven*, and it's a bird with all kinds of folklore attached to it, all over the world. So he could have picked it for any number of reasons."

"Picked?"

"Yep. I'm good, Tommy, but even I get stuck sometimes. I managed to track your Blackbird back to seventy-eight, but there's no record of him at all before then. It's like he popped up out of thin air. It wasn't as easy then to organize a good identity. On the other hand, old records can be a real pain in the ass to work through. I mean, I can pursue it if you want."

"Where did he turn up?"

"Dresden. It was – Oh, yeah, of course you'd know that. Sorry."

He muttered, "*Tal der Ahnungslosen.*"

She seemed surprised. "Valley of the Clueless. They still talk about that over there, like it's some kind of joke. Something to do with radio reception. "

The encounter with Mather in Beverly Hills, asking if he was from the Valley of the Clueless. "Or just one of those things that someone stupidly says, out of habit."

"Yeah, well, anyway: I spent a little time on the folklore thing and the only one that seemed to fit has to do with a legend about Barbarossa, the ancient German king? The story goes that he and his crew are asleep in a cave in Bavaria or Thuringia and when the ravens stop flying around the mountain, the old emperor wakes up and restores Germany to its ancient glory. Kind of funny because it was the reunification that, um, kinda made the difference?"

Lucy repeatedly shifted in her chair, the personification of fidgety.

She's a hunter. She's been hunting and she's bagged a trophy. Like all hunters, she wants to tell her tale. Just like we all do when a perfect op goes like clockwork and the best part is debriefing, show and tell. Lunch can wait.

Lucy's voice filled with pride like a spinnaker in brisk aft air. Tommy nodded approval at technical terms he did not understand, protocols he could not grasp, and a play-by-play that would bring the ultimate tech person to tears of boredom. But no way would he interrupt the presentation.

She was reaching a point. "...And so it dawned on me that the best way to go would be to look backward, rather than guessing at arbitrary points in ancient history."

Ancient? Wow, since when did 1978 become prehistoric? Life was simple then, and espionage a respectable line of work.

She succumbed to a stale doughnut. "I love Germans. In another life, I'd love to be German. Their sense of order, technical skill, their continual drive for perfection: just amazes me, all the time." Lucy paused to add impact to her next line.

First rate story-teller, too.

"Like just a couple of years ago, they created new identity cards, sort of a combination everything – "

"*Personalausweis*, they call it."

"Exactly," she continued. "The new ones have RFID – radio-frequency identification – chips embedded, biometric pictures, sometimes even fingerprints, electronic signatures, on and on. There was a lot of controversy about it at the time, but they're almost impossible to fake."

Dieter would have hated it. So would a lot of Americans. It's called tracking where you are. I bet Lucy's kind of hacking makes her very security conscious.

Lucy leaned forward and her hands began to accentuate punctuation. "Anyway, in Germany, everyone over the age of 16 has to get one. And in 2010, everyone in the country got replacement cards issued to them from the *Bundesministerium des Innern* – Ministry of the Interior – and the Federal Office for Information Security."

"Oh, yeah. The BSI. *Bundesamt für Sicherheit in der Informationstechnik.* It was always fun to deal with those guys. Good people, always helpful. The ones I knew were experts on the best bars and restaurants."

Lucy shrugged. "But of course, there were a certain number of no-shows. People who moved away. People who died. People who somehow slipped through the cracks."

"Or people who couldn't pick up theirs from their local registration office or the *Bundesdruckerei*. That's where they're made now, in Berlin." The concept was delicious. "People like Blackbird, who had a new identity."

She nodded enthusiastically and her eyes sparkled in the glare of the rows of suspended fluorescent shop lights that hung over their heads. "So being the gloriously precise people they are, the Germans kept orderly records of no-shows. All I had to do was look up names of guys about the age of Blackmann."

"And track them back further."

"Yep. That's the beauty of it. I didn't pay attention to the names, because I thought, well, it's an alias, a fake identity. That brought me to the previous change in identity cards, in November, 2001."

Nobody paid attention then. The twin towers in Manhattan were still at the top of everyone's mind.

"It was pretty much the same deal, just not as elegant a card. They plugged in a slew of holographic security stuff." She tapped a couple of keys and a sample image came up on the screen. "Don't you just love the three-dimensional eagle and the holographic shadow pictures? Microprinting, machine-readable zone, kinematic elements. State of the art for the time, really tough to fake."

We did it all the time.

"So same thing. Cards go out. No-shows as usual, a list stored in a dusty old file, city, name, age, gender. I lop ten years off my guess and there's a new name: Rabemann, Josef, from Dresden." She drifted off into technical jargon again, but Tommy listened attentively, even though it meant nothing to him other than to remind him of how obsolete he really was.

One thing to not play the game on general principle, but in the trade, they've got people really good at this stuff, people like Lucy. It's kind of like trying to go one-on-one with an AR-15 when all you've got is a B-B gun. Myra was right. It's time for me to get out. Especially when Lucy says it's getting too much for her and she wants out, too.

Lucy continued. "That brings us to the late eighties, when the *West* Germans came up with a pretty good card for the time, a real departure from the paper identity booklet format *both* sides developed just after the war."

Again she made a few keystrokes and an older type of card appeared on the screen. "These were issued after the spring of 1987. Just a single laminated sheet of paper, but they used some pretty decent microprinting, fluorescent dies, watermarks and look at the engraving on these guillochés. Aren't they gorgeous? Isn't the pattern they make elegant?"

"Yeah, I guess so."

"Well, of course, Rabemann didn't get one of those when they were issued, because he was in the East, in Dresden, right?"

"Right."

"So East Germany collapsed in '89 and the countries merged within the year. All the former East Germans could get a card by applying for one, but the unexpired East German cards were valid all the way through the end of 1995. Josef Rabemann never put in for one."

"Because he was gone."

She beamed. "I know where you're going. The new German government took charge of all the old East German records, obviously for a lot more than 'welcome back to the Fatherland.' And I'm assuming that on their way out the door, the bad guys in East Germany probably did their best to destroy stuff they didn't want the West to find. But Josef Rabemann was in those lists, all the way back to 1978, when he would have been maybe twenty-five, twenty-six."

"And I bet there's nothing before then."

"Exactly. Rabemann appeared out of thin air. Lots of credentials, a vague little bio, but that's all. Sorry, I can't find anything before seventy-eight. I even tried obituaries for the area right around the time, but came up blank. I guess a lot of people died unnoticed."

"Darn nice work, a lot more than I ever could have expected."

"Thanks. It means a lot."

Tommy said, "So sometime after the wall came down, Rabemann packed up and went to the Americans. Or maybe just came in from the cold. But if that was the case, why a whole new identity? As a successful mole, he'd get a hero's welcome, if only because he probably brought a ton of intelligence with him. It's not that the East Germans would put a contract on him. It was the other way around."

Her eyes narrowed. "Unless he went from being a run-of-the-mill mole to a kind of super-mole. I've seen that in corporate stuff, where a company gets someone in, they do their thing, and then go to another company with really first-rate stuff and move up the ladder to being able to feed top-level stuff."

"Really?"

"Really. There's a couple of banks with insiders in the Fed, and some of our defense contractors do it all the time in Asia. Drives the Chinese nuts, so of course, they try to return the favor."

"Wow. I guess I've been away for much too long."

"Um, well, yeah." She sighed and retreated to a diminutive voice coated with melancholy. "Tommy, I've been in love with computers all my life. It's amazing how the technology evolves and kind of sucks you in. One thing leads to another and then, well, look around. You wind up with shit like this, knowing hardly anyone and trusting nobody, paranoid as hell, hiding out with phony identities and layers of security. Then one day you realize it's going so fast and there are so many systems where everyone's in it for themselves. Everyone will lie, cheat, steal because it's not for some noble cause. It's for the game itself and who has high score."

Her voice had become increasingly strident and then mellowed as her eyes misted. "It becomes, well, kind of like a black hole you swim around in because you think you're hot shit and can get away with it, but in the end, it just pulls you in further. I want to quit. I really do. I'm just not sure I can."

A sad silence hung in the air and for long seconds the only sound came from the hum of the lights and a cooling fan on the computer.

Her world isn't really much different than mine. Doc. Sandy. Joseph the Obi-man. The last time he saw his grandfather. Moses Clay. *You don't need a gun. You need redemption.*

Lucy Tramanian pulled herself together. "Screw it. Let's go get something to eat."

CHAPTER FORTY

Emmaus, Pennsylvania

A stout waitress who looked like she could run a no-nonsense farm kitchen waited, pen poised over a pad. Tommy and Lucy held simple menus bound in brown vinyl covers with the Esse Haus Family Restaurant stamped on the front.

Although still early for dinner hour, the restaurant was about half filled, mostly with quiet grey-haired couples who ate methodically and said little. A slate-board sign near the entry proclaimed "Early Brd. Spec. til 5:30" and kept company with a more neatly lettered counsel that the "Hostess Will Seat You."

The dim but cozy dining room consisted of hefty dark-stained pine chairs and matching tables, shiny in high-gloss varnish, in the center and two lines of ancient booths along outside walls. Distractions of a former two-lane farm road that now bore the traffic of suburbia were hidden behind gingham curtains.

Tommy skimmed unfamiliar names on the menu and asked for the day's specials or specialties. He wore a navy blazer, open-collared fitted shirt and crisply creased trousers from which labels had just been removed in a shopping mall restroom.

The waitress shared the easy smile that goes with start of shift and the potential for a substantial tip. "Today the *Getulte Rindbrust* is especially nice. This is a beef fillet, seasoned with onion and parsley, rolled and tied and cooked to tender, with gravy. Also, we have traditional *Bott Boi*, a stew from beef, chicken, ham, potato, noodles and stock from onion, carrots and celery. It's a house specialty. And also very popular are *Leber Kloese*, which are liver dumplings. The liver is seasoned, fried and then cooked in dough to make the dumplings. Very nice."

Lucy said, "The stew sounds good."

Tommy smiled. "I'll have the *Rindbrust* and for the lady, *Bott Boi.*"

"And side dishes? You get two."

Lucy scanned the menu. "Chow-chow and red beet eggs."

"The same. And a bottle of house red?"

The scribbled the order on her pad. "Yessir."

Lucy took a sip of water. "You clean up pretty nice, Tommy." She looked down and softly added, "Look, I'm very sorry about what I said back at my place. I kind of lost it."

"Don't be. I'm not much different. I understand. Times change, time to change. I just want to finish this thing, move on."

She turned her fork over and over. "You never said exactly why you're doing this. Is it revenge or some nefarious assignment? How much does someone get paid to do this kind of stuff?"

"Nothing quite so dramatic. All three of us are burned agents, pretty much kicked out, on our own. One had an idea for a robbery, drug money, which went bad. As it turned out, it was just a con by a guy who's probably being blackmailed by Carter Blackmann. He's promised a reward to get it back, but I'm not so sure."

"What kind of reward?"

"He says a billion dollars, split three ways. We'll see."

Her eyes widened. "A *billion* dollars? Like, with *nine* zeros?"

"Well, not quite, but supposedly close. Like I said, we'll

see."

"Must be some file he's after. God, I can't even imagine. A billion dollars. What about the jet?"

"The Gulfstream? We needed a ride, so the short version is that we stole it. With some really slick help from you, by the way. I really liked the fake domestic flight plan. No customs or immigration when we got in. Cesar was grateful. He's not documented."

She split a dinner roll and clobbered it with cold butter. "Cesar did a great job following instructions. Anyway, to be honest, I was actually kind of lazy. The FAA was tough enough, so to get foreign traffic control involved would have made it more complicated. Sometimes simple is better. Anyway, the Cuban army must be pissed. What's one of those jets go for anyway?"

"They were in a spot. They couldn't claim it without, well, consequences. Now it's mine. I'd say it's worth maybe thirty million or so. They depreciate the moment they leave the showroom, you know."

The waitress returned with two glasses and a bottle of domestic wine. She poured and Tommy sampled his, signaled approval and the waitress promised their meal would be along soon. In the meantime, they could help themselves to the salad bar.

Lucy sampled her wine. "I'm not sure one bottle of wine is going to be enough. What do you plan to do with a billion dollars and a corporate jet?"

"Vanish."

"Ha. That's what your Blackbird tried to do. Not so easy, is it?"

"And what about you? Were you really serious about a long vacation and then some sort of a dead-end job? Seems like the sort of thing that could destroy a good mind like yours."

She laughed. "Maybe I'll do the same thing. Take the

money and run, disappear. Actually, I already have, sort of."

"The money or the disappear?"

"Both."

Tommy lifted his glass in salute and drank. "Good for you."

"You're an interesting man, Tommy."

"I'm curious, though. We were really up against it in Nassau, and there was no way Daniel could have pulled off what you did. You had to get involved for more than a thrill."

She nodded. "Lester Finn. He said you were a big timer, the kind of guy who thrives on adventure. I thought it would be fun to join the game for a while. Besides, you could have had Lester busted in that casino, which would have ruined everything."

"It's all trade-offs. Lester did me a favor, I did Lester a favor, things worked out."

She formed a wicked smile and leaned forward to speak in a low voice. "He went to Vegas, to Atlantic City and finished in Bethlehem. We used shills and we did some jackpots. Good enough for me. But not a billion dollars. You're in a whole different league, Tommy."

H laughed. "Haven't got the billion. Yet."

The waitress arrived with a huge tray and a folding serving station that she opened with a single hand. "Mind your plates. They're hot." After asking the obligatory question, she was told everything was fine and she gathered the serving equipment and left them to their meal.

Lucy organized a napkin and her knife and fork. "This looks wonderful."

"Want to lend a hand?"

"With your – ? Oh, that! Well, gosh, Tommy, I wondered when the other shoe was going to drop. You're not serious."

"I am. Want a job?"

She filled her fork with thick stew and cocked an eyebrow. "What kind of job?"

"We sort of need to break into the CIA, where Blackmann keeps his stuff, and steal the assets of a front company they used called Gulf Chemical and Gas. That's the billion. Well, almost a billion. How about ten percent?"

Lucy chewed her food and then dabbed her lips with a napkin and laid the fork on the edge of her platter. "And I suppose you guys think I'm the only person who could pull this off? For what, maybe almost a hundred million dollars?"

Tommy sawed off a slice of beef fillet and nodded. "Well, yeah. I mean, you did a great job with the jet and all. The 2-2-6-T-K was a nice touch."

"Thank you for noticing." She leaned back in her chair to gather her thoughts and then forward to present them. "It's a very ambitious idea. But I'm afraid I'm not going to be able to help you. Roaming around in low-level government files that are pretty much public information anyway is one thing. But the CIA system is something else. You're talking about tokens with access codes that change every few minutes. Really high level passwords. Telemetry that goes so fast that it can't be tracked. Honey traps like land mines. Encryption that even the NSA admires. One false step and guys in big black SUVs swoop down on you like hawks. Think about it, Tommy: every really, really good intelligence agency in the world would love to even begin to crack it. That's the holy grail and way, way beyond me. Sorry. I guess you'll have to make do without your billion dollars."

They stabbed at food from their respective plates in a tense minute of silence except for the soft clatter of distant dishes and the hum of fragmented conversations.

It was an idiotic idea. She's right as summer rain. Why would I even think the CIA could be hacked? Why would Walter Campos even suggest it? Were we that gullible? Or did he know something? Just hope Serge and Ian don't get upset and come after me.

At last Lucy sighed and offered sympathy. "I'm really, really sorry, Tommy. But I'll give you points for setting the bar really high. Not many guys steal thirty million dollar jets on the way to billion dollar burglaries. Gosh, you should get points just for dreaming it."

Dreaming's one thing. Planning is another. I can hear Paw-paw now. The time to peel your crawfish is before you eat them. Which reminds me...

Tommy pulled the card from Walter Campos from his shirt pocket and felt its thickness. Lucy's eyes found it and curiosity spread across her face. "What's that?"

"A business card. Here, feel it. It seems like it's really thick, kind of like two light cards stuck together. We used to do that sort of thing in the, uh, old days."

Lucy Tramanian took the card and studied it in the dim light of the restaurant. "Wow, Walter Campos. No wonder you think big. He's one of those super-rich guys who has an incredible amount of luck and no one seems to figure out where he gets his information."

"Yeah, but the printer had to have screwed up with the phone number."

She focused on the series of digits and then stared at Tommy. "That's because it's not a phone number. It's an I-P address." To his blank stare, she explained. "Every computer in the world that's on the net has a unique I-P address, sometimes permanent, sometimes transient. That's how information knows where to travel. You ask for something and the request goes out with your return address. Whatever the reply, it knows where to find you."

It was good to actually understand something about computers for a change, but to avoid admitting it, he asked for details.

"Well, first of all, he's obviously hidden it. Not too great, but probably not really noticeable. If you ignore the usual old fashioned telephone garbage you get a series of numbers: 2171478225. Now the problem is where to stick in the periods that make this work. But sets range from 1 to just 255 and there's always four, so something like 21.714.782.25 won't be valid because two of them are bigger than 255. And 2.17.147.8.225 won't work because there's too many sets. Probably 217.147.8.225. And yes, you're right. This card seems a bit too thick."

She handed it back to him and took another bite of her meal.

Tommy looked at the numbers and mentally discarded the parentheses and the hyphen, then spent a few moments trying to find combinations that fit the criteria she defined. *What did Campos say? If you're still interested in a profitable venture, give me a call. Day or night. He wants me to call a computer somewhere.* "So how do we match it up with a specific computer?"

She reached into her bag and found her cell phone, sighed and began to lightly tap the screen. "Why did I just guess you'd eventually ask that question?" By the time she began to use her thumbs to enter a message, Tommy succumbed to temptation and dipped the corner of his napkin into his water glass. After he squeezed away excess moisture, Tommy used the napkin to massage an edge of the card. Within moments, the paper began to separate.

Easy, easy, he told himself. *There's going to be something delicate inside.*

"The I-P is from outside of Galveston, Texas.... Oh, wow. It's registered to Gulf Chemical and Gas. "

She went silent while he gently peeled the card apart and discarded a curled, thinner piece. Then she continued, "It's an actual company, with a website and everything... What *are* you looking at?"

Tommy pulled the card close to his face, winced, then pushed it away. At last he leaned back and extended his hand with the damp card sprawled on his fingertips. She gingerly accepted and cradled it in the palm of her left hand.

Tommy remembered Walter's words. *The files weren't in Langley. He had people on the inside and knew they were someplace else.* "Must be some kind of code, one of those encrypted things. Just a series of letters and numbers, some capitalized, some lower case. Some sort of message, I guess."

He heard Walter's voice. *You're a very resourceful man, Mister Tommy. I admire that in a fellow.*

She looked up and he saw an odd mixture of astonishment, awe and anxiety in her eyes. "I think we're going to skip dessert, Tommy. It's not a code. It's a *key.*"

Tommy slumped back in his chair and realization brought a smile. He saw confusion in Lucy's response when he recalled the party at Lyford Cay and the golf match before it and the words of Walter Campos: *Got your initiation. And now you've got a key.* He marveled at the old man's skill in passing information and could only imagine how much fun it must have been to do it right under the nose of Carter Blackmann.

Lucy began to explain the function of an encryption key to access a computer system, not unlike those used routinely in espionage for ciphers. But Tommy already knew the value of the gift, and how the advantage in the match of wits with Blackmann had shifted. As with a change of wind in a yacht race, the captain who sensed it and responded first unexpectedly gained an enormous advantage.

He looked up and into her eyes and she paused.

"The castle gate," she murmured. "Once we go in, there's no turning back."

Chapter Forty One

On an unmarked service road, snaking for a quarter of a mile through thick stands of naked trees, dark gravel crunched under Tommy's shoes. In the faint, prolonged sigh of air whispering through the forest, a disturbed crow cried out and its *caw-caw* ricocheted through the gloom of a waning late autumn rain. Raw damp clung to the forest floor and softened decaying leaves. Footsteps twenty yards to his left and right were muffled and betrayed only when the heel of a heavy boot fractured a twig.

It was dawn, and the sun had not yet burned through low clouds to chase the chill away.

The service road ballooned into a cul-de-sac where a chorus of bright yellow no trespassing placards haloed a large wooden sign: *Private Property. No Admittance.*

The castle gate. Like yesterday, when Lucy amazed with blithe efficiency using the key from Walter's mole to slip through a back door of Gulf Chemical and Gas. A check of the electronic roadmap, a test of a binary doorknob and so began the process of transferring ownership. The company was privately held by a faceless group, meaning she'd not have to waste time with the Securities and Exchange Commission and major brokerage houses on Wall Street. Because it was just a front company, she suspected and quickly found a side path into the data cellar of the CIA, from which she could roam freely. And completely erase Tommy Kane.

"How about a nice, fresh name to go with a whole new identity?" she had asked.

"No thanks, mine's just fine."

She had looked over her glasses and down her nose. "You know, to erase you, then rebuild, I've got to know everything about you. Everything. You good with that?"

Yeah, what the hell. The old Tommy Kane wasn't much to write home about anyway. It's time to trust.

Private Property. No Admittance. The sign was wired to a broad metal gate that blocked an unpaved path, a path that crept ever deeper into the gray forest, down hill toward a curve and into the private domain of Carter Blackmann. Tommy studied rusted field fence that formed a line in both directions while he paused for thirty seconds.

There's always a trail, even if it's a few breadcrumbs in the snow. Josef Rabemann or whoever he was thought he was safe, because no one is looking any more. Only guys like me. Guys who made it personal. When they shouldn't. So I told Lucy there was always a trail. And she said, "Not when I do it."

Tommy had waited long enough. And then he ignored all the warnings.

Within a hundred yards, the bluish gloom of night's end became the pink blush of a new day. In the bones of the trees reaching to the sky, a hint of pink and orange washed across an otherwise pale eastern sky, and at the intersection of a bridle path, he paused again to allow Ian and Sergei to slip through the woods in something of a floating box.

A lone horse and rider approached from the right. Tommy squared his shoulders, felt the comfort of the Beretta tucked into the waistband at the small of his back, and stood brazen and motionless while Carter Blackmann ventured forward with complete indifference. The director's impressive saddle posture flowed with the rolling back of the animal and he gave no hint of surprise or welcome. When he was within fifteen feet, he pulled up and dismounted.

"Hello, Mister Kane," Blackmann said after a visual appraisal. "I had a sense that we would meet again. Yes. I think it was, what, just yesterday that I told a few associates who came by for drinks that Mister Thomas Kane was expected at most any time." He pulled a treat for the horse from his jacket pocket and fed the animal. "Of course, they expressed disbelief. They thought – now, just stay with me on this – that after you bungled your way out of New Providence, you'd have learned your little lesson and gone to ground, to places where all the little vermin hide, and shiver in fear. Yes, that's what they said all right. Can you imagine that?"

Tommy shrugged.

"Yes, of course. A shrug to say nothing and everything at the same moment, that gesture of uncertainty, that small twinge of unease that becomes all the difference between men such as you and I. You look well, Kane. And speaking for myself," he lowered his voice to a confidential tone, "and you'll promise not to tell the others, I really was rather impressed with that flight plan switch. The Company must have spent fifty or sixty thousand from sorely needed budget to sniff about in Caracas for an aircraft that never existed."

Tommy smiled. "When you're only a teaspoon of static, you sometimes have to make some white noise."

Blackmann looked down, toward his boots, and forced a smile. "Yes, I'm sure. I've seen better, of course, but your departure and reappearance suggest that I may have acted somewhat hastily. Let's walk a bit, shall we?"

Tommy fell in the side opposite the woodland border, which put the horse and Blackmann between him and the trees, and while he adjusted his pace he scanned trees ahead for snipers.

"Tell me, Kane, do you know very much about horses?"

Tommy's eyes followed the trail of the reins from the director's gloved hand to the bridle of the very tall and sleek black horse. "Afraid not, sir," he lied in an accent he picked up at a colonnade on the campus of the University of Virginia. They had chosen a local landmark, The Rotunda, for the rendezvous and took comfort in the anonymity of pedestrian traffic on a large college campus. Passersby were pleased to point them toward the nearby Alumni Hall, where they could complete their impromptu disguise. "But he surely does look to be a handsome animal."

Blackmann smiled. "Dandy, here, is a gelding. A handsome animal indeed, perfect conformation, and a delight to ride, well mannered. But I'm afraid he wouldn't be very much of a hit with the ladies."

Tommy shrugged.

"Ah, yes, of course. You're not a farm lad are you?"

"No sir. Afraid not."

Blackmann allowed his hand to reach out and caress the long bony nose of Dandy. "A gelding is, quite simply, a male horse that's been castrated. Makes them better behaved, so they say. Less wild. More, well, predictable."

"Is that a fact?"

They continued along the bridle path, which was not much more than a neatly groomed surface through a wooded stretch of land. To the left, the woodland climbed a densely brushy ridge. To the right, it trickled out into broad pasture. Blackmann seemed comfortable with the surroundings, but Tommy paid close attention to the trees.

"Are you nervous, Mister Kane?"

Tommy, just call me...nah. Mister Kane is just fine. "Should I be?"

"Oh, yes. Yes, I should say so. This is not the time for the sort of brash behavior you exhibited in the Bahamas. The weapon under your shirt, for example: I'd counsel you not reach for it. Dandy gets skittish, you see, when people nearby are gunned down."

Tommy nodded. "Thanks for the advice."

"And your associates?"

"No idea where they are," Tommy replied in a tone of rueful confession. "We split up. Some things just don't work out too well." *Well it's not entirely a lie. I know they're somewhere up in those woods, but we really did split up a couple of miles down the road.*

"Quite understandable," Blackmann observed. "Intelligence work isn't for lone wolves any more. It's a well-coordinated team effort. My team, for example, is quite at home in these woodlands. Not a unit from The Firm, but my own group. Let's call it a private security service. Somewhere out there, an eight-man crew serves as a perimeter of sorts. Some might say gatekeepers who allow people such as yourself to enter. Whether you see it as a trap or an opportunity is entirely up to you."

I surely hope the transmitter on my jacket got that. I surely hope Yenchenko and Wells didn't pull the earpieces because they weren't excited about Lucy's technology. And I surely don't want to be a gelding.

On a long, sweeping curve, the corner of a pasture bounded by a white rail fence separated what Tommy looked like a large, loose perimeter from the first ring of Blackmann's compound. To the right, open ground of the narrow valley floor offered no cover, no escape and an excellent field of fire. On the left, the trees extended all the way to a distant group of white buildings, very much the way the Ian sketched it on a scrap of paper the night before and exactly as Lucy presented it from a satellite photo the night before that. This would be where the gauntlet began.

I'm still grateful it was the last thing I saw before I left Allentown. The blur of financial stuff on Gulf Chemical and changing my entire history still boggles my mind.

Something moved, just above Blackmann's shoulder, deep in the trees. "I surely do welcome opportunity, sir," he said.

Like the opportunity we took to pick up three orange and blue

*sweatshirts with a big ol' V on the chest and a pair of crossed sabers
on the belly. That and a fistful of colorful brochures and we were instant good ol' alums, just a few beers on the right side of jolly waving
a fistful of cash at the front desk clerk at that chain motel outside of
town. The kid thought Yenchenko was a long-ago interior lineman
and believed it when Serge snarled. Ian faked an American accent
and wondered where the other half of the keg might be.*

Tommy's mind returned to the quiet hum of the motel
room, when Wells unpacked a pair of military-grade SR25
sniper rifles with full noise suppression, night vision and infrared scopes, high capacity magazines and a box of 7.62mm
ammunition.

When I asked where he got them, he calmly said, "One of
those local gun shows at some sort of social club. The bloke
wanted eight and a half, but I bought the pair for seven thousand each. I love shopping for weapons in America, Thomas.
It's a bleeding department store."

More movement. *A deer, maybe a bear?* He ignored
something Blackmann said to listen. The muffled pop of a rifle
shot, fully suppressed. A few moments later, another, absolutely distinct, when Blackmann paused to savor a comment
that had just passed his lips.

Tommy asked, "You got your communications gear back
all right?"

Blackmann registered surprise and pleasure. "Indeed. Indeed we did. A bit naughty of you to run my people around
the airport like that, but I make allowances for that which is,
well, just part of the game. It gives them a bit of experience,
hones their skill, might make them better field people. Some
day."

Tommy longed for another rifle shot but all he heard were
the hooves of the horse at it plodded toward a farmhouse that
sprawled to the right and a series of barns on the left, a hundred yards or so directly ahead.

Blackmann nodded approval to himself and continued,

"And speaking of which, Tommy, it was good of you to return the hostages."

"I thought you said they were expendable."

"Well, I suppose they are, but we do have to keep up appearances in negotiations, don't we? Of course we do, and of course you were not about to leave them to some miserable fate, marooned on an island."

So one theory was wrong. Blackmann didn't get them back himself. He really didn't care.

Blackmann droned on. "You just *had* to involve the local station chief. What was her name? Oh, yes, Tillman, I believe. Well, of course she has been relieved of her duties. However, the trainees are back in the fold, not too much damage, and they'll be sent on to assignments in places we'd rather not think about. To atone for their carelessness. Earn their way back into the agency's good graces."

"But not work for you."

Blackmann chuckled. "No, afraid not. My people don't make mistakes."

"Like Matthias did in Beverly Hills? Oh, sorry, I meant *Mather*."

For the first time in the conversation, tension snuck across Blackmann's jaw. "That was a long time ago, Kane. A very long time."

"Matthias or Mather? I thought they were the same guy. One worked for the East Germans, wet work I heard, and one worked for you."

Blackmann stopped to glare at Tommy, then composed himself by stroking the nose of his horse. "You seem to be well informed, Kane. Very well informed. Now why would someone like yourself even bother, not let this go, just get along with life? You made your point back then, and I was more than willing to let it pass. You went your way, I went mine."

Tommy sighed. "Dieter was a friend of mine."

"Dieter was an East German who took a particular delight in making matters difficult for the British government," Blackmann snapped. "The Americans, too."

The Americans? Why not "us"?

Anger began to surface in Blackmann's demeanor. The horse pulled away from Blackmann's firmer hand and the deputy director thrust the hand into his pocket.

"Dieter Kreutzer was not only Stasi to the core, but in another time would have been a perfect Nazi. He was hardly a pleasant fellow."

Augsburg. The chilly April day at the Fünfgratturm Tower. Dieter muttered verdammte you-something. *Verdammte Juden. Damn Jews.* Dieter was on the wrong side and anti-Semitic to the bone, but he was professional, and he was hunting a mole, long after everyone gave up and went home. And he played a good game of chess.

Tommy traded a bland expression for a cold stare. "Neither was Josef Rabemann."

Blackmann fell silent and looked away and his eyes seemed to search for some distant object he could not find. "I don't think I'm familiar..."

Tommy pressed harder. "Try *Blackbird.*"

But Tommy's blend of anger and control evaporated when an intense sensation exploded on his chest. *What the hell? Like, like... electricity.*

CHAPTER FORTY TWO

Tommy grabbed his left shirt pocket just as the jolt disappeared. When it struck again, he chided himself.

The cell phone. When Lucy handed it to me, she said she had set it to vibrate real strong rather than ring like a regular phone. That way I could feel it in the pocket of my trousers.

Only like an idiot, I stuck it in my shirt pocket.

The phone buzzed a third time and Blackmann guessed what happened. "I'm rather surprised. Your rejection of technology is legendary. I know, I know, if you don't check in – Just be very cautious, Kane. No surprises, all right?"

He waved his hand while Tommy nodded and drew the phone from his pocket.

"Trying to catch up," Tommy said while he studied the little screen. All he saw was a text message: "Don't be left out! Order yours now! New and improved! Environmentally safe."

D-O-N-E.

Blackmann appeared impatient. "Something important?"

Tommy held the phone out to display the screen and grumbled. "Got this thing the other day, but all I get are a bunch of advertisements."

Man, oh man. If Lucy actually pulled it off, we've just won. Not as much as Walter Campos thought, but more than enough. Sergei and Ian are going to be happy. Blackmann is a dead man walking, but just doesn't know it yet. All we have to do is get out of here alive.

Blackmann scowled while Tommy cleared the message and slipped the phone into his shirt pocket. "So I gather you believe Blackbird is somehow connected to – what was that name?"

"Josef Rabemann." Tommy repeated. "You know, Carter, it's amazing how easy it is for field people to grab variations on a name when they need a quick alias. Take the word 'raven,' for example. The German translation is *Rabe*. A raven is definitely a black bird. Raven man, black bird, black man, Blackmann. Even the call sign of your CIA jet is 'Raven'. Lots of folklore involving ravens, lots of different meanings. It's the sort of thing that anyone in the trade would consider, well, *careless*. I wonder what your thoughts might be."

Carter Blackmann forced a placid smile. Tiny beads of sweat formed on his forehead. He gestured toward the fence that ran back along the road they had just walked and toward the white buildings of the farm. With Dandy in tow, the two men detoured from the path.

The clouds had dissipated into a brilliant, clear day, warm for early November, and just a hint of morning fog was withering in the branches of the large oaks that surrounded them and formed a canopy over the bridle path. The scent of humid earth was everywhere, and, still low in the sky, the pinpoint of sunshine sparkled like a lone diamond in the skeletons of trees at rest. In the pasture beyond, a dozen horses grazed peacefully. Blackmann guided Tommy to the fence. "Lovely, aren't they?"

"Yessir, they truly are."

Blackmann pointed. "Now, that one, there, second from the left? Now that's a stallion. He's got all the equipment, you see."

Both Blackmann and Tommy heard two quick pops from the woods behind them and stared at each other. Blackmann cocked an eyebrow and began to smile.

"What's very curious, Mister Kane, is that our stallion is the brother of Dandy. They're very much alike, but with one important difference. The stallion is just a little bit better, and so he stands at stud, passing along the genetic code that makes a superior horse. Dandy is a splendid animal, of course, much better to ride, but in horses, rather like in life, the slightest difference means that some are destined to be revered, honored, given greater opportunity, while others are destined for good and useful service. Wouldn't you agree?"

"Of course."

"Yes. Of course. And some animals are decidedly inferior, of no value, no real worth. They're the ones that need to be culled, to preserve the order and quality of the entire herd."

"You don't say."

Blackmann allowed a long pause. "Now, let's consider you for a moment. I wonder: would Tommy be a valuable member of the herd? Perhaps in our haste to cull, we've misjudged the fellow. What would you say, Tommy?"

"What do you have in mind, *Carter?*"

Blackmann continued to wear a serene smile. "Why to be a member of the team, Tommy. A valued asset. Information is a commodity, you see, and our little unit is quite sophisticated in managing it. We find information of all kinds helpful, a factor in persuasion, an edge in negotiations."

"As in blackmail?"

Blackmann produced an exaggerated wince. "I would suggest that's an unhappy, difficult word. But crude as it might be, let's allow it to stand for the sake of our discussion. You realize, of course, that it's your term and not mine."

"I see. So this business about Blackbird and Josef Rabemann is?"

"Why, a commodity, of course, a product or service traded fairly and reasonably among civilized men. And it just so happens I'm interested in acquisitions just now."

Blackmann's eyes. Unflinching. Utterly confident. Arrogant. The kind of guy who ought to learn that he can't get everything he desires. "Is this the part where I tell you want I want?"

Blackmann looked a bit off-balanced at Tommy's style. "Of course."

Tommy rubbed his jaw, then brightened. "Gulf Chemical and Gas. The entire company, and all its assets."

Blackmann laughed. "Well, now, Mister Kane, that's a bit enthusiastic, wouldn't you say? Perhaps something a bit more realistic? We'll bring you in from the cold, give you a nice case officer position. Country of your choice. Langley if you'd like, or perhaps New York Center. Say the word and we'll get you safely away to a secure location. Ease you into the fold."

Which pretty much means he doesn't plan to let me leave here alive.

Two more pops from the woods. Blackmann smiled even more.

"There, you see? You don't even need to worry about your associates out there. The last of the people connected with Dieter Kreutzer are gone."

Tommy waited a few seconds to give the impression that the proposal had merit. "Yes, but doggone it, I'd know."

Carter sighed impatience. "There can be only one stallion in the pasture, Tommy. It's a fact of nature. Yes. Every so often, someone comes along with dreams and ambitions that create a certain amount of distress, upsets the gentle flow of life, discourages a sense of cooperation and collaboration among people whose influence is, well, helpful to the larger agenda."

"It must be very disquieting."

Blackmann scratched the back of his head. "Oh, indeed. Indeed it is." He turned to his horse. "But you're not like that, Dandy, are you? Good boy. You'll never be king of the herd will you, old chum? But you'll always be a good trooper, knowing the line between valued service and being a difficulty, won't you, boy?" The horse made some noises that suggested agreement. "Yes. And in exchange, you get all the comforts that a sturdy member of the team would require."

I've been in a fixed position too long. Blackmann's tightened his grip on the bridle, as if he expects something to spook the horse. It's become awful quiet in that woodlot. Play the hand. But be careful.

Tommy found an expression of consternation. "I understand what *you* want, *Carter*. But, you know, I'm having just a bit of a problem with the idea of being a gelding. My grandfather had a saying: 'I keep looking at my hands, but all I see is my fingers.' I think I'd still like to have Gulf Chemical and Gas."

Blackmann soured. "Preposterous! The company is worth almost a billion dollars."

Tommy shook his head. "Actually, seven hundred thirty-two million and change."

"I see. And how would you arrive at such a figure?"

Tommy grinned. "Because I stole it from you fifteen minutes ago. Oh, wait: If I took it, then it's not yours to trade. Is it?"

Blackmann's face went ice cold. "You're bluffing. Amateurs like you couldn't even get near it. Those files are quite secure."

Tommy said nothing but continued to smile.

"You had help. You had someone on the inside." He raised his left arm and made a circling motion in the air with his hand. Two people stepped out of the farmhouse and began to walk toward them. "I think it's time you were introduced to a couple of people, Tommy. Let's just find out who's bluffing and who's trapped. What will you wager, Tommy? Your life?" Blackmann tugged on the bridle. "Come, Dandy. Let's get you to the barn."

Paw-paw whispered in Tommy's mind, *"A man with nothin' to lose is dangerous, yeah."*

They became a group of four on a grassy square, near a light gray farmhouse with white trim and black shutters that might have been at least a hundred years old but sparkled newness in the growing morning sunshine. It looked out over a broad valley of pastures and bright red outbuildings. A broad driveway swept past a porch that stretched across the front of the building, but most of the windows were shrouded behind a caravan of black government vehicles and, a hundred feet to the right, an unmarked helicopter rested.

Blackmann was quick with introductions. "I'm sure you remember Mister Lomax from the party at Lyford Cay, and of course, I do hope you remember Myra Fielding. Ah, yes. A good asset never forgets their control officers, do they?"

Blackmann released the bridle. As the horse wandered away, he took half a step back. Lomax showed his hand, which held a Glock that found a point of aim on Tommy's chest.

Blackmann studied Tommy with a blend of amusement and astonishment "I believe you're very much alone, Tommy. It's called the end game."

Tommy studied her eyes and said, "Hello, Myra."

She crossed her arms. "Dammit, Tommy, you just couldn't leave it alone, could you?"

You may be a pain in the ass, but you're loyal, she once told me. Loyal to whom? Her eyes. She's different. She's afraid. Tommy shrugged. "What can I say? Yenchenko had an idea for a robbery, just some dirty drug money, and I went along to help out. Things just got out of hand. They don't launder money the old fashioned way any more, Myra. They use computers and stuff, funnel it through little companies like Gulf Chemical, get away with all kinds of stuff. I made a deal with Walter Campos. He's on the hook to Carter Blackmann, or Josef Rabemann or Blackbird or whoever the hell he is, so I'm doing him a favor. Just here to get a file."

She looked down and muttered. "In the basement."

Lomax's eyebrows shot up and he looked at Blackmann, who registered no reaction at all.

A hard knot formed in Tommy's belly and shoved its way up into his chest. *I've got staff on the inside, Campos said. A mole. Myra. The key came from Myra.*

Blackmann gently said, "I think it's time you surrendered that weapon, Kane. Very slowly, very easy. Ah, that's a good fellow." Blackmann took the Beretta, released the clip and expelled the round in the chamber. "That's better. You see, Tommy, I'm one step ahead of you. The only way you could have gained access is with a key. I've had my concerns about Miss Fielding here for a couple of weeks or so, but now I know for certain that she's not a very helpful member of our team."

Tommy grunted. "C-213."

"Yes."

"But it has nothing official to do with the CIA."

"No, it doesn't. It's a private enterprise. Well, in fact, just here, all around us. We're all patriots, Tommy, and we support our government, our country. A little extra help now and then."

Which government? Which country?

Tommy nodded took a chance. "And I'll just bet that your cellar is stuffed with all kinds of files on all kinds of officials. People in key places, maybe all the way to the top. Politicians. Business people. Civic leaders."

Carter Blackmann suppressed a smile of modesty. "People who at one time or another made a mistake. Committed an indiscretion. Did something that if it were made public would be, well, embarrassing to say the least. Don't be so shocked, Tommy. It's how the game is played at this level." He paused to gather fresh thoughts. "However, I'm afraid you've disturbed things. Quite well, actually. You know for a second-rate field agent, a goon, you've really shown some flair. Just a shame that you're on the wrong side."

"What side is that?" Tommy asked.

Myra cried out, "Tommy, he's not an American!"

I know.

Before Tommy could even complete the thought, Blackmann snapped, "Lomax!"

Lomax whirled, aimed, and fired point blank into the skull of Myra Fielding.

Tommy's jaw dropped. All the air left his lungs in a single gasp. Frozen. Legs in cement. Myra's corpse, sprawled like a broken doll. Dark pool of blood spread across the grass. Blood pouring across her frozen face from the gaping exit wound. Blood oozing over her transfixed eyes and open mouth. Blood that was on his hands as he knelt down and touched her. And then his mind began to wash away the image of her body as it filled with rage. He looked up. Lomax, who held the gun. Blackmann, looking annoyed that someone had littered his lawn.

Tommy sneered an obscenity and didn't care if he lived or died.

Then came the pop. The air filled with a bloody mist.

Lomax. Already dead. Falling to the ground.

Another pop, closer. Lomax's body shuddered and a hole appeared in his chest. The Glock in mid air. Tommy's hand out. Grabbing the pistol as he rolled across the shoulder that once hurt so bad but now took the hit in stride.

When all was still, Tommy aimed the weapon at Carter Blackmann.

From the corner of the house, Sergei Yenchenko stepped forward. "So, Koshka, it is complete. If you wish, I shoot old man, we make depart, get drunk and share story of hunt."

"Where's Ian?"

"Over here," Wells called from the opposite direction.

Tommy looked up to see Ian limp forward.

"You all right?"

"Filthy bugger shot me in the arse. Just a flesh wound. Superficial. I'll be all right. We splashed eight in the trees and counting this bastard, the kill is nine. Who's this bloke?"

Tommy stood to stare at Blackmann.

For the first time, fear in the voice. "Look, Kane – Tommy – let's not be rash. I'm still a very powerful man.